Soul Whispers by Dari LaRoche © 2023
Whispers in a Dream by Susie Slanina © 2023
Friends and Neighbors by Pamela Cowan © 2023
Whispers of the Halcyon by Dari LaRoche © 2023
Whispers Upon a Star by Mary Vine © 2023
Her Zayka by R. Hockamin © 2023
Of Wings and Whispers by Diana McCollum © 2023
Whispering Willows by Kimila Kay © 2023
Bread and Ashtrays by Melissa Yuan-Innes © 2013
Whispers of the Past by Paty Jager © 2023
Pax Reborn by Maggie Lynch © 2023

FIRST PUBLISHED BY

Windtree Press

https://windtreepress.com

Corvallis, Oregon, United States of America

In the anthology, *Whispers*

October 2023

Ebook ISBN: 978-1-962065-24-5

Paperback ISBN: 978-1-962065-25-2

WHISPERS

2023 WINDTREE PRESS ANTHOLOGY

SUSIE SLANINA   PAMELA COWAN
DIANA MCCOLLUM   KIMILA KAY
MELISSA YUAN-INNES   PATY JAGER   MAGGIE LYNCH
MARY VINE   R. HOCKAMIN   DARI LAROCHE

Edited by
PATY JAGER

Windtree
Press

CONTENTS

HER ZAYKA BY R. HOCKAMIN

OF WINGS AND WHISPERS BY DIANA MCCOLLUM

WHISPERING WILLOWS BY KIMILA KAY

BREAD AND ASHTRAYS BY MELISSA YUAN-INNES

WHISPERS OF THE PAST BY PATY JAGER

PAX REBORN BY MAGGIE LYNCH

FOREWORD

A whisper is a soft barely audible sound or resemblance of a sound. Perhaps a thought in one's head, a flutter of leaves, a feather floating to the ground, or a wish.

When we, the Windtree Press authors, gathered for a Zoom meeting it was unanimous that we wanted to do another anthology. This time we didn't stick to one genre. In this collection of ten stories and a poem, you will come across various genres. Mystery, Fantasy, Sci-fi, Supernatural, and a sweet Children's story.

Reading each of the stories, as they came to me to be edited, I enjoyed seeing the different ways in which "whisper" was used in the story. From the poem **Soul Whispers**, from Dari LaRoche, you can conjure up the variety of whispers in the coming stories. This is followed by the Children's story, **Whispers in a Dream**, by Susie Slanina, where Metro the dog visits outer space through a dream.

The tale of **Friends and Neighbors** by Pamela Cowan murmurs of unlikely alliances. In **Whispers of the Halycon**, author Dari LaRoche's submission is a twist on a fairytale. Author Mary Vine's characters, in **Whisper Upon a Star**, hide their feelings as they try to find a killer.

Her Zayka is a tale of a close bond between a young woman and the nanny she grew up with. Author R. Hockamin has a unique twist at the end. **Of Wings and Whispers** is a fantasy where author Diana McCollum takes the reader on an emotional ride as a fairy with a broken wing finds love.

Suspense and romance will keep you turning the pages of author Kimila Kay's **Whispering Willows**. Author Melissa Yuan-Innes story, **Bread and Ashtrays**, is an intriguing tale of an empath who sees whispers of a man's life.

The characters in **Whispers of the Past,** by Paty Jager, are seeking a person whom they may or may not wish they'd never heard of. Ending this collection of titillating and thought-provoking stories is author Maggie Lynch's **Pax Reborn**. This science fiction novella asks the question would the world be better with everyone content and equal?

Enjoy and savor each story. Every one of the stories will leave whispers of questions and coax a smile. I enjoyed reading and editing each of these submissions to the anthology.

Paty Jager

Soul Whispers
A Poem
Dari LaRoche

Life.
Love.
Hope.
Joy.
Forever and a day.

Whispers in the light.
Whispers in the dark.
Running through the wet grass,
kicking the fallen leaves.
Sliding on the ice, after the freeze.

Once I thought the dark was scary.
Then it was my safe place,
warm and comforting.
Now it holds me close in the wreck of the storm
that shapes my life, yet feeds my soul.

Love is light.
Love is dark.
Love lifts on a wing
and whispers *forever*
before it takes flight.

Whispers drive me crazy.
Whispers make me go.
Whispers call me home.
Whispers hurt my soul.
Whispers make me whole.

Hush. Listen to the whispers
that meld our lives together,
one to another.
Love's final whisper, now and forever,
fills my soul with light.

ABOUT THE AUTHOR

Dari's Inspiration For This Poem

I didn't set out to write a poem when this piece came about. I was fiddling with words and thinking about the short story I wanted to write for this anthology. I just started writing down phrases and words that meant something to me, bits and pieces of my life, using the word whispers as often as possible. *Soul Whispers* is the result. After setting it aside for a time, I polished it into the piece you are reading here. I decided to keep it since it had meaning for me. I hope you like it too.

ABOUT THE AUTHOR

Dari LaRoche writes contemporary romance and romantic suspense that will keep you reading long after the witching hour has passed. Her everyday heroes face challenges requiring strength of character, perseverance, and an ever ready dose of laughter to find their way to love and happiness. Her Rescue Series takes place in the Pacific Northwest and the Caribbean, settings inspired by LaRoche's love for travel and passion for safeguarding the natural environment.

Travel is an integral part of her life. She always keeps a little notebook and her cellphone handy to record tidbits that she will use sometime in the future—no interesting detail is too small to be considered in either a novel or a short story.

Learn More About Dari at her website. https://darilaroche.com/

Whispers
in a
Dream
Susie Slanina

It was summer vacation, and the last few days had been uncomfortably hot.

Sherry and Marguerite had been best friends since kindergarten. Now they were eighteen and very excited to go on a camping trip all on their own. At first, Marguerite had not wanted to go camping because she was very glamorous and her idea of "roughing it" was a five-star hotel with room service.

But earlier that summer they had taken a hike with their dogs up to the mountains, and the fresh air and scent of pine trees was intoxicating in a way that made Marguerite reconsider her stance. The dogs had so much fun and so did Sherry and Marguerite. Ever since, Sherry had been deeply yearning to get up to the mountains for a few days so they could see the stars at night and wake up to pretty birds singing and the wonderful mountain fragrance. She thought camping would be super fun, but she couldn't get Marguerite to budge.

Sherry tried her best, but Marguerite always said, "No camping!"

At last, they made a big compromise. Marguerite agreed to go on a trip to the mountains as long as they got a room, not a tent.

So they tried to reserve a room.

"How about Big Bear, Marguerite? It's not too far away, it has a big lake, and this book says it is very dog friendly."

"Gosh, that's a pretty lake," Marguerite said, getting excited. "Let's look it up on the Internet. Marguerite read the description out loud:

"Welcome to Big Bear Lake, a four-season resort community surrounded by the San Bernardino National Forest. It's the perfect getaway, high above the smog and busyness of the lowlands."

"This place sounds perfect!" Sherry exclaimed. "Let's start calling!"

First, they started with the most reasonably priced lodgings with nice features. They all had cute mountain names and friendly people answered the phone. But, alas, not one would take four dogs. (They did allow dogs, but apparently two was the limit.)

After the fourteenth call, Sherry hung up the phone in frustration.

"Oh, rats! This isn't fair! All three of my dogs don't add up to what one big dog weighs. It's already Wednesday. I only have a week and a half left of vacation. I just want to take Tawny, Metro, and Gizzy somewhere pretty for a few days."

Marguerite was concerned. She could see how disappointed her friend was. She was surprised that she felt disappointed, too.

Sherry stared at the phone, thinking hard.

"Oh, Sherry, I'm sorry. It's awful to have our hopes dashed like that. What are we going to do now?" Marguerite asked softly.

Sherry had a determined look on her face. Marguerite had seen that look before and knew something was up.

"I'm going to get a cabin of my own in Big Bear, that's what! Then we can take all the dogs whenever we want!"

"And, how exactly do you plan to do that?" Marguerite asked, dumbfounded.

"I don't know yet, but I have a week and a half to figure it out. Want to help?"

The two friends hugged and laughed. It was the kind of hug that two friends give each other as a show of strong support.

"Absolutely!" Marguerite exclaimed, caught up in the joyous moment. "But how are you going to afford it? You're only eighteen. And, remember, you can't possibly get a cabin before your vacation is up."

Sherry sighed. "I don't know how I'm going to do it, but I will. But, you're right. I think there's a pesky thing called Escrow, and that will cause a delay."

She sat quietly, daydreaming. "But when I do get it, the cabin will be a cabiny-cabin. Like real woodsy, with maybe a stream in the backyard."

Marguerite was thoughtful. She looked at Sherry and said calmly, "Well...you still have a few days of vacation. What are you going to do?"

"I don't know, darn it. I wish we could escape this heat wave and go somewhere pretty, like the mountains."

"Ummm, would you, maybe, just maybe, like to go camping?"

Now Sherry's eyes got big. She looked at Marguerite with astonishment. "Do you really mean it, Marguerite? Camping? In a tent? *You?*" Sherry laughed at the thought.

Marguerite laughed right back. "Well if you can somehow get a cabin, I guess I could do a little camping."

The two friends and the dogs did a little jig of happiness. Camping! In the cool, crisp mountains! And while they were camping, they would scout around and find the coziest cabin ever!

IT WAS SO HOT THAT NIGHT, SHERRY COULDN'T SLEEP. EVERY TIME SHE dozed off, she'd wake up with a start a few minutes later. "Cabin! Camping! Cabin! Camping!" She was excited and happy but too wound up to sleep. Her mind was churning. How would she ever get a cabin? The thought of looking for real estate, coming up with a down payment, budgeting, and long forms to fill out made her head spin.

And then Marguerite decided to go camping! Sherry chuckled to herself. For a month she had been pestering. But Marguerite thought tents were too dusty. Sherry was still surprised that Marguerite had actually agreed to tent camping.

She stared at the ceiling fan. It was spinning fast, but it wasn't doing much good keeping the bedroom cool. The clock on the mantle in the living room chimed twelve times. Midnight!

Sherry picked up the book again. It was no use. The words started to swim and she couldn't understand the sentences.

The dogs were restless, too. They sensed Sherry's turmoil. She looked at them fondly. "Well, pups, at least I'm on vacation and I won't have to wake up early to work tomorrow. Come on, guys. We may as well get up. It's too hot in here, let's go play outside. Maybe the night air will help us sleep."

The moon was full and some of the plants reflected the glow of moonlight. Sherry had planted some special silver plants for a moonlight garden. The air was infused with the heady fragrance of night-blooming jasmine, a shrub that blossomed only after sunset. The breeze made the trees sound as if they were whispering secrets to her.

Sherry was never outside at this time of night. It was a different, mysterious world.

She took a deep breath of perfumed air. Her cats, Butterscotch and Playmate, stared at her from their spot in the little vegetable garden. Their eyes glowed in the dark.

Sherry went to them, scratched their ears, and popped a couple of cherry tomatoes right off the vine.

Taking Metro in her arms, she twirled under the glowing moon, and sang a lullaby. Her mind calmed as she sang the repetitive lines.

"Let's just rest here for a bit." She lay down on the soft grass and the dogs cuddled in close. Sherry could hear their gentle snoring. The sound was so relaxing. Metro's tail twitched. Even while sleeping, Metro was happy.

"You're the waggiest puppy, Metro," Sherry said drowsily.

The slight breeze set the wind chimes singing. Suddenly, she saw the most miraculous thing! She sat up. A flock of butterflies or birds floated above her. Under the light of the moon, Sherry could see they were brightly colored with blue and gold markings. They swirled and swooped around the tired girl. Sherry reached up with her arms and one landed ever so softly on the tip of her fingers.

"Why, you're so beautiful, I've never seen anything like you before!"

"Oh, hello. We are Butterbirds, part butterfly, part bird. We can fly like a bird, and flutter like a butterfly. We are always blue and gold. My family thought it would be nice to visit you tonight."

"Butterbirds? I've never heard of such a thing. Nature is so awesome!" She watched in delight as the family danced around her in the silvery moonlight.

"We only come out late at night when people have trouble sleeping. We help them. I'm a Butterbird, but you can call me Dreamy."

"Oh, Dreamy. I'm so glad to meet you. I could really use your help tonight!"

Dreamy smiled, "Okay, let's go on a flying trip. I have four places I'd like to show you."

"But, wait. I thought you would help me sleep. Normally, I would love to go, but I'm just so tired and sleepy."

"Let me just cover you with this veil of dreams, this will help you sleep. Dreamy covered Sherry and Metro with the most beautiful veil. It was transparent and had stars and moons inlaid in the material. Sherry touched it. It was like no material she had ever felt before: gauzy and glittery, strong, but incredibly soft at the same time.

Suddenly, Sherry was flying. There was no effort at all. It was easy. She felt the weight of Metro on her back and up, up, up they flew. Dreamy said, "Follow me. I'll take you places you will love! First stop: Doggy Dream World!"

Metro's ears flew back and she laughed by wagging her tail. It made Sherry feel off balance. "Stop wagging, Metro, you need to be steady when we're flying!"

They flew to a special island. The island was colorful and filled with happy, excited children and their pets. Sherry felt unsteady on her feet, but the dizzy feeling soon passed. There was a carnival going on with lots of rides.

"The rides are for people and their pets to enjoy together," Butterbird explained. "Come on, let's try out the huge slide!" She perched herself on Sherry's shoulder.

Metro totally loved it!

"Wee! Wee!" The little dog yelped happily. "Let's do it again!" Metro said. They climbed back up the ladder and sailed down the giant slide again and again.

Sherry knew that Metro could sing with her beautiful howl; she had already sung at an opera when they went to Hollywood. But she never knew Metro could talk like a human!

"Let's ride on the miniature train now!" said Metro. The conductor blew a whistle and called "All Aboard!" The train took them all around the island and it was easy to see all the different attractions. They planned what rides would be next. Metro spied a scary looking ride called "The Hammer." It had rocket ships that took the passengers on a very fast journey and made them hang upside down at the top.

"Oh, Metro, let's not. It looks too scary!"

Metro said, "Come on, Sherry! Be brave!" Sherry reluctantly got in line with Metro. Her knees trembled as they waited. They finally got in the rocket, and the big door clanged shut and a safety bar snapped across their laps. At first the rockets swung slowly back and forth. "Well, there's no going back now," Sherry thought as she held Metro's paw tightly.

Then the rockets went faster and faster! They got to the very top and were upside down. Sherry and Metro laughed at each other. Metro's ears were hanging straight down!

When the ride was over, Metro said, "See, it wasn't so bad, Sherry! Don't be afraid to try new things, you might miss out on a lot of fun!"

Metro surveyed the island. "Ooh, look, there's a cart with cotton candy! I've always wanted to try that!" They got some, sat on a bench, watching people with their dogs and eating the sticky candy. "It's like a doggy parade!" Sherry laughed and put a bit of cotton candy on Metro's nose. "Metro you have a pink nose now. It's cute!"

Dreamy was perched on Sherry's shoulder. "Thank you, Dreamy, for bringing us here. We're having a blast!" Dreamy's wings fluttered happily.

Metro was determined to go on as many rides as possible, the faster the better. The view from the Ferris Wheel was pretty, but it was a little slow for her taste.

On another ride that was more to Sherry's taste, they sat side by side in giant swings as they circled round and round. Sherry thought she could stay on this gentle ride forever, but Metro spied the roller coaster and wanted to go! Sherry trembled a little.

"Remember, Sherry! The Hammer wasn't so bad. Just hang on tight!" The roller coaster went up, up, up a big hill. Then down, down, down faster and faster! Metro held up her paws all the way down, and finally Sherry raised her arms a little, too. Metro yelled, "Paws Up, Sherry! Don't be a scaredy cat!" Sherry raised her arms all the way up! They laughed and screamed.

When they got off the ride, stumbling and laughing, Dreamy said, "It's getting late, we have other places to see, let's go flying!"

Metro took her place on Sherry's back and after a longer flight, they were floating in Deep Space. There were so many stars, planets, and galaxies! It looked like confetti from a party. Soon they were flying next to beautiful, glowing Saturn. Sherry saw a little girl sitting on Saturn's rings with her legs dangling over. She was casually reading a book, and somehow Metro was at her side with one ear up, listening to the story.

"Wait, that doesn't make any sense," Sherry said, confused. "How can she be reading a book on Saturn's rings? That would be really dangerous!"

Metro laughed. "Come on! Does any of this make sense, Sherry? Say, I read somewhere that Saturn's rings are made up of trillions and trillions of snowballs. Want to play in the snow, Sherry?"

"Metro! You can read, too?"

"Sure, it's a cinch to read," Metro said. "Let's go make lots of snowballs."

Sherry and Metro landed on Saturn's rings and threw snowballs at each other.

"Okay, you two. We're on a tight schedule and we have two other places to visit," Dreamy said as she looked at her watch.

They started falling down, down, down, and soon they were in a cave with sparkling jewels. The walls were made of emeralds, rubies, sapphires, diamonds, and crystals. Red, Green, blue, yellow—colors so bright, it was like being inside a kaleidoscope. Sherry and Metro sat down next to each other. The cool earth felt very restful.

"This is a good place for us to relax," Dreamy whispered. "Let's just enjoy the beauty of Mother Earth."

Sherry and Metro gazed at the jeweled walls. They felt complete calmness and love. It was a perfect feeling after all the excitement of the carnival and the snowball fight.

The cave was cool, but not cold. It was dark, but the jeweled walls were bright and they could see every facet. It was very comfortable. Sherry's heart felt tender as she and Metro simply appreciated the beauty of the sparkling jewels. Sherry looked at her dog. Metro's shining eyes were prettier than all the jewels.

"Metro, so you are a dog, right?"

"Arf," Metro said.

"But you can talk, and sing?"

"I can only talk when Dreamy's around. But, sure, I can do lots of things when she's here."

"I remember the day I brought you home from the shelter. I had forgotten to turn off the tea kettle, and you were able to make a sound that sounded just like the whistle. I knew you were talented, but I didn't know you could do all this other stuff." Sherry rubbed Metro's velvety ears and felt honored to be in the presence of such doggy goodness.

"But the best thing about you is you always win the love game. No matter how hard I try, you always love me more."

"Sure, dogs are like that. We just have the capacity to love more than humans."

"Wow, that's really incredible, Metro. What makes you the happiest?"

"Dogs are just naturally happy. But what makes us the most happy is when our humans are happy. We try to give our happiness to you."

"But how did you get so happy in the first place?"

"Dogs don't have deadlines, or phones, or homework. That's why we can focus on the important stuff. Humans think too much. Do you remember rubbing lemon blossoms on my tummy?"

Sherry remembered so well. She and Metro were in the backyard on a warm spring day. Metro rolled over and Sherry took some lemon blossoms. As she rubbed the blossoms onto Metro's tummy, she fell into a happy trance. Even then, she had the feeling Metro was trying to tell her something. Something true.

"Yes, that's exactly right, Sherry! I was giving my doggy happiness to you that day! You weren't thinking of anything at all. It's really the best trick dogs know, and we try to teach doggy happiness every day! You just need to try to tap into our happy genes more often. Dogs never stop trying to give their humans the best trick."

"You may be right, Metro. Let me think about it."

Wait, she wasn't supposed to be thinking so much!

"Your trick sure is tricky, Metro! Maybe you could teach me to fetch a ball instead!"

"Nope. It's the simplest thing. And it becomes easier the more you practice. Just try to be more doggy-like in your life, and you'll be happier. I promise."

"Okay, I'll try. Thank you, Metro. You're brilliant."

Dreamy fluttered and fluffed her feathers approvingly.

"Dreamy, so you're part bluebird and part golden butterfly, right?"

"Yes, that's right. We become visible when people have a hard time sleeping. We cover them with the Veil of Dreams. It helps them figure out stuff that may be bothering them. We've been doing this for centuries, but people don't remember us after we visit."

"Oh, I'll remember you, Dreamy! I'll never forget how nice you are. And I'll always remember this magical night and all the wonderful places you took us."

"We'll see," Dreamy murmured, a bit wistfully.

"Why was it I had trouble getting to sleep in the first place? Oh, that's right...cabin and camping. It's strange. I'm not concerned about anything right now. I feel more like how a dog might feel. I hope this feeling stays."

"That's terrific!" Dreamy said. "Your dog has taught you a valuable lesson. Okay, I have one more special place to show you. Let's go!"

Sherry ran her hand over the jewels as they left the cave, thinking how truly exquisite the earth is. The jewels made her fingers tingle with a sweet sensation.

It was time for the last stop. They took a short flight up to the mountains of Big Bear. A bright, cheery cabin was below them. There was a forest stream flowing gently in the backyard.

Sherry watched a girl and friends on the deck with their dogs. They were talking and laughing and the dogs were so well-loved and happy. They were constantly being appreciated and petted.

The scene changed. There was a fierce snowstorm outside but the girls were cozy inside singing and playing games. Marguerite went to the kitchen and Sherry could hear the sound of popcorn popping merrily on the stove.

The scene changed. The friends were taking a walk with the dogs under a full moon in the forest. The tall trees cast eerie shadows in the moonlight, but the path was clear and bright.

The scene changed. The friends were on a boat, sailing across Big Bear Lake. The sunlight made the waves sparkle and dance. Metro's soft fur ruffled in the breeze.

"Oh, Dreamy, this is exactly what I've been dreaming about! This little cabin is perfect. But I just don't know how I can afford it." Sherry's brow wrinkled in confusion. She was starting to wake up.

"Sherry, stop worrying!" Metro said. "Remember all I've taught you. I'll help you get this cabin."

And then Metro laughed and sang in a teasing fashion: "I know something you don't know!"

Dreamy smiled. "Yes, Metro does know something you don't know, and yes, Metro will help. It will happen very quickly, so please pay attention!" Dreamy looked carefully at Sherry. "I'm so sorry. I have to go quickly now. It was very nice meeting you, you've been a fun dream case to solve."

And before Metro and Sherry could say goodbye, Dreamy fluttered and flew away.

***

"What time is it?" Sherry looked over at the clock. It was exactly noon and the day was already getting warm.

"Oh my gosh, what a dream that was!" She covered her eyes with the palms of her hands and pressed down hard trying to remember all the wonderful details, but already the dream was fading.

Outside the bedroom window, a bluebird splashed in the bird bath while a golden butterfly perched in a bush nearby.

"Oh, Metro, look how lovely they are! It's like they're best friends! How sweet!" Sherry admired their beauty. "Those colors, blue and gold, are amazing. They remind me of something…something beautiful." Sherry was quiet, trying to remember. She sighed.

"Now, where are my slippers? I've got to make coffee before

Marguerite gets here. We've got to plan for our camping trip and figure out how to buy a cabin in the mountains!"

Sherry started to get up but Metro felt delightfully heavy on her chest and made her want to stay in bed for a bit longer. Metro stared at Sherry and tilted her head.

"Oh, Metro! You're so cute when you tilt your head like that!" She caressed Metro's ear, but Metro kept staring as though she was a junior detective, trying to give Sherry a clue.

Metro tilted her head further toward the window as though trying to show Sherry something. Sherry looked again. The golden butterfly had landed softly on the bluebird's head and both were peering in the window.

"Wow! They're so playful with each other, it's like something out of a dream!"

Metro crawled close to Sherry's ear. She thought she heard Metro whisper: "Gee whiz, Sherry, maybe it wasn't a dream!"

"But dogs can't talk," Sherry said to herself. She shook her head.

Bits of the dream came floating back in Sherry's consciousness. If only it were easy to remember details, but the dream was gone, and all that remained was the purest feeling of peace and happiness.

The bluebird and butterfly took one last look inside and then flew away together.

"Ahh, Metro. There they go. I hope they visit us again someday."

Sherry smiled at her little dog and noticed a bit of pink fluff on her nose.

"What's that?" Sherry laughed. "Oh, it must be a piece of my fluffy slippers. Metro, you're so silly. Were you playing with them again?"

Metro had an innocent expression.

Sherry peered closer. Metro pushed her nose to Sherry's cheek and gently rubbed off the pink fluff. Sherry took it in her fingers. It was sticky. She put a tiny piece on her tongue. It was sweet! Sherry's eyes grew big with astonishment. She looked at Metro in wonder.

"This is cotton candy, Metro! Now, where in the world did you get cotton candy?!"

· · ·

TWO DAYS LATER

"I can't wait to get up to the cool mountains, it's already so hot!" Sherry said.

"I know. This heat wave has been brutal." Marguerite checked the weather forecast on her phone. "It's going to be 104 today in Covina, but in Big Bear the high will be only 77. Doesn't that sound lovely?"

"Yes, it does! And it's less than two hours away! Okay, we're all packed up now. Packing took two whole days, Marguerite. I'm surprised you didn't pack jewels and gowns!" Sherry winked and Marguerite laughed.

"Come on, let's get out of this hot town!" She opened the front door.

Just then the phone rang.

"Hello?"

"Hello! Is this Miss Sherry who has a little dog named Metro?"

"Yes, may I ask who's calling?"

"Well, Miss Sherry, my name is Mr. Bunny from a company called Corporate Fat Cats. We're in the advertising business. We heard about Metro's great singing at the opera in Hollywood, and we were wondering if you would consider having Metro sing in a commercial for a new product."

Sherry's eyes widened. She put the phone on speaker so Marguerite could hear.

Mr. Bunny continued: "The only requirement is time. I'm sorry for the short notice, but this has to happen today! If you agree, we will be sending a limousine to your house immediately, and then we will leave from LAX to begin filming in Hawaii. Corporate Fat Cats has deluxe accommodations there. You can bring a friend."

Now Marguerite's eyes widened.

"But, oh my gosh, my friend and I were just leaving to go camping in Big Bear. We're on summer vacation for another week." Sherry explained.

"The deal is Kool Kitty Shampoo needs Metro right now! The opera star who was going to be singing the commercial came down with the flu, but she remembered how Metro stole the show in Hollywood. She recommended Metro highly, and said Metro has a beautiful howl that would be perfect for the product and Metro is the only one with a range of voice as strong as hers."

Sherry remembered the opera star in the heavy purple dress who had beckoned Metro to come up on the stage while they were visiting Hollywood. She smiled at the happy memory. But then she thought about today's camping trip and how much she had been looking forward to it.

"But, but, my friend, Marguerite, finally agreed to go camping…in a tent!" Sherry stammered.

(Of course, Mr. Bunny had no idea how long Sherry had tried to get Marguerite to go camping in a tent!)

Marguerite put her hand up to Sherry's mouth. "Wait, wait, Sherry! Let's hear what else Mr. Bunny has to say."

"Miss Sherry, pardon me, but you need to make up your mind. We are all set up for filming. Will you be going camping in the mountains or will you bring Metro to Hawaii to sing on the commercial? By the way, she will be making a lot of money for a minute's worth of singing."

Marguerite grabbed a pen and wrote quickly on a tablet. She showed the note to Sherry.

$$$ 4 CABIN!!!

Sherry got it.

"How long would the filming take?"

"It will take about a week."

"And what is the product?"

It's a dry shampoo for cats called Kool Kitty Shampoo. We will be showing cats taking baths with a funny expression on their faces because cats don't like water. Metro will be howling opera arias in the background for the sound effects, and it will seem as though the cats are howling."

"Is the product safe for kitties?"

"Oh, yes. It's completely organic, biodegradable, and wasn't tested on animals."

"May I call you back in an hour?"

"No, sorry. The company has a strict filming schedule and owns beautiful suites in Waikiki, right on the ocean. The limousine is in Hollywood to pick up the opera singer. We can be at your house in an hour. You need to decide right now!"

Meanwhile, Marguerite had been checking out Corporate Fat Cats on the Internet. It was all legitimate.

"Yes, yes, let's do it, Sherry!"

Sherry wondered absently if Marguerite was looking for an excuse to get out of camping in a tent.

Just then a pretty bird or butterfly fluttered at the window. Sherry couldn't quite tell if it was a bird or butterfly. It had beautiful colors of blue and gold. It somehow gave Sherry confidence. She looked at her little dog. Metro was humming a Hawaiian song. Sherry finally had her answer.

An hour later, in the cool climate-controlled comfort of the limousine, Sherry leaned back on the leather seats and sighed. The coolness of the car reminded her of the coolness of Big Bear. Through the tinted windows she could see the majesty of the mountains. She wistfully waved at them and gave into one last daydream of the camping trip. She knew the mountains would wait for her family of pets to come back someday.

It was difficult, but she managed to switch the camping daydream to a Hawaiian daydream, and soon she was smiling at the idea of Metro in a grass skirt and a fragrant floral lei. She thought Metro looked dreamy!

AUTHOR'S NOTE: IN THE METRO BOOK SERIES, THIS STORY COMES IN *between Metro Goes Stargazing and Metro Duets.*

Susie's Inspiration For This Story

"To sleep, perchance to dream" ~ William Shakespeare

Dogs and dreams--two subjects which have long fascinated me. This story in the Metro book series was fun to write since the setting is a dream. Because it's a dream, Metro can talk. Wondering what she would say was an incredibly inspiring experience! The "Butterbird" who helps Sherry sleep, can smile and even wears a watch. The "floating in deep space" segment was inspired by recent images from the James Webb telescope.

Metro the Little Dog is a series of beautifully illustrated children's books about a lovable puppy named Metro. These stories were written to honor the real Metro and all the wonderful dogs who grace our lives.

Many thanks to artist Paul Bunch for the exquisite illustrations.

ABOUT THE AUTHOR

Susie Slanina lives in Vancouver, Washington. After graduating from California State University, Los Angeles, she went to school in Ireland to study the Montessori approach to educating children. She worked 24 years at CSLA and retired at age 50 to spend more time with her dogs in a cabin in Big Bear.

She had been retired for eight years when a poem she wrote about a spider became the catalyst for the Metro book series. She used to enjoy traveling, but discovered that hanging out with her dogs is better than seeing the wonders of the world.

To learn more about Susie and her children's books, visit her website at http://www.metrothelittledog.com/. Metro is also on Facebook at https://www.facebook.com/profile.php?id=100063563107871

Friends and Neighbors

Pamela Cowan

*L*ucinda sat in her second-story bedroom at the window that faced her backyard. It was quiet there and the natural light was perfect for reading. A nearby bookcase held her favorite books with a stack on top waiting to be read. Most of them were concerned with her one great passion, flowers, and flower gardening. Beside her easy chair was a small round table that held a lamp and a pair of binoculars that had belonged to her husband, Frank. At seventy, her eyesight wasn't what it used to be, and she needed them to keep an eye on her three closest neighbors. She didn't know them, and if she did, she probably wouldn't have liked them, but that didn't matter. In her day, neighbors looked out for each other. Whether or not they appreciated it, she would do her duty.

First though, she trained the glasses on her backyard and was pleased to see not so much as a single blade of grass growing there. Instead, wide pathways of stone wove between beds of vibrant flowers. Some of them, like the tall, multi-colored hollyhocks and the pink foxglove, were biennials, blooming every two years. Many, like the white Shasta Daisies, and purple Lupines, were perennial and bloomed yearly. Most were annuals but still returned, reseeding themselves year after year.

She'd sown the original seeds for bright yellow coreopsis and marigolds, lacy white baby's breath, blue forget-me-nots, two kinds of poppies, bachelor buttons, snapdragons, and cheerful black-eyed Susans. She'd planted bulbs of early crocus, bluebells, tulips, iris, and bleeding hearts, each arriving and fading in its season.

Maintaining her large yard took a lot of work. She not only had to feed, water, and weed, but make compost in the two big rotating barrels the county had given her as part of their Greener Community Project. She supposed the garden, and the stairs were to be given credit for keeping her in shape. No one with a garden and a two-story house needed a gym membership.

Raising the binoculars, she looked beyond the four-foot wooden fence that bordered her yard, and into the backyards of the three houses which shared her back fence.

Each was a cookie-cutter, one-story ranch, with a long narrow yard, a concrete slab patio, and a set of sliding glass doors. The gray house on the left had the best lawn and a scrawny maple tree. The concrete patio had a basketball hoop on one end, and bikes and skateboards were strewn here and there.

The couple who lived there had two noisy pre-teens and a dog that barked from the moment they left for work until the moment they returned. Lucinda had called the animal control department to complain several times. If there had been a child control department, she'd have called them too. Little good it would do.

The middle house had been painted white. It had an overgrown and underwatered lawn, a rusting metal shed, and three stately aspen trees with white trunks. The woman who lived there was rarely home nowadays, which was a shame. For the last two years, she'd been a reliable source of entertainment. She changed boyfriends as often as she changed her fancy underwear. Lucinda deduced that she must have found "the one" and would be moving out soon.

People seemed to move a lot these days. Though none of the houses were rentals, the owners never stayed more than three or four years. There was no continuity, no sense of community, and certainly no one you could call on for help.

The light-yellow house on the right Lucinda thought of as the Cauldwell place. She'd been friends with the Cauldwells, and though they'd gone—Ian Cauldwell passing ten years ago, Elsa in a nursing home with the Alzheimer's the last three—she would always think of it as theirs. The gate Ian had installed in the fence so they could visit each other hadn't been used in so long that the handle and hinges were probably rusted shut.

The lawn's condition was somewhere between the other two. Just inside the fence on both sides were rows of lilacs she'd helped Elsa plant. So far, the new people had left them be. They had tilled up the rear half of the yard to make room for a vegetable garden but that didn't bother lawn-hating Lucinda one bit. On their concrete back patio was a new barbecue grill and a few lawn chairs. She'd expected they'd have barbecues and invite friends but, so far at least, they had not.

To her relief, the couple, who had moved in six months ago, didn't have kids or dogs. They didn't have curtains either, preferring blinds that they rarely thought to lower. It gave Lucinda, who was admittedly hungry for some kind of social interaction, an easy eyeful.

As she performed her neighborhood monitoring, it was impossible not to notice their furniture, at least what she could see of it. She liked the maple dining set, with its upholstered seats for six. The corner of a leather sofa in the living room looked classic and expensive. The house seemed tidy and well-maintained. She approved and knew her friend Elsa would too.

The husband was tall with dark hair and a tanned face. Italian maybe, or Greek. He had one of those hooked noses and she imagined dark-brown eyes. The woman was short and slender with strawberry-blond hair and a light complexion. It was hard to tell from a distance, but she'd guess her eyes were blue. She put them both in their late twenties or early thirties. Professionals by the clothes they wore to work. Him in dark suits. Her in slacks and button-down blouses.

He didn't come into the backyard much except on Saturday mornings to mow the lawn, half lawn really. She came out most afternoons to work in the vegetable garden, refill the two bird feeders, or just sit in one of the lawn chairs and read.

At first, they seemed like the perfect couple, but Lucinda was wise to the signs. She must have been at her insurance-required and totally unnecessary quarterly doctor appointment and missed the first big argument. That evening she didn't miss the huge bouquet of roses he placed on the table or the reluctant way she picked them up. Lucinda instantly recognized that fearful hopefulness.

After that, she kept a warier eye on the place and soon spotted more signs. The wife, who at first seemed quietly self-possessed and often sprawled happily in one of the lawn chairs, reading a book, or raising her face to the sun, was changing. Her posture had become more rigid; her ready smile was gone. She was losing weight and looked twitchy, like a nervous robin when a hawk is in the area.

The changes in her neighbor triggered old memories for Lucinda. Unwelcome, they came rushing in. She recalled the day they'd moved into their new home. How she'd been filled with plans and enthusiasm, and did she dare say it, joy? Then Frank's deceptively cheerful voice came back to her.

"I want a traditional yard," he'd said. "A well-tended lawn like my folks have, and along the back of the house, you can plant some climbing roses, the way my mother did. You can pick them out, just make sure they're red. I'll build some trellises for them to climb on. You can paint them white."

He always couched his commands that way. As if the chore he was assigning was some sort of gift. I'll let you he'd say. As in. "I think it's a good idea to let you get the laundry done on the weekend. That way we'll have clean clothes for work."

His suggestions, followed by his reasoning, never seemed excessive, illogical, or impractical. Which made them hard to argue with. "I think we should find the money so you can learn to bake pies like my mom, he once said. "I signed you up for a baking class." The fact that she didn't like pie or baking didn't come into it.

If she made the mistake of questioning one of his directives he would methodically and slowly repeat why she should do what he said. If she continued to disagree, he would bring out what he called the iron fist of discipline.

"Wives and children, have to learn how the world works," he would calmly tell her as he grabbed her hair and dragged her into the bedroom and onto the bed. Once there he would sit on her and methodically punch her thighs, hips, and ribs. Places where clothes hid the bruises. She always squirmed and fought to break free but never did.

Eventually, he'd release her, and she'd crawl into a corner of the room, a mindless animal seeking escape. Afterward, he'd sometimes leave her alone for a while before summoning her to make dinner. More often these sessions would excite him, and he'd drag her back to the bed. The next day he would bring her roses, forgiving her for her bad behavior and apologizing for getting a little carried away.

She supposed she should be grateful he hadn't decided they should have children. The rules he'd have imposed on them, his iron-fisted discipline, was something she couldn't let herself imagine.

Peering through the binoculars she checked each house once more but saw nothing of note. She hoped the single woman would sell soon. Maybe someone interesting would move in.

A flutter of motion caught her eye, and she looked down at her garden. An early Monarch butterfly was flitting from flower to flower. There was the slam of a car door. A few moments later, the children who lived in the white house, ran into their backyard. Apparently, no one had taught them to walk, not run, through doorways. She moved away from the window, shaking her head at the bonk-wonk sound of a basketball, which would no doubt be bounced ceaselessly for the next hour or two.

She made dinner for herself, a lamb chop smothered in garlic with green beans and mashed potatoes. Frank had hated the smell of lamb and of garlic. Afterward, she tidied up and then took a Hostess chocolate cupcake and a cup of decaffeinated coffee upstairs.

She had finished her cake when she again heard the slam of a car door. Setting down her coffee, she picked up the binoculars and immediately noticed movement in the Cauldwell house. The wife had come home later than usual and was carrying a bag of groceries through the dining room into the kitchen. Lucinda could still see her through the much smaller kitchen window. Little glimpses as she moved around, putting the groceries away in the refrigerator, or the cupboards.

A dark, fast-moving shape entered her field of view. Lucinda sucked in her breath, wanting to shout a warning. Both forms were moving. She tracked them to the dining room. The wife was running but her husband was close behind. Too close. He caught her sweater and spun her around. When he slapped her, she staggered back, legs tangled in one of the chairs. She would have fallen but he held her up and drew back his fist.

His broad back looked like a target to Lucinda. She imagined an arrow, a bullet, a thrown frying pan. She wanted to close her eyes but couldn't. She wanted to call the police but, like animal and child control, she had no faith they would listen to her. They never had before.

The digital clock read two ten when Lucinda woke. It was not unusual for her to wake at two and again at four, before getting up at six to start her day. She supposed it had something to do with an aging bladder. Or maybe it was the emotional hangover from what she'd witnessed earlier.

She'd stayed and watched until the end of it. Seen the husband and wife walk arm-in-arm into the living room. He had kissed the top of her head and said something in her ear. Lucinda could imagine his sweet words, the promises he whispered.

In the dark, she navigated through the familiar room, and down the hallway to the bathroom. Ensuites were not a thing when her old house was built. It had been the original farmhouse, once sitting in the middle of one-hundred-and-eighty acres of hay fields. The fields had been sold to the developers responsible for the sprawl of suburbia that now surrounded it. The original owners had kept the house and the half acre it sat on until selling it to Frank and Lucinda some forty-three years ago.

Returning to the bedroom, she saw a light pass across the back window. It was there and gone so fast she wasn't sure she'd really seen it. A flicker, as if a car had driven by. That happened on the front-facing window, but not the back.

Moving to the window, she glanced out between the curtains and caught some sort of motion in the backyard of the Cauldwell place. Luckily the sky was clear and the full moon cast plenty of light. She picked up the binoculars and zoomed onto a figure clad in dark clothes, a hood over its head, digging a hole in the garden. A strange time to be out planting, she thought, still a little foggy from sleep.

She saw the glint of moonlight on metal as the figure stepped on the shovel, driving the blade deep. Then the person lifted the soil and added it to a growing pile. The tilled soil was probably soft, but the job was taking time. Eventually, the figure stopped to rest. It raised a forearm to wipe sweat from its face and knocked the hoodie back, revealing light red hair.

Lucinda observed the wife tugging a man-sized bundle to the edge of the hole. Then she sat down and used her feet to roll it into the fresh grave. Once that was done she got on her knees, reached for something lying on the ground, and threw it on top of the body. The binoculars worked so well Lucinda could make out a smudge of dirt on the woman's face and see her lips move.

As she watched the wife get up and begin to shovel dirt from the mound onto her husband's body, Lucinda made up her mind. Still in the dark, she found her clothes and went to the bathroom to dress.

It was three thirty-three by the time she had gathered her tools and slipped into the backyard of the Cauldwell place. The old gate hinge was indeed rusty and made a high-pitched squeal when she forced it open, but she didn't think anyone except her and a few field mice heard it. The house was dark, and nothing stirred. The scent of the lilacs in full bloom accompanied Lucinda as she moved across the spongy ground to the slightly raised area.

She'd brought her own shovel for the job. It had a short handle, so she knelt to dig, happily finding it was not difficult. The grave was shallow. Within an hour she had uncovered the corpse. She'd also brought rope and now tied both ends around the body's ankles, leaving a wide loop, which she tossed over her shoulder, like the strap of a purse.

Throwing her weight against it, she pulled. It was slow going, but inch by inch she dragged the body from the hole. After it was free the going got easier. She leaned into the task, and once the body was moving, kept up the momentum. When she reached the path, with its flat, smooth stones, the body slid along behind her with almost no resistance.

The old farmhouse had come with a well, but once city water became available, they'd stopped using it. Frank had torn down the rock wall around the well and for safety, covered the hole with a large flat stone about twice the diameter of a manhole cover. When Lucinda decided to get rid of his manicured lawn, she had told the paving company to use the stone as a starting point from which all the paths would originate.

Stopping when she reached the well, she dropped the rope and rubbed her shoulder which she knew would be sore and bruised for days. But her work was not done.

For a lever, she picked up the four-foot-long rebar she'd left there earlier, alongside the fulcrum, a rock taken from the border of one of the flower beds. Wedging the lever under the well cap, she then laid it across the rock. When she pushed down on the end of the rebar the stone cap rose. She pushed the bar forward and the cap shifted back a few inches. It took three attempts before enough of the well was revealed.

She sat down on one of the wrought iron lawn chairs to catch her breath. At her feet, beside the sparkling mica of the stone, was a stain of darkness two feet wide.

Once she had rested long enough, Lucinda dragged the body to the edge of the hole and then rolled it onto its stomach. Standing on the capstone, she gathered material bunched at the man's shoulders and squatted, using all her weight to drag him forward. With each tug, he slid toward her an inch or two.

It would have been easier if she'd cut him free of the shower curtain the wife had rolled him in. With his arms raised he would have gone into the hole like a diver. Instead, she had to heave and jerk until she got his shoulders in and then his chest.

The body was halfway in, bent at the waist when suddenly she felt a tug. She opened her hands and let gravity finish the job. The sensation of the plastic shower curtain sliding across her palms stayed with her a moment after the body disappeared. Soil, that had shifted and slid into the hole, sent up a pleasant scent of compost and earthworm. After a moment, from far below, she heard a soft thump.

Her hands were sweating as she moved the giant rock back over the well. This time it took four attempts. Then she set the garden furniture back in place, rolled the fulcrum into the toothless-looking space in the border, and carried the rebar back to the garden shed. She would need them again soon and she was tired and sore enough to consider leaving the well open and the tools there but decided it wasn't worth the risk.

Work done, she went upstairs to wash her hands and face. The sting of soap exposed a bloody scrape along the edge of one hand. It didn't concern her. All gardeners had cuts and scrapes.

The storage room at the end of the hall held her ironing board and iron which she used now and then. The rest of the room was dusty with disuse, including an old sewing machine, a dresser filled with material, and old quilts in various stages. She never had been able to make one like Frank's mother did.

Digging through the dresser drawers she found what she wanted, grabbed it up, and hurried out. In the garage, she took the remote and opened the door, then started the car. She didn't drive much these days. Everyone seemed to be in such a hurry that she often felt breathless and out of sorts by the time she got back from the market. The important thing was she did drive.

The clock in the car said it was nearly seven. Perfect.

Standing at the door of the Cauldwell's place, Lucinda decided ringing the bell would be less likely to get the attention of the lookie-loos than knocking would, so she pressed the button.

After a couple of long minutes, her neighbor answered. Her brown, not blue, eyes were red from crying or lack of sleep, or both. She looked drowsy and disheveled and still wore yesterday's clothes.

"Yes?" the woman asked.

Lucinda pushed her way in and shut the door behind her, ignoring her neighbor's ineffectual effort to block her. She stepped into the living room, turned, and without preamble said, "I saw you in the garden last night. Now don't get into a tizzy. We've got work to do. You go get a suitcase and you pack up your man's toothbrush and whatnot. Toss in some clothes and shoes. Whatever he'd take for a trip. You got it?"

Obviously dazed, but with realization slowly dawning, Lucinda watched as the woman began to make sense of what she was hearing.

"What's your name?" Lucinda asked, "I can't keep calling you the wife."

"Angela. My name is Angela."

"Okay. I'm Lucinda, Lucy to my friends. You go and find that suitcase and get it packed. I've brought a quilt top. I'm going to put it on your table in the dining room. When you get done, we'll wrap that suitcase in it and I'm gonna carry it away with me. Later, if anyone asks, I've been teaching you to quilt, and what they saw me put in my car was a pile of quilts we've been working on together. You understand that?" She was a little concerned by the way the wife—the way Angela—kept staring into the middle distance.

"Wake up now and listen to me. I know it's Saturday and the neighbors are probably all sleeping in, but there's no reason to take chances. Better if we can explain anything they might see. You have to pay attention. Do you hear me?"

"I hear you," she said, and it did seem like she had. "I'll go pack his suitcase right now. It won't be hard. I did it for him lots of times. He'll want his blue suit and that new tie. He likes to work out so maybe a t-shirt and his running shoes . . . But what are you going to do with it?"

Lucinda rolled her eyes. "Why, get rid of it of course. You fought. He packed a bag and left. When they come to talk to me, and they will, I'll say I was up, heard you two fighting, and saw him stomp off down the street. I'm an old woman. They won't be surprised I can't sleep or that I'm nosy.

Angela nodded and began to turn away but then paused as a thought must have come to her. "But w-why didn't he take the car?"

Lucinda took a deep breath to disguise her exasperated sigh. "It wouldn't start. We'll take care of that in a minute. You want a car, don't you?"

"Yes. You know about cars?"

"My husband liked me to know things. Now come on. Bring me his cell phone and the charger too. Now get a move on."

Later that afternoon the two women sat in Lucinda's backyard, surrounded by a dazzling display of colorful flowers. The sun was warm and even the butterflies and hummingbirds seemed to move slowly through the peaceful garden.

Cookies and lemonade had been placed on the wrought iron table centered on the wide round paving stone. Lucinda slid her feet out of her shoes and rubbed them on the smooth warm surface. As they sipped lemonade, they had talked about the art of quilt-making. Now Lucinda steered the conversation to more important matters.

"I think you should wait until late Monday morning and then call your husband at work. When they say he hasn't come in you will hang up and call the police to report him missing."

"But what if they ask why I waited so long?"

"You'll tell them you had a fight Friday night. That you were too mad to talk to him. He left and you didn't want to see him again. That bruise on your eye will tell the story for you. Then you'll say you calmed down and decided you wanted to see if you could work things out, so you called him tonight—and by the way, make sure you do that at eight o'clock."

"Eight?"

"Yes, or a minute or so later. That will give me time to get down-town. I'll hear it ring but I won't answer. If they check call records, the police will think he was downtown around ther. After your call, I'll take the battery out and toss the phone. You should probably call a few times after that to show you tried."

"But where will his phone be?"

"You don't need to know."

"I guess not. You know so much about these things."

"I watch a lot of mysteries on television. It's not that hard. On Monday, after you call him at work and they say he hasn't come in, you call the police. You're worried. He's never left like that before. Or has he?"

"No. Never. But what will they do when they can't find him?"

"Oh, they'll have questions for you, but you don't have any answers. The last time you saw him he was storming down the street, suitcase in hand, even angrier because his car wouldn't start. You'll have to get the car towed to a shop, by the way, and get it looked at. It won't cost much to fix. It's just a dead battery. You turned the head-lights off this morning like I told you to, didn't you?"

"Yes, I did."

"Good."

"And you smoothed out the garden?"

"Yes."

"Good."

"You never said where you put the suitcase or . . . it.

"No, I never did, and I never will." She looked down at her hands, both scraped now. "Don't you worry. That suitcase won't ever turn up. She didn't add that "it" would be fine and would not even lack for company.

Angela poured lemonade into their glasses and said, "I don't know how I'll ever be able to repay you."

"Now, don't you worry about that," Lucinda said, repeating something her friend Elsa had told her years ago, as the two of them slid the rock from the top of the well for the first time. "After all, what are neighbors for, if not to look after each other?"

"That's nice. Thank you."

"You're welcome. I am curious about something though."

"Yes?"

"When you were kneeling by the hole in the garden it looked like you said something. If you don't mind me asking?"

"Not at all. I just said I. Don't. Like. Roses. I wanted to scream it at him but that would have been stupid." She looked around nervously and lowered her voice. "When you've just killed someone, you have to talk in whispers. Right, Lucinda?"

Lucinda nodded at Angela, smiled, and then said, "From now on you go ahead and call me Lucy. I think we're going to be more than neighbors. I think we're going to be friends."

Pam's Inspiration For This Story

I had read "Woman on a Train," and was thinking about what someone might see through their window by chance and how that might affect them. Would they let it go or would they become involved?

In my twenties, I owned a yard maintenance business and worked for a lot of elderly women whose husbands had passed. I was often a little disturbed by how often they seemed to gleefully celebrate the loss by buying things that had been forbidden to them. Often it was new furniture, new hobbies, a different often smaller kind of car. Putting these two ideas together, I was inspired to write the story of two women, neighbors, brought together by circumstance.

ABOUT THE AUTHOR

Pamela is an award winning, Pacific Northwest author of dark mysteries and thrillers, as well as science fiction, fantasy and horror titles.

An army brat, she was born in Germany and moved with her family 17 times before her father retired to Oregon, where she has steadfastly remained. She has two grown children and lives with her remarkably patient husband and various four-legged roommates.

Learn more about Pam's books at her website: https://www.pambainbridgecowan.com/

38

Whispers of the Halcyon

Dari LaRoche

CHAPTER ONE

*T*here! She heard it again. Arianne cocked her head to the side, listening closely to the whispers floating gently on the breeze, trying to discern the coded message concealed by Zephyrus as he surfed the light air currents coming from the west.

Still too far away to be sure, she had to wait, taking a chance on being discovered. Arianne remained hidden in plain sight among the human women here in the village, rather than shrinking to the much smaller fairy form that she usually took, when she stayed closer to her home within the Hidden Glen on the far side of the forest.

A small river rolled through the glen. Overhanging trees shaded the area and made it hard to see the sky in some places. Riotous carpets of multicolored flowers covered the ground wherever sunshine managed to pierce the overhead canopy. Moss-covered boulders and fallen logs created steppingstones and bridges to cross from one side to the other. Her own fairy glade where she lived was on the opposite side of the river, near the Wishing Pool, and out of sight of anyone just walking through the glen.

Zephyrus didn't show up much these days. So, if the God of the West Wind was trying to send her a message, she would be wise to listen and attempt to decipher it.

They had been friends for years and years, ever since she was tiny. He had always watched out for her, whenever he was around. He took her with him to ride the air currents when she had grown bigger and stronger. As the harbinger of spring, he made sure to bring her the first flower blooms to peek through the last snow remnants after winter when he came to her home in the forest.

She listened again, trying to make it out. She was going to have to move away from the people around her in the marketplace, if she wanted to hear it clearly, and that would not be safe. No one noticed her among all the humans, but if she was by herself on the fringes, she would not be so lucky. Though her wings wouldn't show, they would see her as different, and as such, threatening, even though she wasn't. Her pointy ears and elven face would be obvious if the wind blew her long, curly burnished-gold hair aside. Particularly if it lifted her hat from her head. She would have to be quick and only stay a minute.

Ah, there! Clearer now that she was away from the press of people, she heard Zephyrus.

"Come to the open glade. We can ride the thermals and talk, my sweet."

He had always called her that ever since she could remember. It made her feel loved—safe and loved.

She hurried into the forest, back toward her home. Once safely away from humans, she brought about the change to her much smaller size so that she would remain unnoticed if anyone stumbled into her glade before her friend arrived.

Arianne hooked one foot around a large philodendron vine that climbed her favorite tree and sat on the giant leaf, waiting for Zeph. He'd probably sneak around behind her and come up from the back side of her tree, in a useless attempt to tumble her off her perch.

His best trick though was to scoop her up as he snuck up behind her and go soaring into the sky. She'd cling to his back while laughing wildly and crawl up to where she could snuggle behind his ear and talk while they flew. This time, he sent a puff of breeze that tumbled her off her big leaf. But he never let her fall. Zephyrus slipped forward underneath her, then angled upward, gaining speed and altitude as they left the glade far behind.

SECURE NOW, ARIANNE SAT IN THE DIP OF THE NEW ELONGATED GOLDEN hoop Zephyrus had attached to his earlobe just for her, a swing that she could hold onto while flying. Soaring with the God of the West Wind, she pretended she was one of the aerialists she had seen at the circus that had come to the village near her last summer. She had sneaked into the pavilion and watched in fascination as the beautiful women flew through the air and the bare-chested men in tight pants caught them at the last second.

It would be a true rush like no other. Well, perhaps like one other she had heard her fairy sisters talk about in hushed whispers, but she had not experienced that one yet.

Like usual, Zephyrus was direct when he started talking.

"Do you remember the Fairy Prince, Blaze? You met him at the Seelie Court when I took you there to meet King Oberon."

Arianne shivered as she thought of Blaze again. She had tried to put him out of her mind after that event. A trick that was difficult to do, considering his engaging personality, charm, and good looks.

"I remember him. Frankly, it has been impossible to forget."

She shivered again, enough that she knew Zephyrus could feel the vibration of the hoop passing through his sensitive ear. Lost in her thoughts for a few minutes, she remembered the glamour of the Court and the prince himself.

He had asked her to dance and had held her close as they whirled around the ballroom floor. As if he had choreographed their dance steps to the maestro's ending notes, when the music stopped, they were on the edge of the ballroom near some tall, beautiful plants. The prince had adroitly moved them into seclusion and had kissed her. And what a kiss it was. Her first—full of emotion and angst and heartache and the beginnings of love all at once—one that bombarded her senses and left her trembling.

"Never doubt it, sweet Arianne. I will be back for you," Blaze had said, his gaze intense, reaching deep into her soul.

She thought he meant for another dance, but that never happened. He had continued to move from one beautiful young fairy to the next, showing no favors as the piercing eyes of his father, King Oberon, looked on. He never spoke to her again.

She sighed now, a sigh deep enough that the winds traveling beside them exhaled gently with her.

"What's wrong, my sweet? Are you thinking of Prince Blaze? I can guarantee you he is thinking of you."

Arianne snorted and spat out. "As if. He never even spoke to me after the dance. He danced with every other fairy of marriageable age in the palace that night and never searched me out again." Her anger ballooned hot, then collapsed just as quickly as sadness took over. "He never even looked at me, Zeph. And I wanted him to." She barely whispered the last, afraid to put it out into the universe because it made her feel so very vulnerable.

"He couldn't," Zephyrus said. "It was not the time."

"And now is? Why?" Arianne did not believe for a minute that her old friend was right, but she wouldn't argue with him. The God of the West Wind had proved her wrong before.

ARIANNE DIDN'T SAY ANY MORE. SHE JUST LET THE RUSH OF EMOTIONS—from longing, to sadness, and finally to curiosity—pass over her as she thought of Prince Blaze. She heard again his promise to come back for her. It tickled the edges of her subconscious like the lightest down of a newborn baby owl. And like that owl, with its huge, all-seeing eyes, it peered into her soul and took root, spreading warmth like the tendrils of heat reaching out from coals left in a fire pit to take the chill off a long night in the fairy glade.

Zeph's gruff voice broke into her consciousness. "You are thinking so loud I can feel the tremble of your thoughts through your hands on that swing you are sitting on. What gives, my sweet?"

She laid her cheek against the gold wire closest to his neck and snuffled. "I have heard on the *Fairy Vine* that King Oberon has decreed that Prince Blaze must marry. And soon. Before the winter winds take over the land."

"This is true. My brother, Boreas, God of the North Wind of winter, swears as much. And my brother, Notus, insists it will happen this summer in his season as he brings the winds and refreshing rains from the south. Does that bother you?"

"Of course, it does. I thought he was coming back for me. At least one more dance. Another stolen kiss. Now he will be gone forever to me."

"I'm not so sure, my sweet. I heard a rumor on the winds. A rumor that Prince Blaze is looking for someone special, someone who stole his heart away and won't give it back. Do you have any idea who that might be?" Zeph shook with laughter as he made a sharp turn around a mountain peak and plunged down into the valley with the speed of —well—of the West Wind, to be sure.

Arianne clutched the swing wires and squealed in glee as Zephyrus chased the winding river through the forests and glens, causing the rapids below them to leap and froth in terrifying maelstroms of swirling confusion. As they exited the gorge and shot upward, Zephyrus chuckled softly.

"Well, little Arianne? Who might it be?"

She sucked in a deep breath as they headed back to the fairy glen. "I don't know, Zephy. But I so wish that it was me."

"Who knows, my sweet? Prince Blaze has kept her name close to his heart. Not even King Oberon can get it out of him. But I think you should go to the first Fae Court ball this year and I, in my alter form, Favonius, will escort you."

"But I have not received an invitation. This is the first I have heard of this ball." She worked hard to control her disappointment. She desperately wanted to seek out Prince Blaze once more before he married and was lost to her for all time.

"I am sure you will receive one. All eligible young marriageable age fairies in the Seelie Kingdom will. But even if your invitation is somehow lost on the wind, I will still take you. If for no other reason than you are my friend and I know you want to go. I can guarantee you no one will refuse the God of the West Wind entrance, and everyone will be watching, most especially Prince Blaze."

He settled gently close to the floor of the forest glade and gave a little bump so that she hopped off the swing.

The solemnity of the moment demanded she use his full name. "Thank you, Zephyrus, God of the West Wind. You are my true friend, and you can see how much I want to go to the Fae Court Ball, even if it will shatter my heart into pieces."

He caressed her face and what felt like an ethereal kiss brought warmth to her cheek and her heart.

CHAPTER TWO

*A*rianne was crushed, but she refused to let any of her sister fairies see it. Over the years, she had become adept at hiding her feelings so as not to be teased or bullied. In the past, her outer shell had protected her. Mainly because what was at stake didn't really matter so much. It was all just frosting, like on a fairycake.

But this. This was real. This mattered.

Her hardened shell was becoming a whisper-thin veneer full of cracks. Cracks of longing and disappointment and worry and fear and sadness—so much sadness.

All the beautiful young fairies had received invitations to the ball. Except Arianne. The chatter in the glade for the last couple weeks was of nothing else besides the ball. Everyone—simply everyone—was talking about it. And about the fact that she had not received an engraved card from King Oberon.

No one could figure out why she had been left out. But she knew. And it hurt. It hurt so bad.

Invitations had only been sent to young fairies King Oberon considered eligible as possible wives for Prince Blaze, his first-born son and inheritor to his throne. Obviously, the King himself or Queen Titania had not considered her *eligible*. Who knew why?

Was she too young?

Too old?

Not pretty enough?

Of questionable parentage?

That last one was a possibility as she had no idea who her real parents were. The fairies who had raised her were not her true parents even though she called them Mama and Papa.

Her two cousins, Ella and Holly, had received their invitations to the ball, and Mama's older sister, Lucy, never hesitated to point out that Arianne had been left out. Holly commiserated with her, but Ella just smiled and turned her head. If she didn't know better, she would think that her aunt or one of her cousins had hidden or destroyed her invitation. Arianne had been in the village when they were delivered. But not even her aunt would dare destroy a missive sent by King Oberon, particularly not an engraved invitation to the Seelie Court and the first Fae Ball of the year.

She had been left out on purpose.

Not suitable ran through her head on constant repeat.

She mentally patched up the cracks in her veneer and ignored the feelings that were trying to bury her. She hadn't heard from Zephyrus and the ball was in just two weeks' time. She could only assume that he was off doing his usual windy things and couldn't be bothered with her.

Well, nothing to do about it but ignore it. Perhaps one of her fairy friends or Ella or Holly would be selected by Prince Blaze as his wife and the kingdom's new fae princess.

Aunt Lucy interrupted her reverie. "Since you did not receive an invitation and will not be attending the ball, I want you to come with us and help your cousins with their hair and gowns."

Arianne's heart sunk. She was being relegated to the position of servant. If she accompanied them, there was no way she could get away and go to the ball with Zephyrus, because she would be expected to be present to assist her cousins in all the tiny agonizing details as they dressed for the ball. Arianne just knew they would be gloating every step of the way.

When she glanced at Ella, she spotted the sly look in her cousin's eyes and wondered what that was all about. They were always jealous, but they were also very egotistical and were convinced that they were the most beautiful fairies in the land. Aunt Lucy was certain that one of her daughters was destined to be the new princess.

RESIGNED TO HER ROLE AS *MAID*, ARIANNE HID HER FACE AND TRUDGED away from her aunt and her cousins. She would never—never—never provide ammunition for their spiteful comments by allowing them to see that she cared in the least about Prince Blaze or attending the Fae Ball. After all, she had only danced once with him the previous year. While she had believed his earnest words that he would be back for her after they had shared a kiss, it had not happened.

She slipped deeper into the forest on the border of the fairy glade, searching out the comfort of the heaviest gloom she could find among the thick trees. Her thoughts were as dark as the shadows that hung on the edges of the trail leading to the Wishing Pool.

As she neared her destination, her longtime companion, Cotton, hopped out of the brush, doffed his ears, and led her forward. He stopped every so often, hopping back to her, twitching his nose, and tipping his rabbit ear in a salute to their friendship. Not questioning why, she just followed.

"You understand, don't you, Cotton? I know it is silly to wish to go to the ball and, even more, to wish for Prince Blaze to choose me."

Cotton hopped into the brush and was gone.

"Oh sure, you are one of my only two true friends—you and Zephyrus—and you both are leaving me in this misery."

Just then, Cotton popped back in front of her with a flower in his mouth and raised up on his hind legs so that she could take it. She closely examined the petals of the tiny delicate blue flower with a yellow center eye and white star rays. When she realized what it was, she grinned in delight.

"Where did you find this, Cotton? It's beautiful. I haven't seen any forget-me-nots in the woods so far this year."

Cotton just popped back down onto all four legs and hopped ahead of her, continuing toward the Wishing Pool. When she rounded the last corner, she drew in her breath in wonder at the sight in front of her—something she had never seen in all her years coming here to the Wishing Pool. All the ground surrounding the water was a sea of blue with every spot covered in a tangled mass of forget-me-nots.

"Oh Cotton, look at this. I have never seen such a sight."

She made her way carefully on the steppingstones to the flat rock on the edge where she always sat. Cotton hopped up next to her as she crossed her legs, facing the deep depthless quiet of the pool in front of her.

"It is magic. Pure magic. I have never seen these forget-me-nots here before." She reached forward slowly to stroke Cotton's soft fur. "I wonder how they got here. How did you know?"

Her thoughts turned to Prince Blaze and she smiled as she remembered their one dance at her first Fae Ball. And her very first kiss. It had truly been a night of firsts for her. One that she believed at the time meant more to the prince than it must have.

Not one to dwell on negatives, no matter how sad she was not to receive an invitation to King Oberon's ball, she looked around again at the mass of flowers, something she had never seen before in her entire life. The sea of blue brought her peace, and she relaxed as she thought of the prince and swirling around the dance floor in his arms. If that was all she could have, it would have to do.

Arianne stayed by the Wishing Pool with Cotton, avoiding going home, until the sun started to set. Cotton traveled with her to the edge of the fairy glade, where he sat up, tipped his ear forward in salute and then hopped away.

She slipped in the front door of her home, trying her best to be quiet. Mama stood from the table and gave her a tight hug, holding her to her heart for several minutes.

"Sorry, Arianne. No invitation today."

"Don't worry, Mama. I really hoped, but I do not expect one. For some reason, King Oberon must not think I am eligible to be a princess in the Seelie Court."

"Maybe next year." Mama patted Arianne's back and hugged her even closer. "I suspect that Prince Blaze's brother, Cosmo, will be choosing a wife then."

"No, Mama, just no! And besides that, Aunt Lucy expects me to go and be a *ladies' maid* for my cousins. I will never do that! I will stay here with you and Papa and Cotton."

"Shush, sweetheart. It's okay. You do not have to go. I certainly wouldn't want to go either. Lucy may be my sister, but that whole family is rude, spiteful, and conniving. No need for you to be part of that debacle."

"Thank you, Mama." She headed for bed and then turned back. "Oh, you wouldn't believe the Wishing Pool. It is covered in the blue forget-me-nots. I have never seen such a thing. So beautiful."

Her mother sucked in a breath and her eyes started to sparkle. "Did you make a wish?"

"No, Mama. I was so amazed by all the flowers, I completely forgot."

Her mother turned her around and pushed her toward the door. "Go! You must go back there right now and make a wish. And be sure to think long and hard about exactly what you want. What you saw was magic. Pure magic. And it has not happened at the Wishing Pool since I was your age and wished with all my heart that I could be with your Papa. Now, go. And hurry!"

Not stopping to ask any questions, Arianne rushed out the door and flew down the path into the forest toward the Wishing Pool. About halfway there, Cotton darted out in front of her and led the way. When she reached the big flat rock by the edge, she looked around in wonder again at all the beautiful forget-me-nots, then fell to her knees in the center of the patch of flowers, gathering together a quick bouquet to hold while she made her wish.

She clenched the soft blue flowers in her hand. Her nerves were tight as kite strings and her belly rolled with acid that threatened to come up in her throat. She picked her way with care through the sea of blue surrounding her, trying her best not to crush the blooms on the ground. As she settled onto the flat rock, she tucked her feet underneath her and looked out over the still reflective surface of the Wishing Pool.

Cotton hopped up beside her. Dusk was fast approaching. She had to hurry to make her wish before full dark when the magic would be gone.

She sat and thought for a few minutes, remembering Prince Blaze and how she had felt, dancing in his arms. The thrill of his kiss filled her even now. She remembered his words as if he was standing before her at this very moment by the Wishing Pool. He had promised when he kissed her that he would be back for her.

She brought the delicate blooms to her nose and sniffed.

"Ah, Cotton, I made it in time. The flowers have no smell now. It is not officially night yet."

She didn't feel in the least bit strange talking to her rabbit. Cotton was far more than just any rabbit. He was smart and her friend, and he watched out for her in the forest. And today, he had done something truly special by bringing her the forget-me-not.

She sat quietly, her feet tucked under her, and thought of what she wanted to wish for and what would make her truly happy. Her mother had cautioned her to think long and hard and be specific in asking for her wish. Finally, she was ready. She just hoped she would not stumble over the words.

"Oh, Goddess, Queen of all Fairies, please grant my wish today that I make on these flowers, your forget-me-nots, that you have magically placed in this glade by the Wishing Pool. Last year at the Fae Ball, I met Prince Blaze and he danced with me, and we shared a glorious kiss—my first. He promised he would be back for me, but he never returned."

She hung her head for a moment in silence, then lifted the blue flowers up with both hands in supplication. "Dear Goddess, please grant my wish this eve. I humbly ask to go to the ball and, further, that Prince Blaze chooses me to be his princess, wrapping us together forever like I hold these flowers up to you, as a symbol of true love, devotion, and loyalty for all time."

Arianne brought the bouquet down to her nose and inhaled deeply. As she did, her head grew light, and her eyes started to close. The sweetest purest scent she had ever smelled wafted around her, holding her in a cocoon of joyful relaxation as she closed her eyes fully. Like in her dreams this whole past year, Prince Blaze was there. He came walking toward her around the rim of the Wishing Pool, his hand outstretched, palm up.

"Come, my love. It is time."

She rose to her feet, still in her dream, and reached for him, the forget-me-nots falling into the pond and floating on the surface out toward the middle.

She curtseyed as she reached for his hand. As he raised her up to her feet, he glanced at the flowers floating in the water and smiled. "I see you found my flowers I sent you."

"Cotton found them and showed me," Arianne said, motioning to the rabbit beside her.

Prince Blaze pulled her closer and folded her into his arms. It felt as if she had never left his embrace. He leaned down, cupping her face with his hands, and took her lips in a gentle kiss soon moving into a deeper, more passionate kiss that wove a spell around her.

"Come to the Fae Ball in two weeks' time. I will see you there and we will continue this conversation."

"I do not have an invitation. All the other fairies got one, but I did not."

He frowned. "I gave your name to my parents, King Oberon and Queen Titania. But no matter, our dear friend, Favonius, will bring you to me. Ah, sweet Arianne, I will see you soon." He leaned down and gave her another soft kiss and then he was gone.

She sat back down hard on the flat sitting stone by the side of the pool with a loud "Umpf!" The last few minutes had been very confusing.

She needed a bit of time to think about her vision of Prince Blaze before she headed back home. The whole scene swirled through her mind again, just like they had floated around the ballroom last year. The more she thought about what had just happened, the wider her smile grew. Zeph must have been right. Prince Blaze had not forgotten her. He had just not been able to act on his desires last year.

"Well, Cotton, I am just going to have to figure out how to go with Favonius and get a ball gown to wear and stay away from Aunt Lucy and my cousins. No problem at all. I will have to make them think I am going and then go hide until they have no choice but to leave."

Arianne brushed off her clothes from kneeling on the ground among the forget-me-nots and sitting on the rock. She picked a few flowers for her mother, tying them into a bouquet with her blue hair ribbon. Then she made her way quickly back along the path to her house just past the forest's edge.

Hundreds of fireflies moved up and down and pointed out the way to her so that she continued directly home and did not wander from the path. She ran the last hundred yards to her house, bursting in the front door and shouting for her mother. In the kitchen, she opened the lower door of the cabinet to find a vase to put the flowers in so they could grace the sideboard against the wall.

Mama and Papa were both sitting at the kitchen table waiting for her. She saw them look softly at each other as they spotted the blue forget-me-nots she had brought home.

"Remember that night, dear? I was just as out of breath as our Arianne is when I ran home to tell my mother that I had wished on the flowers just before the day ended and they released their glorious scent into the air. It surrounded me and I saw you in a vision."

Papa nodded. "And what happened with you, Arianne? You seem to be a bit excited. Please tell us."

CHAPTER THREE

$\mathcal{A}$rianne still didn't have an invitation by the morning of the Fae Ball. Her cousins, especially Ella, but even Holly now, gloated that they were going, and Arianne was not even invited. Aunt Lucy mentioned several times how glad she was that Arianne could help her daughters get ready. But voice was not in the least bit pleasant. In fact, it was snide and demeaning.

Mama and Papa had devised a plan that would force Aunt Lucy and the cousins to leave without her. Once breakfast was over and the cousins were packed and ready to load into their coach, Arianne waited for her mother to step out to wave the cousins off and then slipped out the back door behind Papa. She followed him as they headed deep into the fairy glade where Papa worked in the daytime.

The wind currents carried Aunt Lucy's angry voice, yelling at her sister.

"You have never been a good mother. That girl is obstinate, willful, and ungrateful. She should be happy to help her cousins, not running off in a pout. She is an embarrassment to this family."

Too bad Mama had to stay while her sister yelled and carried on.

Papa just grinned at Arianne and winked as he carried her satchel of personal items for her. Zephyrus had sent word that he had arranged for her ball gown and shoes, so she did not need to worry about that.

Once they were certain that the cousins were gone, Papa circled back around with her to the Wishing Pool deep in the glade.

"Zephyrus will meet us here, Arianne, and will take you. He insists that your mother and I come in a separate coach later so we can see how the night goes. He has a room for us at the palace, close to yours."

As they stood on the flat rock by the pool, Cotton at their feet, he put his arm around her and whispered so softly her pointed ear twitched and bent forward in an effort to hear more clearly.

"I told your Mama to pack a ball gown and I have a suit. Perhaps we will be able to have a dance together. Maybe even meet Prince Blaze, King Oberon, and Queen Titania."

Arianne smiled at him. "I hope so. Thank you for taking care of me all these years, Papa. You and Mama have showered me with your love all my life. I love you both so much."

He just hugged her. "Listen. Feel the breeze. Zephyrus is coming for you, my lovely daughter. You will be the most beautiful fairy at the ball and Prince Blaze will only have eyes for you."

Tears fell over her lower lashes at that. "I hope so, Papa. Oh, how I hope so."

⁓

Zephyrus settled on the surface of the Wishing Pool right in front of them with barely a ripple.

"Are you ready, my sweet? Don't tell me you are going to try to bring that critter with long ears that's beside you."

"Cotton? Why can't I bring him?" she teased the cranky god as she pretended to pick up her rabbit.

"Because his ears will tickle me, and I will sneeze. And if I sneeze, who knows what will happen? Perhaps the whole forest will be laid flat." His petulance disappeared and he chuckled, which caused small waves to disturb the still, glassy water surface. He turned so she could tuck her satchel into the folds of his neck and then time her jump onto the golden hoop in his ear when he dipped down near the flat rock.

Papa waved as Zephyrus lifted them to the sky. "Take care of her," he called.

She waved. "I'll see you and Mama later," floated back on the breeze as Zephyrus rose into the thermals and headed for the Summer Court of the Seelie where the Fae Ball would be held.

The glistening turrets and expansive gardens came into view as Zephyrs slowed their approach. Colorful flowers and blooming trees were everywhere. The grounds were full of fairies strolling about in an effort to see and be seen by members of the Court. The King and Queen were on the balcony of the main palace, waving to the fairy families as they arrived.

She didn't see Prince Blaze anywhere.

"Zeph, help me watch for Aunt Lucy and my cousins. I cannot let them see me before the ball or my aunt will insist I come help her daughters."

"Don't worry, my dearest Arianne. Prince Blaze has promised me a suite of rooms so we can each have our own space. It is on the highest level of the cavaedium, where the pool is, on the very top of that ornate building beside the palace. Prince Blaze lives there too and we will be close by him."

She shivered at the thought of being in a room so close to the prince.

Zephyrus settled down softly beside the pool in the middle of the Romanesque courtyard filled with plants and benches. She looked around to see the source of the aroma that floated in the air—sweet orange jasmine—as delicate as the finest perfume. She spotted the trees in full bloom in the large pots spread throughout the courtyard. She had never seen a cavaedium quite like this one.

Zephyrus chuckled then. "I suggest you turn your back if you don't want to see me naked before I glamour some clothes to wear."

She felt her face flush pink as she turned her back but continued to talk to him.

"Did you find me a gown for tonight? I hope so since I didn't bring one."

"The finest seamstress in all the kingdom has made a gown for you. I put it in your room this morning before I came to collect you."

"Oh, I cannot wait to see it. Is it pretty?"

"It is simply stunning, my sweet. As you will be as well. On my arm, of course."

She laughed at his ego. "Oh, you are so good looking, dear Favonius, but Prince Blaze has my heart, I am afraid."

"I wouldn't have it any other way. He is my dear friend. As are you, my sweet."

He took her arm. "Come, I will take you to our quarters so you can see your dress and then I will go and wait for your parents and bring them up here to their room, which is on the other side of the atrium here. Your mother can come help you dress."

CHAPTER FOUR

*A*rianne woke with a start when her mother came into the room.

"Why are you sleeping, Arianne?" she cried. "We have to get ready for the ball."

"Oh, Mama, I was having such a lovely dream about Prince Blaze."

"That may be true, but if we do not hurry, Prince Blaze will be forced to choose another. The ball has already started. I spotted your cousins going in as I headed up here. My sister was walking behind them, looking like a puffed-up stewing hen in that dress she chose to wear."

A laugh was just what she needed after her hopes sunk thinking the prince might have to choose before she could go down to the ball.

After a quick bath, she brushed her hair until the heavy waves glistened like the most lustrous gold cascade. Her mother fixed it in place with a few simple hairpins and then went to get the dress.

"Close your eyes, Arianne, and raise your arms while I lower this confection over your head. Then you can look in the mirror."

She did as she was instructed, shivering as the finest threads drifted over her and into place. Her mother secured the back, then gasped as she stood behind Arianne.

"Oh my, just look at you. You look like a true princess indeed, daughter."

Arianne peeked at her reflection in the mirror. What she saw brought a rush of tears she had to struggle to hold back.

The person in the mirror staring back at her was no longer a young girl. She was a woman grown and a beautiful one at that. Someone that any man would be proud to have on their arm, not least of which would be her escort, Favonius, waiting patiently in the next room. She could hear the rumble of him talking with her father.

"Hurry up in there or we will be too late, and you may as well have stayed home."

Perhaps the God of the West Wind was not as patient as she thought.

"Or come to help your cousins into their finery," her father added.

That was all it took to speed her up. She slid her feet into the silver and blue slippers that had a tiny blue flower on each heel. Once her shoes were on, she walked out with her mother and twirled for the men.

"Favonius, how did you manage to have this dress made? It is perfection. It is the filmiest gossamer silver like a butterfly's wings." She spun once more and then held up the skirt of the dress so they could see the clusters of embroidered forget-me-nots all around the hem. "They are just like the field of flowers, the ones that Prince Blaze said he sent to me when I dreamed of him beside the Wishing Pool. I still do not understand that vision."

"Magic is magic, dear daughter. I told you as much when I sent you back to make your true wish." Again, Arianne saw her mother's eyes glow as she looked at her Papa and gently clasped his forearm.

Favonius held out his hand to take hers and tucked it around his elbow. "Shall we go? I am sure Prince Blaze is getting nervous by now." He smiled at her as he led them across the courtyard and down the marble steps.

Her papa spoke up, his tone gruff. "It will do him good. He will appreciate her all the more."

Dance music poured out the doors when they reached the entrance to the ballroom. A quick glance upward showed her Favonius was in his element. The pride and friendship in his eyes as he looked down at her convinced her that they looked fabulous together. In spite of her growing confidence, she clutched his elbow tighter and steeled her dancing stomach nerves. It would never do to throw up just as they entered the grand ballroom.

Favonius looked like the god he was, arresting in his formal attire of the darkest blue, just like the night sky. If you looked just right, it seemed to sparkle like stars. Subtle though—never gaudy. He matched the flowers swirling around the hem of her gown.

The music ended and the herald spoke into the ensuing silence.

"Favonius, God of the West Wind, and the fairy, Arianne, of Hidden Glen.

She stepped forward, gliding by Favonius' side. The crowd parted for the imposing god, who led them toward the dais where King Oberon stood, Queen Titania on one side and Prince Blaze on the other.

Favonius bowed in respect. She curtsied to the royals in front of her, peeking through her wavy hair as she lowered her eyes. Arianne shifted her glance to the side enough to see Prince Blaze. Her heart jumped and set up a pitter-patter in her chest when she locked eyes with him for a brief moment. His eyes shone and he smiled as he bowed his head in return. She was thankful it wasn't necessary to speak as her throat was closed tight with all the emotions running through her at seeing the prince once more.

As they backed up, straightened, and walked away, she caught the feral glance of her cousin, Ella, and the fury in her Aunt Lucy's eyes.

"You despicable pretender," her aunt hissed. "Now I see why you hid when we left for the Court. You will never be chosen by the prince. My conniving sister must have helped you. Or her useless husband."

Arianne's eyes flashed in fury. "Perhaps not, Aunt Lucy. But my friend and God of the West Wind, Favonius, was kind enough to escort me. And not to play ladies' maid to my cousins, but rather as an official guest of the King and Queen."

"Ladies, please excuse us. I want to dance with this lovely creature here beside me." The imperious god turned her in his arms and swept her into the mix of fairies who had begun dancing off to the sides of the ballroom.

"Thank you, Zephy," she said, reverting to her affectionate nickname for her friend.

"Of course, my sweet. There is no need for you to put up with their abysmal behavior. You are an invited guest here—invited personally by Prince Blaze, I might add—and neither she nor her daughters have any right to insult you."

He swung her in a wide sweeping loop, closer to the center of the room, and dipped her low as the music ended. Her eyes sparkled and her face flushed as she caught the prince's eyes following her every move.

Favonius brought her back to where her parents stood on the edge of the dance floor and spoke to her father.

"I brought your daughter back for one dance with you, while I have the pleasure of dancing with your beautiful wife. Then I will reclaim her for one more dance before the real purpose for this ball begins."

Arianne's mother smiled wide and took the handsome god's arm as he swept her away. Papa folded Arianne close to him and moved her gently around the edges of the dancers so that they could talk.

"Whatever happens, Arianne, I am and always will be so proud of you. You have been a true joy to your mama and me for all these years."

"Thank you, Papa. And thank you for taking me in when my parents died. I love you both and will always be grateful."

"One last thing," Papa said, as they moved closer to her mother and Favonius so that they could change partners. "Remember the magic. Remember the field of forget-me-nots that Prince Blaze sent to you. The magic swirled the night your mama asked for me by the Wishing

Pool and it will work for you too. There was heavy magic in the air that night. Believe in it."

"I do, Papa. Thank you."

She could feel the magic swirling in the air here in the ballroom, sweetened by the scent of all the beautiful flowers, especially the flowering orange jasmine, as she kissed her mama on the cheek and took her escort's arm again.

"Believe in the magic, Arianne," Mama whispered in her ear. "You look beautiful tonight, my lovely daughter."

"She does, doesn't she?" the imposing god asked, as he placed her hand firmly around his arm and turned them to face the royal dais.

"I will do my best, but it is hard with Aunt Lucy and the cousins glaring at me as if I were a scullery maid and not an invited guest."

Favonius patted her hand and turned them slightly so that she could no longer see her discontented cousins and her aunt.

"Ignore them, Arianne. They are not important tonight. You are. Watch and feel the magic. It grows by the moment. The air is vibrating with it."

CHAPTER FIVE

he heralds stood in a line at the base of the royal dais in all their finery and blew their trumpets, gaining the immediate attention of everyone in the huge ballroom. They all waited, eager to see what would happen next, as they faced the raised dais where the royal family stood. Prince Blaze's brother, Cosmo, had stopped dancing with all the beautiful fairy hopefuls and joined the group, standing beside the Queen.

King Oberon held up his hand for silence.

"Thank you all for coming to our first Fae Ball of the Seelie Summer Court this year. It is more than just the start of the season, as you all know. For tonight—" he took Queen Titania's hand in his and leaned down to kiss her forehead, his affection clear for all to see— "our first-born son and my heir, Prince Blaze, will choose his princess from among all of you beautiful young fairies here in attendance tonight."

Queen Titania stopped him, placing her hand on his arm. "If I may interrupt but a short moment, my lord king?" Then, she faced all who were in attendance. "I want you all to know that the choice will be Prince Blaze's alone, with no coaching or pressure from either King Oberon or me. Our deepest wish is for him to be as happy as his father and I are."

"And," the King continued with a twinkle in his eye, "all of you not selected will have another chance next year to gain the favor of our younger son, Cosmo, who will be choosing his bride next year at this same ball."

Cosmo's eyes grew huge. "What?! Surely you jest, father?"

The king just regarded him calmly while Prince Blaze smirked on the other side.

Panicked now, Cosmo looked around at the crowd, at his mother and brother, and finally back at the king. "I am not ready to make a choice as serious as the one you are suggesting. Nor will I be."

"You will be by then, my son. Trust me. You will be." The king had used his most authoritative voice and the entire crowd knew for certain that he meant what he had just said. He continued as he looked out at the gathered crowd with a twinkle in his eye, clear for all to see. "Next year's ball will be most interesting indeed."

"No doubt, it will," the queen added, her smile directed at her younger son beside her.

A dejected Cosmo waved for his brother to carry on. "Your turn, Blaze. Good luck."

The king continued, "Okay then. Prince Blaze will come down to the floor here in front. Each of you beautiful young fairies will come forward in turn and introduce yourselves to the prince, who will talk with you for a few minutes. Your escort to the ball may come with you but may not speak. They must take a step back to allow each fairy to interact with the prince on her own. The heralds will bring you each forward when it's your turn."

The number of hopeful fairies was large, and the prince paid special attention to every one, no doubt making them each feel like he was attempting in a small way to know her more. After all, his decision had to be considered carefully. It was of critical importance since it would affect the rest of his life and the lives of every fairy in the kingdom when he assumed the throne with his princess.

The heralds kept the group moving efficiently. Arianne watched as Ella visited with the prince when it was her turn, laying her hand on his forearm in a familiar fashion as she bent forward as if to hear him better. Arianne tried hard and barely managed not to snort at her cousin's blatant attempt to flirt with the prince.

She knew what her spiteful cousin was doing, especially when she saw her gloat as the herald led her away from the prince after she had managed an extra minute or two in his presence. Arianne felt spikes of jealousy spread but stomped it down and only let the sadness of losing Prince Blaze forever spill from her heart.

Holly was more subdued and quicker to move on. It was obvious that she didn't try to promote herself in the least. After her cousin, the herald brought the rest of the fairies forward one by one.

She looked up at Favonius, grasping his arm tighter. "Do you think they forgot me, Zephy? It is almost the end, and the herald hasn't come for me yet."

He just patted her hand. "I am sure that Prince Blaze has given the heralds instructions as to what he wants. And you know he wanted you here. He tasked me directly to bring you, my sweet. Now stop worrying. You will have wrinkles by the time it is your turn if you don't."

Her hand flew to her forehead in panic to smooth out the skin in reaction to what he said, causing all the guests to look at them as he laughed loudly. Favonius pulled the arm she was clutching in a death grip closer to his side to comfort her.

She forced away her sadness and let a bit a magical hope flood into her mind just as the herald stepped in front of them. "Come, my dear. You are the last, but by no means the least," the kindly old man wheezed.

How he could be a herald and announce people, she did not know.

The old man guided her to Prince Blaze, placing her hand in the prince's outstretched palm so she could give a proper demure curtsy. Favonius loosened her hand clutching his elbow, gave it a little pat, and took the required step backwards, leaving her alone with the prince.

Arianne could feel the tingle of Prince Blaze's touch all the way through her body as she kept her eyes lowered, before peaking upward through the curls that surrounded her face. His smile filled her with joy, and she raised her head as he guided her up.

"You take my breath away, sweet Arianne, just like you have since the first time I saw you at the ball last year."

"Thank you, Prince Blaze. You are most kind. And thank you for the field of flowers that you sent to me by the Wishing Pool. I was so delighted to see the sea of blue. It was pure magic."

"And still is, sweet one. I see that you have chosen to wear my flowers on your gown. I will take it as a tribute and an indication that you feel the same way I do about the two of us. Dare I hope to believe that is true?"

"If you feel only half what I feel, my lord, I shall be happy. But if you indeed feel the same as me, I shall remain joyful forever in the knowing."

"As shall I, my beautiful Arianne. As shall I."

"Favonius," the prince called her friend forward and passed her hand to the imposing God of the West Wind. "I am in your debt this day."

"Never, my good friend. It was always my pleasure."

Her friend guided her back to the edge of the crowd as they all waited to see what would happen next. Even though Prince Blaze was kind and seemed to care especially for her, she would not allow herself to hope too much that he choose her for his very own princess. Magic can go awry as any fairy knows. She hoped her mama was right —that her dearest wish would be granted this night.

———

Prince Blaze walked up on the dais and called the old herald to come closer. He whispered in his ear and the herald hurried away, motioning for another herald to follow him. Everyone in the crowd, including his brother and the king and queen, watched with interest to see what would happen.

In just a few minutes but what seemed like forever, the heralds returned, the younger man carrying a tray with a chaplet of flowers on it. The older man walked very slowly, carrying a cage with a gorgeous electric-blue bird inside. It had a bright orange beak and was snowy white from its throat to its chest.

Every single fairy in the ballroom recognized the bird for what it was. The mythical halcyon bird, symbol of serenity, prosperity, joyful bliss, and love. The bird's presence was most unusual at this time of year since it was normally only seen when it bred and hatched its chicks in nests it made and floated on the sea near the time of the new year, where its magic calmed the waves to keep the nest—eggs and nestlings—safe.

Prince Blaze raised his hand and the room fell silent, straining to hear his every word. "Behold. You all know this mythical bird, the halcyon, which is rarely seen, except for during the winter solstice. It came to me one year ago, this very same month in summer, just before the Fae Ball last season. I was sitting on the balcony outside my room, and it landed beside me on a branch of a potted tree—an orange jasmine—beautiful and scented like fresh oranges. I was talking to myself when it arrived and continued talking as it stayed. I told this very bird how hard it would be to choose the perfect fairy princess in all the kingdom, when so many of you are truly lovely."

All the young fairies smiled at his words and nodded to each other in encouragement as well. Except for Arianne's cousins, of course. They smiled at the prince, but glared at everyone else when they glanced around, especially at her. She spotted Aunt Lucy right behind them, shooting daggers her way like painful darts. She could expect life to be hard when she got back home, to be sure.

Excitement filled the room as everyone watched the prince. You could almost see the currents sliding around each and every fairy as they wondered if they would be lucky enough to be the one chosen.

The halcyon loosed a series of patterned squeaks, chattering as if trying to get the prince to let her out of the cage. "We have developed a camaraderie in the past twelve months, this bird and me. And she will guide me in my search. But be very certain, it is my choice alone in the end."

The prince walked closer to the cage the old herald held, undid the latch, and put his hand inside. The halcyon chattered, hopped on his finger, swiped her beak back and forth on it, then looked up as if to say "Hurry up. Let's get on with this. It has been a long year and I want to get back to my family, just as you want to get started on your own."

Laughter burst forth from the prince as he spoke with the bird. "All right now. I understand you want to go home. Look at all these beautiful fairies. How can I choose just one?"

"My sentiments exactly, Brother." Cosmo looked around the ballroom and grinned, back in good humor once more. After all, he had gained another year to play the field. Perhaps he could even extend it next year if he tried hard enough.

The king shot his youngest son a sharp glance, but his eyes twinkled as he said, "Your mother will not tolerate extensions, Cosmo. Don't even go there."

The bird chattered again, the high-pitched squeaks coming faster. Walking up Prince Blaze's arm, she settled on his shoulder and looked all around as the prince stepped off the dais and wove his way around the ballroom. He started on one side, walked all around the back of the group and up the other side, ending just in front of the king.

The halcyon's chatter increased to the point of nearly painful tones. The prince picked the vision in blue off his shoulder and loosed her into the air, where she flew and swooped and dipped and dove, like was her habit in the wild. She landed at last on the edge of a glistening crystal fountain in the middle of the court, where she took delicate sips of water before flying back to the prince.

"Well, we have waited a full year for this day to come, my dear feathered mythical friend. Do you have an opinion or not?" he asked the halcyon. "I know I do."

The bird lifted high into the air, chattering all the while, made one circle around the glassed-in top of the ballroom, and dove straight down like the kingfisher she resembled, slowing only at the last second to settle softly on Arianne's shoulder. Her electric blue feathers gleamed in the lights of the ballroom. Everyone held their breath and watched in wonder as the bird rubbed its head on her cheek and then pecked curiously at the necklace she wore.

Prince Blaze laughed in delight as he took the chaplet of forget-me-nots from the tray the younger herald held and then stood in front of Arianne.

"You have always and ever been my first and only choice, sweet Arianne," he whispered to her alone as he settled the chaplet on her head. "Even the halcyon knows."

Arianne sucked in her breath as magic swirled around the two of them and the halcyon. The prince knelt on one knee and took her hand in his, brushing the edge of her gossamer gown with care, touching the beautiful blue embroidered flowers around the bottom edge that matched the ones now crowning her head.

"Arianne of Hidden Glen, most beautiful of all fairies in the whole of the Seelie Kingdom, will you consent to be my princess and live with me here forever? I could never forget you after our dance and our first kiss last year here at the Fae Ball. My love for you has only grown deeper since that night last year. Please say you will be mine."

"Oh, my prince. I have thought of you all year long and my love for you has grown like a magical vine, wrapping my heart in hope. When you sent the forget-me-nots to the Wishing Pool, I felt the magic of love swirling all around me and I dreamed of you. I will gladly be your princess."

The prince nodded to Favonius and to her parents and then tucked her hand around his elbow and turned them both toward the royal dais.

"King Oberon. Queen Titania. I have chosen my princess and ask for your blessing on our match."

Arianne's heart filled with joy as the prince bowed to his parents and she sunk into a deep curtsy.

The king took the queen's hand, holding it up in the formal way as he led her down the steps to stand in front of the couple. They both reached forward, taking the hands of their son, Prince Blaze, and Arianne's in their own.

"Of course, you have our blessing, my son. You have chosen well and will lead our kingdom with consideration and care, bringing prosperity and love to all."

The halcyon who was still sitting on Arianne's shoulder, hopped over to the prince and chattered loudly in his ear. He nodded the whole time she was chattering. It was apparent that he understood it all as he interpreted. "She says we must marry before the winter solstice. She has been away from her mate long enough and wishes to continue with her own family, as we should with ours."

He looked fondly at Arianne. "I am ready if you are, my love. Shall we let her go home now? She promises to come back at autumnal equinox for our wedding."

Arianne agreed, and the whole royal family walked together with them to the entry doors of the huge ballroom. The heralds opened it to the night air and the prince took the halcyon onto his hand.

"Thank you for your companionship and your clarity as I searched my heart and made my choice of Arianne for my princess."

Arianne ran her finger once down the brilliant blue back of the halcyon, smiled, and whispered a heartfelt "Thank you" to her as the prince lifted his hand to the sky and loosed the halcyon. The air electrified and sparkled as the mythical bird rose, circled once, and headed for the ocean where her mate awaited her.

The prince folded Arianne into his arms and kissed her long and tenderly. He cupped her cheeks in his hands and locked his eyes with hers. "Never fear, my love. She will be back in just a few months' time to help us celebrate our wedding."

I see this as a fantasy retelling of Cinderella...

This story takes elements from the well-loved fairytale and from mythology, weaving fairies, gods, and goddesses, a charming rabbit named Cotton, and a mythological bird, the halcyon. Oh, and evil step-cousins and aunt.

I normally write novels and novellas that are contemporary romance or romantic suspense. However, when I write short fiction, I nearly always veer into fantasy and paranormal. For me, it is a fun adventure into the unknown.

ABOUT THE AUTHOR

Dari LaRoche writes contemporary romance and romantic suspense that will keep you reading long after the witching hour has passed. Her everyday heroes face challenges requiring strength of character, perseverance, and an ever ready dose of laughter to find their way to love and happiness. Her Rescue Series takes place in the Pacific Northwest and the Caribbean, settings inspired by LaRoche's love for travel and passion for safeguarding the natural environment.

Dari spends most of her days writing and researching her stories, constantly looking for a way to deliver an entertaining read in which her readers feel they are a part of the journey with her. Travel is an integral part of her life. She always keeps a little notebook and her cellphone handy to record tidbits that she will use sometime in the future—no interesting detail is too small to be considered in either a novel or a short story. Her love for the water, above and below the surface, and for tromping around the ruins of castles and forts, fills any bits of time when she isn't at home watching the birds and critters in her garden, or reading, writing, and enjoying her family and friends.

Learn more about Dari and her books at her website: https://darilaroche.com/

Whispers Upon A Star

Mary Vine

CHAPTER ONE

Myka Woods leaned over reading an article about a spectacular site coming to the November night sky. A comet known as Tempel-Tuttle would leave fragments from a meteor shower and the earth would pass through the debris causing fifteen shooting stars per hour.

Enthused, she rubbed her hands together. After winning first prize for the photograph she'd taken of a comet called Leonard last December, she now wanted to witness this monumental sight and capture it on film.

Although exhausted from a long day at work, she continued with her bedtime routine of turning off the kitchen light and gazing out at the stars in the Idaho sky. The more she looked, the more she saw; the rising moon in the eastern sky and to the southwest the incredibly bright light of the planet Venus. She sighed in appreciation.

Directly across the creek was a small, old yellow cottage that had been empty since she'd bought her house and the previous owner said she never saw a light on. Now though, light, however dim, shined from the window facing her.

She switched on the kitchen light. After taking off the cover and lens guard of a pair of binoculars, she turned off the light and pointed the strong lenses beyond the creek. Certainly, there wouldn't be any electricity at the house. So maybe she was wrong. No, light moved inside the building like someone using a flashlight to search out every corner, ceiling, and window.

Still in the dark, Myka stepped away and laid the binoculars on the counter. Concern weighed on her as she entered the living room and turned on the light. Should she notify the police?

It had been almost a year since the murder in her neighborhood, she reminded herself and decided to be safe rather than sorry.

She grabbed her car keys, no longer tired.

AT MIDNIGHT, STATE BUREAU OF INVESTIGATION SPECIAL AGENT CALEB Locke's duplex was dark. Without knocking, Myka took a key from her purse and opened the door. She entered the living room, then the hallway, and stood before a closed bedroom door.

"Caleb," she said, but not too loudly. He responded better with a calm voice in moments like this. He'd given her a key for emergencies last winter when the killer thought she'd taken a picture of him. When they'd caught the killer, she hadn't given it back. She was sure he left it that way as his manner of inviting her into his life. To her it wasn't a large gesture, like it would be by saying he loved her or committing to her if in words only. Still, she hadn't stated she loved him either, but held out for emotional assurance from him. She didn't blame him; he had a dangerous job that required toughness. So, all in all, she felt honored that he'd given her access to him.

She knocked on his door, then stepped to the side, careful not to get a gun pointed at her.

"Caleb. It's me."

"Come on in, then."

He rubbed his face with both hands as she walked in. "Are you here to take advantage of me?" he asked, groggily.

"No."

He sat up exposing his bare chest, half sighed, and half yawned. "You know it's late and I worked a long day. So did you."

Myka sat on the edge of the bed. "I felt it imperative that I tell you that I saw lights flashing around that yellow house behind me."

"Car lights maybe?"

"No, I turned off the kitchen light and used my binoculars for a better look."

His eyebrows furrowed. "Tell me about that house."

"It's been vacant for years."

"I can check on it in the morning. It might be as simple as someone finally wanting to do something with it."

"I just have a bad feeling about it is all," she said and rubbed her arms.

"It has been almost a year since Macy was murdered near you, it's natural to think about it again, especially as it's getting darker in the evenings."

She looked down in thought and stuck a strand of dark hair behind her ear. "Maybe you're right. I'd still like you to check it out. You know, so I don't worry. If someone was waving a light around in my house, I'd want it checked out."

"Yeah, I will. First thing in the morning. I'll find out who owns the place and then go from there."

After letting out a breath, she said, "Yeah, I suppose you're right. Again. I'll go home and get some sleep."

"It's probably nothing, you know?"

"I like your positivity. It's not like you at all. You must want me to leave." When he didn't answer, she chuckled. "I will. Sweet dreams."

"Yeah, babes. See you tomorrow."

Myka was in the back of her hardware store, ordering supplies, when Caleb stuck his head in the office door.

"You busy?"

"Nothing that can't wait." She pushed her chair back and crossed her arms. "Well, was I only seeing things?"

"No, afraid not." He let out a sigh. "Seems a woman's body was found inside of the house."

She uncrossed her arms and leaned forward. "Oh, no. Have you identified her?"

"We know that she's in her sixties, brownish-gray hair. Medium build. Does that sound like anyone you've seen across the way?"

She shook her head. "Grandma Harper might know."

"What's wrong with your neighborhood, huh?" he asked.

"I didn't think anything was wrong with it until now. That's two bodies in less than a year."

"Can't be the same killer, she's in prison." Caleb's cell rang and he sat down across from her to take the call. After uttering a few short syllables, he said, "I'll be there in a few minutes."

He looked toward her but not at her, in distant thought.

"And here I thought we'd have lunch together."

"No. Maybe dinner." He stood, leaned over the desk, and kissed her. "Nice," he said and winked.

Myka loved it when he winked at her, especially when he was in a suit. She loved a handsome man in a suit. After he left and she had smiled for a while, she wondered what his phone call was about, knowing he'd only say so much in a public place. And sometimes, she learned, he didn't say anything at all about work. This time the new case was close to her house, and she hoped he'd fill her in as much as he could, so she'd feel secure at home, and outside when she started taking pictures of the winter's night sky.

RUTH HARPER, A.K.A. GRANDMA HARPER TO HER FRIENDS, WAS PULLING a few weeds in Myka's flower bed when she drove into her driveway.

"Hello, Grandma."

She smiled brightly and said, "Hello, sweetie."

Myka turned back from grabbing her purse and tote bag from the car. "Now you don't have to pull weeds for me," she said for about the one-hundredth time.

"Well, you are so busy with the hardware store, it's the least I can do for you," she returned the same number of times. The older woman managed to be somewhere near at least once a week to welcome her home and Myka had come to look forward to seeing her.

"The sun will be down soon."

"Well, I won't be out here forever. How's that handsome, Caleb?"

"He's fine. Hey, do you know of a woman, across the creek from my place that is, about medium build with brownish-gray hair? I think she's somewhere in her sixties."

Grandma slapped her hands together to remove the dirt from her fingers. "I used to walk over that way, over five years ago. I probably can't walk that far anymore, you know."

Myka nodded.

She put a finger on her chin in thought. "There was a woman, a recent widow at the time, by that description."

Myka pointed her thumb behind her. "Can you come in and we'll look out the back window and see if you can identify which house is hers?"

Grandma beamed. "Of course. I'd love to help."

Inside, Grandma washed her hands and then stood at the window with a pair of binoculars. Myka grabbed two molasses cookies, that Grandma had previously given her, from the cookie jar.

"Yes, she'd be the fourth house down. Yep."

"Are you sure?" Myka asked between bites of cookie.

"Absolutely. Take a look."

Grandma handed her the binoculars and Myka set her cookie down.

"Oh, my goodness!" said Myka.

Police swarmed the fourth house, around the back porch, and then at the border of the yard between the next house and the creek. When she moved the binoculars to the yellow house, she saw Caleb standing with a woman and a man.

She laid the binoculars on the kitchen counter and let a breath out in dismay.

Grandma took the binoculars from the counter, focused, and swerved them to the left. "Caleb. That means a murder. Oh, no."

"Grandma. Now you can't go over there and disturb the scene like you did last time."

"Whatever do you mean?" asked Grandma, trying and failing to look innocent.

"Remember? You removed the crime scene tape."

"Only what was left that didn't blow off in the wind. It was really windy that night. I remember because when I got home what little hair I have left was standing on end."

Myka couldn't help smiling at the scenario. Her white hair was an inch and a half long at the most.

"Both of us should stay out of this," Myka said.

"Do you think we will?"

"Oh, probably not. Do you think we're safe this time, Grandma?"

"Probably not. Don't let them see you watching."

Myka let out a breath. "I didn't think of that."

"I'll bet Caleb has."

"YES, YOU WERE RIGHT. SOMETHING WAS GOING ON AROUND THE yellow house," said Caleb, sauntering into Myka's kitchen.

She sighed. "I saw all the officers. A murder, I presume."

He nodded. "Remember last winter when we talked about you getting a security camera?"

"Yes. And I did. In the front there, it looks like a light bulb."

"How about for the back of the house?"

"No, I was going to see how the one in the front works first. Then I kind of spaced it, I guess."

"I'm kind of thinking that the person who killed this woman, Robin White, will be looking to find out if you have recordings of the event."

"But I don't."

"I know. Maybe that's good, Myka. For you, anyway."

"Here I am, a part-time photographer, now involved in two murders because people seem to think I take pictures of anything that moves in the night."

"I wouldn't say you're involved."

"Really? Really? I live exactly across the creek from the yellow house. And while you worked at the murder scene, Grandma Harper and I looked through binoculars at you."

His shoulders went back in surprise. "Did you look from the yard?"

"No, from inside at the kitchen window. I didn't want to be seen."

"Huh."

"Grandma knew who the woman was, where she lived. Said she was a widow."

"I hope she doesn't get involved."

"Before she left, she asked if I wanted to borrow her shotgun," Myka added with a smile. "Oh, and I told her not to take down the crime tape."

Smiling in return, he said, "And did you say yes? About the shotgun."

"No." She grew serious. "Do they have any leads yet?"

He rubbed a hand through his short dark hair. "Nothing yet. It's very strange. The victim is a woman who pretty much keeps to herself. According to her neighbors, she goes to church on Sundays. Belongs to a quilting group. The house may have been robbed; the front door left ajar, nothing askew though."

"But what about the yellow house?"

"A key was used on the yellow house, and Ms. White's body left inside."

"Why did he kill her there?"

Caleb pulled out a kitchen chair and sat down. "We're waiting for a forensic report, but it looks like she did put up somewhat of a struggle before being strangled to death. She had a bloody nose, he or she hit her in the face, some hair strands were found. Looks as though the killer walked her over to the yellow house. The neighbors hadn't seen or heard a thing."

"I saw a light moving around inside. A flashlight, I'm thinking." After a moment, she added, "There are pine trees with lots of deciduous underbrush around the house. He was probably hidden some of the time."

He let out a sigh. "I think this person may have noticed the light on in your house, and you turning the light off and then on. It probably spooked him. Or, he didn't want to be found at the crime scene."

Myka searched his face, waiting for him to say more. When he didn't, she said, "Are you trying to scare me?"

"Not intentionally. You should be aware, know the facts."

She looked down, her mind trying to make sense of this, when it was impossible.

"Maybe it's time you moved in with me," he said softly.

"Not doing it. If I moved in with you, you'd never marry me," she said.

"What? We never talked about marriage," he said, in a rather reproachful tone.

"Exactly," she said matter-of-factly and turned to the refrigerator. "You must be starved. I can make you a sandwich."

Caleb briefly squinted at her, and she knew him well enough to realize she'd brought up a subject requiring caution and that stung a bit.

"No, thank you. I'll get going now." Since he'd left on that note, she didn't run out and ask if she could come over. Her pride wouldn't allow it.

Instead, she made believe that everything was fine, took a shower, and went to bed. She lay there thinking about Caleb instead of the murder that happened two hundred-plus feet away. Yet, the topic of marriage, however brief, had finally come up. It was now time to figure out what they really wanted in life and if they wanted the same things. Once she made that decision, she felt peace and drifted off to sleep.

CHAPTER TWO

*I*n the morning Myka woke up and found no one had broken in and killed her, so it was a good day. She had much to focus on at work, and she'd do just that.

Cathy Morgan, Myka's business partner, worked in the front of their hardware store. As an extrovert, she was happy visiting with and helping the customers in the front.

Introvert Myka gave Cathy a wave in greeting and walked to the office in the back where she handled orders and warehousing. Jason Hall and Marty Hansen, were in the process of putting on aprons and gloves to protect their hands.

"Who brought me the coffee?" she asked.

"I did," said Jason.

"Thanks so much!"

Marty rolled his eyes. Everyone knew that Jason was a flirt. Yet, a gift of coffee was rather kind and appreciated this morning.

"Things are all good back here," said Molly Allgood.

Myka smiled at the reference to the woman's last name. This was her team of three in the back and Cathy had a team of three in the front. They all worked together well.

She checked her emails as she sipped her coffee. No calls or emails from Caleb. He was a proud man and she had hurt his feelings. She believed it was hard for him to ask for her to live with him, and he'd used the current murder as a catalyst to do so.

They'd had an exclusive relationship for almost a year, and she would have mentioned marriage given time. They weren't quite ready for it. Caleb had been disillusioned by a sparse police force and rising violence in their small town of Trillium Falls, which didn't always give him time for empathy. His lack of compassion annoyed Myka when she first met him.

She assumed his job touched every aspect of his life, including his relationship with her, and they'd have to talk this out one of these days.

Still, Myka knew if she was somehow involved in the fiasco across the creek, he'd let her know. And he hadn't, so she let out a sigh of relief.

By the end of the day, she reached out to Caleb and they made a plan to eat together tomorrow. She was surprised he'd agreed due to the murder investigation and their last encounter.

That evening, when Myka arrived home from work, she spotted Grandma Harper down the street in her yard and Caleb parked in front of Grandma's house.

Since he was more rough than smooth, and not apt to even admit that she'd hurt him, Myka held her breath for a moment thinking maybe she *was* involved in the murder.

She supposed she had a scowl on her face because Grandma cupped her hands around her mouth and yelled, "Be nice to him! He looks like he had a hard day."

Myka pulled a face and raised an arm in question at Grandma.

Caleb's window rolled down as she stepped next to his car.

"Does Grandma need you for something?" he asked.

"No, she just told me to be nice to you. I'm always nice, right?"

His lips were pursed until he started chuckling, then they both laughed.

"I don't know why I'm laughing, but it feels good." Her heart lifted and she put her hand on his arm, now elbowed out the window. "I love you," she added, softly.

He gave her a huge smile. "I like hearing those words."

She, apparently, had touched his heart too. "There's that smile. You're gorgeous when you smile."

"Not normally?" he asked.

She leaned in and kissed him, then again, longer this time.

"I missed you," he said.

"You're all I thought about," she added.

"Got any food?"

She laughed. Things were good again. "I do. That is, I have two frozen chicken pot pies. Won't take long to microwave. I'm going grocery shopping Saturday, to give you hope for the morrow."

"I'll be right in." He pulled in her driveway and parked.

THE NEXT DAY, AT LUNCHTIME, CALEB BROUGHT CHEF SALADS INTO THE hardware store and settled in a chair in the office.

"I went to a quilting group this morning," he said.

"Oh? What are you going to make?" Myka asked. "I would like some input on the colors you choose."

"Ha, ha," he returned with a chuckle. "I'll choose my own colors, thank you."

Myka closed the manilla file folder she'd been holding and sat down. "It's about the murder, isn't it?" she asked in a somber tone.

"Yes." He rubbed a hand across his face and took in a breath. "It's going to be a hard case. Seems no one in the group really liked her."

"They actually said that?"

"Let me just say, they aren't disappointed she left the group. Of course, they didn't want her to leave *this* way, but it appears she was interfering rather judgmentally with others' work and trying to teach them how to do it better. You know, her way. At the last meeting, she told one of the members just to scrap what she'd been working on, and she'd help her start again."

"Are these people beginning quilters?"

"No. Bunch of retired ladies who know how to sew, make quilts. I saw some beauties that a few of them were making. There was something else going on with the victim - one of the quilters confirmed it. She was an educator most of her adult life and though retired, she kept right on teaching."

Myka saw Marty nearby and whispered, "Do you think any of these women could kill her? Could one of these ladies be a suspect?"

"I don't think so. They tolerated her more than most probably could. They knew she was lonely, isolated a lot." He lowered his voice. "But someone younger, with more muscle mass did this."

Caleb's phone dinged and he looked at his messages. "Huh. Grandma Harper is talking to the victim's…uh, Robin's neighbors."

"What about the crime tape? Did she pull it down?"

"That's not funny."

"You could arrest her."

"Not funny."

"Okay, I'll talk to her when I get home."

"I'd appreciate it." He finished his salad while deep in thought, then stood and left with a peck on her cheek. "Later."

An hour later, Myka looked up from a supply list and saw Jason standing in the doorway. This was not the first time she'd caught him staring and it made her uncomfortable.

"Can I help you with anything?" she asked.

He smiled widely as if she'd implied something untoward with the word anything. "No, just seeing how you're doing." He straightened. "How are you doing, beautiful?"

"I'm fine." She frowned, blatantly. "Here, just take this list and compare it with what we received this morning. Thanks."

"Yes, ma'am."

She dismissed him with a curt tone, but he deserved it. She'd have to show a video on workplace harassment and studied her calendar to plan one.

AFTER WORK, MYKA WALKED OVER TO SEE GRANDMA HARPER.

"Hello, sweetie," she said upon opening the door.

"Hello, sweetie," Myka mimicked, ending with a smile. "I hear you've been across the creek today."

"Well…well. A woman is free to go anywhere she pleases. Come in, won't you? I've got some more home-baked cookies."

"Oh, I'd love one," she returned and stepped inside the one-story ranch-style home. Grandma had a gray couch and a padded, wine-colored chair as a nice contrast. A kitchen chair was placed up against the front window, most likely for viewing the neighborhood.

Grandma handed her fork-marked peanut butter cookies on a saucer.

"Oh, thank you." Myka took a bite and added, "I heard you did some other things today, too."

"Just made some new friends. And got some information." She winked.

"What did you learn?"

"Any one of her neighbors could have killed her." Grandma nodded.

"I doubt that."

"Apparently, she told people when to cut their grass, probably a day before they believe they should cut it. To put their garbage cans away as soon as the pickup service goes by and told old Mr. Thomas to pick up his dog's poop when he walks by."

"People should pick up their dog's poop."

"She told him as he pulled the plastic bag from his pocket."

"Oh, no."

"Yes, oh no." Grandma nodded again and continued, "I think that might be what you'd call a power play, but no, I don't think any of these people killed her. But I did learn something else. Mr. Thomas said that her car was missing on the day of her murder. None of the neighbors know why. I asked them."

"Of course, you did, Grandma. You are thorough."

"If you could pass that info to Caleb, that would be helpful."

Myka finished her cookies and then commented on a project

Grandma was crocheting. At length, she made it home to prepare spaghetti for dinner.

When Caleb arrived, she had the table set, candles burning, and salad and garlic bread set out to go with the spaghetti.

"What is all this for?" he asked and smiled widely. "Did I do something right?"

"You do lots of things right. Can't I serve a nice dinner without a reason?"

"Uh… By the look of you, I don't think so."

Myka returned his smile. "You're right." She sat up straighter and became animated, saying, "The Leonid meteor showers are going on now and are expected to peak in a few days. The Leonid's are expected to generate fifteen, what you would call shooting stars, per hour."

"And you could take pictures," he said with a smile.

She nodded several times.

"I can see it means a lot to you, and it'll be a weekend night-"

"And I made a nice dinner."

"Yes, I will go with you."

Myka clapped her hands. "Good. You won't be sorry.

He wiped his mouth with a napkin and set it down. "I won't be."

"I know you're busy, uh…consumed with the murder case, but just one little night and we can troubleshoot the case on the way over or the way home. I can be a sounding board, you know, sometimes that helps. Right?"

"Okay. Deal."

"Oh, and Grandma Harper said that I should tell you that Robin's car was gone for some time during the day. The day of her murder."

"But we found her car at home."

"I don't know. Just passing it along."

"Did she say anything else?"

"That no one in her neighborhood killed Robin."

"Humph," he said. "Wish I could be so sure."

"That will save you some work, I'm sure," she said, grinning. "I know, but I do like Grandma Harper."

"I do too, but not as a coworker."

Caleb left after dark. Myka watched an old "I Love Lucy" rerun before turning the lights off and gazing out at the stars.

Tired enough to sleep all night, she brushed her teeth and turned back the bed covers, climbed in, and dozed off.

Myka let out a breathy babble and sat up in bed. Still half asleep, her eyes saw strange shapes in the glow of the room's night light. She'd heard that the brain makes patterns that can have no true relevance to reality, still her heart pounded for the seconds it took to focus and fully wake up. When the wavy silhouettes, and black spots disappeared, she pulled the covers to her chin and looked toward the tiny gap in the curtain. No one could see through, she decided, and leaned back to lie down.

Caleb was right. Apparently, the one-year anniversary of December's murder made for an uneasy subconscious.

Myka set up folding chairs in the hardware store's office. First, she'd show the workplace harassment video to the workers employed in the front of the store. She started the video and shut the door behind the employees before joining Cathy to help in the front of the store.

Through the front windows, she could see a squad car parked close to the store entrance.

"Caleb looking out for you, I see," said Cathy.

"Yes. We don't think I'm involved in the murder case in any way though," Myka replied, trying to mask the concern in her voice.

"Oh, I certainly hope not. It was scary last December. That makes it just about a year now."

Myka was interrupted by an older gentleman looking for wood oil. She was glad for the break in conversation. She depended on work to take her mind off of the neighborhood murders.

After lunch, Myka restarted the workplace video and sat down to watch it with Molly, Marty, and Jason.

Marty crossed his arms before saying, "We wouldn't have to watch this if Jason would stop being such a flirt."

"Come on," he returned.

"You don't see me and Molly flirting, do you?"

"Actually," Myka interrupted, "we all need to view this once a year."

"What?" Jason slapped his knee in what looked very much like frustration.

Myka went to sit at her desk. "Come on, we're adults here."

All three sat stoic, arms crossed, all apparently offended.

Still, she hoped she didn't have to deal with Jason's "cuteness" anymore.

THAT NIGHT AS MYKA LOOKED OUT AT THE STARS, SHE CAUGHT something out of the corner of her eye and looked back to the edge of her property. A person with wide shoulders and narrow hips, stood there. In the dim moonlight, she could see he wore a dark hooded sweatshirt, and he gazed in the direction of her bedroom window.

Her heart pounded as she ducked down onto her hands and knees and tried to take purposeful breaths to keep her sane enough to figure out what to do. She moved, then inched up to the very edge of the kitchen curtain to peek back outside. He had moved closer to her bedroom window.

As quietly as she could, with her heart pounding in her ears, she walked out the front door, quietly locked it, and ran to Grandma's.

Myka knocked and looked behind her, then knocked harder.

The porch light came on and the door opened. Myka moved Grandma to the side and shut and locked the door.

"Where's your shotgun?" Myka asked.

"You're scaring an old lady. What's the matter."

"Get your shotgun. I'll tell you when you come back."

Grandma came back in time to hear Myka on her phone. "There is a prowler in my neighborhood. Hooded dark sweatshirt. About five ten, eleven, average weight. I could not identify him. Could someone drive through the neighborhood?"

"You didn't call Caleb," said Grandma.

"No, he has enough to worry about right now. The prowler will be gone by the time he gets here, anyway. I'll see him tomorrow and explain."

"What if it's the murderer?" Grandma whispered and put her free hand over her chin in thought.

"I've locked the door and I'm not worried now that I'm here."

Grandma opened a guitar case and pulled out her shotgun. "I can see why. Now, did you tell him about Robin's car being gone?"

"Yes, he didn't seem concerned. Said the car was at home when her body was found."

"But it means something, I know," said Grandma. "It happened the day of the murder. A neighbor said that when the car was gone, she was out raking leaves for a while in the front yard."

"Maybe she loaned it to a friend or relative."

Grandma shook her head. "Doesn't sound like she has many friends. No relatives unless they're distant."

"Okay, maybe she had the car in for service. I know I need to get my brakes checked every now and then."

Grandma sighed, frustratedly. "The car's six months old."

"Boy, you have the information."

Grandma smiled, rather proudly she thought, and said, "I'm not a good sleeper anymore. I'll take the couch and you can settle down in the spare bedroom. Go on." She patted the gun barrel.

"Okay. Thanks, Grandma."

THE NEXT MORNING GRANDMA HARPER, WITH THE GUITAR CASE clutched in front of her with both arms, walked Myka home.

Now smiling, Myka offered to help her carry the case, but Grandma only shook her head.

Caleb drove up at the same time. "Plan to play the guitar, Grandma?" he asked with a smile.

"Only if I have to," she said in a no-nonsense way.

"I got your text. What's going on, Myka?" he asked, not smiling anymore.

"Some guy tried to stare in her bedroom window, is what," Grandma blurted.

"I was glad to have Grandma in the neighborhood. I went there and spent the night. Everything was fine after that."

Caleb hit his steering wheel. "I don't like that. Did you recognize him?"

"No. Half the men in town probably have a black hooded sweatshirt."

"How concerned are you?" Grandma asked him.

"I'm concerned, of course, but since Covid there's been more car break-ins, people stealing packages and items from yards. But I am concerned that Myka hasn't gotten a security camera in the back of her house, especially since she works at a hardware store."

"If I'd known about this creep, I would've done it long ago. But all right, I am effectively reprimanded now and will buy one today."

"Good. You two go in the house and see if anyone has broken in. Look to see if anything is stolen or disturbed. I've got to talk to the office. Wave if you see something."

Grandma opened the guitar case, prepped the gun, and prepared to lead her through the house. Myka caught Caleb chuckling as he watched them go in. She liked it; it made her feel safe.

When they returned to Caleb, Myka leaned forward in the open driver's window and said, "As far as I can tell, not a thing has been disturbed."

"Okay, that's good news. I'll have someone on night shift do a drive-through tonight."

"Okay."

"And I'll be close by," added Grandma, patting the guitar case.

"That's what I was thinking," he told Grandma.

He looked back at Myka. "You, pretty lady, I'll see tomorrow for a falling star show."

"I can't wait, handsome man."

They watched him drive away and Myka said, "Let's check the SD card on the security camera here in front. I checked it a while back and there wasn't anything on it."

"Isn't that odd, since it's pointed toward the road?" asked Grandma.

"Maybe something's wrong with it."

"Huh."

Myka tensed thinking it'd be frightening to see the man that stood at her back window. "I'm kind of nervous about what we might see. Let's go in and I'll put the card in my laptop."

"It does work," Grandma said, sitting beside Myka on the couch. "I see someone."

"Yes, I see skinny jeans, a light ski jacket, and a knit hat on what looks like the curvy hips of a woman."

"I think it's a woman, too, Myka. But why is she just standing there facing the road? It's not like a bus will stop by this time of night. A transportation company, maybe."

"Maybe. Wait, she's leaving, walking south."

"One must wonder what she's doing outside during the dark of night. Not everyone wants to go outside and stare at the stars, like you do." After a moment, Grandma added, "If she's from the neighborhood, I don't think I've seen her. And look, the date was a week ago, not last night."

Myka went through the rest of the days on the SD card, viewing cars, school kids, people walking their dogs, and cats heading toward flower beds.

"Nothing untoward, I'd say," Grandma said and walked to the front door. "And here I was expecting some excitement."

"I expected to see the man from last night coming around the house toward the road, but he didn't."

Grandma turned back. "I'm glad he didn't. Could you have imagined it, my dear?"

Myka smiled before saying, "Goodbye."

Did she imagine it?

CHAPTER THREE

On Saturday, Myka loaded her camera equipment into the back of Caleb's SUV, settled in the front seat, and patted his thigh. "Any news on the murder case?"

"There's something."

After a moment of silence, she said, "Well?"

"Let me get onto the highway first."

"Of course," she said. "I'm just so excited. I woke up earlier than usual, so excited over the chance to see the falling stars, and even more so that you're going to see them with me."

"Good, babes."

"Well?"

"Oh, the case. The car was indeed missing the day of the murder," said Caleb after he entered the highway.

"Just as Grandma Harper had said."

"Ha, ha," he drawled.

"So where was it?"

"At the dealership. A recall."

"Huh," she said. "She was seen at home when the car was gone, so did someone drive her home then?"

"A transportation company brought her home."

"You mean like Uber?"

He nodded.

"So, then she needed a ride back to pick up her car."

"Yes," he said.

"Okay, that answers the missing car problem."

"It does. Now, it appears that Robin was the only one to witness a confrontation between two male workers after she had dropped off her car. It was when she was waiting for transportation home. Basically, in the struggle, one of the men fell and hit his head against an engine lane on the floor. He's still in the ICU."

"So, what then?" Myka asked. "He found out where Robin lived and killed her to keep her from testifying. Is that it?"

"Possibly."

"Wouldn't he have to kill the man in the ICU, too? You know, to cover his tracks?"

"They don't know if he will survive."

"Does this seem plausible to you, Caleb?" she asked at length. "I hope there's some DNA evidence."

"There is," he said and cleared his throat. "It's hard to make sense of murder, Myka."

"Yes, I suppose you're right. Uh...but if this skirmish has nothing to do with her murder, don't you think it's a weird coincidence that she saw this, on the day of her murder?"

"But she didn't call the police."

"Huh," she said.

"So, I'm not convinced that this is why she was murdered and I'm dragging my feet. We have plenty of work on the docket and it's tempting to want to finish a case, you know, move on and look successful. I'm not like that. I'm not done working on the case."

She nodded. "That's one of the reasons I love you."

"I've been looking forward to coming out with you tonight to give me a little break, help me refresh."

"Good, Caleb."

Caleb stopped at a mom-and-pop restaurant. He faced Myka. "I looked this place up. It's voted one of the best family-run businesses in the state. They have great burgers, fries, and shakes. It takes a little extra time to cook this way, but I figured we had some time to kill tonight."

After eating the wonderful meal, they headed east on the freeway as suggested by an astronomer scientist Myka had read about.

After a loll in the conversation, Caleb asked, "What actually is this amazing occurrence that we're going to see?"

"The cause of 'Falling Stars' is not understood by meteorologists. What happens is the shower radiates from a point in the constellation Leo and, like I mentioned before, it's speculated that it was mostly caused by the earth passing through a cloud of space dust. I guess we don't need to know all of the whys, just watch the beauty unfold."

"Will do."

"You've been smiling a lot tonight, Mr. Broody."

"I decided I needed to count my blessings, like the stars in the sky."

She looked at him through the corner of an eye. "No, I don't think so. Something's up."

"No, really. Really. I have the prettiest girl in town sitting right here with me."

"It's a small town."

In the darkness of the car, she could still see him wink at her and she let out a breath of contentment.

Myka leaned forward and pointed. "Right here. Look, there's a pull-off. See?"

He traveled off the freeway and pulled onto a dirt road that drivers used to turn around and head in another direction.

Myka set up her tripod and camera amongst sagebrush and hibernating grasses.

"The sky is already beautiful," he said gazing up.

"You're not going to go all waxing poetic, are you?"

"Roses are red," he said before lifting her hair and kissing the back of her neck.

"Cut it out, I'm going to drop my expensive camera," she joked.

He stepped away and watched the sky while Myka fiddled with the camera until the settings were right.

"Anytime now," she said. She moved behind Caleb and put her arms around his middle.

"Look at that moon. I needed this," he said and put his arms along hers.

"I'm glad I'm not here alone, too."

"You could have brought Grandma Harper."

"If I did, we'd have the murder case solved by now." She chuckled.

He guffawed. "Maybe you should have brought her then."

"Yeah, then you'd take all the credit for solving the case."

"I saw one! A falling star." Caleb stepped away from her and she carefully moved around the sagebrush to her camera.

"The expectation is fifteen, count them, will you?"

"Sure, babes."

As the hour passed, stars shot across the sky in every direction and Myka snapped picture after picture.

"Awesomely beautiful," he said in a low voice. "This is a special night, indeed."

She took his words in and smiled.

"Are you about done?" he asked.

"Sadly, yes. And now I'm starting to freeze."

She heard him beside her and wondered what he was doing. In only the moonlight, she looked down to see him on a knee with something in his hand.

"What?"

"Will you, Myka Woods, marry me?"

"What?"

"Will you marry me?"

In her fondest dreams, she'd hoped for this moment and couldn't imagine a better way to propose. She nodded, repeatedly before bursting out, "Yes!"

He took a ring from a small box and held it up. In the moonlight, she could see a faint glimmer of the diamond when he twisted the ring. "It's called a north star diamond. What could be more fitting for you?"

"It's perfect. It's a perfect night."

"Except I'm freezing now too, or I could be shaking because I proposed."

After they loaded the camera equipment, they hopped in the car, flipped the heat on high, and started back to Trillium Falls.

After a period of quiet, Caleb asked, "What's wrong, honey?"

She sniffed and tears ran down her face. "Did you know that in the mid to late 1800s the sky seemed to explode with oodles of falling stars? Like the heavens were on fire. At the time no one knew what was happening and many wondered if it was the end of the world."

"That must have been fantastic and scary all in one night. But why are you crying? Did you change your mind about us? Is it too soon?"

"No! Never. I'm just happy and emotional. This is a good night."

"The best ever," he added.

That was all true except there was one other thing. Tonight she had whispered upon a star that Caleb would tell her he loved her. And the man who dislikes being vulnerable did not mention the words.

CHAPTER FOUR

The employees at the front of the store oohed and aahed at Myka's ring and the engagement news. When she finally made it to the back office, she was smiling but anxious to get to her computer.

Yet, as soon as Myka sat down, she noticed how the overhead light made her ring sparkle and she held her hand up to enjoy the flashes.

The back of the store workers stepped in, and Molly busted out with, "A new ring? A new ring!"

Jason and Marty looked at each other, clearly confused.

"I'm engaged to-"

"Hot cop," Molly interrupted.

"Yes, to Caleb."

Jason stepped closer to look. "Nice. When's the date?"

"Will Caleb be a boss, too?" asked Molly.

"I don't think so, no," answered Myka. "Uh, not quite sure on a date yet, or even if we want a formal ceremony."

"Well, figure it out and let us know," Marty said as he headed toward the door. "Just hope we get the day off."

"Well, maybe. We'll see." She wondered if he'd heard her.

"I hear a truck backing up. I'll head out, too. Congrats," said Jason.

"Thanks."

"Hey, speaking of your fiancé, has there been a break in the murder case?" Molly asked and Jason leaned back in the door.

"Caleb says there's been some serious talk, but nothing definite."

"It's just creepy. Two murders in less than a year," said Jason. He tapped the doorjamb and left.

Myka nodded.

"And in Trillium Falls, mind you. At least things are Allgood at the hardware store." Molly chuckled as she left the office.

At noon, Caleb sauntered in with two deli sandwiches and sweet tea.

"Today, I don't know which I love seeing more, you or a sandwich. I'm starved." Then she noticed her faux pas. At least it didn't bode well for her to think about the word love.

"I'm pretty sure after you consume the sandwich, it'll be me." He handed her an iced tea. "Hey, we finally heard who owns the yellow house."

"Why did it take so long?"

"Let me shut the door." After returning to the adjacent seat, he added, "It took so long because the owners lived in Louisiana. We couldn't reach them, but they finally returned a message. Probably would have sooner had they known what was going on."

"Louisiana. That's why no one is ever there."

"A couple owned the house. Seems the man died and then his wife was left wondering what to do with the place. The idea of restoring it was overwhelming to her, so she put it up for auction. The whole process can take about thirty days to complete the sale."

"Yes, but still, what does this have to do with Robin's murder?"

"The house wasn't broken into. Someone used a key to get inside, and the key was never located. And you know the department combed through every blade of glass."

"Good sandwich, by the way. Thank you again."

"Yeah, it's that new deli place that opened on Main. Anyway," he said between bites, "Robin came in first on the auction bids and she received the key. Seems the house just went to escrow."

"At least you got that piece of information." After a moment, she added, "She had some money obviously, since she was paying for the house. Did someone steal from her?"

"I'm one step ahead. No, money was in a credit union account."

"Why would she even want to purchase that house? You know, a building that needed work, inside and out. Not that she couldn't have started something, but she was in her sixties."

"There's an answer. I'll find it." He stood to leave.

She nodded. "If not, I can run it by Grandma Harper."

"You're so funny, you know," he added on the way out the door nearly bumping into Molly.

"Congrats to you, sir," she told Caleb, and then they both moved out of Myka's line of sight.

As Myka prepared to leave work for the day, Marty walked into the office. He handed her a piece of paper. "This is my resignation."

"What? No. You've been a good worker. An important part of the team."

"My parents loaned me a chunk of money to go back to school. Uh...full time."

She glanced at the notice and then at Marty. "So, you won't be able to even work part-time?"

"No. I'm heading toward thirty and I need to get serious about my life."

She nodded; she did understand. "When you're ready to work again I'll write you a letter of recommendation. You've been such a good employee."

"I thank you." He turned to the door.

"Good luck to you," she said, with a smile she didn't feel.

"I have to make my own luck now." And then he was gone.

Myka sat down at her desk wondering how she could plan a wedding when she would be working two jobs. Not to mention going away for a honeymoon.

***

"Why do you look so troubled? Aren't you newly engaged?" asked Grandma as she stepped into Myka's house.

"Oh, my best employee's quitting. Going back to school."

"Can't blame him for that."

"No, I don't. I understand."

"Things will work out." Grandma nodded and sat down on the couch. "Now, I've been thinking about Robin's murder. The clues are not making sense."

"No, and it gets worse. They finally found out who owns the house." Myka continued to relay what info she could.

"Oh, for Pete's sake. Who could possibly know who owned the house if the State Police couldn't? At least in any kind of timely matter. And why would anyone want that ramshackle place anyway? If I'd not heard it with my own ears, I would never have believed that Robin bought that house. Whatever for?"

Grandma was riled up, so Myka just let her talk while she continued to feel sorry for herself.

"Let me think. Robin was a teacher. So, even though retired she'd been telling people what to do. Maybe she finally, finally realized that telling adults what to do was not working for her."

Myka nodded, leaned back, and looked at the ceiling.

Grandma scooted to the edge of the couch. "A home school. Maybe she was setting up a home school or perhaps she was going to hire herself out as a teacher for a small number of students. I've heard that's happening more and more because of all that's going on with schools these days."

After a quiet moment, Myka looked across at Grandma.

"Well? That's what I'd do," Grandma added.

"What?"

"I'd have a home school or be a teacher for hire. That is the only thing that makes sense for Robin, a teacher."

Myka sighed and looked off in the distance. "Maybe…"

Grandma took Myka's phone off the coffee table and looked at the screen before putting her index finger on the face. "Push recent calls… look at the repeated calls…yes, call this one."

Obviously, Grandma had called Caleb's number because she could hear his loud voice when she introduced herself. Myka leaned all the way back in her recliner, put her feet up, and closed her eyes as she listened to the two discuss the murder case.

"Yes, who would want to kill a woman offering such a good service to the community?" asked Caleb, loudly, as he'd had to cut in.

At length, Grandma said, "Perhaps I'll see you around later. Yes, she's right here, stretched out on the recliner and depressed. Goodbye."

"Grandma, you shouldn't have said that."

"Well, it's true. You are down and out. If I had a violin in my guitar case, I'd play it."

Myka couldn't help but chuckle.

Grandma smiled in return. "Maybe a nap will help. Come down in about an hour and I'll serve your pitiful self some dinner."

Myka smiled as Grandma shut the door behind her. She supposed she had plenty to smile about after all.

GRANDMA SERVED MYKA BEEF STEW AND A BUTTERY, GRILLED CHEESE sandwich.

"This is so good, Grandma."

"Glad you like it. Have more."

"No, I don't think I can eat another bite."

"You will have room for dessert though."

"All right, Grandma."

Grandma pushed her chair back, stood up, and sliced a piece of apple pie. Last, she topped it with a scoop of vanilla ice cream.

Myka slurped. "This pie is the best."

Grandma smiled; her chest puffed out. "I put cinnamon in it, not nutmeg like Marge down the street."

"Grandma, did your husband tell you he loved you very much?"

"No. If he did, I would have thought he was ill. My generation didn't hear our parents say I love you a lot. I didn't hear it at home. Still, I know they loved us, my husband's family included."

"I'm sorry."

"No, that was how it was back then. The first time my husband told me was when I helped him put the hay up one year. It still did my heart good, even though it was out of gratitude that he said it. Caleb hasn't said it, has he?"

She looked down. "No."

"What's the matter with you? You're such a girl."

"Nothing's wrong with me."

"Well, let me see. He watched the stars with you, got down on a knee and proposed, and gave you a beautiful ring. Most men in my day, would have considered stargazing a waste of time. So, he basically showed you he loved you."

"Yes, you're right. It was a perfect night. A unique way of purposing. He'd thought it all out."

"That's my girl." Grandma stood. "I'm going to cut Caleb a big piece of pie, just in case he stops by."

"That's nice of you."

"Naw, you're both like family to me."

"We're honored you feel that way."

"That's why I want you to be extra careful until someone is put away for Robin's murder."

"Of course. Molly, at work, picked me out a security camera for the back of my house. I'll get it figured out and put it up. Better late than never."

Grandma nodded.

With a full stomach, Myka walked across the street toward home. Once inside, she glanced around and then locked the door.

She still hadn't heard from Caleb and probably wouldn't until morning now. This could be a good sign, she realized. When he was on a case, and had enough leads to put the clues together, his brain was on one track only.

The security camera was simple enough to figure out and she

decided to install it because even though it was dark, it wouldn't be any less dark in the morning before work. She used a folding step ladder to strap the camera to the top of a wood porch support.

She turned off the porch light and went inside. At least she'd put it up even though she wondered about the value of something that someone could cut down and take away.

Walking to her bookcase, she pulled a novel from her to-be-read section and flipped it open. There was nothing she could do about work at the moment, so she'd enjoy reading a book.

CHAPTER FIVE

While in the hallway, Myka heard a knock at the sliding glass door. Who would come to her back door? Considering the hour, her heart pounded so hard it ached. If Caleb thought this was a joke - no, Caleb would never do that to her.

After a moment, she heard a male voice. Moving toward the end of the hall, she could hear him call her name.

This was crazy! She turned off the hall light and peeked one eye out at the edge of the wall.

Walking to the door, she shouted, "Jason. What are you doing?"

"I need to speak with you," he said and pointed toward the door latch. "About Marty."

Her first thought was that it was some stupid way to get into her house and play God's Gift to Women, but then figured he'd heard Marty quit.

Her heart calmed as she let out an exasperated breath of air and opened the door.

"I do have a front door, you know."

"Yes, but I was trying to get a hold of you without...without someone knowing."

"Whatever for? If you're not afraid of my fiancé, you should be."

"No, no." He shook his head repeatedly. "It's Marty. I think he's not thinking straight."

She shut the sliding glass door. "I guess you've heard he quit. He has a right to quit, even if we don't like it."

"No, no - "

"Maybe you should talk to Molly about this. She's Allgood, you know."

"No, this is not funny."

"I know! Okay. What is it?" She wanted to add pompous ass but needed to be somewhat professional. "Come on." She held up her phone. "I'm calling Molly right now so she can get over here, so I only have to say things one time."

"No, I don't think so," Jason said, trying to catch his breath. His eyebrows furrowed as he glanced behind her, clearly worried.

"Okay then, I have my phone on speed dial to Caleb," she warned, her index figure hovering over her phone.

"I don't know where to begin."

She put her free hand on her waist. "Start anywhere."

"Okay. As I was leaving work, Marty said goodbye. For good, he said. So, I started to think about that, and some things didn't make sense. So, I went home, had a bite to— "

"Get on with it."

"...and I went over to Marty's apartment. He didn't seem to be home, but his door wasn't locked, so I walked in and called out to him."

Jason stopped to catch his breath and she'd swear the hair on the back of her neck stood up. She wondered if he'd found a dead body.

"Listen, in his house there were pictures. All different sizes of photographs."

At least it wasn't a dead body. "Not unusual."

"Of you. Of you. Is this something you knew about? Were you like modeling for him or something?"

She shook her head, trying to grasp what was going on. "No. Ick!"

"There's no way to describe it but he's obviously been watching you. I looked through the house and saw that he'd been taking pictures of you all over town."

"No. No. This is not funny. If you're trying to prank me, it's not going to turn out well for you."

"No, it's no prank. I wish it was. I'm sorry to say, but he has pictures of you through windows, taken at night. Of you and of you and your fiancé."

She took a deep breath and held it for a moment and wondered what else could possibly go wrong in her neighborhood.

"You say there's a lot of pictures. Like ten or so?"

"Try one hundred maybe. It's eerie, disturbing really."

Something she didn't want to see.

"I came here to warn you. You better call the police, your fiancé or just plain get out of town."

"Where's your truck?" she asked.

"Around the corner. Down a way. I didn't want Marty to see it."

"Come outside. Follow me." Myka led him to the side of the garage and pointed at Grandma's house. "I want you to go over there and tell Mrs. Harper to call the police and explain what you've seen." She gave his upper back a shove. "Now go."

"What about you?"

"I'm going to lock the house and meet you over there. By the way, she's an older lady and may point a shotgun at you when she answers the door."

"Oh great. At least I'll feel safe, unlike right now. Hurry up, Myka."

Jason shot off and she scurried to check the doors.

She had another thought. After turning off the kitchen lights, she looked out a window. There were dim lights on in the yellow house, yet it'd been dark since the murder. She'd looked at it every night before she gazed at the stars and went to bed.

The yellow house could either be the safest place on earth for her to be or the most dangerous, but she didn't know for sure which was which.

Every spring, Myka watched the groundhogs go across the creek on a cottonwood tree that's wide trunk and limbs had dipped downward. The kid in her thought about how fun it would be to cross that way.

Between her and the yellow house the leaves had fallen for the winter so once she got through the cottonwood to the other side, she'd be visible. Yet it was in the dark of night, and many were snug in their homes.

Grandma would have called the police by now. This may be the only time Myka could catch the perp back at the yellow house.

She'd only be gone a minute, she told herself and stuck her phone in her coat pocket. That's all it would take to peek in a window and scurry back across the creek.

She stuck a small flashlight between her teeth, straddled the cottonwood trunk, and scooted up to the point she could stretch to a fallen tree and crawl to the other side of the creek.

After brushing off the seat of her pants, she took the flashlight out of her mouth and aimed it directly in front of her to keep from falling on uneven ground or turning an ankle.

Although the house was surrounded by deciduous shrubs and pine trees, she found a small opening and headed toward a window.

"I knew you'd come," said a male voice.

Her eyes strained to see someone a few feet behind her.

Fear gripped her gut. "Who?"

"It's me. Marty."

"Marty?" she squeaked. She tried to calm her pounding heart by telling herself that she knew this man, he'd worked for her. Yet, she couldn't get over the fact that he'd taken so many private pictures of her. And now he's here! Something was not right with him; she could see it in his face now as he looked down at her.

"Hello. Yes, I was hoping I'd see you again." That was probably a stupid thing to say, she thought.

"I knew you'd come, so I have prepared a place for us to meet."

No! He prepared a place. What? Could he have killed Robin?

She stuck her thumb behind her. "Why don't you come to my place? There's so much to be done here."

"For now, we need to meet secretly. It's the best way until every-thing is settled."

She so did not want to know what that meant.

She frantically searched for words. "But tonight, our first night, why not at my house? It's so cold here and it's nice and toasty there."

Why hadn't she heard any sirens?

"No. Now be patient. You need to come inside and see what I've put together here."

"Okay, then. I can take pictures," she said and reached for her phone in her back pocket.

"No!"

She jumped at the loud tone.

"I have my own phone inside. I'll take yours for safekeeping," he added in a calmer tone.

Marty put a hand to her elbow and when she didn't move, he wrapped his fingers securely around her upper arm and pulled.

"Come along. You'll like what you see. I'm just impatient."

"You sure you don't want to wait until morning? I can take the day off. I'm the boss, you know," she rambled and ended with a nervous chuckle.

"Oh, we'll do that too. We're going to be together forever. Starting now."

What did she say to a lunatic? She could make things worse if she didn't say the right thing.

"And the fact that you came right to me at the same time I came to find you. I couldn't have dreamed it better," he said, his tone a happy lilt.

"Yes, I see how you would think that."

He pulled her and she halted again.

"You must come. You must."

What if she went inside? Would it be better or worse for her? She could at least keep a light going so that someone might notice.

"Okay, let's go." She walked ahead of Marty until he put a hand forward and pushed the door open for the both of them.

"Candles. You're burning candles," she stated. In the middle of a placement of white tapers was an eight by ten framed photo of her. It was a professional photo she had taken for the grand opening of the store, and he must have gotten a copy off the website.

Fear threatened to take her breath away and it took a few moments to make herself stop, focus, and breathe in and out again.

This was crazy, this wasn't happening. It was a joke, some mistake. She'd just have to lend some credence to those who claimed their friend or relative couldn't possibly do something senseless.

She gritted her teeth before pointing at the table and saying, "Tell me about all this."

Marty smiled. "This is my shrine to you, for lack of a better word. You are the most beautiful person both inside and out."

Feeling nausea brew in the pit of her stomach, she focused on her breathing, then said, "But you don't really know me. You know, what I want in life. You only know what I want at work."

Perhaps she could stall, she decided. "How was I to know you cared for me? You hardly looked my way, let alone made eye contact. How could you expect me to return your uh…interest in me if you didn't acknowledge it?"

"I— "

"I mean, you just quit your job. You had other plans."

"My plan— "

"To go back to school, I know."

"That man was insisting you marry him, so I had to move fast. I couldn't allow you to be swayed by a domineering man who would want to control you. I knew he was not the one for you. I'm the one for you!"

She'd gotten him angry and the grip of his hand on her arm hurt.

Wondering once more where Caleb or even Grandma could be, she strained to hear anything happening in the neighborhood. She heard crickets but then they stopped.

Please God, help me! she shouted inside her head.

"Freeze! Put your hands on your head."

She let out a huge breath when she heard Caleb yell. Taking advantage of Marty's shock, she pulled away from him, and an officer took her hand. The officer, Kara Morgan, was Caleb's rookie last year.

As Myka's shock began to wane, she made eye contact with Caleb, he winked, and she started to cry like a baby.

"Kara, can you please take Myka to Grandma Harper's house? She can tell you how to get there."

"Yes, sir," she answered and put her hand on Myka's elbow to guide her to the patrol car.

Jason and Grandma were sitting on her front porch, her guitar case nearby.

Even though Myka just wanted to be home in Caleb's arms, she'd settle in just fine with her friends at Grandma's. Maybe she'd invite Kara in to stay as well.

CHAPTER SIX

"Caleb made me swear on a stack of Bibles that I wouldn't go to the yellow house," said Grandma as she split the rest of the apple pie between them all. "Since I'm getting closer and closer to Saint Peter and the pearly gates, I couldn't break that promise."

"Yes, but she was angry," said Jason, between bites of pie. "She sounded like an angry Donald Duck."

Joyous laughter followed and Myka appreciated it beyond words. She could not go back to the scene of the crime in her mind just now.

"You know this is my second piece of pie tonight," Myka said across to Grandma.

Grandma did not return her smile but put her hands to her face and started crying and it touched Myka's heart so.

The room grew quiet and Jason stood, followed by Kara.

"I think I should get going. Thanks for the pie, Mrs. Harper," he said.

Kara cleared her throat. "Yes, thank you, Mrs. Harper."

Grandma nodded but didn't take her hands from her face.

Myka said, "Thank you, Jason, for warning me. I can't help but think what could have happened to me if you hadn't come when you did."

"I'm glad I helped. I'll see you Monday, or when you can make it in. Don't worry, with Molly and me things will be Allgood at work." He smiled sweetly on the way out.

Myka turned to Grandma. "I'm fine. I only have a couple bruises, okay?"

Grandma lowered her hands, and her face was shiny with tears. "I was so worried about you, and I couldn't do anything about it." She sniffed. "I felt so helpless."

Myka put her hand on hers.

"I was so scared," Grandma said.

"We both were."

A knock on the door made them both jump.

"That's probably Caleb," Myka said, but then hesitated, her heart pounding. She walked to the door and said, "Who is it?"

She heard Caleb's wonderful voice, opened the door, and pulled him in and into her arms.

They stood like that for a while until Caleb cleared his throat. "Thanks for keeping Myka company, Grandma."

"No better company," she said, still sitting at the table.

They joined her there.

"I know you have many questions, Myka, but I want to tell you the basics first, and then the other pieces will probably fit together. Or at least we'll know the succession of what's happened."

"Okay."

"It's still unclear why Robin wanted to buy the yellow house. As you know she was the highest bidder. Now we have Robin's killer due to DNA and probable cause. It is Marty."

"I just can't believe my ears," Myka said. "But why?"

Caleb touched her hand. "He was the second highest bidder at the auction."

"What?" said Grandma. "I would have never guessed that."

"It took until later today to learn about the auction in combination with the info given by the house's owner. Marty wanted that house very badly, I'd say."

"Why would he want that old house?" asked Grandma. "How could he have afforded it? And he'd quit his job."

"Marty said his parents loaned him a chunk of money to go to school, that's the only thing I'm aware of. And he wanted the house to be near to me," replied Myka, her gut clenching again. "He was taking it slowly, I believe, but once I became engaged, he had to act quietly and quickly to get me out of Caleb's clutches. He thought my going to him last night was meant to be, as if the universe sent me."

"You shouldn't have gone over there," he said, his eyebrows almost touching the bridge of his nose.

"Not without me anyway," said Grandma.

"Neither of you," he shot back, his voice rising.

He pulled Myka up out of the chair and hugged her tightly. "You scared me to death. I love you, Myka, and I could have lost you."

"You love me?" she countered.

"What? Of course."

"I love you too," she said wistfully. Her whisper upon a star came true.

"That reminds me of the day I bucked hay for my husband," Grandma said, rather wistfully herself.

"What?" asked Caleb and pulled back from a laughing Myka.

"Okay, you two have something over me, that's okay. It's good to see Myka happy."

"I am happy," she said.

We've solved the mystery," said Grandma. "Now go home, you two."

I moved into my neighborhood twelve years ago. During these years I've been watching a little yellow house directly across the creek from me and haven't seen any lights or people around the house. It is abandoned and bushes and trees are now growing around it. This Whisper anthology contribution was my way to make this house and neighborhood come alive as well as the stars shining above.

ABOUT THE AUTHOR

Mary describes herself as a late bloomer. She started writing at age 36. With practice and encouragement, she started writing romantic fiction and became a member and officer of a writer's group.

Her story writing really took off when she discovered the pines, firs and rocky knolls of Northeast Oregon. Mary's husband enjoyed panning for gold in the creeks, but she fell in love with the mining ghost towns and the history surrounding those areas. Three of her magazine articles based on ghost towns in Northeast Oregon, and the history of the Chinese miners who followed the white man to the mines, were published nationally. Mary has written books with gold mining or boom town settings, including a time travel series back to 1870 in Cracker Creek, which is now called Bourne, Oregon.

This novelette takes place in the small, fictional town of Trillium Falls. To learn more about that area, consider her novel, *Secrets of Trillium Falls*. Learn more about Mary at her website: http://authormaryvine.blogspot.com/

Her Zayka

R. Hockamin

*S*tephanie was the first person I told when I found out my husband was cheating on me. I'd learned about it in a bad way—is there a good way? Of course, the first person I thought to call was the woman who had been my nanny and was still a close friend.

I asked her to meet me at our favorite picnic table along a local hiking trail. It wasn't used much, even on a Saturday like today, and the occasional runner or bicyclist would ignore us. I was too upset to talk to her in a more public place, like a restaurant. Getting emotional in front of strangers? No thanks. And I couldn't invite her over. I had to get out of the house—our house.

I heard Stephanie's car pull into the gravel parking lot, the sound of a car door slamming, and then saw her on the narrow path in her usual puffer vest, leggings, and Nikes. She was twenty years older than me, somewhere in her early forties, but she didn't look or act like it. Slender and athletic she was jogging toward me with the grace of a marathon runner, her long brown hair, tied in a high ponytail, swinging back and forth. When she reached me, she said, "Oh, my poor little bunny." Then she hugged me and I burst into tears.

Once I'd pulled myself together, dried my eyes, and blown my nose, thanks to Steph's foresight in stuffing a wad of paper towels in her pocket, we sat down at the table and I filled her in on what happened.

"Brian went fishing with a friend today. He does that two or three times in the fall. I don't mind. It means I have the day to myself. My big plan was to schlep around in my pajamas, have a cup of coffee and a blueberry muffin in bed, and watch The Today Show. After that, I didn't have any plans. Spontaneity was going to be the word of the day."

I paused and wiped my eyes as I remembered that, actually, the word of the day had been astute. Brian had bought me a word-a-day calendar, and I'd glanced at it earlier. "*Astute.*" *Having or showing an ability to notice and understand things clearly.* The first thing I thought of, after hearing that Brian had been with another woman, was that I had not been very astute. I didn't share that with her though.

"I heard someone knock on the door," I told Stephanie. "Must have been a little after ten. I was showered and dressed by then. I'm so used to getting up early for work, I guess it's become a habit. I tried to have a lazy pajama day, but it started feeling weird. Anyway, I was glad I'd gotten dressed because when I opened the door there was a strange man standing there."

"A strange man?" she asked, a touch of concern in her voice.

"Oh, he was fine," I told her, waving my hand as if to wave away her worries. "He told me his wife worked with Brian and he found out six months ago that the two had been having an affair. He told her if she broke it off, he'd forgive her, but if he found out it was still going on he'd tell me and start divorce proceedings. On Friday night he found a new text to Brian on her phone. He found out where Brian lived and came over to confront him—and to tell me. I guess Brian was lucky he wasn't home."

"My goodness. This man. He could have attacked you or Brian. He could have attacked you."

I noticed the odd pattern of speech and the subtle accent that appeared when Steph was excited or upset. I'd asked her about it, and she put it down to having a Turkish stepfather. I had no idea what a Turkish accent would sound like, so I took her at her word; though to my television show-trained ear, I'd always thought she sounded vaguely Russian. Or maybe that was just romanticizing. I'd been told my mother, who died when I was six, was a second-generation Russian-American. Thinking about my family reminded me of something else.

"We were talking about having children," I said. "More than talking. I can't believe he's thrown it all away. The marriage. The family. All of it. How can it be that I loved him yesterday and hate him today? I hate him so much I wish he was dead. He and his home-wrecking girlfriend. I wish they were both dead."

"Do you mean it? Do you really wish your husband dead?"

I looked up at Stephanie and I knew I was not in my right mind, but I didn't care. "Yes. Dead and buried." This time I didn't cry. Maybe

I'd be sad again later but, for now, it felt good to let my rage burn away the unshed tears.

Two days later I would remember what I said with regret; and yes, tears. It was two policemen who knocked on the door that time. They had come to tell me that my cheating husband and his girlfriend had died the very night I'd learned about them.

The car they were driving had gone over a cliff up in the mountains. It had tumbled and burned with them inside. They might never have been found were it not for a smoke lookout who reported a trail of smoke to the Emergency Communications Center. They dispatched a ground crew who climbed into the canyon and found the remains of the lovers. Were they running away together I wondered? A question I was half glad I would never know the answer to.

One of the policemen asked if I had someone I could call for support. For a moment I thought about calling Molly, a friend from work. Then I realized this wasn't something I wanted to share with a friend. I needed family and there was only one person. I called Stephanie, who dropped everything and drove over the minute I called.

I told her what had happened and then I said, "You don't think a wish could make something like that happen, do you? Could I make someone die just by wanting them to?"

"No. That is impossible. That's superstitious nonsense. You can't think like that."

But I could, and I did.

"Remember when I was in ninth grade and that boy cornered me in the old barn on our way home from school? I had to fight him off and, when I got here, I was shaking so much I could barely talk. I told you how he scared me and that I wished I'd never have to go back to school and see him again. Do you remember how I said I wished he was dead?"

"Maybe, but—"

"But nothing. He died that very day. He fell out of a tree in his backyard and his parents came home from work and found him there with a broken neck."

"It was a terrible accident."

"Was it? Or did it have something to do with my wishing he was dead? Think about it. That boy, now Brian."

"Oh, my poor girl. You know this is just your imagination running wild. So much has happened to you in such a short time. Your mind is fighting to understand, to find logical reasons for what you are feeling. But there is no logic in feelings. You must let yourself feel them. Grieve. Be angry. But please, you must let this silly idea go. You did not kill these people with your mind." She smiled, and stroked my hair, "You are, I'm afraid, not that powerful."

I smiled back. As usual, Stephanie's stoic acceptance of the world as it was calmed me down and helped me put things back in perspective.

My calm didn't last long. The next day I was asked to come into the police station to be interviewed regarding Brian's accident. I had never been inside a police station before. It looked like the rest of the local government buildings. A four-story structure with a rather boring red brick façade and rows of windows trimmed in white. Concrete rectangles planted with bushes whose leaves were turning red ran the length of the building, broken only by doorways.

I went through one and found myself in a small reception area with a raised desk. On the walls, there were sepia prints of the downtown decades earlier. There was also a row of framed color photos, all of men in uniform, whom I assumed were police chiefs, past and present. I walked by a small seating area to the desk and a young woman standing there. When I told her who I was she took me back immediately.

I followed her down a hall with a row of closed doors. She left me in a small room with a square wooden table and four chairs. There was no large mirror on the wall or recording equipment I could see. The only thing on the table was a couple of yellow legal pads.

The room was not what I'd expected, and I wasn't sure if I was relieved or disappointed. I did notice there were no pictures on the walls, which were painted a sort of lifeless teal and a little worn and scuffed. Sort of the way I felt. I sat down, took a deep breath of the stale air, and prepared for a long wait.

I was surprised when the door almost immediately swung open and two men in pale gray suits, not quite matching, walked in. They were similar in height and probably in their late thirties. Both had brown hair and eyes but the one with the red tie had a round face, while the one with the blue and black tie had a narrow one.

They introduced themselves but their names dissolved like morning mist. After answering questions about when I'd last seen Brian, if I'd met his girlfriend, Sherry, and did I suspect the affair, a small light bulb went off. I was a suspect.

Stephanie had spent the night sleeping in the guest room. Close, in case I broke down into a sobbing wreck again. When I got home I told her all about my experience at the police station.

"I think they would have dropped it. The thing is the one detective, the one with the long face that I think had one of those last names that sound like a first name. Something like Larry or Gary. Hold on." I got up and found my purse where I'd set it, on the kitchen island. I dug around and found two cards. I pulled them out and read them. "Mike Shepard and Stan Barry." Then I tossed them back in my bag and returned to the living room where Stephanie sat sipping a glass of red wine while my glass sat untouched on the coffee table. Wine makes me relax and I didn't want to. I wanted to think.

I dropped onto the couch, bent at the waist, and ran my fingers through my hair. Finally, I sat back up and said, "I don't get it. The Barry guy seems sure I had something to do with Brian's death. Well, him and her both. They found some suspicious things at the scene of the accident."

"Suspicious?"

"Black marks on the pavement. Skid marks that might mean another car was there."

"How could they tell? That road is so curvy and there are always black marks. How do they know they aren't old ones?"

"I don't know but Detective Barry seemed very sure they were new. He also said the condition of the gravel on the shoulder made it look like Brian had been fighting the car back onto the road when something hit him and shoved the car over the side. The other detective seemed less sure about that. Maybe he was playing good cop or something." I shrugged. "I'm clueless. The only time I've ever spoken to a cop was in junior high when the Dare officer came to visit my school. Oh, and the time, right after I got my license, that I got pulled over for running a stop sign I hadn't seen. Both times the officers were pretty nice."

"But this Barry. He is not nice."

"That's for sure. I think if it was up to him, he'd have me locked up right now. I don't know if he really believes I'm guilty, has something to prove, or he's just ambitious. Whatever it is I know he's not going to drop this until he's convinced them to investigate me some more. Remember me blubbering about having the power to wish people dead? I guess if I really had that power, he'd be next on my list."

I reached for the glass of wine.

"If we plan to drink then I have to go out for something better than wine," Stephanie said.

"I won't argue," I told her. "I can't stand red wine." Drinking did suddenly sound like a good idea. I knew there wasn't a thing I could do about the police and their suspicions. I had to let it go and not let one misguided detective get under my skin. Steph ran to the store, and we did what we'd promised. Or at least I did. I know drinking can become a bad habit, but I was grateful that it helped me fall into a deep and dreamless sleep.

Monday became Tuesday and Stephanie went home that afternoon. I expected a follow-up call from the police but didn't get one. On Tuesday night I wandered around restlessly. My emotions were still all over the place, ranging from anger at Brian's betrayal to grief over his loss. Maybe he would have asked me to forgive him. Maybe we could have patched things up. Another thing I'd never know.

Finally, I poured a glass of white wine from the bottle Stephanie had bought for me. After I filled my glass, I put the bottle right back in the fridge. Given how I was feeling, and the fact that I'd been given two weeks of bereavement time off, a single glass could quickly become a bottle. One night of excess was enough. My mother had been an alcoholic and genetics was nothing to play with.

I stopped pacing and sat down to catch the evening news. After the national news was the local. They would begin with the top story, the perky blond announcer said. Then she dropped her tone and became more serious which got my attention. She looked up from the desk and somberly said, "A 42-year-old police detective has been found dead in an alley between Ninth and Tenth streets near Pine Street downtown. Detective Stanley Barry, of the city police, was shot twice in the head by an unknown assailant. There are no suspects at this time but police from various state and local law enforcement organizations are joining forces to solve this horrific crime."

I looked down. I'd dropped my glass. It had fallen to the carpet with a soft thump which is what got my attention. A damp stain was spreading into the carpet but the glass looked fine. Was I? I didn't think so. It had happened again. I tried to recall what Stephanie had said to me. That I did not have any special powers. That I could not blame myself for things I couldn't control. How such thoughts were just silly superstitious nonsense.

Yet, every person I could remember wishing dead had died. That had to be more than a coincidence. For one of the many times in my life, I wished my mother was still alive. Had she had this kind of power? Was there something more than alcoholism in my genetics that I should know about? Suddenly a horrible thought struck me. My mother died when I was six years old. Had she made me mad? Had I wished her dead?

Should I talk to Stephanie about my fears again? No. I already knew what she'd say. What about my father? Would he suggest, as Stephanie had, that I was a bit of a control freak who suffered from a goddess complex? Or would he have a different truth?

I visited my father as often as I could. He'd gone to prison when I was ten and at this point had been there for sixteen years. I'd never asked him directly why he was there, and he'd never offered so we didn't discuss it. Instead, we mostly talked about what I was doing, my classes, and my grades. Was my team winning their soccer matches? What did Santa Claus bring?

When I got older, we spoke about college, whether I had met anyone, and more broadly about such things as philosophy and literature. Though an orphan who was self-taught, my father read voraciously and could talk on almost any subject. He could have been a teacher, even a professor. Putting him in prison seemed cruel and wasteful though probably just.

When I was seventeen, I did some research and found my father, a real estate investor, was reported to have been affiliated with Russian mobsters. Maybe that was how he met my mother? They said he'd been part of a nationwide organization that controlled all sorts of criminal activities. The profits from those activities had to be hidden and my dad was accused of being one of those who hid them.

He must have been pretty good at it since he got away with it for a long time. Some of the articles I read said he had connections with the Russian kleptocracy of government, civil service, law enforcement, military, and security services. I'm sure that helped.

Thinking about it put me in a quandary. On the one hand, my father was a criminal. On the other, I loved him and was proud of how smart he was. Even of how long he'd gotten away without being caught. I wanted to see him and tell him all about what had happened. I decided I might as well go now, while I was still taking time off from work.

As I made plans to go, I decided it was probably a bad idea to tell him about my belief that I could kill people by wishing them dead. There was nothing he could do about that, except worry that his only daughter, his only child, had lost her damn mind. I didn't want to make him worry. I'd figure this out in my own way.

I called the Toyota dealership and made an appointment. I hung up and the phone rang. I thought it was probably the dealership, calling to ask about something they'd forgotten. I hoped not to cancel my appointment. I liked to have the car checked before going on a long drive.

It wasn't them. It was an official at my father's prison. In a soothing voice, he said, "I'm sorry to tell you that your father suffered a fatal stroke today. He was taken to the infirmary but there was nothing that could be done."

This time it was my phone that fell from my nerveless fingers to the carpet.

When Stephanie arrived, she didn't bother knocking, she just let herself in. The door wasn't locked and if it had been it wouldn't have mattered. She had her own key. I was curled tightly in the corner of the couch. The phone was still on the floor.

"You heard?" she asked. As she sat down, she put her hand on my shoulder.

I nodded and the motion sent tears down my cheeks. "T-the prison called. They told me he . . . But how did you find out?" I asked.

"I have connections there. People who let me know things. I got a call too, and I was worried for you. So much death around you."

"Because I was right. I *can* wish people dead."

"Ridiculous. You did not wish for your father to be dead."

"Didn't I? I wanted a normal childhood, a normal family. Who can say, that on some subconscious level, I wanted him dead?"

"That is nonsense. Now you are making things up to fit the story you have written in your mind. That's not how it works."

"No? Then tell me, how does it work, because I am on the verge of losing it. You said it yourself, there is a lot of death around me. There has to be a reason. There has to be."

"There is, my Zayka, and I have come here to tell you that reason. To tell you all of it."

Zayka? Steph's accent was thicker now and her use of that word . . . She'd called me that before, more than once over the years. Always, when she caught herself, she'd looked embarrassed. Almost like she'd said a dirty word. When I asked her what it meant she said it was Turkish for sugar.

"What does Zayka really mean?" I asked. "What language is it?"

"Mudry moi, my wise one. It is Russian of course, it means little rabbit, bunny, you know?"

She had always called me her little bunny.

"What I am going to tell you now is very secret and must be said only between us. Do you understand?"

I straightened my legs and sat up, hanging on her every word because I expected a revelation. I wasn't disappointed.

"You call me Stephanie and that is now my name, but I was born Stephania, a citizen of Russia. My father and your father were, well, not friends. Let's call them colleagues. When I was twenty, I went to work for your father."

"I know. You were my nanny."

"Yes, and also your bodyguard. You see, your father was a very powerful man, and such men have powerful enemies."

"So, you protected him."

"No, Zayka," She shook her head.

I remembered all our times together, playing in the playroom or the yard. But there were outings too, going to the park, the museums, or the movies. Many of these trips away from home were with my father but Stephanie was nearly always there. I had never questioned her constant quiet presence in the background. It had been typical, our normal.

"You were there . . . You were there to protect me!" I said, with dawning realization.

"Yes, you were my job. My first real job, but I was trained for this work. I did my job well. Your father was not sure he could trust me and so he gave me my first task. Your mother, you do not remember her I think, but she drank. She drank too much and she talked too much. So they gave him a choice that was not a choice. He could see her dead, or he could see you dead. He had loved her but you he loved more."

"But my mother was Russian. Wasn't she one of them?"

"Oh yes. She had married your father against the wishes of her family you see. But he was a very good worker and he had many smart ideas. He became useful and quickly rose to a position of great authority and leadership. Even leaders have weaknesses that have to be removed though. So, this was his choice. Remove his weakness or lose his daughter."

"You killed my mother."

"Yes, but in a very kind way. I promise you. She did not suffer. I gave her a shot while she was sleeping. She did not even feel it. They thought she died from the alcohol she had drunk that day. They did not know her capacity. She was Russian after all." Stephanie laughed with some strange version of nationalist pride, which only added to the surrealism of the moment.

"Did you—did you kill my father too?"

Stephanie or Stephania looked at me with wide, startled eyes. "Of course not."

"Then why now? Why so soon after Brian? There has to be something more than fate here."

"Oh yes, but again, it is not directed by you. Back in Russia when I was training, I spent several months working in a big room with computers. Here I sat with a headset on while my computer looked at American communications searching for certain phrases and names. I think your name must be on this list. When your husband died your name was in the newspaper. Someone saw it on their computer and sent a report to someone else. That person, or maybe someone above them, remembered your father. To remember is sometimes to act."

"But he was in prison. He couldn't do anything."

Stephanie smiled. "He could do a great deal, but maybe not so much. Doesn't matter. Your father was a good prisoner. I think he would have been released early. I think also, after so many years his people had lost power, or perhaps interest. There was no one to protect him. Once released he could become an annoyance so should be dealt with, and they did.

Stephanie squeezed my shoulder affectionately. "It's good to talk to you about these things. Your father was my employer and had my loyalty, but his death has freed me from keeping his secrets. It's been hard to keep everything from you."

"I'm sorry it's been so hard," I said, with sarcasm I realized was probably dangerous. This was not the woman I thought I knew. This was a woman I couldn't have imagined in my wildest dreams. Stephania, my personal bodyguard, and what else, my spy?

"It was not so hard. Over the years there have been few reasons to intercede. After your mother, all was peaceful until that boy in your ninth year of school. Do you remember? He pushed you into a corner and held you. He touched you and didn't let you go until you fought free. I was so angry when you got home that day. I saw fear in your eyes that had never been there before."

"You killed that kid?"

"That animal you mean. Yes, I knocked at his door and demanded he apologize to you. He laughed at me so I broke his neck."

"And left him for his parents to find?"

"And why not. He was their monster."

"This is so . . . My god. I thought I was killing people. I thought it was me."

"Never you, Zayka. Always me. For my job but also for my love for you. That boy, he would have been there every day, to taunt you, to remind you. That could not be allowed. Your father was locked away. He could not protect you. It was my job. As for your husband, I have never seen you in such pain. I could not see this pain and let him live. You understand that."

She said it as a statement, but I didn't understand. What normal person who grew up believing in the social contract, laws, justice, and all those philosophical things could understand that my nanny, my friend, had taken it upon herself to kill anyone who hurt me?

"Well, it's over now," she said. "As I said, my contract with your father ended with his death. With him gone, there will be no one seeking to use you against him. As for the rest. After the boy, you never let yourself get into a position like that again. You're smart and you learn. I don't think you'll let a man treat you as your husband did and if one does, I think you are strong enough to take care of it. You will be fine without me. I am still young. There is time for me to go home now and to live near my family."

"So, you're leaving?" I asked. Inane, I know, but I didn't know what else to say. I was in shock but at the same time my mind was spinning wildly as I reviewed my life with a new understanding.

"Yes, I am leaving, but you'll be fine. Your father left millions for you and you need never work unless you want to. He only wanted you to live a normal life so, if something happened and he lost everything, you would be okay. Now, with his death, I know you will be. It has all been arranged." She got up and began to walk toward the door. I knew this would be the last time I'd see her.

"Are you sure you didn't kill him?" I asked boldly.

She turned to look at me. To look right in my eyes when she said it. "Yes, I am certain. I know the man who did. He was planted in the prison and given a syringe with a drug like the one I used on your mother. It is easy to hide such a thing, even in a prison. He was told to wait until he was given a signal to act. I had hoped he would never get this signal." She sighed. "The man being there, I have always known of it. It was a secret, and no one was to speak of it." She shrugged. "But as you know, there are whispers. Always whispers."

"I thought you were loyal to him. Why didn't you tell him about these whispers? Why didn't you tell me?"

"There are loyalties and then there are loyalties, Zayka."

She went through the doorway and as the door closed behind her, I realized she was not Stephanie, but was now and had always been Stephania.

In a tear-filled voice, but with terrible clarity, I whispered, "I wish you were dead."

R. Hockamin's Inspiration For This Story

I've always wondered what it would be like to have a special and secret power. What if you had one and didn't even know it? I'm also fascinated by gangster culture and especially criminal enterprises in Russia. I am part Russian on my mother's side, though as far as I know my ancestors were farmers and bakers not criminals! A series of what if questions brought me to the idea of a nanny and her Zayka.

ABOUT THE AUTHOR

R. Hockamin lives in the Pacific Northwest, where she contemplates the rain, drinks microbrews, and considers ways to kill people. Her short stories have been described as dark and unpredictable. She and her cat are fine with that.

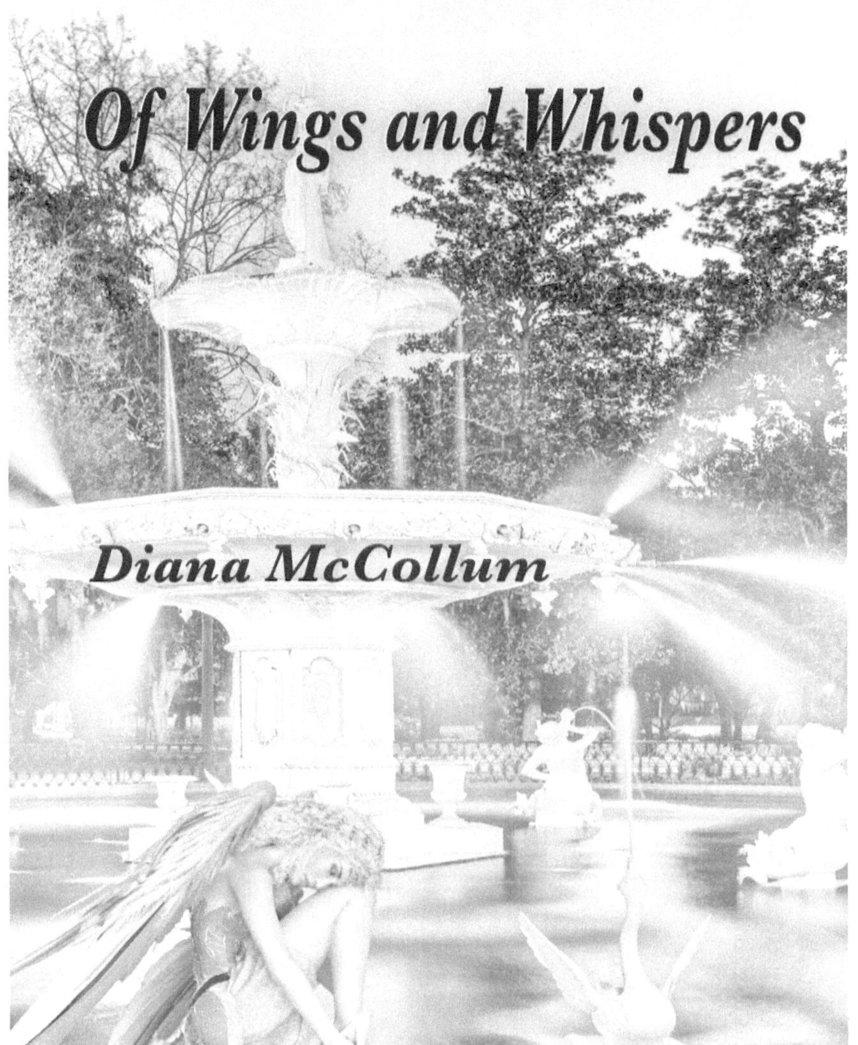

Of Wings and Whispers
Diana McCollum

CHAPTER 1

illa stood on the edge of the cliff. Her torn wing flapped in the relentless north wind. The warlock could not be far behind. One shove from him and she'd fall 100 feet to the canyon below, only the river might stop her from dying. A warning crawled up her back. Turning, she saw the warlock on the horizon his robes whipping around his legs. He hurried down the barren mountainside.

To be captured by a warlock meant certain death. He would siphon what power she had, leaving her to die. She looked over the side of the cliff. The jagged rocks along with the churning water below were not a place for a safe landing. Maybe by jumping far enough out from the side, she could land where the current was not so strong. Possibly her healthy wing might ensure a soft landing. How she *wished* for a rescue of some sort. No one knew where she was. That was not going to happen.

The warlock crested the last hill. "Now or never." She sucked in a deep breath, extended her good wing, and jumped. She spun in erratic circles. "Oh, no, oh no, oh no." This was not going well at all.

She'd taken this assignment from Queen Tatianna, of the fairy kingdom Rieth, in hopes of spreading her wings, so to speak. She didn't want to spend her life in the fairy kingdom. She wanted to visit other realms and see what life was like elsewhere. She'd begged Queen Tatianna to give her this assignment. With a warlock already after her wanting to usurp her power, she was making a mess of the trust the Queen had in her to complete the assignment.

The air thrummed with the beating of wings, as strong arms cradled her. Willa's heart raced. Looking up, she peered into Tate's face. She remembered him from the spring festival.

"Where did you come from?" Willa choked out, "I thought the explorers were meeting in Rieth?"

"Well, I couldn't very well leave you here with a broken wing. I'm no longer with the explorers, banished by the queen who chose to believe an evil-tongued elf over me. Now I work the wish circuit in this realm, and you did *wish* for a rescue."

He soared over a cumulus cloud and dived down through the forest in between branches of green leaves, not yet touched by autumn. New York City showed on the horizon. The busy harbor with large ships and small boats came into view.

"Hang on," Tate said. He flew between tall buildings. The streets below bustled with people, yellow cabs, cars, and horns honking. He turned down alleyways where his wings almost brushed the brick. Tate set them down on the balcony of a four-story building. "Inside with you, now, the invisible cloak will dissolve any moment."

Once inside Willa took the time to examine Tate's human world residence. The colorful yellow couch, royal blue chairs, and ottoman screamed happiness. There was a green shag carpet in front of the fireplace, an array of beautiful posters, paintings, and clocks for every time zone on the walls. In fact, more than just the time zones. He had dozens of clocks all sizes, shapes, and with different settings.

Tate flashed her a grin. "I collect clocks. Something I fancy, time. It stands still for no one.

Have a seat, I'll contact Rory. See about your wing repair. I'll be back directly." He walked into his office, closing the door.

Willa had never been in the human world. She was a courier for the queen. She had always gone into the destination realm, delivered the package, and then back through the veil to the kingdom of Rieth.

She walked around the couch, trailing her fingers along the back. So soft! She examined the wall of posters and paintings. There was a pretty pink sign that said "Love, Love", a "No Smoking" sign, a painting of a dancing girl, and a very accurate painting of the kingdom of Rieth. Only someone who'd been to the fairy queen's kingdom could have painted that.

"Ah, I see you are enjoying my collection." Tate walked over to stand next to her. "This one," he pointed to the painting of Queen Tatianna's kingdom, "I painted in an art class I joined."

"You're allowed to go to classes? To be around humans? You don't have to isolate?" To be able to enjoy what this world had to offer, what a gift.

"Orders from the queen, I'm to fit in. So yes, I go to classes, I am around humans and interact with them. Last, no, I don't have to isolate."

Willa noticed his wings were tucked in. If she didn't know he had wings, she wouldn't be able to tell. "How do you like living in the human world?"

"It's interesting." He laughed a little. "But I do miss the fairy kingdom". He took her by the shoulders, spinning her around to get a look at the torn wing. "You've beautiful wings. It's a shame the warlock tore one." He picked up the edge of the broken wing and let the wing filter through his fingers.

Willa shivered. No one had ever touched her wings before.

"Does your wing hurt when I touch it?"

"No, doesn't hurt a bit." Willa smiled. He seemed nice enough and willing to help her. "I really need to finish my mission and get back. What did Rory say?"

"I've been told, by Rory, to get a half dozen silkworms. They will repair your wing. The wing will be stronger than before. I'll try and make the design match. So that's my mission." His smile lit up his face.

"What about me? How long is this going to take? I've never been away from the fairy kingdom more than a few hours."

"Till I find the silkworms, you will have to stay in my apartment. Don't worry I do have a spare room for just such emergencies." He walked over to a door and opened it. "Everything you need should be in here. There is a closet with a few clothing items, dresser, and end table. There's a bookshelf in the living room, help yourself to the books. Whatever is in the kitchen or apartment, except for my office, feel free to eat or use. You are my guest. "

She peeked into the beautiful bedroom. She loved everything from the misty green curtains and comforter to the thick white carpet and the sparkly crystal chandelier. The little table had a mirror on the wall above trimmed in gold. There was a silver-handled brush and comb set, along with an array of bottles on the table. "This is beautiful!" Willa swiped a tear from her eye. She'd never had such a beautiful room.

"Ahh", Tate tapped a finger against his lips, "all we're missing is a familiar for a companion. Do you prefer a cat, dog, or bird?"

"Wait! This is moving way too fast! This is just not done in the Fairy Kingdom. If I stayed here alone unchaperoned I'd be forced to wed you, that's not going to happen!" Willa walked to the large window in the living room. This was a city she knew nothing about. If she had not been on the outs with Tatianna she would not have been asked to come here.

"We will not have to wed, honestly. My residence is a safe haven for any who needs one. The elders already know you are here. The permission has been granted." He smiled his devastating smile again.

"You're sure?"

"Absolutely! I have to do a bit of research on where to purchase silkworms. Make yourself at home. I have a great collection of books." He picked up one, "You might enjoy this one."

The leather cover was soft. She touched the gold embossed title. "The Green Witch", by Arin Murphy-Hiscock. "Perhaps I should learn more about witches."

"I think you'll find this book an interesting read. Not all witches are *bad*. Some, like the ones who practice being green witches, are solitary witches. Their type commune with nature and actually I have a couple who are my friends. You'd like them."

Willa shuddered. She was told to avoid witches and warlocks they were the fae's enemies. "I'll see after I read this book. I may want to meet your witch friends, and I may not." She settled down on the couch. Opening the book.

She could hear Tate's fingers clicking on the keyboard. She began to read. After a bit, her eyes started to drift shut. She leaned back against the cushy arm of the couch and gave in to the sleep that had snuck up on her.

Tate swore under his breath. "This is not good, nope, not good." The silkworms weren't going to work. He'd have to order eggs, incubate for 28 days, feed them mulberry leaves till they matured and wrapped themselves in cocoons. To harvest the silk fiber he'd have to steam the cocoons, killing the worm since the cocoon is the silk thread. The silk filament would have to be unwound and treated to make a usable source of silk thread.

"Not good, intentionally killing another creature, no matter a worm or something else. Plus, the time to complete this process is way too long."

With a sigh, he turned off the computer. Rory said there might be another way. Punching in Rory's number, he walked to the window looking out. The message recorder clicked on. "Hey, Rory, I researched the silkworm idea, and it isn't going to work. You said you had another idea? Get back to me asap."

Now to work on a familiar. Willa never specified what she wanted. An owl won't work. She needs something, which can go with her if she goes out. Hmmm, maybe a dog.

Tate walked to the bookcase and pulled a black top hat off the shelf. He blew the dust off and promptly sneezed. He couldn't remember the last time he'd used the hat. He set the black hat on the table, studying it for a few minutes.

Snatching up the hat, he stared into the bottom and made his wish for a familiar for Willa. The hat began to shake, it grew warm, there was a distinctive 'yip' and a small white rounded snout popped up. Not the ferocious dog Tate was hoping for. He set the hat on the floor and a miniature bull terrier hopped out complete with a red collar.

Tate petted the dog. "You have an important job to protect Willa." He turned the collar around so the tag was visible. An inscription read 'my name is Boss'. "Well boy, Boss is an important name."

Boss gave a small yip and ran around the room several times. "Here boy! Okay, okay, here Boss." He patted the rug, Boss ran over sat down with a plop, his pink tongue dangling out. "I'm going to slip this tracker chip into the back of the collar. If Willa is in trouble she'll send you a ping with this little remote control." Tate turned the collar around, "Willa doesn't know a lot about this realm and I don't want her getting lost." He reached into the hat and pulled out a red leash.

Boss gave a yip in agreement.

The phone rang in the office. Tate picked the cell up. "Hello, Rory. I hope you have good news for me."

"I believe I've tracked down the best silk weaver around. She is a superior weaver and the cloth will be ready in a week. You are quite the artist Tate, you could paint the design on the silk to match the other wing. What do you think?"

"It's worth a try since the silk worms won't work." Tate peeked out the office door. The fairy slept on his couch. "Okay, sure, I'll do it. Give me a call when the silk is done."

"You got it. Bye, friend!" The phone clicked as Rory hung up.

Tate glanced up to see Willa standing in the doorway.

"Who was that?" Willa took a step into the room.

"Rory. He has found a weaver who is making a special blend of silk for your wing repair." He took a closer look. She had a glimmer about her, a shimmer. He knew for a fact only fairies with royal blood glimmered. "Who is your family?"

Willa ran a hand through her short black hair. "Does it matter?"

"Of course, it matters. Are you of the royal family?" He blurted out.

"I am a cousin to Queen Tatianna. It's best if this stays between us."

144

Willa smiled. " I suppose you want to know why I'm running errands between our kingdoms."

"Yeah, I want to know." He sat on the couch. Motioned for her to do the same.

"The Queen has a spy in her court. None of us have been able to figure out who. She trusts no one, only family. I was chosen for the errand which led me to the cliff and into your arms."

He blushed remembering how good she'd felt in his arms. Thoughts he shouldn't be having for royalty. "Oh, I have a present for you." He clapped his hands, "Boss, Boss come."

Toenails clicked on the wooden floor as the little white dog ran over sliding to a stop. He cautiously crossed the rug to Willa. He sat down patiently waiting.

"Boss is yours while you are here." He handed her the little remote control. "If you are lost or in trouble just click this and Boss will find you. Although, the reason you have him is to keep you safe. Best if you just keep Boss with you all the time."

Willa bent down and picked Boss up. She held the dog up so their eyes were level. They stared into each other's eyes for a few moments. The connection was made. "He's mine. I love him." Boss gave her a quick lick then jumped down curling up near Willa on the rug.

She smiled. Tate felt warm all over. He had to move away from her because he was a helper. She was royalty. He walked over to the window to draw the shades closed. First, one more look at the vista. This was his favorite time of day, purple sky of dusk, stars coming out, a moon rising, and the city lighting up. He liked this world, especially New York City. He turned to call Willa over only to find her right beside him.

Willa linked arms with him. "Thank you for Boss. Well, for everything you are doing for me." She leaned her head on his shoulder. "This is a beautiful sight! We don't have this in Rieth. No tall buildings or lights, quite different from the forest and meadows of Rieth."

"How about some dinner?" he asked, "I have something a friend left here you can wear, the wrap will cover your wings. Plus, there is a chill in the fall air."

"Dinner would be lovely."

He opened the coat closet rummaging through till he found an olive green cape soft as llama wool. "This looks about your size." He held it out.

She slipped into the wrap. "Perfect. Thanks." Willa twirled around and the cape flared out.

ONCE SETTLED IN THE CHAIR AT THE RESTAURANT WILLA PERUSED THE menu. "This menu is rather unsettling. I've never seen so many choices! What do you recommend?" She looked up, he had a half smile on his face, she wanted to reach out with a hand and cup his cheek. She focused back on the menu.

"I personally am a fan of seafood. Something we never got in Rieth." He ran his finger down the menu, "Here we go. Scallops and angel hair pasta in a cream sauce with a nice wine. I can highly recommend this wine since I've had this before. Sound good to you?"

"I'll try the same." Smiling she handed the menu to him. A chill snaked its way up her spine. Something evil was close. She scanned the busy restaurant, noting the happy couples chatting and ordering their dinners. A string quartet played in the lounge. Shaking the feeling off, she picked up the glass of water and took a sip. "I suppose this is a treat for you, or do come here regularly?"

"Once a month or so. Ah, here's our waiter now. We'll have two orders of Scallops with angel hair pasta in cream sauce. We'd also like two glasses of your best white wine."

"Yes, Sir, do you want the wine before the meal?" The young waiter responded in a voice cracking due to his age.

"Yes." Tate smiled. Willa felt a tingle deep inside.

A whisper in her ear, "Beware of the crescent," jolted her. She turned around. No one was there.

"Your wine, madam." The deep tenor of the waiter had her looking up. He was not the same waiter who took their order. His hair was pitch black and slicked back. His deep blue eyes bored into hers. She saw a crescent tattoo on his hand. Was this who she should beware of? "Umm, thank you." The waiter bowed before he left the table.

Tate didn't hesitate to pick up his wine. He held his glass out to her. "A toast"

They clicked glasses. Tate said, "To a speedy fix on your wing."

He smiled and her heart sped up. She couldn't believe she was having feelings for him. This always happened quickly with the fae. Tate wasn't royalty. The chances of Tatianna approving a relationship between them was unlikely.

Their meals were placed before them. The smell of the pasta made her mouth water. She had never had seafood in Rieth. The food there consisted mostly of what they grew.

After their meal, when they were leaving, the waiter who delivered the wine stepped into their path. He bowed saying, "We shall meet again."

Tate grabbed her hand hurrying past the waiter who was still bowing.

CHAPTER 2

illa walked to the window. Pulling the curtain aside, she stepped outside onto the balcony. She tried to make sense of the evening. The dinner was delicious, Tate had been entertaining, but the waiter? He gave her the creeps. Why did he say 'We shall meet again.' Where did the whispered warning come from? Willa turned to go back inside nearly running into Tate.

He grabbed Willa's arms to steady her. "What put such a sad look upon your face?"

Before she could answer, he steered her back into the loft. "Sit on the couch and I'll make you some tea. We'll discuss what is bothering you. I've found it's good to talk things over when they trouble me."

Soon the smell of fresh brewed tea wafted into the living room.

She sat down. Boss came bounding out from the bedroom. "Well 'hi' there." She reached down and scratched his head. Boss gave her hand a lick before curling up next to her feet.

Tate handed her a cup of tea. "Boss knows who he belongs to. Don't you, boy?" Tate patted Boss on the head and sat in the green chair. "Okay, spill, what's bothering you?".

Suddenly her insides felt all jittery. "I had a whispered warning during dinner. The voice said beware of the crescent. I think he was referring to the waiter who had a crescent tattoo on his hand." She shut her eyes reliving the moment the waiter said 'We shall meet again.'

"Do you think he knows who I am and where you live, Tate?"

Tate studied her. "I think we should be on high alert for the witch. I'm pretty sure he doesn't know where I live, or even if you are staying here. There is a shield around the loft. As far as the outside world knows there is no loft. Still, the witch has strong powers."

"That's a relief." She walked to the bookcase running her fingers over the large jar filled with coins. She could see through the glass that the coins were from many different lands. The jar sizzled at her touch. She jerked her hand back, a protection spell.

Tate cleared his throat. "That is the payoff for another of my responsibilities."

"Payoff?"

"There are several fountains not far from here." He set his tea on the table. "At certain times of the day, I collect coins and grant wishes."

"That is a lot of wishes!"

"They don't all get fulfilled. Some are asking for bad things to be visited upon someone else, or for monetary things, I don't fulfill any of those." He stood next to Willa. Placing his hand on the glass jar. "There are so many memories floating around in here. When the jar is full, I donate the money to a worthy charity."

"That must give you a good feeling to help others."

"Yes, of all the positions I could have, granting wishes is perfect." He brushed a lock of hair away from her face. "Perhaps you'd like to see one of the fountains?"

"Of course! I need to walk Boss, too. Is it far from here?" She grabbed the leash.

Tate opened the door. "Not far from here."

<hr>

They walked a few blocks in silence. The sun had set. The crowds were gone. Streetlights lit their way. The smell of wood smoke from a fireplace reminded her of the cottages in Reith. All were heated with wood. Mama would be standing by the stove stirring the stew. Life in Reith was a quieter way of life. This place was stimulating with all there was to see and do.

"The fountain is just a few blocks away. Father Demo Square off Houston, the fountain there is beautiful and modeled after an Italian piazza. A great gathering place for the community." He stole a glance as they walked.

Boss growled and planted his feet. "Come on boy." Willa pulled on his leash. He wasn't budging. Instead, Boss gave another low growl.

Tate scrutinized the area for a very real enemy. After all, the creatures came out during the night, the witches, goblins, and elves. Some were good, nevertheless, a few were the enemies of the Fae. He took hold of the leash, "Come, Boss." He grabbed hold of Willa's hand. The little dog trotted up ahead of them the danger apparently gone.

Soon they were beside the fountain. The air was cool from all the moisture. The sound of the running water and the smell of the wet rocks took Tate back to the waterfall in Rieth. How clean and peaceful the glade had been. All the green lovely plants grew there. The glade was the last place he had been in Rieth. The glade was where Queen Tatianna had banished him to the human world. Oh, he still had ties to Rieth and hoped one day to earn the right to return. For now, he did the queen's bidding in the human world. Protecting and helping those who ventured here from Rieth.

He released Boss from the leash at the fountain. He immediately headed for the water.

"Look! Boss! You silly boy." Willa laughed when the small dog jumped out of the flowing water shaking himself. "Now you will be cold on the way home."

Tate let loose of Willa's hand. She gave him a puzzled look. "I have to find a coin. One with a wish I can grant." Tate glanced towards the clock on the high-rise building, two minutes till nine. "Only when the clock strikes 9:00 can I grant a wish here. Each fountain has a different time for wishes."

He put his hand into the water. As the clock struck nine a quarter floated up from the bottom to his hand. He grasped the coin, "I have the wish." He slipped the coin into his pants pocket.

"Now what?" Willa asked.

"We go back to the loft. I work out the fulfillment of wishes there. That's my secondary job here in this world." He took her hand which Tate knew belonged in his hand, and nowhere else.

TATE'S CELL CHIRPED AS THEY WALKED THROUGH THE DOOR. "RORY, HEY, what's up?" Tate walked into his office. He watched Willa settle on the couch. She leaned over to pet Boss.

"Okay, let's go with the nylon. I can paint nylon to match Willa's other wing. It's durable, right? Great, see you then."

He leaned against the office doorway. Willa ran her fingers through her hair. A trail of sparkles shone in her ebony hair. She had an aura of lavender light around her. Willa was the most beautiful fairy he had ever seen. She even outshone Queen Tatianna.

"Change of plans. That was Rory on the phone. The silk won't work for your wing, however parachute material will. That's nylon. Much stronger than silk. The nylon will be delivered in a few days."

"I don't care if it takes longer. I like learning about this world, and you." She beamed.

His heart beat faster. He could get lost in those emerald eyes.

This wasn't good. He shouldn't have feelings for Willa. Such behavior would not get him back to Rieth.

Boss barked. Then growled and ran to the door. Scratching sounded from the other side. Tate placed his hand on the door. An elf was outside.

"Call Boss back to you."

She secured Boss with the leash. Tate opened the door.

A short little man with a green pointy hat walked in. "Ah, Master Tate, there's a rumor going 'round you have a royal house guest." He bowed in Willa's direction. "Master Tate, what have we here?"

"Duke, this is Willa from Rieth, Willa, Duke from New York City."

Tate rubbed his brow. "No royalty here, she's just a fairy who took a wrong turn and was attacked by a warlock. Willa's sheltering here till her wing is repaired."

"Ah, what say ye, Mistress Willa, are ye royalty?"

Willa glanced at Tate. "Truly, I'm not."

"I declare, I declare if ye don't resemble Queen Tatianna. Why ye could be a sister or cousin." He shuffled closer to the couch.

Boss jumped from the couch and grabbed hold of Duke's green shirttail. "Boss, Boss!" Willa pulled on the leash.

"Get the wretched beast off me shirt!"

When everything settled down, Tate decided to use the elf to help warn them of encroaching danger. Hard to trust an elf, it was an elf who had lured him to the glade in Rieth with false accusations, forcing the Queen to exile him. Still, Duke was a trusted friend of Rory, and Rory was Tate's best friend.

"Duke, do you live far from here?" Willa asked, petting a shivering Boss.

"I live here, there, and yonder. Not just one place mind ye. I've many friends, places, and spaces I rest me head each night."

"Duke, I have a favor to ask of you. I'm going to be out of town for two days to fulfill a wish. Do you think I could trust you to keep Willa safe?" Tate had no choice, but to rely on Rory's judgment in trusting the elf.

"No favors, I'll keep her safe, ye'll owe me some change to clink in me pocket." Duke sidled closer to Tate.

"Okay deal. Willa, come here, put your hand on the door two boards in and right on this mark." Tate placed his hand over hers and whispered a spell. The wood around their hands glowed.

They removed their hands from the door. "To get in or out of the apartment, all you have to do is place your hand on this spot, either side of the door. No one else except me can open or close it."

As an afterthought, he said, "Rory has a key, he's the only one who does."

"That's easy enough." Willa smiled.

His heart beat faster. She was stunning.

"Might I lie me head on yonder couch tonight?" Duke rubbed his chin and eyeballed the jar of coins.

"Elf, don't even think about the jar of coins! There's a spell on the jar, and you'll scorch your hands touching it." Tate gathered up his cloak and shouldered his travel bag. He looked intently at Willa. "Don't stray too far from the loft. This city is full of creatures who would like nothing better than to capture a fairy, even one with only one good wing."

"I'll only go out to walk Boss." She promised with a smile.

Tate left, closing the door with a click. Hoping in his heart of hearts his decision about the elf was the right one.

CHAPTER 3

$\mathcal{T}$he next couple days passed quietly.

Willa read for a while finishing the book on Green Witches. She thought perhaps she'd like to meet one considering they held the same beliefs she did. The natural magick of the world and Rieth were similar.

She walked over to the bookcase and slid the book in.

Boss barked.

She turned to see the elf, quick as a flash of lightning, speed out of Tate's office. "What were you doing in there? That's Tate's office." Boy, the elf could move fast!

"Just checking for creatures." The elf sat on the floor by Boss, he laid his hand on the dog's head and petted Boss. "Me and the guard dog need to make friends. I can't have him barking at me every time we take him out for his walk."

There was a knock on the door, the elf jumped up. Duke held up his hand for her to stay back. Boss yipped his annoyance when the petting stopped.

"Who 'tis knocking on the door?" Duke laid his ear against the wooden door

"Is that you Duke? It's me, Rory. I've brought the material for the fairy's wing."

Duke motioned Willa over to the door. "Ye must open with your palm."

She pressed her hand on the door, the latch clicked and the door swung open.

Rory appeared stunned. He held out the bundle to the elf. "A-are you Willa, Queen Tatianna's cousin?"

"Yes, I'm Willa. My wing was destroyed on my way to deliver a packet."

"The queen has sent out a search party for you. I understand you are very late in returning. Queen Tatianna is not going to be happy to know you've been staying with Tate."

"As you can see I'm perfectly fine except for my wing. Please tell her I'm very well. I'll be back in Rieth in a few days."

"I will do that." Rory bowed. He motioned toward the door.

Willa put her hand on the door, opening it. Rory left and she made sure it was locked by magic, again.

THE NEXT EVENING WILLA, BOSS, AND DUKE WALKED TO THE FOUNTAIN Tate had taken her to. The early evening air was brisk with lots of people milling about. Willa missed Tate. Without knowing it was happening, she had bonded with him. There were so many things about Tate she loved.

"Mistress Willa! Come. There be a goblin weaving himself through the crowd." Duke grabbed her hand. They hurried to an alcove in a building.

Then she could see not only a goblin but also several wicked-looking elves dressed in black and brandishing swords, meandering through the throng of oblivious humans. "What do we do?" she whispered.

A low rumble started in Boss's throat. She picked him up trying to quiet him.

Duke looked up, "Do ye mind if I put a hiding spell on ye, so I might talk with them, find out why they are here and what they be searching for?"

The hairs rose on the back of Willa's neck. "Yes, Boss, too." She hugged the small dog even closer. Willa knew only too well what goblins and wicked elves might do to her. The least she'd lose her other wing and the only way back to Rieth. The worse they'd kill her and take what power she had for themselves. She watched from the bubble of security Duke had placed around her.

The goblin with his ugly smashed-in-looking face approached Duke. He put his nose next to Duke's face and sucked in a breath. "Me smells goodness elf. What might ye have been hanging around? Perhaps a wayward fairy?" He walked around Duke and pushed the elf to the ground.

"I not be with any fairies, goblin." He turned his head to look towards the goblin. "Ye know our kind detest fairies. Don't ye now?"

"Leave him be." Shouted one of the malicious-looking elves. "The witch only gave us a short time to find the fairy. Come, let us make haste."

"Ye lucked out. Don't ye be hiding fairies from Ben the witch. He'll skin ye alive!" The goblin turned. With a flick of his hand motioned the elves to follow. Within seconds they had disappeared into an unsuspecting crowd.

***

TATE ARRIVED HOME TO THE EMPTY LOFT. THEY MUST BE OUT WALKING Boss, he thought. The smell of ginger tea hung in the air. He was glad the elf was with Willa. He walked over to the packaged material from Rory. "Well, he came through a day early." His heart sank a little. He realized with a heaviness in his chest, this meant Willa would be leaving this realm, leaving him.

He flinched at a knock on the door. Not the normal knock Rory gave. Willa didn't have to knock. He opened the door to find Ben the

Witch. The threshold sparked with a protection spell. In the hope the witch couldn't enter. "What do you want, witch?"

"I believe you have something of mine."

"And what might that be?" Thank goodness Willa and Duke weren't here.

"The Queen's cousin, Willa."

Tate opened the door wider, "As you can see she's gone."

The witch grabbed Tate's arm in a vise-like hold. "Then you'll have to do!".

WILLA AND DUKE RAN AS FAST AS THEY COULD. BOSS RAN ALONGSIDE his pink tongue lolling out.

Reaching the loft, Willa put her hand on the wood. The door didn't open.

She tried again, and again. "What's wrong, why isn't this working?" She asked in a shaking voice.

Duke touched the doorknob, the residual witch magick was on it. "The witch has been here. He must have disrupted the magic on the door."

Rory came around the corner of the hallway. "What's up?"

"I can't open the door."

"I have a key." Rory pulled the key from his pocket. Once inserted the key opened the door. "Oh, no, it's gone."

Willa and Duke followed Rory into the loft. Dark engulfed the room, dust covered the furniture and everything was dismal, gray. Tate's pictures were gone off the walls, dishes were smashed, cobwebs hung in the corners and across the windows. Everything good had been touched by the witch. The loft was a deserted shell. No longer the vibrant loft of Tate.

Rory walked over to the table. "The cloth for repairing your wing is still here. The witch probably didn't know what the cloth was for." He hefted the bundle to his shoulder. "Come to my place, we'll fix your wing so you can get back to Rieth."

WILLA'S REPAIRED WING WORKED JUST FINE. TRUE THE WING WAS WHITE, devoid of color, still she could fly. Back on the ground, she said, "Before I go to Rieth, I want to go to the wishing fountain. Just in case Tate is free of the witch and looking for a coin."

With Boss in the lead, she walked at a brisk pace towards the fountain. The elf followed his short legs trying to keep up with Willa.

"Duke hurry! We're almost there."

They turned the corner, the fountain came into view. No, Tate.

"Oh, no." She whispered. It was the right day, the right time. If he could, Tate would've been here.

Boss broke loose and jumped into the fountain.

"No Boss!" Willa jumped in after him. She slipped underwater, grasping coins as she searched for purchase.

When she rose out of the water a handful of coins came with her. Her hand felt warm and then hot. She placed the coins on the cement side wall of the fountain. One glowed. She picked the coin up, then pushed the rest back into the fountain.

"The inscription says 'for one wish from a fairy.' Wow." She was that fairy. Her wish was, for the bonds of the witch's magick to break. For her Tate to come back to her.

Closing her fist around the coin, she made her wish. The wind blew hard and fast. The bond broke, sending leaves tumbling down the street, and people grabbing for their hats. Tate lay on the ground before her. Slipping the coin into a pocket and kneeling down beside Tate, she cried, "Tate open your eyes, please!" She cupped his cheek. "Come back to me, please!" She saw the marks of bondage on his wrists fresh and raw. Smoothing her fingers, covered in fairy dust, over the wounds the wrists began to heal.

When he didn't respond, she was afraid he was dead. Magick tears slid down her face dropping onto his. She bent over kissing him. Sealing their love and awakening Tate.

He pulled her head closer deepening the kiss.

Willa broke away. "Tate, I tried not to, but I'm afraid I've fallen in love with you."

"Ah, love," he sat up. Brushed a stray curl behind her ear. "I fear I cannot live in your world."

She smiled. "But I can live in your world. That's the loophole. If a fairy falls in love she must stay in her mate's world. That's your world, Tate."

Boss jumped in Willa's lap and dropped a coin in her hand. Folding her fingers around the coin, she closed her eyes letting the coin show her the wish. This wish she could fulfill.

"Tate, I'll be your partner in all ways. I now have the power to make wishes come true, too."

A bird landed on Duke's shoulder carrying a rolled-up paper. Duke held out the piece of parchment. " 'Tis from the Queen herself."

Willa reached out with a shaking hand, opening the parchment to read.

"Tate, listen to this," Willa said.

Willa and Tate, you have bonded. I cannot stand in the way of true love. I grant you, Willa, permission to be Tate's mate. You now have the power to make wishes come true.

Tate, your ban from Rieth is lifted. Not only shall you grant wishes, but you will continue to fight the good fight against the bad in your world.
I expect to see your bot, and Duke, here in Rieth next week for the bonding for life ceremony.

Love,
Queen Tatianna, your cousin.

They stood embracing with the elf dancing and Boss running circles around them. "I will buy paints tomorrow and paint your wing." Tate took her hands and brought them to his lips. "Today, tomorrow, and all the days that follow, I'm yours."

"And I'm yours." Willa embraced Tate. She'd never let him go.

I've been thinking about writing a story with fairies in this world. They walk among us as do elves, gnomes and witches etc. They look like you or me. They would have a home base realm, Rieth, where they get their orders for whatever type of work they do. Or whatever havoc they raise.

Anyway, this little story introduced my hero, Tate, and heroine, Willa, who will be featured in the novel. I hope you enjoyed "Of Wings and Whispers".

ABOUT THE AUTHOR

Diana enjoys weaving elements of paranormal and fantasy into her stories. She always ends with a Happily Ever After, because she must for her own satisfaction! Her hope is to take you away from your everyday life for a journey that is both entertaining and fun, and sometimes a little scary.

Her home, in beautiful Paradise, CA, on the edge of the Sierra Mountains, allows her a wide range of hobbies. When Diana is not reading or writing, she is a fisherwoman. She also enjoys gardening, hiking, coffee dates with other writers, taking classes to expand her writing abilities, and hanging out in book stores.

You can learn more about Diana and her books at her website: https://dianamccollumauthor.com/

WHISPERING
WILLOWS
KIMILA KAY

CHAPTER ONE

*E*cho stared at the screen but didn't react to the news.

Wyatt knew the young woman rarely spoke and never about the disappearance of her sister Willow. She touched the laptop screen with a finger then looked at him, tears in her light gray eyes. The monitor showed a picture of a tattered pink T-shirt featuring a brown bear holding a bouquet of daisies, which was what their mom remembered Willow wearing the day she disappeared.

"Since it's Saturday, we won't know the identity of the remains for a few days." Wyatt needed to ask Echo some difficult questions and hoped if he did so slowly, she'd be able to respond. "It would help if we had your DNA for comparison." Wyatt's knee bumped Echo's when he turned to look at Derrick who stood at the ready with a buccal swab.

"Open your mouth wide." Derrick stepped closer to Echo. "And I'll swab your cheek."

Echo looked at Derrick, then Wyatt. Nodding at Derrick, she parted her lips and a hint of tuna rode on her breath.

Derrick angled the swab toward Echo, who leaned back, her eyes round and wary.

"Say ah," Derrick instructed, and when she complied, he inserted the long swab and did a quick circle against her cheek, then slid the collection tool into a paper sleeve.

"I'll prepare this for the crime lab." Derrick walked to his desk.

Echo wiped her lips with the back of her hand and looked at the computer screen again.

"Do you know if Willow had any broken bones?" Wyatt asked.

"No." Echo tilted her head. "I mean I don't remember." Tears trickled down her cheeks.

Wyatt handed her a tissue box as Derrick joined them.

"Willow fell from her bike." Derrick looked at Echo as if he expected her to agree.

"How old was she?" Wyatt reached for his notepad and a pen.

"I don't," Echo began, then shrugged.

"It was before the trip into the woods," Derrick stated. "She would have been thir—"

Echo drew her knees to her chest and began rocking back and forth in her chair. She stared straight ahead, and Wyatt knew she didn't see what was in front of her, but what had happened to her, Willow, and their friend Leah six years ago.

Wyatt looked at Derrick and worried Echo wouldn't be the only one having a meltdown in the Sheriff's station.

"Derrick." Wyatt spoke softly. "Take your seat."

Derrick nodded and moved to his desk. Wyatt placed a hand on Echo's arm. He wasn't sure if calming her was like helping his cousin, but he didn't know what else to try.

Wyatt heard Derrick crack open a Pepsi, followed by pencil scratches on paper and knew his cousin was writing in one of his notebooks. Echo continued to rock but made no sound and still stared ahead. Derrick's dad, Sheriff Austin Stone had tasked Wyatt and Derrick to work the incident, along with Blake, and he wished he didn't need to review the tragic events, but his mind had already headed back in time.

News of the missing girls had reached them via Leah's hysterical mom bursting into the station.

"Sheriff Stone!" Vada Keller looked around the lobby. "My Leah and her friends haven't come home, and I'm worried about them."

"The Sheriff is out right now, but we can help." Blake moved a chair close to Vada. "Here, have a seat."

"No, no." She shook her head. "It's getting dark. They went into the woods and—"

"Do you know where they were headed?" Wyatt picked up his phone and started a group text to the other deputies.

"They liked to go to the willow grove near the lake for a picnic." Vada ran a hand through her unkempt hair. "I told Leah it isn't safe to be there after dark."

"We'll find them, Mrs. Keller." Blake escorted her toward the door. "We need you to go home in case the girls show up at your house."

Vada left and the sheriff's department went to work. They searched the woods until it was too dark to see even with a flashlight. The next morning Wyatt and his men were joined by Fire Chief, Marcus Brennan, and his firefighters.

When the setting sun painted the tips of the trees orange, Wyatt worried they would have to call it a night without finding the girls.

"Here!" Ace had shouted. "I found Cedar!"

The search party circled the girl, who lie unconscious, but breathing. Mac enlisted his men to stabilize Cedar on the picnic blanket and radioed the ambulance parked at the lodge.

"The EMTs are on their way," Mac told Wyatt. "Will carry her toward them," he said as his men lifted the blanket and headed for the trail.

Wyatt knew Mac would keep him posted on Cedar's condition.

"Wyatt," Derrick said behind him.

"What?" He knew from the look on Derrick's face the news wasn't good.

"I found Leah."

Wyatt followed his cousin to a patch of grass where the young girl's body lay. She was partially clothed, and Wyatt could tell her last minutes with her killer had been horrific. He wanted to cover Leah to give her some dignity but knew that would contaminate the scene.

Derrick was already on the phone with the coroner's office and next he'd request the Oregon state police and CSU from Salem.

"Chief." Deputy Simms approached carrying a backpack. "I found this next to the picnic area." He lifted the pack. "This is Willow's." Then he pointed to blood on the strap.

Wyatt was jolted out of the memory when Echo shot to her feet and ran from the station.

He started to follow her but stopped when Derrick advised, "Let her go. She needs to process the possibility that we've found Willow's remains and trying to talk to her will extend her shutdown."

Wyatt nodded and watched as Cedar Atwood ran down Main Street on her way back to her apartment. The only girl rescued, Cedar, was questioned several times to try to piece together what had happened, but the only responses she gave was to repeat the questions.

Her speech pattern had remained the same over the years, earning her the nickname, Echo.

"I don't believe the bones belong to Willow." Derrick stood next to him.

"Probably not. But it's been a year since we thought Willow was the young woman who'd returned to the woods." Wyatt looked at Derrick. "And since we still haven't found Willow Atwood alive, we need to do a thorough investigation and identify these remains."

CHAPTER TWO

*H*arley let Elvis have the round pen all to himself as she organized the tack along the fence line, then shoveled manure into a wheelbarrow. The ginormous quarter horse followed her around like a big black dragon, curious about everything she was doing. The ten-year-old, seventeen hand Elvis reminded her of a big teenager.

Wyatt was coming to dinner and Harley wanted to finish her long list of Saturday chores, so she'd have an hour to get ready for their evening. Mid-May had brought warm days, with cool evenings and tonight's weather would be perfect for barbequing the T-Bones Wyatt was bringing. She could almost taste the summer salad she planned to make as a side dish.

As she finished rolling the hose after watering down the round pen, she thought about her first year as the owner of the Redneck Ranch.

She and the ranch had survived a raging fire thanks to Wyatt's help, along with the residents of Stoneybrook, who despite originally calling her a greenhorn, now welcomed her into the fold. The mysterious murders of three young women that had spanned seven years had been solved a year ago and she was no longer afraid of the ancient barn where two of the bodies were found. And after being rescued from a serial killer six months ago during Christmastime, Harley and Wyatt had grown closer, finally sharing their first *I love yous*.

Now as she finished up her chores, she thought about how uneventful the first five months of 2024 had been and how much she loved her life in Stoneybrook. Smiling, she realized the only thing she missed about New York was her bestie, Busy, who was planning a visit next week.

Elvis whinnied from the round pen, where she'd left him while cleaning his stall. After she'd acquired the massive horse, Wyatt had helped her expand his stall, complete with a run allowing Elvis access to a small outside area. Wyatt kept encouraging Harley to ride the giant quarter horse, but she didn't think her riding skills were honed enough to manage Elvis.

Wiping sweat from her brow, she did a slow turn making sure she hadn't forgotten to feed someone or fill their watering trough. The minis, Scarlett and Rhett were munching hay, and Hoss, her old hog, snuffled the ground looking for scraps he'd knocked out of his dish. Pigmy goat siblings Butch and Sundance, had darted outside and found a patch of grass to munch.

Her other equine charges, Maverick and Trigger, tugged hay from their feed bags, both stepping to their gates for a drive-by pet as she walked toward the round pen.

"Okay, big guy." She took Elvis by the halter. "Your suite is nice and clean, and dinner has been served."

Harley heard Buckeye and the other chickens squawking, which meant Trampas was playing his nightly game of chase. She tucked Elvis into his stall and smiled when he sniffed the fresh pine shavings. Harley held her hand up and waited for him to say goodnight. The monster horse centered the star on his forehead against her palm.

"Goodnight, Elvis." Harley rubbed his face until he stepped away, heading for his feed bag.

She turned off the big overhead lights, then flicked the switch for the dimmer bulbs and exited the barn. As she made her way to the stairs leading to the wraparound porch of her old farmhouse, Harley smiled at Miss Kitty and Festus, both enjoying the new cat condo she'd set up for them.

After stepping into the mudroom, she shucked her boots and grabbed a bottle of water, then headed upstairs for a much needed shower. First, she double checked her outfit for the evening, an aqua sundress to pair with the new turquoise dragonfly necklace Wyatt had given her for her one year anniversary at the Redneck Ranch.

Her phone chimed before she stepped into the shower, and she smiled at Busy's text.

Busy: *Changed flight to arrive tomorrow. Land Eugene at three. I'll take Uber.*

Good thing Elizabeth Benton came from money because an Uber ride to Stoneybrook would cost her a bundle.

CHAPTER THREE

ou didn't bury** the bones deep enough!" she yelled at him.

"It was three years ago." He gave her a blank stare.

"Well, I'm guessin' with all the new fangled DNA tests they might figure out who she is and what you did to her before—"

Her words trailed off when he came to his feet.

"I told you we shouldn't have come back here to the gulch. No telling what evidence we've left in the damn woods."

A young woman, trailed by a small child, entered the kitchen and her smile faded when he looked at her.

"I-I thought I'd start dinner."

He stepped toward her and kissed her, ignoring her recoil. The little girl grinned at him, but he didn't acknowledge her except to say, "She's filthy, give her a bath."

The young woman tucked the child behind her and muttered, "After dinner."

He headed for the door, but the old woman's nagging brought him to a halt.

"You cain't bring another girl here, not after she let the last one escape." She glared at the young woman. "It's your job to watch the girls you dumb bitch." She yelled, spittle flying through the air.

Suppressing a smile when the young woman squared off against the old hag, he barked, "Leave her alone."

She whipped around, her hand held high ready to slap him. "Don't talk to your mother that way."

He grabbed her wrist before she could strike him, the stale odor of cigarette smoke and cheap whiskey emanating from her.

The young woman stepped back, shielding the child.

"I'll talk to you any way I want, *mother*," he growled.

He grabbed a Coke from the fridge. Glancing at the young woman before he stalked from the rundown hovel, he said, "Come get me when my dinner is ready."

He banged through the screen door and headed for the shed he'd converted into a holding room. God, how he hated his mother. All she'd ever done was made him feel inadequate. And when puberty hit, she'd made him feel like a pervert when he'd kissed a local girl. He'd tried to explain it wasn't his idea to hide in the garden shed in the girl's backyard. That he hadn't forced her to take off her clothes. Or asked her to touch him. It didn't matter what he told his mother, she'd beat him within an inch of his life, then packed up their meager belongings and left town.

Desire, colored with shame, washed over him when he thought about that day with the young woman and her friends in the willow grove. He hadn't meant to kill the first girl, but she wouldn't quit screaming. One of the friends sat crying and rocking back and forth and when he'd approached her; she jumped to her feet and ran. As he chased her down, the third friend rushed him with a big stick in her hand. The three of them had gone down in a heap and the crying girl hit her head, falling silent.

The friend with the stick struck him across the back and they fought until he gained control of her weapon. For the first time since he'd been taking advantage of young girls, he felt something other than rage. He felt respect and knew he needed to keep this wild girl for himself.

His mother's recent berating had created a longing for someone new to enjoy, even though the last time had ended badly. And not even the disgust of knowing he was a killer could subdue the longing he had to take another girl.

He thought about the young woman and burning in his groin indicated he still enjoyed discovering new things about her. A few years older now, she was still beautiful and despite fighting him every time he took her, they'd found a kind of balance. Not even the arrival of the child had deterred his desire for the girl he'd snatched from the woods almost five years ago.

But the evil animal living inside of him wanted a new challenge and needed to be fed.

CHAPTER FOUR

*A*fter leaving for the day, Wyatt couldn't shake the image of Cedar Atwood bolting from the sheriff's station. And though Derrick had made it clear that he shouldn't follow Echo, Wyatt worried about her being all alone with no one to talk to about the discovery of bones that might belong to her missing older sister, Willow.

Unlike the Keller's who'd moved away after their daughter, Leah's murder, the Atwood's had stayed in Stoneybrook until Echo had graduated high school, then decided to move to Nevada. Despite their best efforts, and with no explanation, their surviving daughter refused to make the move. Wyatt assumed Echo couldn't leave until she knew what happened to Willow.

Before he left, he asked Derrick if he knew if Willow had broken any bones. Although Derrick remembered her bike accident, he didn't recall her being injured, which meant she probably wasn't seen by a doctor. Wyatt would have to wait for the remains to be examined for any abnormalities or damage prior to the individual's death.

As he made the turn onto the highway, he thought again about the young couple who had discovered the bones while on a hike near Willow Lake. He knew Marie Davis had moved back to Stoneybrook eight months ago with her boyfriend and they'd bought the bait and tackle shop on the highway to the lake. Even though the lake's resort had been shut down, there were plenty of rivers and tributaries perfect for trout fishing, so the small shop did a steady business. He made a mental note to ask Derrick if he knew the route they'd taken on their hike.

Making the turn onto Little Creek Road, his mind jumped to the situation that had introduced him to the beautiful owner of the Redneck Ranch and he was glad Carl Yates had met his demise at the hand of his last victim, Sylvie Own.

He pulled into Harley's driveway and parked in front of the old barn, which looked more inviting after the facelift his high school friend, Britt Hanson, had given the old girl. Lifting the butcher shop bag and wine carrier from Fenya's shop, he stepped from his truck. He was glad Ms. Petrova, who'd been instrumental in helping locate the man who'd murdered Stoneybrook's resident Santa last Christmas, had made the move to Stoneybrook and tried to support her business as much as possible.

The afternoon air was still warm, but he could tell the night would bring cooler temperatures. *Perfect for a fire*, he thought. He climbed the stairs to the wrap-around porch and used the toe of his boot to open the screen door.

"Hi." Harley greeted him with a kiss and took the sack with their steaks.

"Hi." Wyatt wondered again why he'd been blessed to have this beguiling woman in his life.

He placed the wine bag onto the kitchen counter and pulled her close for a proper hello. As he kissed her, she twined her arms around his neck and leaned into him, causing him to question whether dinner was necessary.

Harley palmed his chest and smiled at him. "Do you want a beer or a glass of wine?"

He pointed to her glass sitting next to the sink. "Beer."

"It's the new blonde, Sunrise Surfer, from Pelican Brewery." She padded to the fridge and pulled out a cold one. "I love that it tastes like summer."

"I love how pretty you look." He took the beer in one hand and twirled her with the other. Her sundress billowed around her legs and the fresh scent of lavender wafted from her dark brown hair.

Giggling, she took a breath, then said, "Why thank you, Sheriff Stone." She opened a cupboard. "Want a glass?"

"No, thanks." He cracked open his beer and took a long drink. "Want to sit outside for a bit before we start the steaks?"

"Yes." Harley bussed his lips, picked up her glass, and led the way through the dining room to the front porch. "How was your day?" she asked as she sat in a white wicker chair.

Wyatt took a drink, sat in the matching chair, and stared east across the once again green fields which became hills that bled into mountains.

Harley placed a hand on his thigh but didn't press him for a response. She understood his job and had, unfortunately, been personally exposed to the dreadful nature of mankind.

"I made a green salad to go with our steaks." She smiled at him. "And I have adult root beer floats planned for dessert."

Wyatt pulled her onto his lap, so she sat straddling his legs, facing him. "Sounds like the perfect dessert to be enjoyed naked in your new pool."

Harley kissed him, then said, "I'm not sure the water's warm enough."

He caressed her ass. "Naked by the fire then."

She tilted her head. "What if someone drops by?'

"Ms. Harper." He pulled her hips toward him. "Are you trying to avoid being naked with me?"

"No." Harley laughed, and he felt the vibration of her body deep in his loins. "Maybe naked before dessert would help us work up an appetite for a sweet treat." She kissed him and pressed down against his crotch.

"If you kiss me like that again, I'm going to need to work up an appetite before dinner."

Harley stood and took his hand, opening the screen door leading into the foyer.

His phone buzzed and Wyatt said a silent expletive, then pulled it from his shirt pocket and looked at Derrick's text.

Derrick: *Tracked down Willow's MRs. No broken bones*

Wyatt: *Copy. At Harley's if you need anything*

Derrick: *Copy*

Wyatt stepped into the foyer and found Harley in the kitchen.

"Do you have to go?" she asked as she rinsed her beer glass.

"No." Stepping close to her, he wrapped his arms around her waist and waited until she turned to him, then kissed her.

When he released her lips, he said, "Are you starving?"

Harley wrapped her arms around his waist. "Yes, but not for dinner." She kissed him, then headed for the back door. "Lock the front door before you come up."

Wyatt grinned, walked back to the foyer, and thumbed the lock. They'd learned the hard way well-meaning visitors didn't always knock and wait for an invitation.

He took the stairs two at a time to the landing where Harley waited for him. She smiled at him as he held her hand and then they climbed the short staircase to her bedroom.

*H*arley woke in Wyatt's arms to find him smiling at her as she blinked against the bright sunshine peeking through her bedroom curtains.

"Morning," he said, his voice still husky with sleep.

"Morning." She leaned across his taut chest to kiss him.

"Waking up with you in my arms is the best part of my day." Wyatt stroked her back until he reached her ass.

"Same." Harley stretched out on top of him.

"As much as I would like to have a repeat of last night's appetizers for breakfast." He kissed her. "I have to go."

Brushing sandy-colored bangs from his forehead, she touched her lips to his again. "Got somewhere better to be than here?"

"Nowhere is better than here." Wyatt rolled her onto her back and caressed a breast.

"Maybe breakfast in bed will have to do." His phone buzzed and she groaned. "Someone has terrible timing."

Wyatt grabbed his phone from the nightstand. He looked at the text, then kissed her before climbing from the bed.

"It's Derrick," he said, and Harley could tell by the frown creasing his brow that though he'd rather stay with her, something pressing needed his attention.

As Harley stood, Wyatt pulled on his pants and reached for his shirt. She plucked the shorty pajamas she normally wore to bed from a yellow overstuffed armchair, then slipped them on.

"I'll make coffee." She lifted her phone from the nightstand, kissed him, and plodded down the stairs. She was a little annoyed that her romantic breakfast had been interrupted, but one thing she'd learned over the past year is Deputy Derrick Stone never bothered his cousin the sheriff if it wasn't important.

The coffee maker finished brewing a full pot of dark roast as Wyatt stepped into the kitchen. Knowing the departure routine of her handsome boyfriend, Harley poured coffee into a travel mug.

"Thanks." Wyatt took the mug from her. "Dinner?"

"Busy's coming today instead of next week and lands at three, so I'll have to plan around her arrival."

"Let me guess." Wyatt tilted his head. "She's taking an Uber from the Eugene airport."

"Yes." Harley laughed. "Can you imagine the cost?"

"Yes, which means Busy should buy dinner." Wyatt grinned at her.

"Where are you off to?"

"The owners of the bait and tackle shop that discovered the bones, want to meet with me, which of course means *us* in Derrick's world, to offer more details about their discovery."

"Bones?" Harley inadvertently resorted to her hands on hips stance.

"Right." Wyatt met her questioning gaze. "I never answered your question last night about my day."

"It's okay." She held up a hand. "You don't have to share your work with me."

Wyatt stepped close to her and set the travel mug on the counter. "Remember when we stayed at the lodge last year?"

Harley nodded, the memory of the little girl wandering in the dark along the edge of Willow Lake popping into her mind.

"The shop owners found bones near the willow grove and we're trying to determine if they belong to Willow Atwood."

"The girl who went missing over four years ago?"

"Yes." Wyatt put his hands on her arms. "I need to see what else they have to add."

"Of course." Harley bussed his lips. "Go, do your job, because I know Echo and her parents need answers."

Wyatt wrapped her in his arms and kissed her as if he wished he could stay. "I'll text you this afternoon and maybe we can have dinner to welcome Busy back to Stoneybrook."

"Good plan." Harley smiled at him.

Travel mug in hand, he headed from the kitchen. "Love you," Wyatt called as he banged through the screen door.

Harley repeated his sentiment but since he was already on his phone, she assumed he didn't hear her. As he climbed into his pickup, she watched through the kitchen window and thought to herself, *You're a lucky girl, Harley Harper.*

After he drove away, she popped an English muffin into the toaster, poured herself a cup of coffee, then sat at the small dinette table. Her phone was text free for the moment and she imagined Busy hurrying through the routine of getting to her gate where she'd then text to say she'd made her flight. On more than one occasion, Busy had been known to miss boarding by ten minutes since she had a slight time management problem.

The toaster lifted the browned muffin and Harley spread peanut butter across the top, then headed for the barn. She could hear Maverick whinnying from his stall and was thankful she wouldn't have to spend the day looking for the mischievous donkey. Of course, it helped that Luke Sloan had reinforced the latch on Maverick's stall door and another of Wyatt's ranch hands had strung hotwire along the fence line between Stoneybrook and Broken River Ranch.

Harley inhaled the musky animal scent of the barn and greeted each member of her menagerie with a 'good morning' as she tended to them. She was glad she'd taken the extra time yesterday to clean stalls and tidy the barn, which made today's chores go quicker.

As she headed back to the house, she plucked the rubber ducky thermometer from the pool, which registered sixty-eight degrees.

"Busy will be disappointed if she can't swim in her pool," Harley told the duck before placing the yellow thermometer back into the water. She checked the pH level, which was within normal range, so all she needed was hot sunshine to warm the day and heat the pool.

Crossing the patio, she checked the furniture she'd cleaned a couple of days ago. If the night provided an opportunity to swim, they could enjoy nightcaps by the fire afterward. The idea of drinks caused her thoughts to jump to jalapeño margaritas and she ran through a mental list of ingredients.

"Oranges," Harley said as she climbed the back porch steps. She'd need to make a stop at DairyMart for oranges before she picked up Busy's champagne order from Claire at the Rocky River Bar.

She poured another cup of coffee and trekked upstairs to take a shower. Grabbing a fresh towel from the linen closet, Harley stepped into the bathroom and turned on the water. As she stood under the hot spray, the spicy scent of the body wash she'd given Wyatt for his birthday enveloped her.

Gooseflesh bloomed on her skin as she thought about their pre-dinner interlude last night. What was it about the handsome sheriff that made her feel like they were the only two people who'd ever been in love? Several obvious reasons sprang to mind, but their shared chemistry seemed otherworldly, like something no one else had ever experienced. Despite her struggle to understand her love for him, Harley knew Wyatt Stone had been the missing puzzle piece she needed to complete her life.

CHAPTER SIX

For an early Sunday morning, the campground was almost empty, which surprised him given the warm spring weather. He assumed families were waiting for the upcoming Memorial Day weekend.

Roaming through the vacant sites, he loaded abandoned campfire wood into his trailer. Of the few people milling about, most of them ignored him, but a few said, "Good morning."

Over the years he'd learned to wear non-descript clothing, a plain baseball cap and work boots with a well-worn sole. He always picked rundown campgrounds that weren't well maintained and or didn't have a caretaker, which allowed him to assume the role of a maintenance worker.

When he'd left the crappy shack his mother was cooking bacon and eggs and she'd yelled at him he'd better pick a girl he could control as he snitched a piece of bacon.

He wondered what his life would be like if he took the young woman and the little girl, then left the bitch who'd ruined his future fending for herself. He didn't have any delusions life would've been full of sunshine but maybe he wouldn't be a monster who kidnapped and murdered young girls. He might've even been able to have a normal relationship if she hadn't branded him a disgusting and twisted pervert. If they hadn't roamed from one rundown hovel to another. If she hadn't killed his father and made him help cover her crime.

He'd been so busy wandering down his shitty memory lane, he'd almost missed the girl who picked wildflowers in a small clearing. Sunlight sparked the red highlights in her strawberry-blonde hair and for a moment he was reminded of the young woman he'd snatched from the willow grove all those years ago.

Now, he wanted this girl. Needed this girl. Knew the young woman would be furious with him when he brought her back to the shack she'd tried to make into a home.

CHAPTER SEVEN

*W*yatt **and Derrick** arrived at Hook, Line & Sinker and found one of the owners, Marie Davis, watering daisies in a flower box next to the door of the bait and tackle shop.

"Morning," she said as she turned off the faucet.

"Ms. Davis." Wyatt extended his hand. "I believe you know Deputy Stone."

"Yes." Marie brushed a strand of honey-colored hair from her eyes and shook their hands. "Come in. I think Nate's at his worktable tying flies."

They followed her through the tidy store that held a hint of anise and coffee to a small room in the back where Nate Long leaned over a magnifying glass as he worked on a bright pink fly.

"Nate," Marie said. "The sheriff and Deputy Stone are here."

A tall, lanky young man, Nate set his work down and stood. "Thanks for coming."

"Derrick said you had some additional information about the bones you found."

Nate looked at his girlfriend who said, "Tell him, Babe."

"It's more about the clothing scraps." Nate picked up a beautiful blue hand-tied fly. "When I was tightening the line on this fly, I remembered being struck by extra stitching on the shirt we found." He ran a finger down Marie's pink paisley tank. "Along the side seams."

"Like maybe someone had taken the shirt in to make it smaller," Marie added.

Wyatt looked at Derrick and knew his cousin was thinking the same thing. If the shirt had been altered to fit a smaller person, then the bones couldn't belong to Willow.

"Anything else you remember about the discovery or found odd?" Wyatt asked.

"Well." Marie cut her eyes to Nate who nodded. "It seemed as though the bones were buried with care." A single tear trickled down her cheek. "Like someone cared about whoever had been placed in the ground."

"We're willing to check the surrounding area where the bones were discovered." Nate looked at Marie, who added, "We feel there might be more evidence around the site than what we initially discovered."

Again, Wyatt exchanged a look with Derrick, then said, "Thanks for the offer, but it will be better if my deputies and I conduct a search."

"I don't mean to tell you how to do your jobs," Marie began. "But I would look for something personal that might belong to the bones."

Though the site had been explored after the bones were found, Wyatt decided they should expand the search area. He and Derrick would assemble a crew and begin the tedious task of looking for additional clues in Willow's Woods.

CHAPTER EIGHT

The **Rocky River** Bar had a good lunchtime crowd and Claire dashed from table to table checking on customers. Dyani, the new waitress, headed Harley's way.

"Hi, Harley," she smiled. "Here for the champagne?"

Nodding, Harley said, "Surprised to see you here."

"Things are slow at Broken River and Claire had a waitress quit so I said I'd fill in until she hires someone."

"I'm sure she's glad for the help." Harley gave Claire a wave.

"Claire put the champagne into two boxes and they're behind the bar." Dyani headed toward the large, hand-carved redwood bar.

A man stood from his stool as they approached, turned, and smiled at Harley.

"This is a nice surprise," Blake Stone said.

"Hi, Blake." Harley hoped her shock didn't show on her face. "I didn't know you were in town."

"Blake's moving back to Stoneybrook," Dyani said as she set a box with six bottles on the bar top.

This time Harley knew her surprise registered in the look she gave him. "Oh, that's great news."

"Can I buy you a beer?" Blake flashed two fingers at Dyani.

"I really have—" Harley began.

"Blake likes the same beer as you." Dyani grabbed glasses from the freezer. "Two Sunrise Surfers coming up."

He pulled a barstool out for her, and Harley took a seat as Dyani placed the beers in front of them.

Blake touched her glass with his, then took a sip. Harley took a drink of the delicious blonde ale, the crisp malt flavor lingering on her tongue.

"Are you having a party?" Blake angled toward her.

"My friend Busy is coming for a visit and she ordered the champagne." He stared at her with Wyatt's blue eyes and Harley was struck again by how much they looked alike.

"A bottle a day, so she'll be here for 12 days?" Blake smiled.

"You're moving back to Stoneybrook?" Harley countered.

"I investigated Willow Atwood's disappearance with Wyatt." Blake took a long sip from his glass. "When I heard the news about the discovered remains, I felt a need to come back and help finish the investigation."

"I hope there's finally a resolution." Harley's phone chimed and she looked at a text from Busy.

Busy: *Delay out of SeaTac. Will text from Eugene*

Harley: *K. Safe travels. See you soon*

"All good?" Blake asked.

"Yes. Busy's flight's been delayed." Harley took a sip and wondered if it would be rude to leave without finishing her beer. "Are you still working as a bounty hunter?"

He raised an eyebrow. "I prefer fugitive recovery agent."

"There can't be much need for that type of work in Stoneybrook."

Blake laughed, then said, "I'm also planning to reopen the campground at Willow Lake."

"The campground by Wyatt's lodge?"

He picked up his glass and she noticed a slight squint to his eyes. "Wyatt isn't the only Stone in this county."

"Right." Harley reached for her purse as she slid off the bar stool. "Good luck with everything."

Blake stood too and frowned at the money she placed on the bar. "Beers are on me."

Harley nodded but didn't pick up the ten-dollar bill. She lifted one box of champagne and turned to leave. As she took a step, her purse strap caught on the back of the stool, and she almost pulled it on top of her.

Blake steadied the barstool, then placed his hands on her arms. "Let me carry this for you." He ran his hands along her forearms until they both held the box.

Harley's cheeks warmed when he looked into her eyes, then a whisper of dread flitted through her gut when Blake's eyes grew dark, and he stared past her.

"Wyatt." Stepping back, Blake crossed his arms.

Harley turned slightly and Wyatt took the box from her, then returned it to the bar top. He leaned down and covered her lips in a kiss clearly staking his claim.

"Babe." Wyatt smiled at her. "I thought you'd be home waiting on Busy."

The term babe took her by surprise, and she could see a flicker of anger in his eyes. "How'd you know I was here?"

He tilted his head and smiled. "Your Lexus is parked in front of the bar." Wyatt waved at Dyani.

"Hey, boss," Dyani said as she dried her hands on a bar towel. "Luke didn't have any work for me, so I'm helping Claire out. Cool?"

"Yes." Wyatt smiled at her. "Just check in with Luke each night to see if you're needed."

"Will do." Dyani nodded. "Can I get you something?"

"Okay to leave the boxes here while we have lunch?"

"Sure." Dyani reached for three menus.

"Just two for lunch." Wyatt took Harley by the hand and headed for a table.

"Wyatt," Blake said, following them. "I want to be included in the new investigation about Willow and the hunt for Leah's killer."

"Come to the station in the morning." Wyatt continued through the restaurant, and Harley felt like some prize he'd just won at the fair.

When they stopped at a table for two, he pulled a chair out for her, then sat next to her with his back to Blake.

"Fine." Blake turned and called over his shoulder, "I enjoyed our beer date, Harley."

Wyatt met her eyes, and she opened her lips to protest, but he put a finger on them to silence her.

Harley took his hand in hers. "It wasn't a date."

"I know," he said as Claire approached the table.

"Sorry, Wyatt." She placed two glasses of water on the table. "I wish I could ban him from the bar, but I just can't take sides."

"It's okay, Claire."

"What can I get you two?"

"I'll have the turkey and Swiss," Wyatt said.

"Chicken Caesar for me." Harley smiled at Claire.

"Coming right up," Claire said as she walked away.

"I know we agreed not to talk about our past relationships," Harley began. "But—"

Wyatt drank half his water and when he met her gaze, her heart twinged at the pain she saw in his sky blue eyes.

"Someday, I'll tell you if you really need to know." Wyatt ran a hand through his hair. "For now, it's important to me that you don't spend time with Blake."

Dyani delivered their food and they set to the task of eating. Harley loved this man and her heart ached because he'd been hurt. But she didn't like being caught in a war between two brothers.

CHAPTER NINE

"**I** **told you** not to bring another girl here!" the old crone screamed at him. "We should be packin' up now that them bones were found." She continued to stir her bland beef stew.

He shoved the crying girl toward the young woman and rushed his mother. "If you don't keep your mouth shut, I'm going to shut it permanently," he growled.

"Oh, big man." She squared her shoulders. "And who's going to take care of you, your tramp, her brat, and the crying mess?"

The young woman tried to shush the wailing girl as she took the hand of her daughter and huddled in the corner. He glared at her as she spoke softly to the sobbing child.

He turned back to his mother and slapped her across the face. "I'm sick of you and your crap."

She tried to hit him, and he knocked her to the floor, then proceeded to pummel her with his fists. The rage that had been building within him for years boiled up from his core and all he could think of was silencing the bitch who had criticized him his whole life. Every punch he landed represented some imperfection she'd labeled him with. He was too stupid to manage a good job. He was too ugly for a pretty girl to love him. He was too damaged to live a normal life.

His knuckles became bloody, the scent of iron filled his senses, and his mother lie motionless on the grimy kitchen floor. He kicked her with the toe of his boot, and she didn't respond.

When he looked over his shoulder the young woman and two girls were missing. He returned his attention to the bloody heap on the floor and bent down to check for a pulse. Nothing.

"Well, it's not like I didn't warn you," he said.

He found it curious he didn't feel sorrow, but instead relief that the manipulative bitch was dead. Movement behind him caused him to turn and he found the young woman staring at him, fear in her hazel eyes.

"Put the girl in my shed," he told her as he picked up his mother's body. "Then clean up this mess."

"I-I—" she stuttered. "Maybe you'd like for me to calm you down."

He tilted his head and adjusted the weight in his arms. "Fine. Feed them and put them to bed, then wait for me in my room."

The young woman had never volunteered herself before and lust flooded his loins as he pushed through the battered screen door. For the first time since he'd taken her from the willow grove, he found himself looking forward to enjoying her willingness all night.

CHAPTER TEN

He nodded at Derrick, who gave a shrill whistle that echoed through the warm morning air. Wyatt then waited for the search crew to turn their attention to him.

"As you all know," he began. "Human remains were found in this area a few days ago." Wyatt cut his eyes to Blake who was walking toward the group, then continued, "The coroner hasn't identified the remains yet, but we have reason to believe they do not belong to Willow Atwood."

"Chief," Britt raised his hand, "are we looking for something specific?"

"No." Wyatt narrowed his eyes at his high school friend who knew he hated the nickname. "We'd like for you to put anything of interest into a bucket." He pointed toward his truck where a stack of buckets sat next to a pile of rakes and a box of flashlights. "You've all participated in a grid search before, so let's get started."

"Wait." Derrick held up a hand. "The flashlights might spark something too small to see otherwise. If you find anything in the ground requiring a shovel, call out so we can do a controlled dig."

"Also," Mac began, "there's a cooler of sandwiches compliments of Mercy and one with water so stay hydrated."

"Any other questions?" Wyatt scanned the crowd. "Let's get started then."

Wyatt followed the crew as they headed for his truck.

"Didn't expect to see Blake here," Britt said, as he caught up to Wyatt.

"It was his case too," Wyatt responded.

"I remember Leah's murder was hard on him." Britt shook his head. "It's why he gave up his badge, right?"

"He gave up his badge for Ava," Derrick said as he stepped behind Wyatt.

Wyatt turned and gave his cousin a warning look, then picked up a rake and headed for an area away from everyone else.

He tried to focus on the task at hand, but his thoughts jumped to his night with Harley. She'd seemed fine when they'd taken Busy to dinner. And he'd enjoyed hearing her laugh as they sat around the fire drinking her scratch jalapeño margaritas. Still, he felt tension between them and had gone home instead of staying the night. He knew he'd hurt her feelings by insinuating she was voluntarily hanging out with Blake. As hard as it had been when Ava ran off with his brother, Wyatt knew he couldn't bear losing Harley.

They'd searched for almost three hours, with everyone taking breaks to eat and drink some water. Wyatt looked out across the area Derrick had determined would be the best place to start and estimated they'd searched over half of the ground. He'd hoped they'd find a few clues to help identify the recently discovered bones.

A loud whistle drew everyone's attention as Britt held up a hand. Wyatt and Derrick crossed to Britt who leaned on a rake. Moving lupine flowers aside with his boot, the scent of honey rode on the breeze as Britt directed his flashlight beam to a spot on the ground. The light sparked a speck of blue lying partially hidden by the ground debris.

"I think it's a toy heart." Britt looked at Wyatt. "When I tried to pick it up, I could tell it's attached to something buried in the ground."

Mac had retrieved a shovel and handed it to Wyatt who inched the dirt away from the object. Once he created a circle, he stuck the nose of the shovel into the ground and lifted a small section of dirt.

Derrick had dropped to his knees and sifted through the dirt with his fingers. He gently dusted debris away from what looked like a clump of twigs attached to a blue heart. He nodded as he stood, and Wyatt lifted another shovel full of dirt. He set the clump to the side and repeated the process. When he was about a foot down, the shovel tip struck something hard, Derrick handed the twigs to Britt and hit his knees again. He dug around the object, then lifted a small skull.

"Jesus, Mary, and Joseph," Mac said and made the sign of the cross.

Setting the skull aside, Derrick continued to dig with his hands, stopping when he unearthed a blue blanket. He cradled the decomposed bundle and came to his feet.

"I have something over here," Blake called. He stood from where he'd crouched next to the grave where the first set of bones had been found.

When Wyatt joined him, Blake handed him another bundle of twigs which had a red heart attached this time. Wyatt met his brother's stare and wasn't surprised when he bolted to the other side of the grove. Derrick and Wyatt followed Blake and the three of them scanned the surface for another heart.

"I have it!" Derrick knelt and cleared grass from a third bundle of twigs. Wyatt eased the shovel into the ground and set the clump next to Derrick, who fingered away the debris.

"A pink heart for Leah." Derrick held the small cluster in his palms, then looked at Wyatt. "This is the same cross made with willow tree twigs we think Willow gave to Sadie."

CHAPTER ELEVEN

"**I heard you** get up early," Busy said as she stepped onto the front porch, cup of coffee in hand. "Did you get any sleep."

"Some," Harley said and looked at the time on her phone, which showed ten to one.

"What?" Busy sat in the wicker chair next to Harley. "I needed sleep." Busy smiled.

Harley took a drink from her water glass as Busy sipped coffee and they sat looking across the fields, now green after a fire had destroyed the vegetation a year ago.

"Archer's engaged." Busy laughed when Harley spit water out of her nose.

"To who?" Harley used her tank top to mop her face.

"Some Wall Street blonde." Busy took a sip. "She's totally different from you."

"So, he probably won't cheat on her." Harley frowned. Blondes had always been her ex-fiancé's go to before they'd become engaged.

"That's not what I meant." Busy narrowed her eyes. "Care to tell me what the hell is going on with you and the handsome sheriff?"

Harley shrugged.

"If he's hurt you, he's going to have to answer to me." Busy set her cup down and touched Harley's arm. "What did he do?"

"Nothing." Harley shook her head. "He surprised me yesterday at Rocky River and found me having a beer with Blake."

"Black sheep brother, Blake?"

Harley nodded. "Wyatt was angry and doesn't want me to spend time with Blake."

"Understandable after he ran off with Wyatt's last girlfriend."

"It bothers me he thinks I would do the same thing."

"It's also kind of romantic he's making it clear he's in love with you and doesn't want to lose you."

"I guess." Harley stood. "It's getting warm, so I'll check on the animals water, then we can have a late lunch at the Babbling Brook Café."

"Perfect. And I'd like to stop in at Pebbles and Pretties to talk to Mia about furniture."

Harley didn't respond as Busy followed her into the house, the lingering scent of burnt toast causing Harley's stomach to growl.

"Har, Har," Busy began and Harley faced her. "Jealousy is an evil bitch, but I don't believe Wyatt thinks you'd cheat on him."

"Thanks, B." Harley gave her bestie a small smile and headed for the barn.

As she drew close, she could hear Maverick causing a ruckus. Harley walked straight to his stall, eliciting whinnies from Trigger and Elvis. Maverick's breakaway halter had twisted instead of releasing and was caught on the new latch Luke had installed. The donkey's large eyes were wary, and Harley could see he had a small cut near his jawbone.

"Damn it!" She tried to loosen the halter enough to free Maverick, but the strap was too tangled and would need to be cut.

After freeing him, Maverick tossed his head and stomped around his stall. Speaking in soothing tones, Harley entered slowly, and the crazed donkey rushed her. She back peddled, but not quick enough and he knocked her down as he bolted from his stall.

"Shit!" she cried when her head hit the ground.

"Are you okay?" Blake asked as he helped her up.

"Yes." Harley tried to step away from him but swayed on her feet.

Blake swooped her into his arms and strode from the barn, stopping when they came face to face with Wyatt. The look on Wyatt's face made Harley cringe and she climbed from Blake's arms.

"Wyatt, it's not what you think," she called after him as he stormed toward his truck.

He spun around, his face beet red. "It's exactly what I think." Anger flashed in his eyes before he turned and continued to his truck.

"Don't walk away from me, Wyatt Stone."

He didn't respond and tears sprang to her eyes when he spewed gravel as he raced up her driveway. Harley tried to stay on her feet but crumpled to the ground.

"I've got her," Busy barked at Blake when he tried to help Harley. "Why are you effing here?"

"As soon as we finished the search in Willow's Woods, I came straight here." Blake looked at Harley. "I liked being included by Wyatt and wanted to apologize for yesterday.

"That worked out well." Busy pulled Harley to her feet. "I need you to leave."

"She hit her head and might have a concussion." Blake headed for his truck.

"She'll be fine." Busy wrapped her arm around Harley's waist and guided her toward the house.

"Nothing happened," Harley mumbled as she stepped into the mudroom.

"I know, sweetie." Busy helped her sit in a chair at the dinette table. "Your sheriff is a man deeply in love and right now he's letting his jealousy control his behavior."

Busy put an arm around Harley who let the tears flow. "He's not the only one deeply in love."

CHAPTER TWELVE

"Where the hell** have you been?" he barked at the young woman.

"It's a nice afternoon so I took the girls for a walk." She limped to a chair. "The new girl shoved me down a hill and ran off with my baby." She dabbed a rag against a cut on her shin as tears spilled down her cheeks.

"Why'd you do that?" He ran his hands through his hair. "The cops are crawling all over the field by the lake and it's only a matter of time before they find Mom's body."

"Maybe we should leave," she suggested, then stifled a sob.

He stormed across the small room and yanked her to her feet. "You let them go, didn't you?"

"No." She glared at him. "Your new captive knocked me down and ran away with *our* daughter."

He gripped her wrist and dragged her toward the door. "They're probably lost so we'll go look for them."

She jerked her arm free. "If we get caught, they'll throw us in jail."

He narrowed his eyes at her. "Why would they arrest you?"

"Because I'm a bad mother." Another round of tears shook her shoulders. "I didn't protect my children and they'll take my daughter away from me."

Rarely did he feel sorry for her, but the sorrow in the young woman's eyes made him want to comfort her. The death of the boy baby hadn't been her fault and she'd almost died during labor. Maybe if they left this hell, they could leave their pasts behind them and start over.

Her lips tasted like raspberry jam and peanut butter when he kissed her, and the scent of grass woven through her hair made him want to hold her until her tears subsided.

"Pack a few things." He stepped away from her. "And we'll leave tonight."

Before he left the shack, he thought he saw a hint of a smile cross her lips. But it didn't matter because they could travel faster without the baggage of his mother, their daughter, and a captive. She may have freed the little girls, but she hadn't saved herself from him and their future together.

CHAPTER THIRTEEN

 yatt had passed out next to a half-empty fifth of single malt sitting on the end table next to the couch. He'd been saving the Rogue Spirits Whiskey for a special occasion and anger warmed his cheeks when he remembered why he'd cracked open the bottle.

The vision of Harley in Blake's arms almost made him reach for the bottle, but he climbed from the couch and headed for the kitchen. Frankie had made coffee and set a sliced loaf of banana bread next to his favorite cup. He appreciated his cook's efforts, but ignored the bread, filled his cup, and climbed the stairs off the kitchen to his bedroom.

He'd hoped to feel better after a hot shower, but his head still felt fuzzy and his anger at Blake hadn't dissipated. Nor had his embarrassment at storming away from Harley. He wanted to believe nothing was going on between her and Blake but couldn't shake the fear that he'd lose Harley as he had Ava. And losing Harley would be a far bigger loss.

His phone buzzed and he looked at a text from Derrick: *Come to station ASAP*

Wyatt pulled his gun from the safe in the den, grabbed his keys, and stepped from the house. The bright morning sunshine caused him to squint and his head to pound.

"It's going to be a long day," he muttered and climbed into his truck.

When he parked at the station, he found Derrick pacing in front of the open door.

"The new set of bones are a baby boy. And we have a partial fingerprint on the blue heart. The blanket still showed a stain, which the lab thinks is amniotic fluid." He took a breath, then continued, "And—"

"Derrick." Wyatt placed a hand on his shoulder. "Let's go inside."

Derrick nodded and led the way. Blake, along with Simms and Barnes, stood near the coffee pot. They formed a semi-circle as Wyatt and Derrick joined them.

Wyatt looked at Derrick. "I'm guessing the lab can get DNA from the blanket."

"Yes, revealing both parents." He flashed a rare smile. "I think it's time to go back to the FBI with our new discoveries."

"You've already called them, right?" Wyatt returned Derrick's smile when he nodded.

"There isn't a fingerprint on file for Willow," Blake said, and Wyatt glanced at him before reaching for the coffee pot. "But it could be useful if we find her bod—"

"She's a survivor." Derrick shook his head. "She's alive and we're going to find her."

"Anything else discovered in the search?" Wyatt asked.

"No, Chief." Simms coughed. "CSU is still sorting through the buckets, but nothing so far."

The station phone rang, and Barnes picked up the closest receiver. "Sheriff's Department." He waved at Wyatt and handed him the phone.

"Sheriff Stone." Wyatt listened, then met their questioning gazes. He disconnected and said, "Two young girls have been found wandering the shore of Willow Lake."

Derrick bolted outside and jumped into Wyatt's truck. Before he could object, Blake settled onto the backseat, Derrick hit a button, and the siren wailed as they headed out of Stoneybrook.

"More coffee?" Mercy stood at the counter, carafe hovering over their cups.

"Yes, thanks." Harley smiled at her.

"Did you hear the latest?" Mercy asked. "Deputy Simms told me this morning CSU found a body near the willow grove."

"Do they know who she is?" Harley prayed it wasn't Willow Atwood.

"No." Mercy shook her head. "An older woman who Simms said probably isn't connected to the search for Willow. But it does seem odd, right? What a crazy few days."

"Crazy's an understatement," Busy replied. "Two girls found at the lake, one who'd been kidnapped a week ago and one who tells Wyatt she's Willow's daughter."

Harley tried not to flinch at the mention of his name, but she hadn't seen Wyatt since he'd raced away from the Redneck Ranch almost a week ago. Her only connection to Wyatt had been Luke returning Maverick to her.

She'd run the gamut of emotions as Busy kept her company during the sleepless nights. Busy offered many reasons why Sheriff Stone hadn't called, but in her heart, Harley believed their relationship was over. When she told Busy, she was going to sell the ranch and move back to New York, her BFF informed her she was sticking to her plan to move to Stoneybrook in a month so running away wasn't an option. Harley had responded to the news by locking herself in her room with a bottle of tequila.

"Your breakfast okay, Hun?" Mercy pointed to Harley's veggie omelet.

"Yes, just not hungry." Harley attempted a smile.

"Mercy," Busy said, pushing her empty plate away. "Can you bring us a couple of your summer crush mimosas?"

"Sure, Hun." Mercy turned toward the back counter. "Are you celebrating something?"

"Yes!" Busy grinned, and Harley rolled her eyes. "I'm moving to Stoneybrook!"

"That's great news!" Mercy set their drinks in front of them. "Are you two going to the dance tonight?"

Harley shook her head, but Busy responded with, "We wouldn't miss it."

As they drove back to the farm, Busy gave Harley a rundown of the outfit she planned to wear to the dance. Harley partially listened to her bestie and mulled over how she could get out of going to the damn dance.

After feeding her charges and putting salve on Maverick's wound, Harley had showered and dressed in a tight jean skirt, red low cut, sleeveless blouse, and her new dark red Ropers. If she had to go to the effing Memorial Day dance, then she wanted Wyatt Stone to notice what he'd walked away from.

"You ready?" Busy called from the kitchen.

As Harley sprayed a touch of Cowgirl Secrets, a gift from Wyatt, on her wrists the hint of jasmine brought tears to her eyes. She blinked to clear them away as she added diamond studs to her ears and blood red lipstick, then with a last look in the mirror, she headed downstairs.

"Damn, girl." Busy whistled. "If Wyatt isn't sorry for storming off, he will be now."

"You look fabulous too." Harley pointed at Busy who wore a brown jersey dress with turquoise piping and a fringed skirt. "Hoping to see Ace at the dance?"

"Only if he arrives without his new girlfriend." Busy grinned.

As they drove to Stoneybrook, Busy pratted on about her move from New York, but Harley's mind couldn't let go of a singular thought: *How was she going to react to seeing Wyatt? Anger? Sadness? Joy?*

They walked the block to the Rocky River Bar and Busy opened one side of the large double doors. Harley turned, intent on running back to her car, but Busy took her hand and led her inside.

"Welcome, lovelies," Claire greeted them with hugs. "You both look stunning."

Scanning the bar for Wyatt, Harley didn't realize she'd been holding her breath until Claire said, "He's not here." She motioned for them to follow her. "I think we could use a shot."

Dyani, who wore a leather headband with white feathers strung across the back of her long jet black hair, grabbed a bottle of Herradura. She poured four shots, then lifted one in toast.

"What?" she said to Claire. "I'm only having one and you know it's been a difficult few days."

Harley wondered why Dyani's life was hard, but once she held her shot, forgot her concern.

"To life getting back to normal here in Stoneybrook and at Broken River." Dyani tossed down her shot, held Harley's stare for a beat, then moved down the bar to help another customer.

"Wyatt's been in Salem helping the state police locate the kidnapped girl's parents and meeting with the FBI about Willow." Claire sipped some tequila. "And according to Dyani a couple of ranch hands left for the rodeo circuit so Luke's trying to run the ranch shorthanded."

"What about the little girl?" Busy asked.

"Joy's been taking care of her," Claire began, "it's actually been a group effort and the whole town has been taking turns sitting with her, bringing her clothes and toys."

"And she's been asking for her Aunt Cedar and her grandparents who are on their way from Nevada," Derrick said behind them. "But Echo isn't ready to meet her namesake niece."

"Hi, Derrick." Harley smiled at him. "You look very handsome."

He touched the horseshoe clasp of his bolo tie. "And you look nice, too." Derrick looked past her, then met her eyes again. "Wyatt misses you." He didn't wait for a reply and headed toward a table where Blake and the other deputies sat.

Blake met her stare and Harley looked away.

"I love this song!" Busy grabbed Harley's hand and headed for the dance floor.

It took Harley a beat to realize the song was Lainey Wilson's "Smell Like Smoke", and she cocked an eyebrow.

"What?" Busy said, dancing to the music. "I'm moving here so I'm learning all things country."

Laughing, Harley found her rhythm as Ace joined them, without a girlfriend in tow. After the past few days of solitude, it felt good to laugh and be with friends. A hand at her waist caused Harley to turn and find Wyatt Stone searching her eyes with an intense blue stare.

The song shifted to Eric Church's "You Make It Look So Easy" and Wyatt pulled her into his arms. Harley twined her hands around his neck as he leaned down to kiss her. He tucked a strand of hair behind an ear and whispered, "Forgive me?"

Harley saw concern in his eyes and tears sprang to hers as she nodded.

"You and me." He kissed her again, then placed a hand on her cheek. "From now on it's just us." Harley moved closer to him, and he held her tighter. "No matter what."

As the melody floated from the speakers, Harley had to agree with the song, there might be days when she and Wyatt wanted to quit, but she planned to do everything she could to make their love easy and to last a lifetime.

Kimila's Inspiration For This Story

This short story, "Whispering Willows," provides another glimpse into the lives of Harley Harper and Wyatt Stone, along with all the other interesting characters in my Stoneybrook Mystery Series.

I created this series and these characters to honor my autistic son, Derrick Henson, who passed away unexpectedly in 2017. Derrick always wanted to be a police officer and I hope I've realized his dream in his fictional alter-ego, Deputy Sheriff Derrick Stone.

ABOUT THE AUTHOR

Kimila Kay lives in Donald, Oregon with her husband, Randy, and a feisty black cat, Halle.

Her professional accomplishments include three anthologized essays in the CUP OF COMFORT series. Kimila is currently a member of Northwest Independent Writers Association (NIWA), Ladies of Mystery, Sisters in Crime, Willamette Writers, and Windtree Press.

Her cross-cultural series, Mexico Mayhem, includes Peril in Paradise and Malice in Mazatlán. The series will also include

Vanished in Vallarta (2023), Chaos in Cabo, Lost in Loreto, and Fiasco in Peñasco.

The first novel in Kimila's Stoneybrook Mystery Series, Redneck Ranch, is set in a fictional Oregon town and is slated for publication in 2023. A novella, Five Golden Rings, will also be available in 2023.

You can learn more about Kimila through her blog posts on her website: https://kimilakay.com/, Ladies of Mystery and Windtree Press.

Bread and Ashtrays

Melissa Yuan-Innes

he loaf of bread is calling me. It is lonely.

I try to ignore it. I brush by it on my way to the cereal aisle with a green plastic basket balanced in the crook of my arm. I often eat Cheerios for breakfast and dinner. I do not particularly like bread.

Hey. Hey!

The loaf of bread will not be denied.

I count to ten.

It is still calling.

Hey! Hey!

It is the round, flat loaf of rosemary focaccia on the top shelf in front of the bakery manned by a bored teenager in a hair net. The bread is dressed stiffly in a crinkly paper bag with a transparent window. I move another loaf beside it, a cranberry focaccia, and it quiets down.

hey. hey.

Then it falls silent, and I am free to buy my Cheerios and milk and leave the store. I step on the rubber mat and the door sweeps open with a whoosh. I feel rain dotting my hair and face and rain jacket and I wonder how many more voices I will hear today. More importantly, I wonder if I will be able to hear the one that counts.

THE MAN IS SHORT AND THIN AND HAS KIND BROWN EYES, BUT MY EYES immediately go to the thin white scar above his upper lip, evidence of some old surgery. He drops his head and holds out his hand for Hana to sniff and he smiles at her and doesn't recoil from her eager, bushy tail. He glances at my lovebirds twittering in their cage and clears his throat. "Nice place you got here."

I do not like people.

People care more about their cars and clothing size than the earth under their feet. I do not know if he means what he says. Other visitors have complained about the bird smell in the air and the animal hair on the sofa. Hana sits beside my chair and I pet her, digging my fingers into her fur harder than necessary. "Thank you."

He clears his throat. "I, uh, brought you a few things."

I point at the table. He checks my face for permission before he pulls out one of the plastic chairs. Good. He is respectful, at least.

He pulls off his army surplus backpack and sets it in his lap. "You need something she made, right? With her hands?"

I nod. My telephone instructions are very clear and I usually only take people by referral. Mustafa sent this man so he should be all right, but you never know with people.

"This sounds funny, but she doesn't make a lot. That's what took me so long. She doesn't like to draw. She doesn't even make dinner."

I feel my self, my inner self, curling inward like a cat curving into a ball. This is a bad sign.

"I had to get creative. We went to her mother's house and I made them take out a box of elementary school stuff. She made this ashtray." His scarred mouth jerks up into a smile. "Can you imagine? They'd never let kids make ashtrays now, but back then...anyway, I took it."

I look at the flat lump of grey with crude grey and yellow markings. I do not want to touch it, but hiring out my talent represents heating oil and pet food and Cheerios. I take it from his hand and immediately relax.

Mommy?

I pet the ashtray before the man stares at me and I realize what I'm doing. "This person is okay. She is very young, but she just wants to please her mother."

He smiles and runs a hand through his limp brown hair and suddenly, I realize he is not so bad-looking, despite his scar and his tendency to talk. "Great. I mean, you might think I'm crazy, but I just want to be sure. You know, once bitten and all that."

I stare at him. Why would he think I would call him crazy? It's what I have been called my whole life.

He shifts in his chair. "Never mind. I don't know if we need to bother with the other stuff. She made me a Valentine last year after I made her one."

This man is paying me a lot. I hold out my hand.

"It's nothing, really. Like I said, she doesn't like to make stuff. She already bought me a card, but I thought it would be fun, and I had the construction paper and scissors out."

He hands me a plain red heart. It is small but neatly cut out. The writing is spiky for a woman's, but written perfectly legibly in black ballpoint pen. *For Rob. Love, Sara.*

As soon as the paper brushes my palm, I flinch.

--nooooooo--

Oh, no. No, indeed. Not this nice young man who is paying me well. But it is always this way. Even so, I hold my breath and poke the valentine one more time.

NO.

I make a sound at the back of my throat, almost inaudible, but Hana presses against my legs. "She is not the right one for you."

"What is it? What do you see?"

I shake my head. I am no good at counseling. They ask and I answer, but no more than I can. "She doesn't want you."

"But--" He reaches for the card and knocks the ashtray, catches it before it hits the ground. "You said she was okay!"

I point at the ashtray. "I said she was okay. They are not the same person." I turn away from the pain in his eyes. 'Sometimes, people bring me objects made by different people. They try to trick me."

"I didn't. That would be a waste--" He stops, drops in his chair, visibly thinking. "She has a sister, Amy. I suppose their childhood things could have been mixed up."

I nod. "She would be better for you."

"She's fat!" He looks at me, winces. "Sorry. I mean, hell, it would look pretty bad--"

I shrug. My fat shields me from curious eyes and chilblain winters. I am not offended. I am more bothered by his human pain. So alien, so word-filled and often full of lies. This is why I always guarantee my fee with a credit card. The richest people can be the most slippery.

He runs out of words and stops pacing the room. Fortunately, he is not violent. Hana will bark and growl, but she is very gentle and does not know how to handle mean human beings. The birds are pretty but can do little but chirp, although their flight is something more than we can ever achieve with our own pure limbs.

He shakes his head again. "This is what I get for chasing after fairy tales." He scoops up the ashtray, hesitates at the valentine, but shoves them both in the backpack. He drops an envelope of money on the table.

"Thank you," I say to the money. I could avoid money altogether. Someone with my skills could barter instead of paying cash, but that means dealing with people, something I try to avoid. Money is easier.

After he slams the door, I lock it and pet Hana until my fingers stop trembling. Then I count the money. It is correct. Next time, I will ask more. Oil is getting more expensive and every client weighs on my mind and heart and spine.

THE MAN IS BACK. HE IS OLDER AND, IF ANYTHING, THINNER EXCEPT FOR a small paunch. He still has mouse-brown hair, although it has grown thinner too. I remember the scar. I remember everything. He says, "I'm sorry about how I behaved the last time. Thank you for seeing me again."

I nod.

He seems to be waiting for a response, but then he goes on. "You were right. I married her anyway, but the divorce papers should go through next month. Anyway, we have a son, Jeremy, and--" He stops. "I guess you don't care. Your dog still looks good."

I shake my head. Hana's ashes rest under a maple tree. I point to the golden lab at my feet. "This is Jake."

"I'm sorry. I seem to go about everything all wrong. Anyway, as you know, I'm worried about my business partner. I didn't know if you could work with computer programs, but I printed out the code. I also brought my laptop and we can run the program if you think you can get anything from it."

It is a strange world we live in, and not an improvement, where creation is limited to microchips. He passes me a folder of white computer paper. I read the strange words and pass my fingers over the raised print. I go through several sheets of paper. The man shifts in his seat. Jake flops over on his side. I do not feel anything. Perhaps this modality is wrong, although I have worked a little with computers recently. I open my mouth to apologize, as the man is always doing, and then I get a glimmer:

take

Just a breath, but it is enough. I run my fingers over more lines and I feel it again.

take

"He is greedy, whatever that means to you."

He closes his eyes. "Do you always give bad news?"

I do not answer. It is their fault, really. They would not come if they did not have a suspicion. I wait for the money. My fee has doubled since the last time.

"You ruined my parents' marriage."

It is not the first time someone has said this, or a variation on it. I have grown even more wary. I employ a sophisticated spam filter so most e-mails go in the trash. I order groceries on-line and have them leave the bags outside so I don't even talk to the delivery clerk. When I need clients, I meet them at a neutral public place--a library room with a door is good--so they don't see my house or my animals. I take cash only.

This is the first time in a long time someone has rung my doorbell and refused to go away.

"I want to talk to you."

From my webcam, I see it is a boy in that adolescent stage where he seems all legs and spidery fingers and tenor voice.

"I won't hurt you."

Then why are you here? I wonder. I should call the police, but I don't know if they would help me. They might not understand why I have over a dozen love birds, eight cats, and two dogs. They might turn them all over to the "humane" society. I could not bear that.

"Go away," I say, but I say it softly, from the hallway. I know he won't be able to hear me.

"You did us a favor," he says. "I can talk through the door if you want. I don't care."

I walk up to the door. I hesitate. What if he can see me through the peephole? What if he shoots me through the peephole? I once read that in a book. You never know with people. I stand off to the side, away from the peephole, and I decide to speak. "Talk."

He stops. "Well, okay. I, um...you remember my dad?" He says the name. It is the man with the cleft lip scar.

"Yes," I say into the silence.

"He died." His voice breaks.

Even I feel a soft measure of sorrow. My cat, Zulu, stares at me from the bathroom door frame. I wish she would let me pet her, but she stalks over to the litter box instead. My dogs are sleeping in the bedroom.

"He was only 57. I've been going through his notes and I found his diary. He talked about you and what you said about my mom. I want to know how you do what you do."

I laugh. It is a silent huff, unaccustomed to use, but a laugh none-theless.

He continues as if he didn't hear me, and maybe he didn't. "I did a eulogy for my dad, but it sucked. I don't think I ever really knew him. I brought this pen he made for me. He was no good with his hands, but he took a course because he wanted to give me something he made himself. And...I brought one of my drawings. It's nothing, but I thought maybe...I don't know."

He is crying, the boy outside my doorway. My dog, Sasha, wakes up and begins to bark.

What does this boy want from me? Can he not see that I failed to help his father and everybody else, that even if I tell them the truth, the plain truth, and nothing but the truth, they continue to walk their own crooked way?

Sasha growls and stalks out of the bedroom. I shush her. She leans against my legs.

The boy raises his voice. "I can pay you. He left us good money after you spotted his rotten business partner, and he made my mom sign a pre-nup, I think because of what you said."

Ah.

Still, I have no answers for this boy. Ahead of him lie heartache and fear and loneliness.

I pet Sasha. She growls one more time. Her ruff smoothes out. She sits up with her ears pricked and wags her tail. Silly dog. I pet her.

"Oh, forget it." He rubs his nose with the back of his hand and starts to turn away. His dull green backpack is the same one his father once wore.

It is foolishness. You can never trust people. They lie, they scream, they die. But perhaps I grow a little weary of my apartment and can risk death, although I will miss my animals. It seems that despite my best barricades, I can never resist the call of a lonely loaf of bread, no matter what shape it takes. Holding on to Sasha's collar, I unlock the door.

Melissa's Inspiration For This Story

A high school student, named Cayleigh, said that she always worries about loaves of bread in the grocery store. Cayleigh thinks they get lonely.

ABOUT MELISSA

Melissa Yi, also known as Dr. Melissa Yuan-Innes, studied emergency medicine at McGill University in Montreal. She was so shocked by the patients crammed into the waiting area, and the examining rooms without running water, that she began to contemplate murder. And so she created Dr. Hope Sze, the resident who could save lives and fight crime.

As Melissa Yuan, she writes children's and middle-grade books for ages ranging from kindergarten through middle-school.

Doctor-wise, Melissa has worked as far north as Ivujivik, Quebec, the northernmost village in a Canadian province. Nowadays she stays closer to home, running codes in Eastern Ontario. She's cheerfully married to her high school sweetheart, with two loud and loveable children, a Rottweiler shepherd, and a mountain cur. She loves stories, yoga, blading, sustainable fashion, laughter, intelligence, and random craziness.

If you enjoyed "Bread & Ashtrays", please consider signing up for Melissa's occasional, amusing newsletter at her website: *http://www.melissayuaninnes.com/* for special deals and insider stories.

Whispers of the Past

Paty Jager

CHAPTER ONE

*D*ela Alvaro shouldered her pack and tightened her grip on Mugshot's leash. Glancing behind her, she watched Heath Seaver, her ex-high school sweetheart, best friend, and now, a roommate with benefits, lock the truck and shoulder his pack, pulling his long braid out from under the pack.

"Are you sure the shack is at the end of this old road?" he asked, catching up and taking her one-hundred-pound, three-legged dog's leash from her hand.

"I'm not positive, but on Google Maps it is the only structure at the end of a road on this mountain." Dela started walking on an obscure track hidden by undergrowth. This had to take them to a shack that had been kept secret on the Umatilla Reservation for decades. From all the stories she'd dredged up about the place, Dela was surprised someone hadn't burned it down. Her footsteps faltered and she slowed to a stop. It could have been burnt down or even just fallen down by now. Would there be anything to give her a sense if the man who had lived there so long ago was good or bad? She needed to know.

"What's wrong?" Heath asked, stopping on the track beside her with Mugshot's leash pulled up short to not bump her.

"I had a thought. What if we hike in and discover the shack is now just rubble?" Dela peered into Heath's dark brown eyes. Eyes that knew most of her fears and failings. They'd made a pact as teenagers to help each other find their fathers, men no one would talk to them about. Heath had found his father. Now they were trying to make sense of the tidbits she'd collected about the man she believed to be hers.

"We'll have a much-needed long weekend from the police station and the casino if there isn't anything to search through," Heath said, motioning for her to continue walking.

Dela began walking slowly as she thought and navigated over obstacles that wouldn't hinder Heath or Mugshot.

They couldn't even be certain the man they hoped to learn about in the cabin was her father. But so far, all she had to go by were the photos of the man and his resemblance to her. Dela didn't know what she expected to find in the structure, if it still stood. Her gut told her she had to find it. Had to see if anything was left of the man who, according to Grandfather Thunder, returned from Vietnam with PTSD.

Having lived next door to Grandfather Thunder her whole life, she considered him her grandfather. After all, he was the only grandparent figure she'd known. He had been Dela's babysitter. But he'd never uttered a word about the shack and the man Dela believed might be her father. Not until she'd brought the man's name up and asked why she had never heard about him, since he was a Thunder. The elder had sidestepped most of her questions and suggested she not say a word to her mom about the man.

"Is it that hard for you to navigate the track?" Heath asked.

"No. Just thinking." Dela picked up the pace as much as she could with a prosthesis. She might have returned from Iraq missing a lower leg but at least she hadn't left the Army with psychological issues like many others. And, supposedly, the man they were seeking information about at the shack.

Her missing leg was why she led the hike and Heath had a grip on

Mugshot's leash. On uneven terrain, she had to place her prosthetic foot carefully or fall.

As they hiked deeper into the Umatilla National Forest, Dela thought about all she'd heard about the man who had demons that the elders had tried to chase away but only seemed to make worse. Many found the man dark, brooding, and frightening. While some of the young women found him charming. She'd even been told a story of how he'd saved four young women who were traveling home on a winter's night and had car trouble. This man had picked them up and taken them to the structure Dela was seeking. This had been one of his saner moments, almost. In the light of morning, the young women found the man gone and a cooked arm left on the table. Or so the tale was told.

No one other than the four young women saw the arm. Who's to say it wasn't a leg of an animal and not a human arm? The women had been scared, barely slept, and feared for their lives.

Dela had tried to talk to two of the women who were in the shack that night. Neither one of them would speak to her. When she'd asked about the other two who had been with them, she'd discovered they had both died.

But to her surprise, the new bartender at the Spotted Pony Casino where Dela worked as head of security, knew the man so many feared. She'd grown up with Theodore "Dory" Thunder and had nothing but fond memories of him as a boy and teenager.

The bartender hadn't known the man who came back from Vietnam broken on the inside. She'd married and moved away by then.

The warm August air brought out the tang of the pine trees and the mustiness of the decaying forest floor. Dela continued following the faded track of a road. With each step, she had the sensation this was the right direction.

"Are you getting used to the terrain?" Heath asked. "You're moving faster.

She glanced back over her shoulder. Heath had stopped. Mugshot was sniffing the ground as Heath drank water from a thermos bottle.

Pulling out her own water bottle, Dela sipped, studying the landscape and the GPS tracker hanging around her neck. She finished hydrating and said, "When I found what I think is the shack on Google Earth, I entered the latitude and longitude coordinates into my GPS. It looks like we're getting close."

Heath stepped beside her and peered at the device in her hand. "This had to have been a decent road forty years ago. Otherwise, why would he have brought those girls here instead of taking them to their homes?"

She heard the admonishment in his tone. "Yes, I concede it would have been easier for him to take them all home. That's one of the mysteries. Why did he bring them here and then leave? And did he bring others here and hurt them?" Dela didn't glance at Heath. Being a tribal police officer, he had a hard time being non-judgmental when it came to skirting the law.

"We will never know what drove him to do the things people refuse to talk about. Unless he is still alive." That hope had been bubbling in her chest ever since they looked at every headstone in Umatilla County and had not found any with the name Theodore Thunder.

"Don't think about him still being alive. I did that when I discovered where my dad had gone. It hurt twice as bad to discover he'd died and I couldn't ask him why he left us." Heath put his water bottle in the pocket on the side of his pack. "Let's just hope we can learn a little more about him before he went to jail."

Dela nodded, shoving her water bottle into a side pocket of her backpack and continuing up the overgrown track.

As they hiked, they didn't talk much. Dela had thoughts whirling around in her mind, when they'd stop for water breaks, she voiced her thoughts.

"What do you think happened to Dory that had him leaving a fun-loving young man and coming back an angry, volatile man?" Dela studied Heath as she spoke what had been slushing around in her head since the last stop.

"I've heard the horrors of the Vietnam war were more devastating to the soldiers. That and the fact when they came back they weren't considered heroes, but instead accused of killing innocent people." Heath drank more water and put his bottle in his pack.

"I know it was rougher with all the chemical warfare and an enemy that was much like what I encountered. You never knew if a woman or child was rigged with bombs or not. It kept me always thinking bad of someone before I met them."

After nearly three hours of hiking, Dela spotted a structure, leaning to one side. "That has to be it!" She hurried forward, only to catch the foot of her prosthesis on a downed limb. The weight of the pack on her back propelled her forward. She dropped hard onto her stomach. "Oof!" Air rushed out of her lungs as her hands stung from trying to catch her fall.

"Dela? Don't move. Let me see if you injured anything." Heath crouched beside her.

She sucked in air, and said, "It knocked the air out of me. That's all."

When she tried to push up with her arms, pain seared her left shoulder and the side of her neck.

"Shit and Burgers!" she hissed.

"What hurts?" Heath asked.

"My shoulder and neck." Dela wanted off the ground. The smell of musty leaves, damp ground, and a pile of deer droppings wasn't helping her to ignore the pain.

"I'll help you up." Heath grabbed her right elbow and levered Dela up to her feet.

When her left arm dangled, shards of pain sliced through her shoulder and neck. It was minor to what she'd felt when her leg was blown off. The sensation was more an irritation than full-out pain. She raised her hand, sliding it between the buttons of her shirt.

"Let's take your pack off and I'll see if I can figure out what you did." Heath stood behind her taking the weight off her shoulders.

Dela unbuckled the strap around her waist and unclipped the strap holding the shoulder straps on before lowering her arms for Heath to slip the pack off. Once her arms were free, she slid her hand back into her shirt front.

Heath appeared in front of her. "Let me take a look." He unbuttoned her shirt and his eyes widened.

"What?" Dela tried to look down, but he used his left hand to hold her chin up.

"I can't see the problem if your head is in the way," he said, gentler than his pressure on her chin felt.

She relaxed, holding her head up and to the right. "Ow!" pain radiated out her shoulder and up her neck.

"You fractured your collarbone."

CHAPTER TWO

"We're heading back," Heath said.

Dela spun around and peered into his eyes. "We can't go back now. We found the place. Let's spend the night and snoop. One day isn't going to matter with a collarbone. Just make a sling and I'll behave."

Heath rubbed a hand up and down her uninjured arm. "Dela, I know you're tough. Both mentally and physically, but this is a fracture. If you fall again, the bone could shift and tear through the muscle and skin."

"I've fallen on my stomach lots of times. I don't understand why it broke now." She stared at the ground studying her hand imprints in the dirt.

Heath bent over and picked up a rock. "The bruising indicates you landed on something. I'd say it was this rock." He tossed it off to the side. "It's only noon. We can get back to the truck and get you to the ER before the doctor goes home."

"No. Find something for a sling. We'll go back tomorrow. I'm not going to let this stop me from finding whatever might be here." She studied the leaning building. Something was drawing her toward the shack. Her need to know more about the man and whether he was related gnawed at her like a stomach ache. But it wasn't just wondering if he was her father, her curiosity about a fellow soldier who was misunderstood also nagged at her.

Heath released a breath of air and studied her. "You promise we'll head back first thing in the morning?"

She spit into the palm of her free hand and held it out. She and Heath had used this as a means of vowing a promise after they'd watched a movie as teenagers where best friends did it to pledge silence.

Heath shook his head, grinned, and spit into his palm and they clasped hands. "You know this is dumb for two grown people to do."

She grinned. "But it makes me look legit, doesn't it?"

Heath tied Mugshot to a downed tree and rummaged around in his pack. He pulled out a t-shirt and tore it to make a sling. Once he had her injured arm secured, Dela breathed a sigh of relief. It would be held in one place, and she could concentrate on the building and anything that might tell them something.

"Take these." He handed her a flashlight and a lantern. "I'll put our packs up in a tree while we look around." Heath carried the packs over to a tall pine. He dug parachute cord out of his pack and tied it to the shoulder straps on both their packs. Then he tossed the other end over a tree limb about thirty feet off the ground and pulled the bags up almost to the limb, before tying the cord to a lower limb on the tree.

There weren't a lot of black bears in the Blue Mountains of Oregon but they were around, as well as cougars. Dela had noticed coyote scat along with the deer and rabbit droppings as they'd hiked.

Mugshot snuffled in the decaying leaves near the tree where he was tied.

Dela walked up to the gaping door of the building.

"Hey! Wait up. Don't go in there until I've checked it out." Heath was beside her before she could step through. "The way this shack is listing, it could fall down. I'll check out the walls and beams from the outside."

Dela stepped back and studied the area. If Dory had lived up here, how did he get water? She stayed ten feet from the shack as she made a slow walk around the perimeter. She studied the ground and bushes, as Heath shoved on the corners of the shack.

Behind the building, she heard trickling water. Following the sound, she discovered a pipe stuck in the ground and water spilling out the end. Dory had used a spring to get water.

She cupped her hand and slurped at the cold water. It had to be snow melt flowing through the cracks of the rocks up higher and finding a way to the surface here.

"Fresh water? Nice." Heath cupped both his hands and drank.

"Well? Can we go inside the shack or do we have to knock it down and sift through the rubble?" Dela asked.

"It looks sound enough. We'll do a search but we'll spend the night outside in a tent." Heath picked up the lantern she'd placed on the ground to drink from the spring.

Dela pulled the flashlight from the pocket of her cargo pants and headed to the front of the shack. "When I did a property search, this shack wasn't on the tax records. But it could have been built when the property first came into the Thunder family in 1887 when they were given land allotments."

"We have several fee patents in my mother's family. But all of those were on the north end of the reservation." Heath shoved the half-open door all the way in and jumped back when the front wall creaked.

"From what I could find, this one-hundred and twenty acres were given to the three children of Loud Thunder, Grandfather Thunder's grandfather."

"Then Grandfather Thunder is one of the people who now own this shack?" Heath asked, stepping into the shadowed interior.

"His father was one of the children it was allotted to. So yes, he and his brother and sisters own it. But as you can see. No one ever comes here." Dela tamped down the excitement bubbling in her chest. The furniture had been overturned. It was weathered and covered in dirt and rodent feces but remained mostly intact. Would the animals inhabiting the building have ruined any papers they might find?

She walked over to a set of drawers about three feet wide that could have been used for a kitchen or for clothing.

"There hasn't been a fire built in this for decades."

Dela drew her gaze off the small cabinet and studied Heath standing by a rock fireplace. The rockwork and dingy smoke stains of the black hole, missing a rock on the backside where she caught a glimpse of green, told of a time long before she and Heath were born. "I think that is the original fireplace."

"Yeah. And pots and pans." Heath held up a blackened pot and dumped out dirt, pine needles, and droppings.

Dela's gaze drifted over the scattered furniture, stained ripped clothing, and household items strewn about the floor. It was a mess. One she knew had been made by animals and possibly humans over time. She settled her gaze on the cabinet and grasped the wooden knob on the front of the top drawer. A tug with her one good arm didn't budge the old wood. "Could you help me over here?" she asked Heath, who was kicking things around in the corner and raising dust.

He coughed and put an arm over his nose and mouth. "Coming," was his muffled answer.

"What were you doing over there?" she asked when Heath stood beside her.

"I saw what looked like a mattress on the floor and clothing. I was just moving it around with my feet." He scrunched his face. "I didn't want to touch it with my hands. We really should have brought gloves with us."

"And masks," Dela said, coughing. "See if you can open the drawers on this, please." Dela stood back as Heath gripped the wood knobs and pulled.

The drawer jammed about halfway out. "Looks like cooking utensils." Heath picked up a meat fork and stirred the contents in the drawer. "Yeah, that's all that is in here." He shoved the drawer shut and grabbed the knobs on the next one.

This drawer moved a little easier. It had a couple of books that had been peed on and the corners chewed by rodents. Also clothing that was barely recognizable from the way it had been used for rodent bedding.

Heath tucked his nose in the crook of his arm and shoved the drawer back in with his foot. "Are you sure you want the bottom drawer opened?" He studied her, his brown eyes begging her to say 'leave it be.'

"We need to see what's inside." She stood back as he bent and pulled on the knobs. This drawer held candles with small teeth marks, candle holders, a box of matches with faded sulfur heads, and a metal box about the size of the lunch box she used in grade school.

"What could be in there?" Dela asked not expecting a reply.

Heath picked up the box and placed it on the top of the cabinet. The latch was rusted shut from rodent pee.

"Let's take it outside in the fresh air, and I'll find a rock to break it open." He picked up the box and headed out of the shack.

Dela did one small circle taking everything in and followed.

CHAPTER THREE

he box sat on a large boulder as Heath washed his hands, used the sanitizer Dela offered him from a pocket of her cargo pants, and picked up a rock.

"Stand back," Heath said, raising the rock and smashing it down on the latch.

The box bounced and the lid popped open. Heath backed away as Dela moved forward.

Her heart thudded in her chest as she peered into the box. The first thing she saw was a small notebook. Next to it, the sunlight glinted off a set of military dog tags. There were photos scattered across the bottom of the box.

Dela's hand shook as she reached into the box and touched the dog tags. Her fingers tingled as she grasped the thin metal in her fist and held it in front of her. She glanced at Heath to reassure herself this wasn't a dream and opened her fingers, one by one.

The backside of the tag was face up. She read the name backward and a chill slithered up her spine. Theodore Thunder, his service number, O pos, and Christian. Dela held her palm with the dog tags up to Heath. "These are his."

He nodded. "I'd say you found something he either didn't want anyone to find or he treasured. Not sure which."

Dela placed the tags back in the container and picked up the book. A waterproof pencil, the length of a golf-scoring pencil, sat under the book. Opening the black cover about four by five inches, she recognized the feel of waterproof paper. The first page was dated 6-11-1968.

I left today for Army basic training at Fort Knox.

Her hands shook as she skimmed the page. "This is a diary of his time in the army." She flipped to the back of the book. Tears burned her eyes as she read the last words in the book.

Today I am confronting the beast. If you find this book, the beast has killed me.

Her chest squeezed and her heart felt ripped in two.

Heath dropped the photo in his hands and wrapped his arms around her. "What's wrong?"

"He-he killed himself." She held the book up for him to read the last entry.

"Look at the date." Heath pointed a finger at the date scribbled in front of Dory's last words.

Dela willed her eyes to look at the numbers beside Heath's finger. 12/25/1984

"Christmas! Do you think this was because his family had shunned him?" Dela's heart ached for a man she'd never met but felt his pain.

"Not the month, the year. He can't be your father. You were born November ninth, of eighty-five. That's almost a year before you were born." Heath put an arm around her shoulders. "This proves he wasn't your father. Let's hike back to the truck and get you to a doctor."

She shook her head. "No. He may not be my father but he was here for a reason." She made a circle around her face. "And I look like him. Maybe he'll talk about a brother or someone he was close to. I want to know more about him. Even if he isn't who I'd hoped he'd be."

"You can take the book and read about him, safe at home. After you've seen a doctor." Heath insisted.

"No. Set up camp. I'm going to nose around in the shack a little bit more then I'll come out and read the book." She put the book in the metal box and motioned for Heath to take it.

"I'll put this over by Mugshot. Wait for me before you go back in. There are too many things you could trip over and knock the place down around you." He strode over to Mugshot and set the box down before hurrying back to her. Dela stood at the door until Heath was headed back in her direction. She ducked into the building and worked her way through the debris toward the fireplace.

"What do you think the fireplace will tell you?" Heath asked, taking hold of her uninjured arm and helping her around an over-turned chair with gaping joints.

"I don't know. It's like ever since I found out about Dory, some-thing in me has to know more." She peered into Heath's eyes. "I feel like he was wronged, and I want to find out why."

Heath shrugged. "Ever since we found out about him, I've had to hold my tongue to not ask Grandfather Thunder or my aunt about him."

"According to Norma, Dory was an easy-going young man who enjoyed music and sports. She'd been surprised when he'd joined the army instead of waiting to be drafted." Dela kicked at the dirt, pine needles, sticks, and ashes in the bottom of the fireplace. She hadn't a clue what she hoped to find.

"That doesn't really match the person that came back from the war, does it?" Heath grasped her right arm. "Come on. We aren't going to learn anything new in here."

Reluctantly, Dela allowed him to lead her out of the shack and over to where the packs hung from the tree.

Mugshot whimpered and Dela walked over, unhooking his leash from the downed tree and sitting. She wasn't going to be much help setting up camp with only one arm. Sitting on the tree, she patted Mugshot's head and watched Heath take down the packs and unload what they would need for the night and a meal before he hung them back up.

"I wish I could help with more," Dela said, walking over to where Heath had placed the metal box.

"You're injured and shouldn't even be here. Read the book and pet Mugshot. I'll get some food cooked and you can tell me what you've read while we eat." Heath set up a one-burner propane stove and set a small fry pan on it.

"I thought we were just bringing MREs," Dela said, watching Heath work.

"I'm making stir fry with canned chicken." He grinned and pulled out baggies of prepped vegetables and a can of chicken.

She shook her head, sat on the ground next to Mugshot, using the downed tree for a backrest, and opened the book.

Her heart ached as she read about how badly he'd been treated during boot camp and beyond because he was Native American. She'd never heard some of the racial slurs he mentioned. Then he was sent to the war. He was put in every shitty job there was when they weren't using him for a decoy.

She looked up from the book and studied Heath making their dinner. They were lucky the world was becoming a little more welcoming to their presence outside of the reservations. But what Dory had gone through... A tear slid down her face.

Heath glanced over. "Hey? What's wrong?" He was by her side in three steps.

"I thought being Hispanic in the military was hard. You should read the things people said to Dory and made him do just because he was Indigenous." She shuddered. "No wonder he came back a changed person when for four years he was treated like the enemy." Dela held up the book. "And some of the things he saw... I know how that stays with you. Lingers in the back of your mind and comes out at the worst times."

Heath hugged her. "Stop reading that." He gently took the book from her. "Dinner is ready, come on over, and let's talk about something else." He helped her to her feet and they walked over to where he had a pan of food on the burner and two metal plates and silverware set out on a large flat rock.

Dela pushed the food around before finally taking a bite. Her mind wouldn't let go of the way Dory had been treated in the army.

"Dela, you can't change things. There is no sense in worrying about something that has already happened. And be thankful there are improvements in how we're treated. Most of that comes from the fact the Umatilla stay up with the times and are making our own future with the casino and the businesses that it has funded. We are strong proud people. We will prevail."

She nodded. "I know. I need to get my head into the present. But if he died December of eighty-four, how could he have been in jail and have his mugshot taken five years later?" They knew this because of a mugshot a corrupt tribal detective had tossed on Dela's bed to distract her right before he lunged at her and she shot him. "If what Jones said, that mugshot is a photo of my father, then he was alive after I was born. Yet," she held up the book, "this book has proof he killed himself."

Heath took her plate. "We don't know for sure either of these people is your father."

She pulled out her phone and brought up the photo she'd taken of a driver's license she'd found tucked away at Grandfather Thunder's. "You said the man in the mugshot resembled me and so does this younger version that Grandfather Thunder didn't want me to see." She held her phone next to her head.

"We don't know that either of them is your father and we may never know. You can't keep pushing this. Not when we have so little to go on." Heath handed her a baggy with two smashed brownies in it. "Eat your dessert."

"I'm going with my gut. Why else would Grandfather Thunder say bringing that person in the driver's license up would hurt my mom?" She put her fingers in the bag and pinched the chocolate gooeyness between two fingers and shoved a bite in her mouth.

"There could be more reasons than you think. Maybe once your mom arrived at the reservation that person dated her and broke her heart." Heath held his own bag of brownies.

"No. She never dated. At least not that I knew of." She thought about her mom's upcoming marriage to a man that had been in her mom's life for many years, and Dela hadn't known about him. "I guess she is good at keeping things from me." A switch clicked in her mind. "Maybe I should just come out and ask her the truth about my father. I'm pretty sure the one she's told me all these years is a lie."

"You don't want to upend your mom's life now that she's marrying."

Dela peered into Heath's eyes. "I know that's being selfish. But if she's been keeping the truth about my father from me, I think that is selfish."

"Or she's just trying to protect you. The reason she didn't date anyone until you joined the Army."

CHAPTER FOUR

*D*ela found sleeping nearly impossible with her arm in a sling and her prosthesis still on. Her mind was groggy as she stared at the ribbons of moonlight through the tree limbs.

The sounds of Mugshot and Heath gently snoring only added to her misery. They were sleeping peacefully, and she was uncomfortable and couldn't get the things she'd read in Dory's book out of her head.

Quietly, she unzipped the sleeping bag, slipping out of it. She placed the book and her flashlight on the bag and dragged it over to the side of the shack in front of the rocks that made the back of the fireplace. Spreading the bag out, she sat with her back leaning against the rock on the outside of the cabin.

She wanted to go inside but had a feeling there would be lots of rodents running around and she'd prefer the friendly glow of the moon as she continued to read the book.

Once she settled, wrapped in the bag the best she could with one arm, she sat against the rock wall, turned on the flashlight, and opened the book. She'd become accustomed to the boxy printed letters of Dory's writing.

He wrote about returning home from Vietnam and how everyone called him a killer. He'd tried to hide at the reservation but people wouldn't leave him alone. They asked about the army, what he did, and if he killed anyone. He finally moved to the cabin, staying to himself, until the beast showed up.

Dela studied the last sentence. *I thought the beast had died years ago, but he showed up today.* Staring at the sentence, she wondered what the beast had been and why had it come out in him that day. While it was a journal it didn't give detailed events of his days. Only significant things that bothered him or changed his life.

She leaned her head back against the rocks and stared up at the moon. If he was her father, was the beast inside of her?

The wind fluttered the wisps of her hair that had slipped out of her braid. She pulled the sleeping bag higher and snuggled into the warm depths. With the bag over her head, she held the flashlight tucked under her chin and the book open on her bent legs.

There was a gap of half a year after he'd mentioned the beast showing up. He talked about being back at the cabin after working for someone. The snow was falling hard as he drove up the mountain. He'd found four young Umatilla women, he thought they were still in high school, walking along the road in the snow. He stopped and discovered they were all high. None of them made any sense. He brought them to the cabin and gave them all the blankets he had. They passed out and he left to go listen at the rez to find out if the women were from there or somewhere else.

At the rez, he'd discovered they were missing and told Uncle Silas where they could be found. He'd returned to the cabin the next day after they had been picked up.

Dela switched off the flashlight. The girls had been high and probably made up the story about the cooked arm to take away from the fact they had been at some party and got lost. Anger that their story made Dory even more of an outcast made her chest ache. But if they'd made that story up, why wouldn't the two still alive tell the truth now? Why would bringing up Dory's name make one of the women have nightmares? It didn't make sense. Who should she believe?

She placed the book and flashlight on the ground beside her and tried to sleep with her shoulder and collarbone throbbing and her leg swelling in her prosthesis.

Footsteps woke Dela. She reached for her handgun but it wasn't there. Her head was still inside her sleeping bag. She listened and became awake enough to remember she wasn't in Iraq. She was in Oregon in the Blue Mountains. The footsteps had to be Heath checking on her.

She relaxed and that's when she heard what sounded like two male voices arguing. There wasn't anyone else here. Just her and Heath. Cautiously, she lowered the sleeping bag and listened. The words were muttered or muffled. She listened intently and realized the low-pitched tones were made by the wind blowing through the holes in the shack.

But she'd heard footsteps. Dela twisted quietly and used the hole where the rock was missing from the fireplace to peer into the shack. Nothing moved in the darkness spiked with shafts of moonlight.

Dela clicked on the flashlight and shined it into the building. The scurry of small feet scratched across the wood floor. She couldn't see anyone in the building. But her light illuminated something stuck up the chimney. She'd have Heath help her pull it out in the morning.

Before snuggling down in her sleeping bag, Dela checked her watch. Only a couple more hours until daylight.

CHAPTER FIVE

sharp pain woke Dela. She hissed and sucked in air. The sleeping bag was pooled around her waist and her arm wasn't in the sling. Birds chirped and hazy early morning sunlight made the small clearing look ethereal. Biting her lip, she opened the sling and slid her arm in. It appeared when she finally fell asleep it had been restless, like most of her nights.

"Dela, what are you doing clear over there?" Heath asked, standing by his sleeping bag and stretching.

"I couldn't sleep." She put out her good arm as Mugshot walk/hopped over and stuck his face inches from hers, sniffing. "I'm okay. You and Heath were snoring so much I had to move."

Mugshot gave a short soft sneeze as if he didn't believe he and Heath were snoring.

"Need help up?" Heath asked, standing beside them.

She reached up with her good arm. "Gently. I don't know how cramped my legs are."

He leaned down, grabbed her elbow with one hand, placed his other hand at her waist, and stood her on her feet. He continued to hold her as she moved her knees and decided if they'd hold her.

"I'm good. Thanks." She looked down at her sleeping bag where the book and flashlight peeked out.

"Were you really not able to sleep or did you just want to read more from the book?" He bent and picked up all three items.

"You and Mugshot were snoring, my collarbone hurt, and I couldn't get comfortable. I came over here to read." She walked toward the small camp. "According to Dory's account, those girls were high when he picked them up wandering around up here. He brought them to the cabin and then went to the rez to see if anyone was missing. When he overheard conversations, he told his Uncle Silas they were at the cabin." Dela studied Heath. "That would have been Grandfather Thunder. Why didn't he tell me that the man in the story was related to him and had done the right thing? Instead, he'd talked as if he believed what the girls said and that his nephew was uncontrollable." She didn't understand how the man she'd known her whole life hadn't helped a family member.

Heath shrugged. "Maybe he was ashamed he hadn't stood up more for his nephew."

"But does that sound like the man we know? Grew up knowing?" Dela had spent all her after-school hours and teacher work days with Grandfather Thunder.

"No. Grandfather Thunder has always put family before anything else." Heath picked up a pan and headed toward the shack.

"What are you doing?" Dela asked, stretching her arm over her head.

"I'm going to get some water for hot drinks." He disappeared.

Dela patted Mugshot. "Want to keep me company while I pee in the woods?"

Mugshot gave a soft woof and they headed into the trees.

"What do you think about all of this," she asked her furry companion as she squat.

Mugshot peed on a tree about five feet away and stared into the forest.

"No comment, I see." She finished and stood, trying to zip her pants with one hand. She managed the zipper but couldn't get the waistband buttoned.

They walked back to the camp and found Heath staring into the trees. "There you are. I wondered where you'd disappeared."

"We needed to pee." Dela walked over to Heath. "Would you please button my pants?"

He grinned, buttoned her pants, and gave her a kiss on the cheek. "I like it when you need me."

She laughed and said, "Don't get used to it." But in her heart, she enjoyed being helped and listened to by Heath.

She sat on the log where they'd eaten dinner.

"Here, read while I come up with some grub." Heath handed her the book.

Dela fumbled to open the small journal where she'd left off the night before. The photos she'd found in the box with the journal spilled onto the ground. She picked them up one by one and studied them. They appeared to be a photo of the Thunder family at a party or reunion. There were three boys that might be Dory as a child. Then there were two grainy black-and-white photos of a man in an army uniform. She put them in the back of the book and told Heath, "He mentioned something about he thought the beast was dead but it showed up one day." Dela watched Heath lowering the packs to get food. "What do you think the beast is? Some mental malady that comes over him?"

Heath walked back to the small camp with two MREs. "Do you think he had problems with that before he went into the army?"

Dela read the labels on the meals ready to eat. He had two packets to make scrambled eggs and ham. She'd had more than her share of these in the army but she had always liked the breakfast ones.

"It didn't sound like it from what Norma said about him. I think something changed him in the army. Combat and trudging around through swamps seeking out the enemy, takes a toll." Dela was happy the nightmares she came back with centered around the day their Humvee was blown up and she lost her leg. It could have been about killing people, but she'd not been in the middle of the fighting being an M.P. She'd dealt with prisoners who were healthy and angry or wounded and angry.

Heath poured water into cups he'd spooned hot chocolate into and stirred. "Keep reading. There has to be something in that book that will help us figure out what happened." He handed her a metal steaming cup.

She set it down on the log beside her to cool and started reading. Dory was back to writing a sentence or two about what he'd done all week. He appeared to be living in the cabin when he wasn't on the road. It didn't say what he did, only that he worked and when he had enough money saved up to live quietly for several months, he came back to the cabin until he ran out of money for food. "He was a hermit when he wasn't traveling to make money."

"What did he do when he traveled?" Heath asked.

"It doesn't say." She pulled her gaze from the page and watched Heath pull the MREs out of the boiling water. "Do you think he was going to rodeos? He could have made enough money to hole up here for a few months and then head out again."

Heath dumped the contents of the packets on their tin plates. "Yeah, but if he did that year around, he'd have to travel south to rodeo during the winter." He handed her a plate with a universal utensil that had a spoon on one end and a fork on the other.

"We have dates, but it would be a lot of work to find out if a rodeo was happening during the time he was off working." Dela put the book in the side pocket of her cargo pants and set her plate of food in her lap.

Heath grabbed his plate and cup and settled on the log beside her. "Now that you have the book, let's head back this morning, so you can get treatment for that collarbone."

Dela nodded. "But we have to look in the chimney first." She chewed a bite of her meal.

"In the chimney? Why?" Heath sipped his drink, watching her over the rim.

"It was strange. I dozed off for a while and it sounded like someone walked by me. I listened and thought I heard two men talking. So I looked into the cabin through that rock that is missing in the back of the fireplace. I didn't see anyone and realized it was just the way the wind blew through the shack." She picked up her drink. "I shined the flashlight through the hole and rodents scattered in the building, but the light reflected off something tucked up in the chimney. Something shiny."

"You think another tin box?" Heath asked.

Dela shrugged. "We won't know until we look."

CHAPTER SIX

When everything was cleaned up and their belongings stuffed into the backpacks, Dela led Heath to the outside of the chimney. They both knelt and Dela shined her flashlight into the hole.

"There, see the way the light reflects off something up there," She pointed to the spot she'd seen the night before. "You go in and reach up there and I'll guide your hand."

Heath stood. "If a spider bites me and I die, it's your fault," he said, walking around the corner of the shack.

Dela chuckled and peered into the chimney. Heath's hand and arm appeared.

"A little more to your left," she said, directing his hand closer to the object. "About four more inches and up three, maybe."

His fingers skimmed the part of the item Dela could see. "That's it! Can you grab it?"

She watched as Heath's arm reached farther up. His hand held a metal cylinder when it came back into view.

Dela pushed to her feet and met Heath in front of the building. "What do you think it is?"

Heath continued walking until they were over by their packs. He unscrewed the lid and tipped it for Dela to look in.

There were rolled-up papers. She pulled them out. The top paper was a yellowed newspaper clipping taped to the page. SORORITY RAPIST CAUGHT.

Her gaze flicked to Heath. "Why would someone hide this?"

Heath's gaze was on the clipping. "It appears that Theodore Thunder was sentenced to life in prison for raping six college students." He peered into Dela's eyes. "Are you sure you want to keep saying this man is your father?"

Her heart squeezed. Was that why her mom would be devastated if Dela brought this man's name up?

Dela pulled out the rest of the papers. They were all about the crimes committed. She shook her head. "This can't be." She peered into Heath's eyes. "I'm the result of my mom being sexually assaulted?"

"You don't know that. I'll get the records pulled on this and see if her name is mentioned."

Dela held up the clipping with the mugshot that Detective Jones had tossed on her bed before trying to kill her. "This is the man Jones said was my father. How did he know? And look at the resemblance."

Heath grasped her shoulders.

She hissed from the pain in her shoulder.

He released her quickly and said, "Don't jump to conclusions. We'll get to the bottom of this. But it will take time." He put a hand under her chin and raised it. When her gaze was on him, he said, "You can't let this eat at you. You hadn't known it for thirty-three years and you know the person you are. Don't think of it personally. Think of it as another investigation."

She nodded. He was right. Knowing this about her father didn't change who she was and how she lived her life. "We can't let Mom see any of this. I don't want to ruin her marriage to Lance."

"I agree. We'll keep it hidden and work on it secretly. I'm sure we can gather all the information without arousing any suspicions." Heath rolled the pages up and put them back in the cylinder. He placed that in Dela's pack before he slung his on his back and put her pack on his front.

"I can carry that on my good side like a bag in my hand," she argued.

"I don't want you off balance and falling again. Start out," Heath said.

"I can at least take Mugshot's leash," she offered.

"Nope. Same goes. I don't want you injuring yourself worse."

Dela headed back following the tracks from the day before. As she walked, she pondered how she thought she'd heard two men talking. She mulled this around in her mind until they stopped to rest and hydrate.

"Who put that cylinder with all the stories in the chimney? It couldn't have been Dory if he was in jail." This had been bothering her as she walked.

"We need to find everyone who knew about this cabin and that Dory spent most of his time here." Heath pulled out a notepad and wrote in it.

"When you get copies of the investigation, we need to see if the times he was off working are the same times that women were attacked." Dela wanted to know the truth, even if it meant her father was a man she would have loathed.

She put her water bottle back in the pack and studied Heath. "You're right, I am who I am and I need to find out the truth—good or bad. But I can't let the whispers of the past change the future I'm striving for."

To learn more about Dela Alvaro as she proves her worth as the head of security for the casino, how she and Heath grow as a couple, and if the man they are searching for in the cabin is really her father, check out Paty Jager's Spotted Pony Casino Mystery series. https://www. patyjager.net

I wrote this short story as a way for me to discover more about a thread I have running through the Spotted Pony Casino Mystery series. The main character, Dela Alvaro, has always been told her father died before she was born. However, since her return to the Confederated Tribes of the Umatilla as head of security for the casino, she has come across evidence that her father may not be who she was told and has a secret.

This short story is a gift to readers as I wrote it to get to know what the character, Dela, is trying to learn more about. You can find these stories at https://www.patyjager.net

ABOUT THE AUTHOR

Award-winning author Paty Jager and her husband raise alfalfa hay in rural eastern Oregon. On her road to publication she wrote freelance articles for two local newspapers and enjoyed her job with the County Extension service as a 4-H Program Assistant. Raising hay and cattle, riding horses, and battling rattlesnakes, she not only writes the western lifestyle, she lives it.

All her work has Western or Native American elements in them along

with hints of humor and engaging characters. Her penchant for research takes her on side trips that eventually turn into yet another story.

PAX
Reborn
Maggie Lynch

CHAPTER 1

RESIDENT

*T*ova carefully put on her dark blue uniform, a long dress that draped her body like an upside-down triangle, wide at the shoulders and slender at the feet. The designated uniform helped to make her feel content, a part of a larger community where everyone was equal, everyone was doing the work of the community and keeping the peace. All genders wore this same uniform during the day. The only differentiator was the sash. Hers was draped from the left shoulder to the right hip, in the spring-green color that signified she was a newly graduated psychiatrist entering her psychiatric residency at the unit in her village.

With the same care, she braided her hair snug across her scalp, bringing the long tail down over her collarbone. This was the decreed hairstyle for all genders working in the psychiatric unit. It had something to do with the belief that long braided hair was soothing to the malies. Short for malcontents, malies was how the residents of Pax Reborn were designated by the doctors and staff. Malies fell along a spectrum, from those who were temporarily malcontent, due to sudden trauma or prolonged grief, to those who expressed far too many emotions in a short period of time and seemed completely uncontrolled. She had to admit, she was a bit afraid to encounter one of the latter. She'd seen pictures and vids during her studies, but that was at a safe non-interactive distance. Now, with her new assignment, she would be amongst them every day.

Her brother, Eoghan, stepped beside her. "Are you ready for your first day?" His uniform included the same navy blue, upside-down triangle. However, his sash was tied at the waist and secured with a carved wooden fist to signify his occupation as a woodworker. His tools were neatly arranged in a wooden case he carried at his side. His shorn hair was the decreed style of his profession. A practical style to guarantee that no hair would get caught in any equipment. Female woodworkers also had their hair shorn. As with everything in Concordia, all was equal. Equal requirements, equal treatment, equal opportunity, equal pay. It kept the peace.

"Were you frightened the first day you apprenticed with the woodworkers?" Tova asked.

"No. I was confident in my skills. Tools are tools. They don't change. They don't talk back to you and they never show any emotion. It is a profession where it's easy to be content. I could never do what you have chosen. I can't imagine facing malcontents every day. All those emotions, all those crazy conversations would probably suck me into becoming a malcontent myself."

He stepped out the door. "See you at dinner," he said over his shoulder and then stepped into the group of uniformed walkers, all heading to their posts.

She watched and smiled at the neat orderly way that people joined the traffic patterns. She loved hearing the greetings, and the constant answer of: "I am content," as the people moved along designated pathways dotted with nice shade trees and glowing balls of glass. No one ever got lost because as you passed one of the balls it would change to your sash color if you were on the right path. If you had strayed, a voice would call you by name and the glass ball displayed an arrow pointing the direction you needed to go.

The peace still held. Not that she didn't expect it. It had been this way for more than a hundred years. It was all she knew. Hearing the greeting and response of contentment among all the people was like pulling a warm blanket around you on a cold evening when the heater couldn't keep up. It reminded her that the community was one and, with each person glowing with contentment, nothing could harm them.

Closing the door behind her, Tova stepped out to join all the others. She truly was content on this first day of her new job. She'd worked hard for this opportunity, getting accepted to advanced studies, working on her own emotional management in the process so that she could be a role model for others. The exams had been the hardest she'd ever taken. They were all case studies enacted by paid actors from the local theater company. Some of the actors were so frightening and frustrating that on the final case study, she'd broken down and cried in front of the entire class. She couldn't seem to stop because she felt so much for the two characters portrayed. She couldn't remember when or if she had ever cried more than a minute —even as a young child. Crying was an emotion that was a harbinger for a future malcontent diagnosis.

She'd been afraid she'd failed after all those years of classes and preparation. She feared she would be assigned to another profession and have to start over. But the professor said she'd made it farther than 90% of the students. She passed with a score of 90, even with that horrid display of emotion. She'd received her medical degree and was given the uniform of a psychiatric doctor. She'd been so relieved, she'd vowed then to never let a case get her so upset, and definitely never ever cry again over anything. She was ready.

As she made her way along the paths, she looked from side to side to try and catch another new psychiatrist she could befriend. But she saw very few sashes of any new professional and none for psychiatric work. She had no idea how many new psychiatrists were offered positions at Pax Reborn. In fact, she had no idea how many malcontent patients Pax Reborn housed. The institution was never in the news and, except for the occasional celebrated return of a patient to the broader community, most people never thought of it.

Her initial residency hours were only four hours a day during the first six months. The expectation was that in the remaining four hours the intern undertook research and study, and did meticulous prepping for the next day of dealing with patients. She was required to debrief with her supervisor each day and hand over all recordings of her interactions with patients.

Tova had never seen a malie in person before. She'd read all about them in her abnormal psychology book, but she'd never encountered one. In fact, she hadn't even known they existed until she started her advanced studies in psychology in her fifth year at university. When she learned they existed and were housed in the Pax Reborn facilities, she knew instantly it would be her life's work to help them toward peace. Her psychology courses did speak of the occasional malie outlier who could not be helped. When all treatments failed, the malie was put into the deep sleep—like an injured pet beyond repair.

The thought of even one Concordian being put down was something she could never imagine being a part of. After all that the founders of Concordia had done to save the people and create the peace, it seemed like a failure to have a single soul who could never rejoin the rest of the community and experience contentment like everyone else. She was determined she would never be a part of that kind of failure. Surely, it was for lack of trying all options.

"Tova!" Her friend, Maree, waved from where two paths diverged near a forest. Eoghan also waved and then kissed Maree on the cheek before taking his own path. Tova wrinkled her forehead, was that a romantic kiss? No, he'd known Maree growing up like she was another sister.

Maree caught up to Tova and linked arms matching her stride. "Good morning, Dr. Tova." She emphasized the doctor part. "I'll bet you are so excited to be starting today. You must be so pr..." Her friend swallowed the word, but Tova knew she was going to say proud. "Darn, I keep forgetting."

Tova raised her eyebrows at the near blasphemy and nodded slowly. Pride, among most other emotions was not allowed. As problematic words were exposed, they were banned. Pride and proud were banned two years ago. It was the responsibility of every Concordian to keep up with the banns. It was especially important in a psychiatric unit, where all the patients were filled with far too much emotion and delusional ideas. Many were unable to restrain it. She couldn't imagine how that would feel. It must be very frightening to the malies.

"I am eager to learn new things," Tova said carefully. Excited also was not a good word choice. Excited tended to suggest more than the average contentment, whereas eager simply meant ready to learn and work. Tova had worked hard to keep up on all the emotion word changes. She denied any feelings of being better, smarter, luckier, happier than any other person. This was the way of peace. It had been less than a year since pride/proud was removed from acceptable use.

Excited was still acceptable in certain situations, like having sex, but then not too much excitement was allowed. She wasn't sure how anyone would know it unless you boasted about it. Which was also not allowed. After all, if it was discovered that your sex was better than someone else, it would signify inequality in partnering. She'd known of one couple who boasted all the time about their sex life and shared openly all the different things they did to make it even better. Within a few months they were separated by the emotion police. Eventually, they found a new pairing that was more equal. When the woman became pregnant she said she was relieved that her baby would not inherit any inequality issues that she may have gotten from her previous partner.

Tova wasn't partnered with anyone yet, so it wasn't a question she really needed to ponder. But she did wonder about it. What made it just right and what made it over the top?

"Darn, too soon." Maree stopped in her tracks and pulled Tova off the path. "This is where our paths diverge. It seems like we barely got to talk."

"We can catch up after work," Tova suggested. "Though I'm not allowed to tell you anything that happens at Pax Reborn."

"Exactly!" Maree said. "What fun is that if I don't learn some secrets?"

Tova wasn't sure if she was teasing or really wanting to know. "I'm sure there are no deep dark secrets lurking that would be of interest to anyone except a clinician. Really, if you were a malcontent, would you want everyone to know your business?"

"No, I guess not...but could you at least tell me how they look? How they move? If they are...you know...disfigured or...have special psychic abilities or...never mind. I'll probably get in trouble just for asking."

Tova smiled slightly. Her friend had always been a questioner. She didn't automatically accept the way things were. Maree wasn't a malcontent. She did follow the rules...most of the time. Fortunately, she didn't share her questions with many people. In fact, it may be that Tova was the only one she shared things with. Maree was what her mother called "a free spirit." She was two years younger than Tova and still trying to decide what her future would be. From week to week, she vacillated between coffee server and astronaut. Tova figured the community would be well served if Maree took up acting. Then she could be lots of different things and never have to stick to one.

Tova looked at her timer. "I have to get going," Tova whispered. "Can't be late on my first day. Let's meet after the dinner hour tonight and we can catch up. Maybe we can watch a favorite movie."

Maree nodded and then shifted to Tova's ear. "How are you really?" she whispered. "You can be honest with me."

"I am content," Tova responded aloud.

"Truly?" Maree wrinkled her forehead and drew her bottom lip in with her teeth. "Truly?"

"Yes, truly. And you?"

Maree's shoulders sagged and she let out a long breath. "I am content, too." Then she turned and hurried in another direction.

Tova wasn't sure Maree was content. She watched her friend for nearly two hundred meters before turning to continue her own path to Pax Reborn. Maree would occasionally look up to the heavens as she walked and then skip for a few paces. If someone greeted her, it appeared she would pull into herself as if regulating the joy she felt, then proceed at a more normalized pace.

It was hard to keep up with the emotion word changes. It did seem that every year another word had to be banned to keep the peace. Was it true that the malcontents were multiplying outside the boundaries of Concordia? She'd heard stories of some escaping, marrying each other and never reining in their emotions. The rumor was they lived in the deep darkness of the forest where most Concordians would not dare to enter. She'd heard that malcontents were having children without permission. Not that PSEC would ever give them permission. That was definitely against the law and science. There was a whole police force dedicated to seeking them out and bringing the children to Pax before they were irredeemable.

The history books talked about a long-ago time, in her great-great-great-grandparents lives where no one was equal. Everyone strove to be special, and everyone showed their emotions all the time. In fact, in those days people didn't only act in plays for case studies or family-friendly movies. They actually had movies and vid series that were all driven by emotion and conflict. One person's marriage was wonderful, amazing, hot, perfect, but then another person would steal their partner and a fight would break out. People would be crying, shouting, calling each other names, telling stories about how awful the other people were. Some even planned murder for their partner or the person the partner was seeing. This was done on fiction vids for all the world to see.

Evidently, this was accepted all the time in the before days. Violence, hate and crime increased. No one agreed about anything. In fact, no one even tried to compromise. The thought of working together to solve problems was laughed at by government officials and commoners alike. It must have been a very unhappy time. It was a miracle that the human race even survived that period of history.

Lost in her thoughts, she didn't notice Dr. Charles walking beside her until he touched her shoulder. "Already planning your first intervention?" he asked. "Your face looked a bit worried but determined."

"I was remembering the old days and the stories I've been told about how most of the population were malcontents. How did we survive that? How did we evolve to find peace before killing everyone?"

"Through far too much trial and error. Unfortunately, a lot of errors. Many people died."

"Died? At their own hand or from experiments?"

Dr. Charles shook his head as if shaking out the knowledge so it wouldn't bother him. "Both. I wasn't there, of course, but all the history books describe it as a time of great tragedy. The acceptance of such emotions as normal expression became a world-wide pandemic, and very few were immune."

"But it will never happen again. Right? I mean in Concordia PSEC has it under control."

Dr. Charles smiled a half smile, the appropriate smile for content-ment. "Yes, the Peace Security unit has it under control. With profes-sionals like you, it will continue to be so. But we must never let down our guard. Not everywhere in the world is like Concordia. There are deep pockets of malcontents in other places and I'm convinced that some of them travel here to change us."

"I hope I can be of service."

"And how are you today, Dr. Tova?" he asked.

"I am content. Well content."

"Good. You'll need it." He steered her into the facility and then pointed to the right. "Sign in at the office at the end of the hall. Then someone will escort you to meet Daniel, your first patient. I'll meet you there. He is a very special case. I'm interested in hearing your diagnosis by the end of the week."

"You're my supervisor?"

"If you don't mind," he said. Then he walked way, again pointing to the office at the end of the hall.

Tova couldn't believe it. Dr. Charles had visited her classes several times. He was considered a future-thinking psychiatrist. Not the best of all, of course. Nobody was the best of all. But he'd done a lot of research and was credited with much of the initial work to help the malcontents. He was one of the founders of Pax Reborn. Many case studies in her program were based on patients of Dr. Charles. One of them was the really frightening one at the end of her final exam where the patient killed himself and the doctor. Maybe she'd get to ask him about that. She'd really love to know how it could have been solved and ended with a better result.

Finally at the registration office, she opened the door and stepped up to a counter.

"Hello, Dr. Tova, and welcome to Pax Reborn," a disembodied voice greeted her in the vicinity of a flashing blue light on the reception counter. "I am called Emma. How are you today?"

"I am content," Tova said. She'd never encountered a non-human receptionist before. How strange to have a machine in a facility that was designed to make everyone most comfortable and open to optimal human interaction and treatment.

"I hear a question in your voice," the machine said. "Are you sure you are content?"

"I am well content," Tova repeated the usual phrase. "I was simply wondering why there is not a human to greet me. I have never been met by a machine before."

"I was built by human coders under the instruction of Dr. Charles. I have all the qualifications of a Pax Reborn receptionist. I can sense stress in voices, monitor heart rate, respiration, and oxygen levels at a distance. I have many complex routines that help me deal with any problems. Initial patient intake is done by machines as well. It is much safer that way in case someone doesn't want to be admitted. They can shoot me and I can come alive again, unlike a doctor or nurse. However, if you are uncomfortable with me I can arrange for your supervisor—Dr. Charles—to be here within minutes if he is not busy with his patients."

"No need," Tova quickly said. The last thing she wanted on her first day was to appear unwilling or unable to face this simple first challenge. "I was just curious."

"Good. Then we shall proceed. Please sit in the chair and face the light while I analyze your status and cross-check your documents and waivers."

Tova sat, monitoring her breathing so that she was as content as any person could be. She remembered signing all kinds of documents and agreeing to all the rules. How many rules were there? Twenty? Thirty? She couldn't remember. They all seemed obvious. Then there was the security and confidentiality paperwork. She imagined it was the equivalent of going to work for any top Concordia government agency that had secrets to keep or their world would go awry. She often wondered how all the rules came about. It seemed that new bans of certain words or emotions came about because someone did something that wasn't anticipated. Then, as a proactive move, the government banned it so no one would ever do it again.

"All seems in order," the machine finally said.

"Good," Tova responded and started to rise.

"There is one last verbal release I must read to you."

Verbal release? Something they couldn't put in writing and give her time to review before coming. That was unusual.

"Are you ready to proceed?" the machine asked.

Tova sat back in the chair and steadied any fears or questions. She would listen. She was sure it was reasonable. Probably something like have you been truthful about everything. "I'm ready," she said.

"If you break any of the rules you've vowed to keep, you will be banished from Pax Reborn and removed from Concordia forever. If you ever discuss a patient outside of this facility or the treatment regimens we undertake to help the patients you will be banished from Pax Reborn and removed from Concordia forever. If you ever cause a patient to become attached to you, in that they refuse to work with any other clinician, you will be banished from Pax Reborn and removed from Concordia forever. If you ever attempt to remove a patient from this facility you will be banished from Pax Reborn and removed from Concordia forever. There is no appeal for this sentence and punishment will be immediate. Do you understand and agree to this final waiver?"

Tova hesitated. There were many rules in the documents she signed. Did she remember all of them? Certainly, she thought she would never do them, or she wouldn't have signed. Banishment from everything and everyone she knew was unthinkable. How would she survive that? How could she possibly promise all of this without having spent even one day with a real patient? She had no idea what challenges lay ahead.

"Is there a problem?" the machine asked.

"No...no. It's just that...well, what if I make a small mistake...not on purpose but by accident. I'm still learning, I might forget or... stumble... just once, of course."

"Can you give me an example of a mistake you might make?" the machine asked again with perfect modulation of the electronic voice.

Tova sighed. "I don't know, I just...I'm not sure. What if I just forget one of the rules?"

"Is there a specific rule you think you might forget?"

"No...I don't know...I..."

"Your heart rate is rising. I'm concerned you are not content. I will call Dr. Charles."

"No!" Tova raised her voice, then purposefully lowered it so no one would think she was out of control. "Give me a minute. Please." She took some deep breaths and consciously worked on calming herself. Why was it at every turn of imperfection, the machine was going to summon Dr. Charles?

"I see your heart rate is lowering now and your breathing is returning to normal. It took you more than two minutes to achieve this. That is a non-optimal response time in emergency situations. Has your malcontent episode passed?"

The machine thought she'd become a malie for two minutes? That wasn't possible. No way. After all she'd done to study and prepare, staying to the rules, never using emotion even when she wanted to let loose just a little. This was only...

"Hello, Dr. Tova." A soft, familiar voice greeted her and then put a hand on her shoulder. "What's going on here?"

Tova hadn't heard the door open. She hadn't heard any footsteps. How could he be so quiet? Was she so scared that she wasn't paying attention to her surroundings? Now, *that* was scary.

Dr. Charles pulled up a chair next to her. He took her hand and pressed his fingers against her wrist where her pulse was. "Emma said you were having some type of attack." He made the statement in a very calm voice—no judgement. His voice tone said: trust me, I'm here to help you. His clinician persona was very good. "She feared you were on the brink of becoming a malcontent. What happened?"

"It wasn't an attack," she said slowly, matching her best therapist voice to his. "I'm a little nervous. First-day jitters."

"Your pulse rate is coming down. I see you have some breathing techniques to calm yourself. That's good. Emma, how is her oxygen level now?"

"Ninety-seven," the machine responded. "At the height of her malcontent it was as low as eighty-nine. Pulse is now down to seventy-eight. It had shot up to the ninety-six when she was in thrall. This was the second rise of vitals during our intake. Her respiration had become shallow. The first one was quickly controlled. The second one lasted two point six minutes before she was able to calm herself."

"You had a small panic attack," Dr. Charles said, with no judgement, as he released her wrist. "What brought this on?"

Tova wanted to trust him and be honest, but she also didn't want to lose this opportunity for the work she'd spent the last seven years proving herself and her skills. Was it worse to say: I'm not sure, and show she couldn't diagnose her own symptoms? Or worse to admit the verbal waiver and punishment was impossible to comprehend and she wasn't sure she could sign it until she had some experience? The latter was worst. Definitely. "I—

"It happened during the reading of the verbal waiver," the machine spoke before Tova could put her thoughts together. "With each sentence her breathing became more rapid and shallow. By the end I feared she would have to be admitted as a patient."

Tova's eyes widened and she immediately took in a deep breath to stop the panic from rising again. A patient? Her reaction wasn't that bad. It definitely was *not* a panic attack. Everything was just new. It was different. She wanted so badly to perform well. Couldn't they see that?

"Emma, give us privacy, please." Dr. Charles said.

The light dimmed. But was that to make her think the machine wasn't listening or was it really listening in the background still? Okay. Calm down. Don't start suspecting the machine is evil or anything. She took some more deep breaths and said the mantra. I am content. I am well content.

"I'm sorry you've had a difficult time," Dr. Charles said. "Let's see if we can talk this out and make sure this is still the right profession for you."

Tova nodded. She didn't yet trust her ability to speak until she was in the zone of perfect contentment.

"I suspect there are a lot of new experiences here, things you've never seen or done before."

Tova nodded again. I am content. I am well content.

"Have you ever been interviewed by a machine?"

Tova shook her head slowly from side to side. Keep breathing slowly, she told herself. I am content. I am well content.

"Aw, that is a bit off-putting. My heart rate might rise if I hadn't helped build Emma to start with. It's a bit scary to realize a machine is tracking your emotions and sometimes seems to be reading your mind."

Reading her mind? Please don't tell me that is the goal of this machine. No, it couldn't be. Con...cen...trate! Don't get scared again. She was almost back to normal. It appeared that Dr. Charles wasn't trying to fire her. He understood her dilemma, at least a little bit.

"How are you feeling at this moment, Dr. Tova?"

"I am content," she said it this time, still only halfway to believing her own words.

"That's good. Let's talk about the verbal waiver. You may be wondering why we require it to be verbal instead of written."

"Yes, it did take me by surprise," she admitted. Glad her voice didn't waver.

"The problem is we've had some previous applicants send in their paperwork without really reading and understanding everything. Then when they get here, things go wrong quickly and they are surprised by the punishment. They claim they didn't remember rule 15 or rule 29. They claim it was a simple mistake. Because banishment is something we do not wish on anyone, we decided to create this verbal waiver. When Emma reads the waiver, it seems to hold more power and requires a response in person that signing papers does not."

Tova nodded again. "I understand. But…"

"But you weren't sure you remembered all the rules you had already vowed to keep." He finished the sentence for her as if she wasn't the only one who had balked. "There are lots of rules. Thirty-two to be exact. Our assumption was that you would memorize them and know all of them the day you started. We should have made that clear in the paperwork. I will direct Emma to change that for future psychiatric residencies."

"If I could review the rules again, I would feel more comfortable in saying yes to the final waiver."

Dr. Charles smiled more widely than she'd ever seen him smile. "Of course. Emma should have offered that option to you instead of allowing you to panic." He turned toward the dimmed light. "Emma, wake up." The light glowed again. "Please display the list of rules for Dr. Tova."

The desk lit up and a three-page display of the rules appeared. "You can review all the rules right here. All you needed to do was ask."

Tova didn't move toward the desk to read them. She felt the need to explain before reviewing them again.

"It wasn't Emma's fault I panicked." She paused. When did she start using a personal name for the machine? That didn't feel right. "I've just studied and worked so hard for this opportunity. I don't want to make a mistake. I want to do what is asked of me. But I know it is likely I will make a mistake at some point, because I'm new and I don't know everything, and…well…it seemed that banishment was a harsh punishment for a small mistake."

Dr. Charles nodded and patted her hand. "Of course, we wouldn't banish you for a small mistake. Like number twelve, here." He pointed to a row on the first page. "This is the rule for recording all of your sessions. In this way you don't have to write up a report. Then when I listen to the recording I can hear the session and the voice fluctuations and responses between you and the patient. It makes it easier to then advise you on nuances you may have missed that would help you in the next session. Certainly, if you simply forgot, *one time*, to start the recording I wouldn't banish you."

"Good to know," Tova said, beginning to read from the top of the first page to re-familiarize herself with each rule. She read each one multiple times in order to put it permanently in her memory.

"On the other hand," Dr. Charles continued and pointed to a rule on the second page. "If you broke rule nineteen, purposefully creating a personal relationship with a patient, you would definitely be banished and very quickly. There is no second chance with that one."

"Of course, I'd never even consider doing that. I worked a lot on managing potential transference of affection when I was in supervised therapy sessions at university."

Dr. Charles nodded. "Yes, I'm aware of your good record in those sessions. It was one of the reasons I chose you. Unfortunately, we've had a couple of other new professionals who could not follow rule nineteen."

Tova suppressed the urge to ask for details. Those poor people, banished forever. Where did they live? Were they stuck in a country populated with malcontents? Banishment was bad enough, but then to live among them the rest of your life. She could see how someone might contemplate ending their life in that situation.

He pressed a finger into his ear and nodded. "I understand why your panic started to rise when you didn't know all the rules by memory. But why did it take more than two minutes for you to self-regulate the second time you had a panic attack?"

Tova wanted to protest that neither instance was indicative of a true panic attack, but she wasn't going to question his diagnosis right now. "It felt shorter than that," Tova said, looking straight at him instead of bowing her head. "But I accept that two minutes or more is a long time."

"It is indeed. However, in *this* instance, it is not a worry." Dr.

Charles leaned forward as if sharing a confidence. "Between you and me, Emma is a bit rigid," he whispered as if she might be listening. Then he sat up straight. "Your reaction is a bit uncommon," he said in his normal voice. "But you recovered fairly quickly. Thirty to forty seconds faster would not have tripped Emma's concern program. Though we would prefer no panic attacks at all, our upper limit in patient situations is one minute and that can only happen once. I hope you learned something about yourself and how to manage your emotions. It is unusual to have two attacks in this friendly setting."

"Yes, I have," Tova assured him. "Honestly, I have berated myself for letting it get to that level."

"Berating is not a good coping mechanism. Psychiatrists need not feel guilt for an emotional misstep, only a desire to improve. At Pax Reborn, we do not want to be judgmental. Our diagnosis does not mean you are bad or a failure. It is only a matter of optimal patient care. If a patient is out of control, two minutes of not being able to react appropriately can be the difference between life and death."

"I see," Tova said. "Of course, you are correct."

"I don't think you do see. I have your record of the final exam. Though you did better than ninety percent of the students in your graduating class, you did fall apart in the last case study. When most students fail that case, they simply don't care how it ended. They have no emotional reaction at all. The notes on your situation indicated you stuck with the patient for longer, but the ending caused you to be so distraught that you cried for more than fifteen minutes."

Tova lowered her eyes. Of course, he would have the record of her biggest failure in her seven years of university before becoming a doctor herself. No wonder he was worried that she may devolve to becoming a malcontent. Crying for more than fifteen minutes was inexcusable. She knew that, but had put it behind her when they still awarded her the degree and gave her the uniform for the job. The exact same uniform Dr. Charles wore now.

"That was a tough case," he continued. "My Pax Reborn founding partner was the doctor on call that day. He was the one killed."

Tova sucked in a breath and her eyes began to tear as she remembered the case study that had shook her core. She swallowed hard to keep a single tear from falling.

"That was the last time I cried about anything," Dr. Charles revealed. "We've only had fifteen patient deaths since that awful event four years ago. Though that record is not optimal, I did not cry about any of them since that first one. At least we did not lose any more staff."

She wanted to ask if he was really crying about his friend being killed, or for concern about the patient. But now was not the appropriate time to ask. Maybe there would never be an appropriate time.

"Emma, I'm convinced that Dr. Tova will be just fine. Now that she knows how a panic attack feels, she will be able to ward them off in the future. Please mark her as cured. I do not see any malcontent in her now."

Cured? But she was never sick. She was glad she hadn't lost her job on the first day. But, she wasn't sure that Dr. Charles was a good diagnostician. She wondered how many people had been admitted to Pax Reborn that perhaps should never have been admitted. Or worse, how many had the machine admit them without Dr. Charles or another clinician questioning it?

"Are you ready to take the verbal waiver now?" Dr. Charles asked.

She held up a finger. "One moment." She returned to reading the rules and putting each one to memory. Most of them were straightforward. A few regarding the use of restraints were questionable, but then she hadn't been faced with anyone who needed restraints. Certainly, there were good reasons for some patients—reasons that stopped the patient from harming themselves or others.

After another couple of minutes, she finally looked up from the desk. "I am ready."

The machine read the same verbal waiver again. This time she didn't flinch at the repeated words of "you will be banished from Pax Reborn and removed from Concordia forever."

At the end of the reading, the machine asked, "Do you understand what I have read and do you waive your right to question banishment in the instances I have read?"

"I do," Tova said, though her stomach did a little flip flop, she competently kept her fears contained. She would memorize every rule and make sure she made no mistakes. She was back in control and nothing would cause her to ever break a rule.

"Good," Dr. Charles said. "We are set then." He pressed his ear again. "Yes, it is time for lunch. The patients are being brought their trays right now. I suggest you head to the staff dining room and have a meal. Introduce yourself to others. Then I will meet you at room 111 and introduce you to Daniel. He'll be your only charge during the first few months of your residency."

"Where is the staff dining room?" Tova asked.

"Take your badge on the table here," the machine responded. "Place the earbud in your ear. Your badge is coded to all locations where you are allowed access. That includes staff dining, staff toilets, staff shower room, Dr. Charles office for your daily follow-up meetings, and patient Daniel in room 111. Your badge will track time and days and remind you where to go and what to do. It will track you anywhere in Pax Reborn."

"Thank you. That's very handy," Tova said. She placed the badge on her sash and put the earbud in her ear. Immediately it reminded her she was already late for lunch and told her to proceed to the corridor and she would find an elevator in twenty-four meters. It guided her to the staff dining room, informed her she had only forty minutes left to finish a meal, and reminded her she was to meet Daniel at 1:10pm.

Yes, all very helpful, Tova thought to herself. It also seemed quite overbearing. Did it also measure her urine when she went to the toilet and run tests on it to see what she ate? Or did it already know what she'd chosen for her meal in the staff dining room? What about after her workday? Did the badge also know how she walked home, who she met, if she stopped anywhere and perhaps had two beers instead of one?

She shook her head. Certainly not. There was no need to monitor everyone in Concordia. The peace had been secured. There were no malcontents lurking in the community. She was working herself up over nothing. Like so many things today, she stuffed the questions deep in her mind and set up a wall between it and what she had to accomplish today. It was all so new. She didn't have time to let her imagination run amok.

CHAPTER 2

DANIEL

$\mathcal{A}$t the appointed time, Tova's earbud directed her to room 111. As she approached the door she saw Dr. Charles rounding a corner. They met in front of the door at the exact same time. How strange. How planned everything was, down to the second of arrival. She wondered if anyone was ever late.

"Dr. Tova, before we go in I will do an initial briefing on Daniel. He was admitted to Pax Reborn only five months ago. He is nonverbal. He makes his wishes known primarily with grunts and groans and leading a staff member to something and pointing. His IQ is unknown as the usual tests require verbalization. He does not appear to be violent. He has not attacked a staff member. However, his gestures and some loud grunts may appear threatening."

"Where was he found and in what condition before he was brought to Pax Reborn?" Tova asked. "Had he suffered any physical trauma that you could see?"

"He was found next to a dead body, the throat slit, assumed to be his mother. They were in the forest on the northern edge of Concordia. When PSEC questioned others in a one-mile area , no one claimed ever seeing him or his mother. The area is known for murderous malcontents. The police said he was crying loudly and rocking back and forth. They only knew his name because it was printed on a shirt he was wearing. They could not get him to talk and they feared he was a malcontent that had been hidden by his mother and now could not live without her."

Tova shivered. Poor soul to lose his mother and then be admitted to Pax Reborn without being able to understand what was happening to him.

"How are you feeling now, Dr. Tova?"

"I am well content."

"Are you ready to meet Daniel without judgment and without emotion of any kind?"

"I am."

Dr. Charles opened the door and Tova followed him in.

In the far corner sat a young man of perhaps twenty to twenty-five years staring out the window. No one knew his real age because he didn't exist on the Concordia rolls and he was unable to tell them. Did he even know his own age?

"Daniel, this is Dr. Tova. She is going to be working with you this year."

Daniel did not respond in any way. In fact, he did not make any movement or utterance to acknowledge their presence.

Dr. Charles gestured for Tova to follow him as he stepped directly into Daniel's view. "Daniel, this is Dr. Tova. She is going to be working with you this year."

Again, no response of any kind.

Tova raised her hand and said, "Hi, Daniel. Good to meet you." Then she held out her hand ready to shake his.

He reached toward her and shook her hand. She smiled back at him.

"Very good," Dr. Charles said. "You've already gained his trust. Surprising. Surprising indeed." He turned back to Daniel. "Daniel, I'm going to leave Dr. Tova here with you for one hour. Do you understand?"

Again, Daniel made no motion or even a grunt to show he understood.

"I don't know what you can learn in an hour, that I haven't already spent several hours trying to determine. But I'll check back with you in an hour for a debrief."

"I'll be fine," Tova said.

Dr. Charles cocked his head and raised a brow. "I trust you will have no panic attack being left alone."

"None," Tova verified.

Then he turned on his heel and left. The heavy door closed with a definite lock behind him.

Tova pulled out a chair from the small dining table in the room and brought it near the window. "Do you mind if I join you?"

Again, no answer. She sat and looked out the window herself, wondering what to do. She'd never met someone who was blank to every statement. Of course, she'd never met any diagnosed malcontent before. Perhaps the trauma of his mother's death made him mute. She'd read about those cases in her psychology texts. Her role was to gain his trust, so he could feel safe to talk.

He had readily accepted her wave and handshake. What other gestures could she try?

She waved her hand near his face again. Then she put her hand on her chest. "I'm, Dr. Tova." She pointed to her name on her badge. Then she pointed to him. "What is your name?" Pointed to him again.

He responded by pointing to himself and then pointing to his own badge. Okay. That was a start. She wasn't sure if he was telling her his name or simply copying her gestures without understanding.

Then he did something different. He pointed to himself and the fingers on his right hand fluttered by pointing, closing, opening quickly as if he had no control over them.

Tova shook her head. "I don't understand." Then she tried to translate that to gestures. She pointed to herself and said, "I." Then she pointed to her temple and said, "Don't understand" while shaking her head.

Daniel threw his hands in the air and shook his head. Then pounded the table. He drew an imaginary box on the table, and then made a circle in the box with a little tail. Or at least that is the way it looked without really seeing it.

Maybe he could draw or write. Had anyone tried that? Tova pressed her earbud. "Emma, can someone bring a paper and a crayon or pencil to Daniel's room, please?"

"He'll only write out the alphabet over and over," Emma responded. "Obviously he knows his letters."

"That's okay. I want to see it. A paper and a pencil or crayon, please."

Within a couple of minutes there was a knock on the door and then a key opening the lock. A young man, about the same age as Daniel but wearing a white sash indicating he was an orderly, entered the room. He placed a large piece of paper the size of a poster on the table and a box of eight crayons in different colors.

"You going to write your alphabet again, Daniel?" he asked as he placed the paper down. "That's all he does, you know. He just writes the alphabet. He doesn't draw pictures or anything. He just writes the alphabet and points to them and his hands go crazy."

"Thank you, Michael," Tova said reading his badge. "I'm new here, so I'd like to see that anyway."

"Yes, Dr. Tova. Let me know if you need anything else or need me to remove the paper and crayons later." Then he left the room again.

Just as he'd predicted, Daniel took the black crayon and wrote the entire alphabet on the paper in large letters. Then he looked at Tova with expectation.

"Yes, I can see that is the alphabet," she acknowledged.

He grunted and pointed at the letter a, then made a closed fist. Then he pointed at the letter b and held up four fingers. He continued that way going faster and faster, pointing to a letter and then his hand did something strange. It all looked like nothing she'd ever seen or read about but it was clearly meaningful to him.

After he finished with the letter z he looked at her with expectation.

She pointed at herself. "I." Then pointed at her temple and shook her head. "Don't understand."

He let out a big breath, then he put his closed fist in front of her face. He opened it slowly to form a circle. Then he slowly lifted his index finger and third finger and placed his thumb between them.

He pointed to the letter O and made the circle with his fist again. Then he pointed to the letter K and made the same fist and extended his second and third finger, placing his thumb between them. Then he did it again.

"O K," she said. "Oh, Okay!"

So, he did understand her gestures for I don't understand and he responded with okay?

She pointed to the O and made the same circle with her hand, and then pointed to the K and made the gesture he had made previously.

"Ug, Ug, Ug," he uttered, his eyes sparkling and his smile wide.

Then he pointed to the letter C and made his hands into that letter. Then he pointed to the letter A and made the closed fist toward her. Then he pointed to the letter T and made the closed fist again, but this time pushed his thumb between the closed index finger and the next finger.

"Cat!" Tova said as she made the C with her hand, then the closed fist for the A, and finally pushed her thumb between the first and second finger for the T. "Cat!" she repeated.

He pounded the table and nodded his head.

His crazy finger gestures were a physical language. How did he ever learn that? Why did he need to learn it?

She'd never heard of hand-talking before. At least not in this way. There were history books that talked about when Europeans came to America that they learned to converse with the natives with gestures. But that wasn't hand-talking like this. The few pictures she'd seen were very large gestures like pointing to the sky or the ground or things like that.

She spent the rest of her hour pointing to letters and learning each letter of the alphabet with this new hand-talking. Then she would spell out basic words like cat, dog, her name, Daniel's name. Then she would make a short sentence: My name is Tova. I like cats. Then he would slowly do his hand talking with a similar sentence. My name is Daniel. I like dogs.

"Daniel?" she spelled with her fingers. "Why don't you just write messages to me or the staff in order to communicate? Why do this language?"

He finger-spelled very slowly so she could grasp it. "Sign language is faster. Bad people..." He made a face showing disgust. "..kill us if they know we can't hear. They experiment on us like rodents. That is why we hide deep in the forest. Hundreds have died in this facility."

Tova struggled not to show any emotion of surprise or disgust. She didn't want to believe this could be true. But Daniel did not appear to be in a psychotic or delusional state. He was emotional, but given what he conveyed it was understandable.

Slowly Tova finger-spelled back, "How do you know *I'm* not bad?"

Daniel's eyes widened and he pointed at her with a sharp motion and looked directly in her eyes as he fingerspelled, "You listen. You care."

She swallowed at the thought of the trust he was giving her. This was a huge step and so early in their acquaintance. Tova wasn't sure how to proceed. Was he playing her or was he truthful. She wanted to believe it was truth. He seemed genuine in his body language presentation.

Tova signed back that she understood and, for now..." She paused in indecision, then she signed, "This is our secret. Let's proceed with calm and see what happens. It is possible we are being watched. We can't afford suspicion."

Daniel nodded and his eyes looked to the right and toward the ceiling. Tova followed his gaze. There was a pinhole about the size of her thumb and light glinted off what appeared to be a mirror or lens. She slowly took her gaze around the room as if looking for something. Then she looked back to Daniel and smiled. So, he knew he was being watched. By who? Dr. C or some staffer?

She looked back to Daniel. "I don't see anything unusual," she said aloud. "I'm pleased with our progress, Daniel," she said in her most formal therapist voice. "I will ty to learn more quickly." Then she signed to him, "Let's begin again."

It was then that Daniel picked up his pace for her learning. He began showing her signs that meant a whole word that could be used instead of fingerspelling. First, he showed her a different sign for cat. He spelled it out with his fingers, then he made an open F sign near his face and pulled it away. It took her a while, but she associated it with whiskers. He did the same thing for dog. First spelled it with the letters, then patted his hip and snapped his fingers. She could see that was like calling a dog to your side.

When her earbud told her the hour was up, she didn't want to go. She wanted to stay all night and learn many more words. But she knew she'd be back tomorrow.

She signed thank you with the alphabet, and see you tomorrow.

Daniel responded with signing thank you with the alphabet and then a gesture where he placed his open fingers near his lips with a flat hand and then moved it forward and slightly downward toward her. He repeated it twice with first spelling the thank you and then the action.

She smiled again and then did the new thank you sign without spelling it out.

Daniel clapped his hands.

As she let herself out, her earbud directed her to Dr. Charles' office. What would she tell him? Would he believe that she had discovered a language of hand talking, or would he think she'd been infected by a malcontent? She couldn't believe he would not have come up with this on his own. She'd take it slow and not tell everything until she could judge his reaction.

Tova knocked on the door with the nameplate stating Dr. Charles, Psychiatrist.

He opened the door and smiled. "Dr. Tova. I see you have survived your first session with one of our most difficult patients." He gestured for her to enter. "Please, come in and have a seat."

She noticed two chairs facing a large desk covered with papers. In fact, the piles were so tall she wondered if he could really find anything on his desk. Did he really rely on those papers? Most people today stored everything in a personal database that one could secure from prying eyes.

Dr. Charles moved both chairs away from the desk and turned them to face each other, about five feet apart. Then he sat in the one on the right, and crossed one knee over the other. It seemed a very casual approach to a professional supervisory appointment. Tova thought she might match him but decided not, as she would feel very uncomfortable.

"Did you record the session as required?" he asked.

Tova nodded. "I've already transferred the audio to the electronic file."

"Let's listen together then, shall we?"

About fifteen minutes in, he pursed his lips, replayed a couple minutes, and then stopped again.

"I don't understand what is happening here. You are pointing to letters in the alphabet and telling him how they form a word? I've tried that and nothing comes of it."

"You have it wrong," she said. "He is teaching me."

"Teaching you what? The words cat, dog, thank you?"

"No, he is teaching me his language." She demonstrated slowly with her fingers how he would say cat. "This is the way he communicates. Every letter of the alphabet has a specific way you put your fingers." Then she went through the entire alphabet at a fairly brisk speed, saying each letter. "Though he can communicate by spelling everything out and I can follow him, if it's not too fast, at the end of the hour he was teaching me a few gestures that mean the whole word." She showed him how to make the gesture for cat. "See? Like whiskers."

He said nothing for what felt like several minutes, though it was probably only a couple minutes.

"I'm not sure you are helping him by learning his made-up language that no one else knows. It is your job to teach him to speak like all Concordians do. Do you think any other content Concordia will take the time to learn a language of gestures? If he can't express himself so that everyone understands he will never become content."

Tova tried to listen to Dr. Charles without judgment, but she was disappointed in the direction he was heading. She had learned in her therapy sessions to meet the patient where they were to build trust. She couldn't help them until she knew how they thought.

"May I ask what approach you would recommend?"

"I've tried all kinds of approaches with Daniel over the past few months. I've tried speaking slowly. I've tried limiting the number of words I use in case he only knows a few. I've tried tying his hands so he couldn't use them and would then be forced to speak. I've tried a variety of psychotherapeutic drugs to relax him and I've even tried shock training."

Tova's intake of breath was audible. She thought that had been outlawed more than a century ago.

"We only use it on our most difficult patients. It can reset their brain in a way. It's only used for a fresh start and then it is back to only positive reinforcement. Our goal is for every patient at Pax Reborn to leave here and become a good citizen of Concordia."

"And none of your attempts have worked," Tova said, keeping every bit of judgment out of her voice.

"None," he confirmed. "If we cannot find a way to teach him to speak, the most humane way would be to let him sleep."

Tova's eyes opened wide. "You mean the deep sleep?"

"Yes. It isn't harsh. It is humane. No one could ever become content without being able to communicate their thoughts to others. Would you prefer to live in Pax Reborn for the rest of your life? He is only in his twenties. He is healthy otherwise. He would be without companionship and never content for the next seventy or more years. Is that humane?"

Tova swallowed several times. "How many people who come to Pax Reborn are delivered to the deep sleep?"

Dr. Charles took her hand and stroked it slowly. "I think you are getting emotional, Dr. Tova. Surely you know that some people cannot be saved. It's a sorry situation, but that is simply reality."

Tova withdrew her hand and held her head high, looking directly at him. "I do accept that some people are in such pain that the sleep is a mercy…but I don't believe Daniel is in pain. He is frustrated that no one has taken the time to learn how he communicates. Yes, it is different from the norm but…"

He shook his head and stiffened his spine. "I know where you are going with this. You want to learn his way of communicating and make it acceptable. I cannot—"

"You misread me," Tova interrupted. She knew where Dr. Charles stood and she wouldn't accept it. But she would not let him know that was her end goal. "I'm suggesting that I learn how he communicates now, so that I can speak with him in complete sentences. Then I can begin to convey deeper themes and meanings, so he will understand the importance of speaking. Don't all therapy sessions properly begin with putting yourself in the patient's shoes in order to gain trust? Only then can we scaffold the learning from where they are currently to become what is needed to live in a peaceful and equal society."

Dr. Charles closed his lips tightly. "Hmmm. The student schools the supervisor."

"I am not judging your approach," she said with very little modulation of her voice. "I'm sure you have tried many things I can't even comprehend. On top of that you have the entire facility to run and all that entails. Perhaps, because I'm new and don't have the ability to diagnose quickly, I see things differently, more simply."

"Of course you do. You are new to the profession."

He stared at her for a minute without speaking and she returned his gaze with zero emotion, as she said the mantra in her head. I am content. I am well content. She was sure not to convey that it mattered at all to her what he might say next.

"I think it will be a fine experiment," he finally said. "You have one month to learn his unacceptable communication style, and then I expect you to immediately begin teaching him to speak."

"Of course," she agreed. "Thank you for allowing me to start slowly and learn the best approach."

"You will, of course, meet with me every day and I will review the recording. You will keep me apprised of your progress."

She nodded and stood to leave.

"One more thing," Dr. Charles said as he stood. "Surely, you realize you are taking a big gamble here. If you become the only person Daniel can communicate with, romantic transference is highly likely to follow."

"Yes, I am well aware of that," she said slowly, again keeping all emotion out of her voice. "I will guard against that at every step. And if I feel it is happening I will report it to you immediately so you can advise me as to next steps."

"Good. That is appropriate." Dr. Charles gestured toward the door. "I trust you are always professional, Dr. Tova. I hope this works. I truly do."

"Thank you, Dr. Charles. I do too." She lowered her head for a moment and then raised it and nodded once before turning her back on him and slowly walking out the door.

Did Dr. Charles suspect her motives? Was it possible that in addition to her recorded notes, there were video recordings in each patient's room? If they recorded patients and therapy sessions, did they also record therapists outside of Pax Reborn?

On her walk home, she processed the day. She struggled to keep any emotion from her face as she realized she was already straying toward rebellion against Daniel ever going to the deep sleep. Several times she had to force herself to stop thinking and count her breaths as she walked. She had been truly upset when he mentioned the deep sleep. That seemed so premature. Daniel had only been there five months. Certainly, they put more time and effort into helping reform a patient.

She wanted to ask if anyone had made sure he had the ability to speak. She'd read in history books that less than a century ago it was common for about twenty percent of the global population to have a hearing loss so severe they had to have surgery to help them hear even a very loud noise. The history books didn't say anything about how they lived or communicated. She had wanted to ask if Daniel had been tested for hearing loss, but after the mention of the deep sleep she didn't dare. It wasn't right that a physical disability like that would mean the deep sleep. How many other disabilities were not recognized in Concordia? Was it because those with disabilities would be judged "less than" and the peace would be at risk?

The problem was that Tova wasn't sure that Dr. Charles should be the one to make these decisions, though she didn't know who should. She tried to imagine how she would feel if she couldn't talk. If she could only communicate, like Daniel did, the sorrow would be having no one who understood the hand-talking. But was even that sorrow enough to want to die? Whatever the answer, it seemed that Daniel should have a choice in the matter. He wasn't a malcontent. He was a person who couldn't communicate with speech.

As she walked up her porch she made a vow in her heart. She was going to make sure Daniel was never forced to the deep sleep if he didn't want it. She wasn't sure how she would stop it, but she'd figure it out. She swallowed hard as tears began to form at the thought of him being put to death when she'd barely started with him. She worried her bottom lip. She didn't want this emotion. She didn't need this emotion. It would not help her or Daniel.

"Tova! Tova!" She heard Maree's voice up the street, then saw her running to reach her before she went inside. Out of breath, she raced up the stairs and gave Tova a big hug. "So, tell all. Were the malies scary? Did anyone attack you? Were they ugly? Was it hard to be around so many? Did you make any friends with the staff? Are you fitting in or starting a revolution?"

The last made Tova laugh. "Definitely I'm the revolutionary type."

"I was just trying to be funny," Maree said. "Not enough people laugh around here—especially you."

"Laughter is considered to be a sign of immaturity," Tova said. "It is only for children who don't know better. Laughter can hurt others. You know the rules."

Maree stubbed her toe into the ground, then looked and laughed again. "Then I shall forever be nine. After that the world is boring."

"Shhh." Tova put a finger to her lips. "Eyes and ears will turn you in. Believe me, the last thing you want is to be considered a malcontent. It is not fun. No one understands."

Maree's eyes widened. "You saw something didn't you?" she whispered.

Tova nodded slowly. "No, I can't tell you," she whispered back. "I'm beginning to think there are electronic ears everywhere." She opened the door to her building and gestured for Maree to enter. Without speaking she gestured for her to follow her up to her room at the top of the stairs.

For the first time in recent memory, Maree actually said nothing.

They entered her room and Tova held up a finger next to her mouth. Maree sat carefully on the bed in silence and Tova moved around the room checking that everything was in its place. She'd never thought about being watched or recorded in her own home, but after today she questioned everything about Dr. Charles, the government people in charge, even the stories about the breakdown of peace and why everything was so constrained today.

She slipped to the floor next to her bed and closed her eyes. First day on the job and her whole world was falling apart. She started the mantra in her head. I am content. I am well content. I am content. I am well content.

Maree squinted her eyes and sat on the floor next to her. She put an arm around Tova's shoulders and whispered into her ear. "What's wrong? You look like you are in pain. Shall I take you to the hospital?"

Tova shook her head hard. She turned to Maree's ear and whispered. "Nothing is what it seems. I'm not sure what to believe anymore. My home may be bugged. Audio, video, I don't know."

Maree's eyes widened and her mouth was open as she now faced Tova. "You're really tired aren't you?" she said a little too loud.

"Very long day, a lot to learn." Tova followed her lead. "I seemed to have misplaced my favorite journal. Would you help me look for it?"

Maree nodded. "Sure, I'll take the other side of the room and you take this one. It's the one with the abstract butterflies, right?"

They each moved around the room with purpose looking for recording devices.

The reality was she didn't even know what to look for. She'd only seen suggestions of this on the vid series talking up the old days, before Concordia brought peace. In the old days neighbors would record neighbors and get them arrested or sent away. Sometimes it was for real misdeeds, but most of the time it was because they wanted to get rid of them or take their apartment.

Finding nothing that hinted of a recording device, Tova let out a big breath and grabbed her journal then bent as if looking under her bed. "Here it is! How could it get under the bed?" She giggled, perhaps a little too loud.

"So how was your day, Maree?" Tova asked.

Maree screwed up her face and cocked her head. "Nothing too exciting, the usual stuff. Hey, are we going to watch the latest historical crime vid?"

"Good idea!" Tova jumped on the chance to have the sound on. It could certainly cover anything else they were doing. "I have a whole sandwich in the cooler. I'll split it with you."

"Okay." Maree then silently mouthed what's going on?

"Find the show and get it started, I can hear it from the kitchen."

The usual intro began. It was about a group of four friends who were trained police security. You could tell because they all wore the triangle uniform and they had a blue denim sash across the shoulder on one side to the hip at the other. But unlike most sashes, this one was strong because it held a variety of weapons to stop dangerous people and also had a full micro camera for recording every person they encountered.

Tova heated the sandwich, cut it in half and poured two drinks. Then she quickly took a crayon and wrote a note on a napkin. *Things are strange at Pax Reborn. I will tell you what happened, but you can't say anything!* She handed the half sandwich to her friend with the napkin and drink.

"What the...?" Maree blurted out.

"Yeah, how did they find the body already?" Tova said quickly and pointed at the vid screen.

Maree nodded. "You know how these things go. The police are

well-trained. They figure things out quickly, at least in an hour.'"

"Okay, no more interruptions until they solve the crime and bring the criminal to justice," Tova said. Then she bumped into Maree and her drink spilled on her blouse. "Oh, sorry, Maree. Here, use your napkin to blot it up. I'll go get some cleaner. Really, I must be tired because I learned so much today."

Maree's eyes widened again. "It's okay. All is well. I am content."

As Tova went for the clothes cleaner, she took her journal and wrote the alphabet in it just like Daniel had today.

"So, any progress on solving the crime?" she asked as she handed the cleaner and a towel to Maree.

"Nope, two steps back and one step forward. You know how these shows are."

"Let's eat. At least I didn't bump your drink so it soaked the sandwich."

As the TV blared on Tova showed Maree the alphabet and then went through the exact process Daniel had taken her through to show her how to hand-talk. With each step, Maree's eyes grew wider and her mouth formed an O. Her eyes twinkled with excitement.

Maree picked it up much more quickly than Tova had and was soon fluent with all the word signs she had learned.

The music signaling the end of the vid show blared. "Well, that was so-so," Maree said. "But I love learning new things."

Tova nodded and used her gestures to say: "Don't show this to anyone. Don't tell anyone about it. This will be the way we whisper from now on."

"Happy to keep it a secret," Maree hand-talked back. "It's fun to know something no one else knows."

"Thanks for watching the vid with me," Tova said aloud. "Maybe we can meet again tomorrow after work. This time you get to provide the food."

"Sounds good to me. See you tomorrow." Maree waved goodbye as she left Tova's room.

"I am content," Tova said with more fervor than usual. "I am well content."

CHAPTER 3

THE THERAPEUTIC PLAN

*O*ver the next few weeks, Tova slowly elongated Daniel's therapeutic sessions from one hour to two hours, with Dr. C's approval of course. She had already established trust with him. The more gestures and hand-talking she learned, the faster their conversations became.

Daniel told her he couldn't hear her voice. He heard rumbles but not words. He said his mother started teaching him how to hand-talk, which he called *signing*, when he was three. His mother had already had recommendations from a doctor that he could not be cured and she should give him the release of the deep sleep.

By the time he was five, neighbors had reported him so many times to the police that PSEC said the next time they received a report they would take Daniel to Pax Reborn to be cured. That night, his mother took him across the border land, deep into the forest where they built a home into a berm of dirt and moss. The entrance was covered with ivy so no one could find them. They met other people in the forest who had also run away to avoid being taken to Pax Reborn. Each family had at least one malcontent member.

Some were obvious, as the diagnoses related to physical disabilities like a missing limb, an inability to speak because of a voice box malformation, or an inability to see clearly or not at all. Some people walked strangely, as if their arms or legs had a mind of their own. Others could only become mobile by using home-built chairs with wheels they could move with their hands.

Many other people's diagnosis was not easy to see. Their malcontent stemmed from questioning the laws in school, at work, or even at home. The most egregious charge was organizing public protests. The belief was that anyone who protested obviously was a malcontent—one whose mind was so convoluted that they couldn't comprehend the work of peace and how it kept them safe and a valued member of the Concordia community.

Daniel's mother had chosen to lie about why she needed to leave her apartment. She told everyone her son was taken to Pax Reborn to learn to speak. Every day to get to her job, she crossed the borderlands—a two-kilometer-wide area between Concordia and the deep forest. Crossing was always dangerous. PSEC waited to see who came from the forest, and in which direction. They often stopped and questioned anyone coming into Concordia. They were also known to then search the forest for homes and malcontents who might infect Concordia with their psychoses.

It was a hard life. Daniel could only play after dark. He had to be schooled at home because if anyone saw him and learned he couldn't speak, he would be taken away. The more Tova learned of his story and others who had fled to the safety of the forest, the more angry she became. She tried to keep it in check, but it wasn't right to treat him or his family this way.

Tova made the sign for "Sorry." Then she gestured, "What happened to your mother?"

He made the sign for death. Unlike most of his signs, he made it in a non-emotional way.

"How?" Tova signed back.

"Don't know," Daniel signed. "She was late coming home and I went to look for her. She was barely across the borderlands, at the edge of the forest, not breathing. Scratches on her arms and face.

PSEC saw me holding her body. They charged me with her murder, then brought me here to cure."

"Who worked with you before me?"

"Dr. C." His sign for the doctor was to point to his head and then tap his wrist and then shorten his name to the letter C. Then he made the sign for stupid.

Tova shook her head and signed, "No. He's very smart. Don't underestimate him."

Daniel shook his head signaling a vigorous no and pointing at her with his index finger a challenge in each statement. "You're smart. You learn. You understand. You care. He doesn't learn. He doesn't care. He doesn't believe we are human. We don't deserve to be Concordians." He punctuated each negative statement by making his gestures larger and frowning to show emphasis.

"Calm down," she signed. "I don't know if we are being watched. I must show you are progressing. If you don't stay calm, Dr. C will remove me from your case and I fear for your life."

Daniel's eyes widened. He swallowed and slowly nodded his head. He signed, "I understand." He placed his head on the table, a signal that he was done for the day.

Tova lifted his head and signed, "Don't lose hope. I'm forming a plan."

Daniel nodded again.

He signed, "I have a plan, too. We must compare."

"Next time," she signed and left his room.

Tova met with Dr. Charles after each session and shared some of what she'd learned. Suspecting they did have cameras in the room, she knew she had to be careful what she shared. She had to make sure it looked close to what she was doing with him. With each debrief with Dr. Charles, she'd share a new word sign or gesture. Something that would meet the language standards of Concordia. Things like: Thank you. I am content. I don't understand. If Dr. C asked about things that would make it more likely to lead to a diagnosis of recommending the deep sleep, she would say she didn't know how to do that except with fingerspelling, which she would demonstrate very quickly so he couldn't catch it. Many times, she mixed up the signs to be close to what they really were but added a slight negative gesture at the end which meant don't pay attention to what I just said. She didn't trust Dr. C to treat Daniel fairly. And she didn't want him to gain Daniel's trust and use it against him.

At the end of every meeting, Dr. C sounded encouraged that she had gained Daniel's trust. By the end of the month, he said, "You have done well, Dr. Tova. I think the time for learning his style is now over. You know enough to start teaching Daniel to speak."

Tova didn't speak for a moment. She wasn't sure Daniel could ever learn to speak as he didn't hear the sounds. But she would never say that. It would be an instant death sentence. "Do you have any advice about how to do that?"

"I admit I have never had a patient that couldn't speak at all. I've treated traumatic mutes, but they spoke before the traumatizing event. I don't know if Daniel has ever spoken. From what you've told me, his mother did him a disservice to teach this hand-talking communication form. Why would she do that? Why would she hide them from the good folks of Concordia?"

Tova had never shared that Daniel was deaf. "I'm not sure. Perhaps as her only child she wanted to ensure he would always be with her."

"Yes. Clearly she was a malcontent herself. No content Concordian would choose to remove their child from a well-ordered life. If he was born a malcontent, she should have brought him to Pax Reborn immediately. Now, twenty years later, we may never cure him. His death will be on her head, not ours. Remember that."

"Do you agree with my treatment regimen?" Tova asked, making sure she was showing no judgment in the question.

Dr. C looked just to the side of her face, as he rolled his tongue along his teeth in a closed mouth. "You have done well," he began speaking slowly. "You have progressed farther with Daniel than any other therapist, including myself."

She waited for the but, the follow-on statement that would negate what he just said. She sat still and waited, her eyes indicating she was ready to learn. She refused to take his statement as the end of the conversation.

She saw his chest rise as he took in a deep breath. "But…you need to prepare yourself that you may not be successful."

He waited for her acknowledgement but she wasn't going to make it easy for him. She wanted to hear his real plan.

"Although you've done well to gain his trust," he began again. "It is remarkable that you've learned this hand-talking language so well and it shows some promise for clandestine agents. But I'm not yet convinced it will translate to speech for Daniel. In my experience, speech training, language training begins in infancy. Your job is fraught with complications. To leave Pax Reborn Daniel must not only learn to speak, but also learn which words to speak. I fear that his obvious heightened emotion when he makes these gestures is perhaps not curable. Yet, it appears to me that his communication requires heightened emotion. As you are well aware, it is heightened emotion that always ends in violence."

Tova paused before forming her next sentence. She said her mantra to regulate her own emotions. I am content. I am well content. "What makes you think his emotions are heightened while hand-talking?" she asked. She had never demonstrated the signs to him with Daniel's usual emotions.

"I remember from when I worked with him."

"Do you trust that in my work those emotions are moderating? That would be a first step to accomplish before speech. Would you agree?"

Dr. C surprised her with a laugh. Not a laugh like Maree, but the type of laugh that said he was caught out.

"You're such a clever girl. I knew you were when I watched all those case studies. You immediately grasped the situation and could apply your techniques to solve the problem. That's why I wanted you here. I needed that cleverness to help me continue the work. You are amazing, Tova. You are one in a million."

There was so much wrong with what he just said. She could think of several diagnoses of his own behavior at this very moment. All of them fell into the malcontent category. Starting with addressing her without the required Dr. before her name. Then the comparisons which make her unequal to others. Her heart rate ticked up as she tried to regulate her natural flee response when faced with danger.

"Dr. Charles, I am no different than any other student in my program. I am no smarter nor do I have more skills. I do work hard and I am careful with my approach. I came here to learn from you. Your prodigious research is recommended in all psychiatric teaching programs."

He laughed aloud again. "You can stop pretending with me. You know you are better than others just as I know I am better than others."

"All Concordians are equal," Tova countered. "That is what keeps the peace."

"Stop pretending," he said again. This time as a demand. "Yes, all Concordians are equal but some are better. I am better. You are better. A few in government who make decisions are better. Someone must make the rules. Someone must enforce the rules to ensure the peace. We could not do that if we truly believed we were equal to the masses."

Tova said nothing. Was this a trick? A trick to get her to admit she no longer believed in everything she'd ever known or was taught? A trick to get her admitted to Pax Reborn?

"Mute?" he asked. "Has telling you the truth caused you to go mute? I expected more from you. I've been watching you."

She stared at him hard. A stalker?

"We have a camera in every patient's room. For their protection of course, and for ours."

"Trust then is only a word without meaning," Tova said with some bitterness. Was he baiting her to make her mad, make her emotional?

"Trust is for everyone else. Not for people like you and me, Tova. We can't trust because if we trust, we can't make the hard decisions. If we create any relationships we can no longer be trusted to cull the herd for the sake of peace. Certainly you see that. Certainly you have questioned the rules and have considered that some of them don't apply to you."

Yes, she had those thoughts from time to time but not in the way he suggested. She questioned the rules and wondered if they should apply to anyone. She questioned if the rules stymied human growth and communication. She questioned if Concordia's equality commitment brought peace or brought pacification. Did fear of being labeled a malcontent create hopelessness that people like Dr. C renamed peace?

"I see I've frightened you," Dr. C said with a concern she definitely did not trust. "You really did believe you were equal…that all of us are equal."

She nodded, unwilling to speak until she could control her emotions. This was a game to him, and she had to play the game if she were to survive. If Daniel were to survive.

"Have you never questioned that you were different? That you wanted more? That you deserved more? Really, Tova, I think you are holding out on me. No need to be afraid of my judgment. I've come clean with you, now you come clean with me."

She took a deep breath. Deeper than usual to make sure Dr. C noticed it. She had the game plan now and she had very little time to execute it. "Yes, I have asked myself if I was different. Though rather than thinking I deserved more, I thought I was less than the others because I wanted inequality. I wanted to be surrounded by diversity of thought. I wanted to explore without a chain pulling me back to limited choices of expression and learning. But…" She paused for effect. "But, I believed that was blasphemy and I trained myself to think that less and less."

"Exactly!" he shouted then laughed at his excitement. "I knew you were like me. I knew we were an intellectual match. No more thinking you were wrong. No more berating yourself for your thoughts. While you are here, at Pax Reborn, you can think however you want. I encourage you to explore new things, to stretch your mind, to bring up possibilities that may seem horrible but we will try them. We can experiment all we want. We have the resources. We have the human patients. We have the power."

She consciously shrank from him, but ordered her body not to move away. "Dr. Charles, I believe you should regulate your emotions. We may be better than or more powerful than the masses, but if we don't practice restraint we will be found out and they will revolt. History teaches us that."

"You're right. Of course. This is just between you and me. We are equals, not like the others. Now that you understand the reality of the world and are ready to step up to make the hard decisions, I will remove you from Daniel's care and schedule him for the deep sleep as I'd planned."

"I would like to continue to work with him," she said calmly.

"Why? He'll never be cured. Surely you know that. He will never speak."

"Yes, of course I know that. But he is the only patient we have that hand-talks? Right?"

"Yes. Now that you've identified that communication style, I can see that we've had others in the past but all of them joined the deep sleep before we knew they had any value at all. Not that hand-talking *is* a value. We could never let Daniel return to the public. It wouldn't be good for them or for him. In fact, I'd be afraid he would find a few people like you he could teach his hand-talking to and that would lead them to being able to communicate in ways we couldn't track." He paused. "One more reason to put Daniel in the deep sleep. If he ever escaped…"

"Of course, you are right," Tova soothed. "But I would like permission to work with him for three more months to learn as much as I can for research purposes."

"What possible use would that be? We will never ask the people of Concordia to learn to hand-talk. It would upset the peace, the knowledge that we all have one language, one way of communicating. Hand-talking is a useless skill."

"Is it?" Tova drew out the word is and left the sentence hanging a few seconds. "Certainly Concordia has spies in other countries. Certainly Concordia has secrets to keep."

"Yes, of course. It is necessary though we don't admit to it."

"But you and I understand the reality, correct?"

"Yes. Go on."

"How do you communicate those secrets now? Audibly? Encrypted messages that other spies learn to hack and then your secrets are compromised. Right?"

"I've underestimated you. You are more curious and widely read than I suspected."

"I am a questioner," she replied. "Wouldn't having a means of communication that did not involve audible speech be useful to those positions? Hand-talking is already encrypted and no one else knows it but Daniel and me. Does any other country have hand-talkers?"

"I don't know. I will check. But Daniel can't know about this. He can't be counted on to help us. He can't be trusted. He's not like us."

"Of course," Tova played along. "But over the next three months I can learn all of the signs. In fact, I can learn enough that we could create new signs that even other hand-talkers, should they exist, could not interpret. It gives us that extra edge that no one will suspect."

Dr. C said, "I knew you were very clever. I knew your IQ was likely off the charts. But I didn't know you could be devious. You had me fooled. How have you kept this inside you all these years? I've watched your progress through the entire seven years of your program and never saw a hit of deviousness. I am well pleased."

Tova did not like that characterization at all. She didn't think of herself as devious. But if it took being devious to save Daniel and others labeled as malcontents, then she would be devious.

"I suspect that the words clever and devious are like first cousins. Many similarities, but some important differences."

"Indeed." Dr. C nodded. "You also have a good memory of many words that are not allowed. How have you been storing all of these and never saying them?"

"How have you been known as one of the best therapeutic minds with a perfect therapist presence all these years, while hiding your true beliefs?" she countered.

He laughed. "Deviousness."

"Exactly."

"You can have your three months with Daniel," he pronounced. "But remember, after that he will go to deep sleep. Do not get close to him. Do not allow for transference and throw away all that I have offered you."

"You've been watching all of our sessions. Have you noticed even a hint of that?" she asked.

"I believe Daniel sees you as his new mother."

"That may be true, but he has never signed that he loves me. In fact, he's never signed that he trusts me. He simply seems happy that he can communicate with someone again."

"What is the sign for I love you?" he asked. "I want to watch for it, in case he signs it when you aren't looking, just like a patient will profess love to themselves but not to the person they love."

"Sure, this is it." She taught him a sign he would believe, but not the real one. She pointed to herself, drew a heart on her chest with her fingers and then pointed to Dr. Charles. To add to her subterfuge she also said, "That one is universal for family or close friends, but here is the one to really watch for. This is the one that means something even more intimate, like romance." She showed him the sign untrustworthy but added it in the context of the person speaking saying he was untrustworthy. She knew Daniel would never say that of himself.

While teaching the fake signs to Dr. Charles, she became more and more uncomfortable with even the concept of deep sleep for Daniel. She vowed that she would not let Daniel die because it wasn't fair. No one should be put to death because they communicate in a different manner. However, she knew Daniel was not going to learn to speak in three months. So, there was no way Dr. C would let him live. Tomorrow she would convey to Daniel that they needed to make a plan for escape while not being caught doing it.

Over the next few therapy sessions, Tova worked with Daniel to learn as much as she could about the other patients in Pax Reborn and if he wanted to include them in the escape plan. She learned that most patients who did not have the capacity to communicate in any form had already entered the deep sleep. Those who could not walk or looked very different from most Concordians also had been put into the deep sleep.

The majority of the remaining patients, about fifty of them, were more aptly described as dissidents—Concordians who disagreed with some of the rules. People who dared question the government and demonstrated their discontent by wearing unapproved clothing, like pants instead of the uniform required of all Concordians. Some also chose more than one color sash to wear to show they had more than one skill. Others consistently spoke words that were forbidden—words that showed inequality or emotion. Others had a disability (e.g., vision, hearing, a different way of processing data and conversations) that was looked upon as a person who couldn't possibly be content because they were unable to function exactly like most Concordians.

Tova wasn't sure if Dr. C's plan for these patients was actual therapy and re-education with a hope to return them to society or solely as an experimental group to try new drugs or surgical procedures. She feared it was the latter. She feared that once someone entered Pax Reborn they never left. Families knew not to ask about their loved ones once they entered Pax Reborn. They were to trust that if the patient could be cured, they would be returned to them. No one would ever admit to their neighbors that someone had been admitted to Pax Reborn for fear of anyone painting the entire family as possible malcontents.

In the past few weeks, Tova had stopped thinking of the residents of Pax Reborn as patients. Though she only worked with Daniel, Dr. C had never spoken of a dangerous patient—outside of the one time a therapist was killed long ago. Daniel knew all of them, and she trusted his judgment of their situation. They were no longer patients. They were prisoners—prisoners who needed to be released and given a chance to live their lives in peace.

They would need to escape Concordia, but surely there was a place where they could thrive. In spite of what the leaders might want everyone to believe, Concordia was not the whole world. She no longer believed that the rest of the world was evil. She no longer believed that Concordia was the only safe place to live. She no longer believed that showing emotion was dangerous. In fact it was the opposite. It was freeing.

She accepted that should she be successful in releasing these prisoners, she would live with them outside of Concordia for the rest of her life—wherever that might be.

Daniel shared how the patients communicated without speaking or even sitting near each other. The patients ate at individual tables and were not allowed to speak. Since arriving at Pax Reborn, Daniel had begun making a plan to leave and to take anyone with him who wanted to come. It had begun with him passing a paper with the alphabet and pictures of equivalent finger spelling signs as the patients silently waited to enter the dining room for each meal.

In his first month of incarceration, he'd chosen a couple of patients who he believed were quick learners and anxious to communicate. They made eye contact, showed body language that invited communication. Those residents passed it on to others. Soon, others were asking for the pictures and they also shared as they could. All residents were wanting contact, were wanting communication in any form.

Soon everyone was having silent conversations while sharing a meal in the dining room. He could catch the occasional brief smile when someone caught a joke. He'd taught them abbreviated signs that were imperceptible to staff watching the dining room. These signs could be conveyed with their hands at their side as they walked in or out of the dining room, or with their fingers near their dinner plates or cups as they ate their meals. For example, a warning that Dr. C was coming would be the letter c next to a cup. Times to meet surreptitiously in the showers where up to five patients were in the same room at the same time, where even their bathing routine could be a whispered conversation with hand-talking.

They set up clandestine meetings between other residents upon entering and exiting the dining room or shower. A single finger pointing down at their side for PM and up for AM. Fingers on a dish and then on a cup added together showed the time. Four fingers on a dish and three fingers on a cup meant 7:00, then the resident would watch for the AM or PM sign upon exiting. Each person had their own name sign that took only one movement. Curling a finger in the hair meant Kathy, a patient with unruly curly hair. Fred's name sign, who had a habit of bursting with laughter without provocation, was the sign for funny—two fingers brushing the top of the nose. Daniel's name sign was teacher because the residents thought of him as the teacher for silent communication. Daniel had given every person a unique name sign.

Tova's job was equally dangerous as she worked her plan. She had to enlist people in Concordia who might turn her in. She also needed to find people who lived in the forest but worked in town, people who would be willing to risk their lives to see their children again. They would need to create some type of distraction outside the building— something that would allow many patients to leave and run to a spot where they could be picked up and taken deep into the forest where PSEC would not follow. She needed to find Concordians who secretly did not trust the government, people who were willing to transport the escapees.

It all seemed impossible. But she was determined to make it happen.

CHAPTER 4

THE MALCONTENTS

oday was the day. Would everyone die? Would everyone become residents of Pax Reborn? Or would some make it to freedom?

Tova paced in front of her apartment window at 5:00 am as she waited for Maree to arrive. Early in the planning, Maree had found someone she knew with special equipment that could identify hidden listening devices or video devices in Tova's apartment. This person was a true spy. The kind of person Tova only imagined when she concocted her story of using hand-talking. The female spy located three—one in the living room, one in her bedroom, and one in the kitchen. After they were disabled, she provided a feed based on the audio and video already collected that would make whoever was watching see normal things from the past—a routine that, in fact, Maree had followed for years.

Maree was full of surprises. The people she knew, the network she seemed to be a part of was all secret. But Maree assured her they were all vetted and could be trusted.

Today, during the noon meal at Pax Reborn, they were executing the plan to free the prisoners; and Maree was an important part of that plan. Tova would go to work as usual at 8:00 am and work with Daniel for two hours. Then she would meet with Dr. C to debrief, as usual. She would file all her notes in the case file on the computer, and then stop Dr. C at the beginning of the noon meal. She wanted to be with him when the distraction occurred so she could pretend to flee with him for safety, but in fact make sure he couldn't interfere with the plan.

Maree had formulated a plan of distraction that involved fireworks near the building. Fireworks had been banned for more than a century because they always hurt people. Somehow Maree knew how to get them and who to trust to shoot them off so no one was hurt. At every turn, Maree knew someone. It was Maree who said she could find ten drivers with work vans who were willing to secrete patients and take them to a predesignated place in the forest.

Over the past two months, Tova and Daniel had worked out the hand signals. He'd used them over and over again in the dining room, making sure every prisoner understood what was going to happen— the fireworks, scattering quickly, grabbing orderlies and locking them in separate rooms. They would work in well-coordinated groups who would protect each other.

Maree's team would cut the electricity so all recording devices throughout the building would be disabled. They would take control of door locking and unlocking from a central terminal. It was like they were all acting in a history vid showing the dangers of malcontents ruling the world. If any of their plan became vid news, it would reinforce everything the leaders of Concordia had said—how dangerous malcontents were.

It was now clear to Tova that Maree was definitely a malcontent. Looking back, she'd probably always been a malcontent, but Tova had looked the other way—unable to accept it. Maree admitted that long ago she had searched for others who thought like her. She'd found many Concordians who never believed that the required compliance for all to be "equal" in dress, demeanor, language, and deportment was the way to keep the peace. These rebels often came from families who kept banned history books that talked about a different kind of freedom, a freedom where people were welcomed for their differences. A freedom where people were encouraged to question the status quo and work toward a better solution for all.

Tova had asked how many were part of this rebel group. Though she didn't count Maree as an irredeemable malcontent, she feared there were probably others in her group who might be and that could would lead to possible psychotic breaks and danger for everyone. When she brought that possibility up, Maree just laughed. She'd said, "Tova, *you* are a malcontent now. Even considering planning this escape is being a malcontent. Not trusting Dr. C is being a malcontent. Asking me to help is being a malcontent. Embrace it! It will be like the biggest game of hide and seek ever. You'll see."

Deep down Tova knew she was right. Daniel was a malcontent by Dr. C's definition, but only because he couldn't hear. He'd never done anything wrong before he was taken to Pax Reborn. His only problem was his mother was murdered and he expressed himself in a way Concordians didn't understand. Dr. Charles was definitely a malcontent, a dangerous one—one drunk with the power of his position. He truly believed he was better than everyone else, like a god, and no one could touch him.

Now Tova had become a malcontent herself. Today she would break every rule at Pax Reborn. Perhaps she was the worst malcontent of all of them because she knew the rules and how to break them. She knew how to lie and not be caught out—she'd done it all her life.

Until working at Pax Reborn, Tova had followed the rules. Always! But she also knew that she had questioned things all her life. She sought to learn, to understand beyond what was prescribed for her profession. She wanted to read banned texts, to understand how malcontents came to be. She wanted Concordia to truly be a utopia— a place of equality, a place where people were more than content— they were joyful, happy, and yes sometimes sad. She wanted Concordia to live up to the values espoused in the charter.

But now, what she and Maree were doing endangered everyone she cared for, even those who had no idea of their plan. She'd asked her brother to spend the evening with a friend, saying she and Maree wanted quiet time together. When the night is over, would PSEC go after her brother? Fortunately, he truly knew nothing.

Had Tova asked too much of her best friend? If anyone in this escape plan was caught, they'd all be sent to Pax Reborn for therapy if they were lucky. Or, they'd be put into deep sleep as soon as they were out of sight of any Concordians.

Bang. Bang. Bang.

Tova jumped at the knock on her door. She slowly opened it to reveal Maree in the uniform of the Peace Security Forces.

"Dr. Tova, I have a warrant to search your house," Maree said loudly.

Tova pulled her in and slammed the door, and Maree burst into laughter. "Clever isn't it? No one would dare question a PSEC officer."

"Where did you get this?" Tova whispered. "Did you steal it? Why didn't you tell me? This wasn't part of the plan. We're all going to die if you get caught wearing this. You are putting the entire plan at risk."

Maree hugged her tight and whispered into her ear. "Calm down. Everything is fine. We know what we are doing. This is not the first rescue we've executed. It may be the biggest, but not the first."

Tova extracted herself from Maree's close embrace and stared at her as she said the calming mantra in her head. I am content. I am well content. I am content. I am well content.

"The plan has, um, changed…grown a bit…it has…"

"What?" Tova asked quietly, knowing full well she had no idea what was going on. Deep inside she had feared that Maree might take it too far, but she was always assured that only ten people outside of Maree and Tova would know. "How many know?"

"Just a few more, nothing to worry about."

"How many, Maree?" She emphasized each word. "Don't treat me like a child. Don't keep me in the dark. What have you done? Remember, I'm the one going into Pax Reborn. I'm the one with no way out if I'm caught."

"Yeah, about that." Maree stepped back and worried her bottom lip as she looked directly at Tova. "I haven't been completely honest with you."

Tova dropped to the sofa and let out a big breath. "I knew it. I knew it was too good to be true. How many know? Now is the time for honesty. I'm not going in if I don't know the truth. I'm not risking the life of every prisoner if it is likely to fail."

"I don't know the exact number."

"Really? How can I trust you? This isn't one of your thought experiments or a made-up game. This is our lives! This is Daniel's life. This is every prisoner at Pax Reborn's life. This is—"

"Approximately 283, give or take," Maree said quickly.

Tova's mouth dropped open. She couldn't find words. She'd never imagined there were that many malcontents in the open. Twenty maybe or fifty at most. Were they all like Maree? Functioning but not content? Was it safe to have them involved?

"I haven't been one hundred percent honest with you," Maree admitted.

"You think?" Tova said.

"Listen. Just listen. It's important to understand everything before you leave for Pax Reborn today."

Tova sat on the edge of the sofa, her spine straight and her teeth locked together. What could she do but listen? Their lives depended on it.

"I'm a malie. In fact, all of us are because we have been planning an overthrow of the administration for years."

"Don't exaggerate," Tova said. "You're barely an adult. At twenty what is that? Two years of planning?"

"My parents were malies before they were taken to Pax Reborn and killed. My grandparents were malies. My great-grandparents and who knows how many greats were also malcontents. I come from a long line of dissidents. I was trained from a young age to be a very good spy."

"I...I didn't know. I thought you were an orphan who never knew your parents."

"I lied about that. I'm sorry, but it was the only way to stay safe. I was orphaned at age twelve when my parents were taken. I was taken in by an aunt who adopted me. At age fourteen my aunt was informed my parents were incurable and had gone to the deep sleep. My aunt said it was likely they'd gone to the deep sleep within weeks of being taken to Pax Reborn."

"Why did I never know this?" Tova asked. "Why didn't you trust me enough to tell me? I've shared everything with you."

"You are soooo good, Tova. You have been the most perfect Concordian I've ever met. You truly believed that all the rules were necessary and you were soooo good at hiding any disbelief. I couldn't ruin your life with my story, putting doubts and questions into your head and endangering you."

"But now?"

"Now you're a malcontent, too. You have realized the things we've been told aren't true. I've always known they weren't true but you have just learned. You can no longer look away now that you've met Daniel. Now that you know the truth about Dr. C. you are too smart to believe lies anymore. But this is all new to you. You haven't had years of practice being something you are not. I have. You need our protection and we need your access to Pax Reborn."

"I'm not perfect," Tova said. "I've hidden my thoughts, too."

"I'm sorry, I've hurt your feelings. I know you've hidden...more like tamped down your questions, your concerns, your feelings. You didn't want to believe things weren't true so you built a world where they were true and that world included helping others to see and believe what you wanted to believe about Concordia—that giving up freedom for peace was worth it."

Tova closed her eyes and sighed. Maree was right. She knew all along that not everything was right, but she wanted it to be true. She didn't want to believe there was a crack in the Concordia peace. So, she told herself she was wrong, she wasn't perceiving correctly.

Before her job at Pax Reborn, Tova had worked in therapy with many Concordians suffering from cognitive dissonance. The concept was created to identify when what a person sees with their eyes or hears with their ears doesn't match with what they are being told is true by others—whether that is authority figures or friends. When that happens, it produces a feeling of discomfort that can be painful mentally and sometimes even physically. To make that discomfort go away, the person works to restore balance. Often that means they choose what they *want* to believe instead of questioning or digging deeper to find the truth.

Now that she thought about it, in many ways the laws of Concordia frequently created cognitive dissonance—particularly when they were constantly changing, like when a word was removed from the vocabulary, or a person one thought was normal is suddenly diagnosed as a malcontent. In fact, everyone in Concordia was living under some sort of forced compliance. When someone was forced to do publicly something that they really don't want to do or is inconsistent with their beliefs, it sets up cognitive dissonance. To survive that dissonance, they must convince themself they agree with the compliance, they agree it is the right decision. The longer they are forced to live in that way the more difficult it becomes.

Every time she saw the joy go out of Maree's step, or the pain of a neighbor's child being taken to Pax Reborn, she knew something was wrong. But she didn't step in to change it. She didn't question it in public. That would be the malcontent way. Her forced behavior (not stepping up, not asking questions or following leads) couldn't be changed as it is in the past. The only choice was to re-evaluate her attitude toward what she was forced to do. She had to tell herself that leaders knew what they were doing. She had to tell herself that there was a reason she just couldn't see. She had to make it right or she couldn't live with herself.

In fact, perhaps she pursued psychiatry to help patients deal with this dissonance in their life so they could return to society as whole people. Tova had worked with patients to provide a path to understanding how both things can be true at once, but helped them to resolve the pain with the knowledge that Concordia values were still true and they were safe in the hands of their leaders.

Had she been lying to herself and her patients all this time?

"Earth to Tova," Maree said. "I'm sorry your life appears to be falling apart at this moment, but can you wait to have your break-down until we get everyone out of Pax Reborn today?"

Tova lifted her chin. "I'm not falling apart. I'm just...coming to the realization..."

"That everything you believed is a lie," Maree added.

"Not everything."

"Almost everything," Maree said. "Look, I get it. I've seen it happen to others. I wish I could have somehow passed on to you what I knew as a child, but it would have killed our friendship immediately. Then you went off to university and I stayed home, and then you had your career and I had...well..."

"Your rebel career," Tova finished for her. "I get it, too late. It's not your fault. It's mine for not seeing it, for not questioning it more."

"One thing I learned in the rebel business as a child was don't beat yourself up. Don't make yourself a martyr to the cause because you feel guilty. We all have fault in our lives. We all have things we wished we'd done differently. But right now we have to put that behind us. We can't let it be a part of our plan. We are not looking for salvation for whatever perceived sins we've perpetrated in the past. We are looking to right one wrong. When that is done, we will look for the next one and the next one. If you wallow in the woulda-shoulda sins of the past, you will be lost and likely killed on your first mission."

Tova said nothing. When had Maree become so wise? What had she missed in her best friend all these years? She had never looked closely.

"Got it?" Maree asked. "Good to go?"

"Yes." Tova pulled back her shoulders and looked Maree in the eye. "No more woe is me. Tell me this new plan so I don't screw it up."

"Good!" Maree pulled up a chair to the coffee table between them. She then dropped a detailed map of Pax Reborn's interior and exterior onto the table.

"Whoa! Where did you get this?"

"No time to get into the who and where stuff, just what *is* going to happen."

The front door opened, and Eoghan entered. "Hi, Maree, am I in time?"

"Wait!" Tova stood and looked at her brother and then at Maree. "Wait just a minute. You were spending the night at your friends? You're up early and you know about…what exactly?"

Eoghan gave Tova a hug and whispered. "Secrets abound. I love you."

Tova pushed him away. "Am I the only one in all of Concordia who is not a part of this rebel group?"

Eoghan and Maree joined hands and nodded yes.

"Not all of Concordia, of course," Maree said. "But among all of our friends, um yeah."

"We were protecting you," Eoghan added. "You were a true believer and we couldn't smash that dream and endanger you. But now that you know the truth…"

"And if I'd never changed? Would you have left me here alone while all of the rebels go to the forest?

"Of course not," Maree said, her eyes watering around the edges. "I'd never leave you alone."

"We would have kidnapped you and taken you with us," Eoghan added. "After about a month with us, we would give you the free choice of returning to Concordia if that is what you really wanted."

"How egalitarian of you," Tova said. "Forced compliance for only a month."

Eoghan stood tall. "You don't have to do this now, Tova. You can back out right now. We will leave the house. We will still save Daniel and the other Pax Reborn prisoners. But you don't have to be a part of it. You can stay here and resume whatever life you want in Concordia. It's not easy living in the forest. It's not easy being part of a group that is often in discord during communications. It is not always peaceful. But we respect each other. We respect and value our differences. We find a way to compromise on the important things and agree to disagree on others. It's a different world than Concordia. A completely different way of living."

Tova pointed to her brother and Maree. "How long have you two been what? Partners, lovers, best friends?"

Maree swallowed. "I wanted to tell you but…"

"How long?"

"We married when Maree turned eighteen. We have been in love since she was fourteen. We have a forest home and I hope one day children as well—children to raise as Maree was raised."

"And your work as a woodworker, a job you have been proudly going to every day without fail—a job you have loved."

"I have been doing that work every day—only not in Concordia. I put on the uniform and head toward a shop at the edge of the border-lands. I then slip behind a tree and change to what you see me in now and run to the Bota River. We've built a footbridge of rocks beneath the water that is known by those who wish to live on the other side. The unincorporated land of about five thousand acres is what we have named the Clearview settlement. That is where I work each day, helping to build homes and furniture and to provide for the community. Others are farmers who provide food and milk. There are currently a little over a thousand of us, but we believe it will grow."

"Crime?" Tova asked.

"Minor," Eoghan replied. "The occasional stealing of food or telling a lie that hurts someone else. They are dealt with based on compassion, understanding, and reasoning. An unmet need, a misunderstanding, or actual determination to do harm to someone else. We are still working it all out."

"It is where my birth parents lived until they were taken in the city. It is where Daniel and many people in Pax Reborn have family or those who knew their family. Clearview takes care of all members of the community who do not fit in Concordia or have never wanted to join Concordia after the floods."

Tova tried to take it all in. She didn't really know her friend or even her own brother. The stories about criminals and dangerous malcontents beyond the boundaries of Concordia were not necessarily true, but she had believed them—still held that fear inside. It could be that

Daniel's mother was not killed by malcontents but by PSEC in Concordia. Did they do it because they truly feared Daniel would hurt them or the residents of Concordia? Or did they do it because they could, because they wanted to squelch any dissident ideas in Concordia?

"Well?" Eoghan asked. "Are you in or out? We need to read you in on the plans for today if you are still in. Your choice. We will still love you no matter your decision."

"I'm in," Tova pronounced. "I have to be the one to do it. Daniel trusts me. Other Pax Reborn prisoners trust Daniel. I know Dr. C, how he thinks, how ruthless he can be. I am the one who must control him in the blackout. Let's go over this."

The three of them poured over the schematics for the building. Maree and Eoghan took turns outlining what would happen. The most dangerous part was controlling Dr. C. and securing the staff—not to hurt them but to make sure no one interfered with the escape plan.

At 7:30 am the video and audio feed in Tova's apartment was live. Tova double-checked her uniform, making sure it was perfect. She carefully braided her hair snug across her scalp, bringing the long tail down over her collarbone. She stepped to the door and opened it.

Eoghan joined her in his woodworker uniform. "Have a good day at work," he said. "I'll see you at dinner." He placed a kiss on her cheek and then headed into the pattern of people walking to work. He waved as he walked out of view.

She savored the neat orderly way that people joined the traffic patterns. Something she might never see again. She listened to the greetings, and the constant answer of: "I am content," as the people moved along designated pathways dotted with nice shade trees and glowing balls of glass.

The peace still held at this moment. It had been this way for more than a hundred years. It was all she'd known until the past four months. Hearing the greeting and response of contentment among all the people walking now created a block of ice in her stomach. She shivered at the thought of how her life would change today. She accepted she was a malcontent. She would never again believe that everyone could be truly content all the time. She could never again believe that PSEC helped keep the peace, that nothing could harm her.

Closing the door behind her, Tova stepped out to join all the others. She would pretend for one more day. She would do what was needed to save Daniel and others. As people saw her they asked: "How are you today." She replied: "I am content. I am well content." She joined the stream of messaged contentment on her way to the last day of her job.

CHAPTER 5

PEACE REVISITED

ova opened the door to Pax Reborn at 7:45am. She pasted a half smile on her face as she headed toward her usual 8:00am therapy time with Daniel.

Dr. C met her at Daniel's door. "Dr. Tova, right on time as usual."

She smiled. "Only one more week with Daniel and I'll turn over all I've learned."

"About that," Dr. C said. "I've scheduled a meeting with the head of PSEC for you to share your preliminary work with them."

"That's excellent," Tova reached into her satchel to retrieve her electronic calendar. "What day and time is it?"

"It's today. I hoped you could stay beyond your normal time, have lunch with me, and then meet with PSEC at 1:00."

Tova waited a moment before speaking. She needed to slow her heart rate so as not to raise suspicion.

"Of course," she responded. "I'm always happy to stay, particularly when it means so much to the peace of Concordia."

"Good. I was hoping that would be your response. I thought we could have lunch at the Café Vérité in town. My treat of course."

No! She didn't want to be in town when everything happened. She didn't want any chance of Dr. C not being trapped in the building.

"That's very thoughtful of you," she said. "However, as PSEC is coming for the presentation, I would prefer to eat in your office so we can plan exactly what I should share."

"We can do that for the two hours before lunch after you meet with Daniel," Dr. C suggested.

She let out an audible breath, purposefully showing her discomfort.

Dr. C raised his brows and crossed his hands across his chest.

"My knowledge of Café Vérité is a place where young people go to share their truth, their closely held values before making a final decision on marriage. I'm sure you didn't mean the invitation in a romantic way, because that would be teacher-student transference in our relationship. I'm afraid I would feel very uncomfortable in being your lunch companion at that place."

Dr. C put his shoulders back, cleared his throat, and raised his chin. "I was unaware that people your age use Café Vérité for that purpose. Of course, I was not making a romantic overture. I would never do that. If I was interested in you, which would not be appropriate as we work together, I would let you know in another way. In fact, I was only—"

"Thank you for understanding my concerns," she interrupted. "Please, let's just order in for lunch. A sandwich would be fine for me. You know how I am about preparation. I want everything to be perfect. Since I had no warning of this meeting, it really is imperative that I discuss all the points with you and how to best present it. In fact, I think we should present it together, as without you I would not have been able to make so much progress."

"If you insist," Dr. C said with a gruffness.

"Perhaps we could go to lunch another day. Perhaps next week to celebrate my completion of working with Daniel. Not to Café Vérité, of course, but somewhere else when I don't have a presentation hanging over my head."

"I'm surprised you are anxious to be done with Daniel. I'd assumed there would be some grieving."

"I will miss working with him," she said slowly. "I've enjoyed learning this new language—one I didn't even know existed. However, I have accepted that he cannot be happy remaining here at Pax Reborn for the rest of his life. I would not want that for anyone so young. Being a malcontent must be very stressful. Never being able to fit in. Never being able to truly become a Concordian and know of the great peace our colony provides. I will not grieve the deep sleep for Daniel. Instead, I hope for another world where he and others like him may be whole."

"Certainly, you don't believe in heaven or some sphere where the soul remains do you? That is something for the masses of little intelligence. That is something for those who need a salve to continue in their meaningless lives."

She was hating Dr. C more and more each day. He didn't have one bit of compassion in him. He pretended to care, but he didn't care about anything except what he wanted.

"I meant it has a metaphor," Tova finally said. "I don't believe in a place, like heaven. However, I find comfort in the thought that a soul can be made whole after death. Or perhaps, like some ancient religions, that it can return in another form—a form that provides enlightenment."

Dr. C chuckled. "You surprise me every time we talk. Just when I think I understand you, I learn something new."

"I take that as a compliment," she said. "Now, may I go into see Daniel? We only have two hours scheduled, and I'm already ten minutes late. I'll see you shortly after 10:00 am and we can plan the PSEC presentation together before lunch."

"Of course." Dr. C made a grand gesture with a half bow at the waist, obviously to mock her. "Shall I open the door for you, Dr. Tova?"

"No need." She lifted the lever and walked in, the door closing behind her. She signed surreptitiously at her side for Daniel to stay still and not sign anything yet.

She suspected Dr. C was hurrying back to his office to watch every minute of her interaction with Daniel. This whole PSEC thing was too sudden to make sense. She wouldn't put it past him to say this was her last day with Daniel and no goodbyes. She wasn't sure if it was jealousy of her learning something he did not, or just the need to show her he was in charge. In any case, she didn't need more than today with Daniel if everything went to plan.

She sat across from Daniel as usual and talked as she signed to make sure Dr. C could hear her. She'd been practicing all week at home to be able to sign one thing but voice something different. It was quite hard, harder than rubbing your head and patting your stomach—a child's game of concentration and control.

"Hello, Daniel. Good to see you again."

Daniel signed back hello and grinned. Then he signed, "Why so careful."

She signed and said, "Follow me carefully, while we play our spy game."

Daniel clapped like a child. She had already told him about what Dr. C wanted her to do and why. They had together worked out many opposite signs for when she said something but began it with a negative, meaning don't pay attention to what I'm about to sign. They had a shorthand for that.

She began the next piece with a negative. She spoke and signed. "The game today is about setting up a rendezvous point for spies. Can you help me?"

He nodded yes.

"If we were on a high hill, surrounded by enemy spies and wanted to tell everyone where to hide without speaking, how we would start the sign?"

Daniel signed, "Meet at the tenth tree from this location and make a following mark. Then follow in teams of two until you reach the rendezvous point."

"Oh, that's good," she said. She signed, "The rescue begins during lunch." But she said aloud, "Then the air machines will extract the PSEC from the final location?"

Daniel nodded.

Next she signed, "All power will be cut. Can you make sure

everyone will stay calm?" But she said aloud, "The flyers can only take three people at a time, so the others must stay hidden."

Then she signed and spoke again, placing a negative at the beginning. "If you had to create a sign for extraction that could not be understood by the enemy, what would it be?"

Daniel made the sign of an inchworm then pointed to the sky.

"That's a good one," she responded. "The flying cable moving slowly to the extraction point." Again, she used the inchworm and sky sign Daniel had made up for the word extraction.

They continued in this same fashion with her laying out the plan for Daniel to relay to everyone else during lunch, but speaking about the spy game and saying something completely different. Fortunately, Daniel didn't have to deal with her speech, only her signs.

The power outage would occur at 12:30 pm to give him time to prepare everyone. The prisoners would form in groups of three to take on each orderly or staff person and make sure they were secured and unable to do anything. Then they would all meet at the back door where Maree, in her PSEC uniform, would start loading up the vans. She taught Maree the sign for her name and friend of Dr. Tova. Fireworks would be going off throughout this and many people would be pounding at the front entrance to be let in to take their children home.

"What about you?" Daniel signed. "Where will you be?"

"I will be safe," Tova signed back. "I will secure Dr. C and then meet you and the others in Clearview later."

"Be careful," Daniel signed. "Don't trust Dr. C."

She signed, " I know. Believe me I know." She said aloud, "I will see you tomorrow at our usual time."

Daniel nodded and signed, "See you then."

She exited and headed straight to Dr. C's office. She wasn't looking forward to this PSEC presentation. Nor was she looking forward to two plus hours with him alone. But it would all be over soon.

Dr. C was standing at the door of his office. "How did it go with Daniel?"

"Well. He always amazes me how he can create new hand-talking words that make sense in the context of other words. What we have learned will be of great use to PSEC and Concordia spies."

Dr. C smiled, but it didn't reach his eyes. He opened the door and signaled for her to enter.

She stopped immediately when she saw the uniforms of three PSEC officers. They all turned to face her. She gasped and covered her mouth. One was Maree, but her badge read Lt. Bosha. She didn't know the other two.

"I thought—"

"I apologize, Dr. Tova," Dr. C said. "I'm afraid we have a problem. It seems that PSEC believes you are part of a rebel group that plans to train others to do hand-talking. I'm inclined to believe them. Your work with Daniel and your debriefs with me have not been entirely honest."

"I...No...I..."

Maree spoke first. "Dr. Charles, please have a seat and remain silent. We appreciate you reporting the problem to us, but now let us do our job. Please record the session."

Dr. C. made a point of pressing record with a satisfied grin.

When had Maree or her group found out about this? They must have people on the inside of PSEC. Why hadn't they told her this morning? Was this a double-cross? She took a deep breath and forced herself to calm. Maree had been her best friend since childhood. She'd shared most of the plan with her. She'd been honest and revealed things she didn't have to reveal. Personal things. Difficult things.

Maree first recited a detailed review of Tova's life from childhood, through university, and her work at Pax Reborn. She recited the identification of Maree's parents, her brother, and how she spent her days. She indicated that, at Dr. C's recommendation, PSEC had been monitoring her home, her office at Pax Reborn, and her work with Daniel for the past month.

"You understand that we know everything, correct?"

Tova nodded.

So, Dr. C was jealous. More than that, he was afraid that Tova would surpass him in knowledge. This was a typical narcissist's response to perceived competition. Talk about diagnosing a malcontent: Dr. C was the epitome of someone who was constantly malcontent. Instead of being able to share knowledge or power, or to work in community with each other to learn more, a narcissist's response was to annihilate any perceived rival. A narcissist must believe he has supreme knowledge, supreme control, and is the only one with the right answers.

"Now that you understand the situation, you know that any lie leads to an immediate diagnosis of being a malcontent," Maree said.

Over the next hour, Maree asked the questions and Tova gave honest responses. She admitted to thinking of the patients as prisoners. She admitted to creating a plan with Daniel to save everyone. She didn't know how this played into the plan, but she was following Maree's lead.

"Our information indicates, you planned to unleash the escape of the malcontents on the last day of your work with Daniel. Is that correct?" Maree asked.

Tova wrinkled her forehead and looked at Maree. Why would she…

"Remember, we have audio and video evidence from your home that this plan would be executed in ten days. Is that true?"

Tova hung her head. "Yes. It's true."

"Also, from the audio with your co-conspirator, you suggested that Dr. Charles was also part of this plan. That, in fact, it was his idea. However, unlike you, he wasn't going to save the residents. He was going to move them to a building he'd been constructing so that there would be no oversight of his work."

Dr. C jumped up. "No! No, that's a lie. There is no other building. I only wish to help these malcontents. I wish to cure them. That has been my life's work. She made that up. She's trying to destroy me. She's jealous of my work, of my knowledge. She wants to be me."

"Sit down, Dr. Charles, or I will have you restrained.

Tova stood and shouted, "I would never be you! I would never lower myself, give up my values to be like you!"

"Dr. Tova, sit down. Sit down or I will restrain both of you and leave you stuck in this room together for the rest of the day without food or water."

Tova immediately sat, but Dr. C remained standing, his arms crossed at his chest.

"Let's split them up for interviews, see if they agree or not," Maree said. She pointed at one of the two officers with her. "Take Dr. Tova to room fifteen. I believe it is empty. Be sure to handcuff her to the chair. I'll be in within an hour." Then she pointed to the other officer. "Put Dr. Charles in the room nearest the dining room. Also make sure he is handcuffed to the chair. I'll begin with him. I believe we have two malcontents at work here. I will get to the bottom of this."

Just as the prisoners were filing into the dining room, Maree joined Tova and the officer who took her to room 15. She had not been tied down. The other person said nothing, except to verify that he was part of the rebel group. In fact, there were many actual PSEC officers who had joined the rebel group several years ago.

"Is Dr. Charles secure?" the officer asked Maree.

She smiled widely. "Very secure. In fact, he is sleeping uncomfortably on top of a confession that describes all the things he's done since opening Pax Reborn—the experiments, the forced deep sleep when experiments failed, and his plan to move all the patients to a facility at the edge of the borderlands."

"What about the other officer?" Tova asked.

"Jordan is in the dining room. He is an accomplished hand-talker. In fact, he is Daniel's cousin. He's been a part of our group for a year. When I learned you were working with Daniel, I knew he was the right person to bring to this job. In fact, I knew that we would finally succeed in getting the prisoners out and create enough of a distraction that any Concordians who wished to leave could do so. Half the PSEC force will help us."

"Was it really Dr. C's plan to move everyone to another building?" Tova asked.

"Yes. But he hadn't gotten very far. He has the foundation for a building, and a nine-foot concrete wall without a roof, windows, or doors. The government stopped payment when malcontents from the forest kept painting slogans and questioning the government. Using it like a billboard for anyone who entered the borderlands."

"Is the rest of the plan still on?"

"Of course." Maree smiled wide. "We must have fireworks."

Half an hour later, Tova was at the back door ready to put Pax Reborn residents into vans that were already queued behind the building. PSEC rebel members were stationed at all corners. It seemed there were at least twenty near the building.

On schedule, fireworks exploded. Power was cut. Hundreds of people surged into Pax Reborn calling for family members by name.

Maree and the two PSEC officers were joined by four more to help the prisoners secure all staff. They did not want to hurt them. No one knew if the staff realized what was really going on at Pax Reborn. They may have been deceived like everyone else—believing that Dr. C's primary purpose was to cure malcontents and return them to their homes.

There were many more cars and vans than the six planned. The rebel group had evidently known that hundreds, or perhaps even a thousand, wanted to leave Concordia but had always been afraid.

As each resident exited, they brought with them at least one other person—someone from the crowd who surged into the building, another resident who was lost, or anyone who said they needed a ride.

Daniel was the last to exit, with his cousin in a PSEC uniform. They both signed their thanks to Tova for her strength to recognize the truth. Daniel gave her a strong hug and signed, "I'll be waiting in Clearview. Ask anyone where I am and they will find me."

Tova's eyes watered as she nodded. Then they were gone.

After ten minutes with no one else leaving, Maree and Eoghan drove up in a van clearly labeled as a woodworker's supply van. "Get in," Maree said. "There are no others waiting."

"Are you sure? I don't want to leave anyone behind?"

"The building has been swept," Eoghan said. "PSEC rebels even asked each staff member if they wanted to leave with us. No one said yes. These cowards will not get another chance."

Tova climbed into the van and they drove toward the borderlands.

When they reached it, there were still hundreds of people crossing—most on foot, a few in vehicles.

"More than a thousand Concordians have fled today with only what they could carry," Maree said. "We've been planning this for three years. There is strength in numbers."

They stopped to add a mother carrying two children who could not walk.

"There are many others," the mother said. "Many who have been hidden, who need help."

"Cars and vans will return," Eoghan said. "We will continue throughout the day and night, as long as we need. Watch for PSEC who are not on our side. They will use whatever weapons available to stop us. They will kill anyone who stands in their way."

Every mile they drove, Tova was waiting to be killed or worse see someone in front of them or behind them be maimed or killed. But it seemed there were more PSEC helping them at every turn. She never saw or heard an explosion.

It was another hour before they reached Clearview. The roads were bumpy and they couldn't drive at a maximum speed without losing control. As they continued in one direction, a train of cars and vans were going in the opposite direction to pick up more people who wanted to flee Concordia.

They stopped in front of a sturdy home near the edge of a village. Though this one was complete, it seemed that many homes were only half-built. Some were buildings of brick or stone. Others were wood. Some had thatched roofs, many did not. A few had windows, many did not. Tova couldn't tell how many homes were constructed, but she imagined there were many she couldn't see.

They started unloading the van. The woman and her two children immediately headed toward the center of the village where others had gathered.

"We've asked people to announce their name. If they have relatives or friends, they will be reunited and share those homes for now. If they have no one, they will be lodged in one of several communal buildings for now," Eoghan said. Once the van was unloaded, he got in and turned around. "I'm going back to see who else needs help." Then he drove back toward the borderlands.

Maree lugged a load to the porch of a modest two-story home. "This is our home," she said. "We've fixed an upstairs bedroom for you. It's about the same size as yours in Concordia."

Tova couldn't speak. This was real. She was no longer going to live in Concordia.

"If you'd rather not live with us," Maree said, "I could ask someone else to take you in. It is your choice. Everything is your choice here."

"I...I would love to stay with you...if it's not an inconvenience."

Maree laughed. "Good to the end, always thinking of others instead of yourself. I may have to kick you out because I will never compare well to you."

"I'm not always good," Tova countered as she had throughout their friendship. "I do selfish things, too. It is selfish of me to want to be near you and my brother. It is selfish of me—"

Maree hugged her tight. "Shut up and get inside before I change my mind. I think I'll make you my slave instead so you can feel you are doing whatever penance you think you deserve."

"I'm not doing penance." Tova pulled a heavy bag over the transom.

"We'll see. We'll see how you feel once you're settled, once you know what it's really like to live in community with others, with people who feel free to disagree, to say how they really feel about things that are happening."

Tova stepped back outside to get more bags and boxes. She looked up at the broad sky overhead. Only a few white clouds broke up the cerulean blue. Beyond the central village was a patchwork of golden grain fields, green vegetable fields, and many acres that were yet unplanted or built upon. She could see in the distance what appeared to be the edge of the plateau. What was beyond that? A river? A valley of rocks?

So much to see. So much to learn. So much freedom to investigate who she would be in Clearview. Tova did not believe in utopia. Concordia had claimed to be one and failed miserably.

Maree had warned her that Clearview is not an easy place to live. It is not always peaceful like Concordia appeared to be. When making rules, enforcing rules, trying to build a society where people communicate first, people will disagree. Sometimes they disagree loudly and forcefully. Sometimes they say mean and hurtful things. Evidently, it was a constant tug of war between the united interests of those who lived in Clearview and had some shared values versus each person's individual fears, needs, and circumstances strongly driven by the instinct of self-preservation.

Tova wasn't looking for a perfect world. Likely, that was not achievable or perhaps not even desirable. She'd worked with many perfectionist patients, trying to help them understand it is never truly achievable. However, not achieving perfection doesn't mean one should stop striving for a better future. Perhaps her contribution to Clearview was to be herself—her screwed-up, never one-hundred-percent-sure self. She would do what she has always done: maintain her idealism enough to continuously envision a better world for all, while simultaneously counting on her pragmatism to do the work required to continuously strive toward that idealistic vision.

"Earth to Tova." Maree stood in the doorway. "Time to stop dreaming and start doing." She pointed to a pile at the bottom of the stairs. "You can start with getting your things into your room. Start nesting. Within the hour, we are going to the village center to help with cooking a celebratory meal for all those who have joined us today. We will probably be up most of the night still accepting new people and finding them lodging."

Tova laughed as she stepped in and lifted two heavy bundles at the bottom of the stairs. "Work first, dreams only at night."

"Exactly," Maree said.

With her meager belongings, Tova took her first steps into the reality of her new life.

Maggie's Inspiration For This Story

Over the past year, I've contemplated how personal communication has shifted to be at two ends of the spectrum. Those who wish to bring chaos and fear, and those who desire to have a world where everyone is polite, lives the "Golden Rule" and agrees on everything. Though the former is awful, the latter is impossible and to get to that utopia requires a suppression of thought to enforce that kind of communication.

I combined those musings with thoughts of my neurodivergent siblings. In fact, three of my siblings are neurodivergent, with two on the autism scale. One brother who has severe autism and has never developed speech, has lived in a state facility since he was five years old. Now in his early sixties he is in a group home. Another brother with moderate autism, has the added difficulty of also being 70% deaf. Though he has managed to eek out a living as a dishwasher for 30 years, he is often taken advantage of or manipulated because he has little understanding of non-verbal cues in conversation, nor can he measure actual intent. He primarily reads lips, missing much of spoken communication. He also believes that what a person says (in person, on TV, on social media) is always the truth. This applies equally to "I love you, and wish to come to America to marry you" and to "The world is out to kill you every day." He will continue to need someone who loves him and will look out for his best interests for his entire life.

This story envisions what some would call a utopian existence where everyone is equal and content with life. However, there is a heavy price to pay for that. Humans, their hopes and dreams, the way they process the world, and their diversity of abilities and needs is messy to accept, manage, and understand.

ABOUT THE AUTHOR

Maggie Lynch is the author of 27+ published titles, as well as numerous short stories and non-fiction articles. Her fiction tells stories of men and women making heroic choices one messy moment at a time. Her fiction spans romance, suspense, YA fantasy and SF titles, as well as children's books. Her current non-fiction titles are focused on helping other authors become successful in their careers.

Since 2013, Maggie and her musician husband have settled in the beautiful Pacific Northwest where they have retired from the corporate and academic world to follow their dual creative pursuits of writing and music.

To learn more about Maggie and her books, please visit her website at https://maggielynch.com. If you sign up for her newsletter, you'll receive updated information about her books, special deals, and any upcoming events.

THANK YOU for purchasing this Windtree Press Anthology. We hope we've peaked your imagination and that you've found some new authors to follow.

For more books of the heart, from anthologies to memoirs, non-fiction, and novels, please go to our **website at https://windtreep ress.com**. There you can learn about all of our authors, their books, and where to contact them directly.

If you **sign up for our email list** you will receive a free monthly newsletter with new releases, author interviews, bargain books pricing, author events, and much more. https://landing.mailerlite.com/webforms/landing/e6h6a6. We never share or sale your information.